The Prophecy

When the Marked is found amongst the Maples,
And the armies of the east shall walk again,
With the Enderdetag alignment in the heavens,
Then shall be the end of good men.

When the Oracles crypt shall be opened,
And the choices we make must thrive,
The powers of evil shall be woken,
And no one alive shall survive.

From the innocent the savoir shall waken,
To the Bards he shall appear,
To reunite the Gems of Thamous,
And destroy the Lord of Fear.

The Game

"Come my dearest of siblings, it is time to start the game; roll the dice sister," cackled the leather skinned hag as she sat before the hearth.

"Clunk and yet another clunk; a six and yet another six!" squeaked her ancient sib amid the decaying scent of her own rotting flesh. "I have thrown a magic twelve. We are playing months so the game will last a year."

"Now it's your turn youngest of us three," added the first as her talons picked out wriggling maggots from her cheek. "Though you do not talk, pick a card so that we may play... Well done sweetie, you are at your sharpest today I see... Now, youngest of our eternal dead, turn the card and let us feast our eyes upon the greatness of the one you have chosen to lead the way."

"Oh, I don't believe it!" screeched the second of the foul crones. "You mumblecrust! We are shackled from the start. Look at the paltry card our sister has chosen. What can the odds be against such a miserable and miserly start to the epic game we have decided to play?"

"It cannot be helped," groaned the first. "Our sweet dumb sister has always been a poor chooser. We withered spawn can only hope that Mother deems this game worth playing, for 'She' knows best and always has done."

"Let us hope the round is better than the last time we drew this card for then we almost lost control of the outcome," sneered the second of the sinuous swine.

"But still the ending was a good one, so roll the dice again," demanded the first.

The silent third smiled and winked while she sat and sharpened her blade.

And So It Began

Enveloped by an encroaching sea fog, two misty eyes struggled to focus the available light through milk centred lenses that had succumbed to the passage of time. The weary globes stared at the crimson inked words scrawled on a crumpled piece of vellum and sought to confirm the message they conveyed. The lines, no doubt penned in blood, had summoned the aging warrior to a secret rendezvous atop of the highest tower south of the Grey Mountains. As best as the maudlin knight could judge he had followed the instructions to the letter despite the apathy brought on by melancholy and weakened essence. The recent loss of the two dearest to his heart continued to sap his soul and yet he had still deemed it necessary to meet with the author of the note, an unknown entity who had demanded contact in order to save the Realm from destruction. Reading the words for umpteenth time that day the highborn knight retreated into the impenetrable shadows cast by the crenelated walls of Parandor's Tower of Enlightenment. All was still at the midpoint of the night and little of Mona's light forced its way through the heavy cloud cover that rolled up and over the city from vast ocean beyond the Estuary of New Beginnings. A trembling hand dropped and searched for the reassurance of a trusted blade that hung from a leather belt; one that had seen more summers than most men could ever hope to witness. The brain does strange things to old heads. Deep moods had added to an ever increasing forgetfulness, made greater since the meaning of his life had been ripped from his grasp by the sweating sickness that called each winter.

It was the smell that first caught his attention, long before any sound hit his drums or visions appeared before his gaze. Having deliberately hidden his form deep within the shadows, the life learned artisan of stealth knew how difficult he would be to spot when the one who craved an audience ascended the spiral steps to pinnacle of the tower. The scent that tickled the lining of his nostrils was unlike anything common to the Capital. He was sure he had encountered something of its ilk way back in his early days serving the Royal Guard, yet this aroma seemed different in a way he could not identify. Inhaling deeply, a hint of sulphur and decay reminded him of time spent on patrols on the edge of the marsh lands and around the death pits beyond the city walls. Once many years previous he had come across a snake, killed by some unknown assailant and left to rot on a rock by the side of a pool of stagnant water. The tinge of a similar stench stirred a fading memory. Further analysis was interrupted as the sound of a light footfall on the spiral steps penetrated the wax lined channels of his ears and caused both drums to flutter. Seconds later a hooded shadow rose up and took command of the centre of the observation square. Deep gasps, part induced by the effort of the climb, dominated the still air of the otherwise silent night. The shadow stopped, sniffed, and turned to where the old knight hid amid the dark.

"I am most pleased you chose to come," rasped the mysterious other. "I know you are there. Step forward out of the black and reveal yourself."

Despite the heavy disguise there was something in the nature of the voice, perhaps the odd way that consonants were clipped by the tongue, which reminded the knight of one who walked the Court. Yet try as he might he could not identify who it was who wore the cowl and hessian habit that hid all features of recognition. Even the stranger's height and build seemed indiscernible in the gloom of the mist filled night. With no other option available, gnarled knuckles curved around the faded leather of his blade's hilt and drew the steel. He stepped out of the shadows.

"Who are you," he demanded? "Your message spoke of vital information concerning the safety of the Realm. What is it you wish to say and why such subterfuge and secrecy?"

The hidden one snorted and raised two gloved hands. There was no weapon visible and the knight felt the better for it.

"First let me offer you a gift," began the other. "It is common knowledge amongst those who plod the halls of the Citadel that you have not slept much of recent. In a pouch beneath my habit I have powder, one that has served many others and that can help you forget the pain you carry with you each long day and night. Aid me in my task and it will be your reward."

"I need no such help from you, one who refuses to show his face and seeks to hide his voice."

"So be it, but first hear me out," grated the other's voice. "What I am about to reveal will be to our mutual benefit. Help me save the Realm old man, for there are not many who have been chosen in this way."

"Stop talking in riddles, foul creature of the night. Get to the crux of the matter and tell me what it is that I should know. Why send me this letter."

"First slip your blade back into its place of rest," continued the other. "I am unarmed and there is no need to fear me. Once I have your agreement to do as I request, I will reveal my true identity and we will leave as friends. The world that we know is about to change for ever. To ensure the right outcome please listen to all that I have to say before casting judgement."

"Spit out your message then for the cold penetrates my marrow."

The other lifted a glove and pointed to the north wall of the tower.

"Step forward with me to yonder stone for there is something you must see before you will believe what I am about to tell you."

"You go first while I watch your every move," ordered the knight.

Through the crisp air the old man stepped, never once taking his eyes off the pungent cloth that moved two steps ahead. Once the untrusting pair had reached the imposing wall, a gloved hand rose and pointed to a distant nothingness.

"That is where it begins, can you not see? Beyond the Grey Mountains. From the Dragonas and beyond it comes..."

"My eyes are not as good as yours. I see nothing out there but the black."

"Then lean a little forward and look to the North Gate. Tell me what you see there."

The old knight bent forward and in doing so dipped his head an inch. A hand gripped the crown of his skull as would a gauntlet round an axe. Pain pulsed through whitened hair and parchment thin skin. Three circles of induced agony burned beneath the hand and dropped the knight to his knees. Yet as he tried to scream no sound left his lips. Stunned but still conscious, two cloudy eyes gazed upon a thick rope that had been tied to a metal ring, long ago fixed to the stone of the tower's floor. Seconds later the knight felt the noose slip around his neck. Two rough hands searched amongst his garb and retrieved the ink scrawled vellum. With ease those same hands then lifted the knight from the ground.

"Why?" his lips moved, but no sound came.

Had he been younger the knight would have shat in terror but having lived long enough to suffer the punishment that comes with age he resigned himself to his fate. At least he reckoned his end would be quick, a snapped neck after been thrown from the crenulations. Whatever had gripped his head had induced a strange paralysis for not a single limb would respond to his efforts to shift them. Rough hands lifted his not unsubstantial weight and slowly lowered his bulk over a gap in the stone. The rope tightened and the knight began to choke. The old man knew it would take some minutes before he would pass from consciousness. His killer had denied him the quick end he had so expected. Unable to struggle he dangled while the voice from above rasped out it final message. It was beneath his dignity to thrash.

"You want to know why? Well that is not for you to know. You have served my purpose and for that you will be forever remembered."

While eyes throbbed and neck veins pulsed the old knight's life ebbed away. The other waited until the end before pulling back the cowl that hid a well-known face from the eyes of world. Two bloodshot eyes looked to the distant north while a sinister half laugh lisped through parched lips. The other then turned and a soft footfall padded across the stones and on down the steps.

All was quiet atop of Parandor's highest tower save for the scratching of the rope upon the stone as the knight's corpse swayed in the wind.

1.

A mind that has many foul secrets locked in the tortuous crypts of its underkeep cannot rest in peace; and so it was that Llyat Emgar woke with a start, his thoughts shot into existence as by some strange unearthly pult. It was the same each morning now, ever since a recurring dream had begun to plague his sleep hours. Over recent weeks it had occurred with an ever increasing frequency until now it visited him every night. It was as if some great evil toyed with his mind and had at last taken control of his senses. This thought troubled Llyat for the reality was that he never felt in control of anything anymore.

The youth rolled over onto his back and looked at the thatched roof through his glazed over eyes. Feeling then returned to his right arm on which he had lain. The numbness and tingling sensation passed as did the morning fatigue that was another feature of his wakening. He rubbed his eyes and yawned as wide as the entrance to a cavern. Then while his breathing returned to normal he threw back the coarse and itch-filled sheepskin blanket that covered his naked torso. In one swift movement he swung his legs out from off his hard wooden bed, sat upright, and allowed his feet to touch the cold knotted planks that passed as floorboards.

Llyat yawned again while he surveyed his surroundings. In the gloom of the small stone built room he saw that his parents had already risen and that their bed was empty. He looked across the shadows and then to the small opening in the wall, his window to the outside world. There he saw the yellow disc of Solaris as the god rose on the distant horizon. From that one simple fact he knew that he was late for work. He jumped from his bed and threw on the olive green hessian rags that been strewn across the floor the previous night. The daily washing of his pits at the stream would have to wait. He could put up with his own smell for one day for he did not expect to meet anyone of significance during the long and arduous toil that lay ahead.

Having slipped into his pair of worn leather boots Llyat bounded through the door and into the living space beyond. This second room contained little except for a table, three chairs, and two large wooden cabinets, one for food and the other for utensils. A stone hearth sat in one corner but there was little else worthy of note. The Emgar family, a simple unit of three, had very few possessions. Llyat's father, Rukave, and the fourth of that name, had often told his son that he had always worked hard to better his family and he still strove to drag them out of their impoverished Maplehill existence. Work for a rustic family, even though everything they could grow was in great demand, did not pay well. Rukave, his wife Lyrusa, and son Llyat, tried to live a good honest existence and were almost content with their simple lives. They had each come to realise that only the rich and privileged would, or could, ever escape from the land and visit the city of Parandor.

Llyat raced through the living space of his family home, if such a basic bug hut could be called one. Pushing open the solid wooden door that led outside, he stepped over its threshold. There he paused and marvelled in the magnificent light of Solaris as it hit him with its full morning glory. He stood for a while to take in its heat and the smells of the village that as always struck the inside of his nose like the punch from a gauntlet. It was a most unique combination of pig shit, mixed with burning wood, and intermingled with the strong sweet smell of maple. The majestic trees grew in abundance throughout and around the village and gave Maplehill its name. It was a very specific aroma, a perfume that once experienced was never forgotten.

Maplehill was one of three villages that lay along the banks of the water called the Tiaryer, a river which journeyed a great distance across the verdant grasslands towards the Capital. The inhabitants of the three, Maplehill, Ashview, and Oakwood, had always helped each other to survive as best they could, given their dire poverty and all that they were forced to endure. All three hamlets contained only a few dilapidated houses. The largest of the settlements was Maplehill with its six buildings, farm, and watermill. Even amid such a desperate existence the people of the quiet and sleepy villages found ways to face life with remarkable fortitude.

Looking down the dirt track and away from his abode at the top of the hill, Llyat could see the rest of the village below, the path which snaked through its five buildings and on towards the farm, the water mill, and then to the river. He watched the few people that moved below and knew that he would have to hurry if he was to reach his destination in good time to start his daily toil. Being late for his labour he feared getting into another argument with his father about his family's dire financial state and his contribution to its survival. It was always the same. Every time that Llyat got into trouble at work, either from misapplying the harness to the horse, or planting the wrong seeds in the wrong season, his father would repeat the same tale of despair about how poor they were and how much they needed the pitiful income that Llyat brought into their house. He sometimes wished that he could escape his family and find work elsewhere in the Realm but employment outside the three villages was limited and Llyat knew that he couldn't leave his parents to struggle on alone. He also knew that without the money that he brought to their table they could not buy food and without it they would just starve. It was as simple as that and it was a most miserable life for a seventeen year old dullard.

Llyat broke into a run. He raced down the winding track that passed between the scattered maples and on towards the village centre. All the way down he felt the heat from Solaris on his back. It did not take him long to reach the bottom of the hill where he paused to catch his breath by the village stocks which were empty as usual. The last person to have suffered there was a disgraced Lord who had been caught trying to escape from the Capital and who had committed unknown crimes against the Sovereign Ruler, Phauless Gylewu. That had been many years past and was now but a distant memory. The Lord had lasted four days in the stocks without food and water after which his corpse was taken away as meat for the hunting hounds of the Sovereign's army. No crime went unpunished in the Realm. Even the slyest and most skilful thieves knew that they would all in time be caught. It was just one of the certainties of life.

Leaving the stocks and lost in his lateness, Llyat ran past the blacksmiths workshop, then the Red Mare tavern, and the houses that belonged to the three other families that inhabited the village. They went by the names of Castor, Darcha and Heyn. The largest of the three houses and the only one to have a second floor, belonged to the Heyns. There were five members of that family and the head of the household was called Vostag. His wife, Ruta, tended to keep her own company. Vostag ran the smithy and there was not a single weapon or farming implement that he could not forge. He was proud of that fact and provided sturdy weapons for his three boys, Fiat, Grophaldo, and Methladon, who acted as the defence force for the three small villages. Little trouble ever came to Maplehill, Ashview or Oakwood, except for the odd nighthowler or skyfawn; yet Vostag had trained his sons well in the art of combat for he had been taught those skills himself by his own father.

The Darcha were a complete contrast to the Heyns. They numbered only two, the mother Catriana and her daughter Maria. Their abode was the smallest in Maplehill and given that there were only two members in that family it seemed right that it should be so. Catriana was also the landlady of the Red Mare tavern and had never married. It was suspected, and speculated on, that Maria was either her bastard daughter from some client that had passed by her place of work, or as other rumours suggested, Maria was not Catriana's child at all, but that of her sister Elita who had died the previous winter from a septic skyfawn bite. Elita had left her sister the Red Mare on her deathbed and as both Ruta Heyn and Mal Castor had relayed in their gossip, Elita had also bequeathed the ten year old Maria to her sister's care.

Mal Castor was the wife of the bastard born Denius Castor. They were the third family that that resided in the small village. Their thatched roofed house was identical in design to that of Llyat's parents on the hill but it was in an even greater need of repair. There was a large hole in its roof that let the light from Solaris into the living space but also water when it fell from the sky. Llyat knew that the Castors were even worse off than his own family and that Denius was fit only for the simplest of work given his apparent limited intelligence and skills. Mal was also pregnant with child which would bring another hungry mouth that they couldn't afford to feed. Although all in the village were destitute, those who could afford to help the Castors did so in any way that they could; such was the rule of rustic life.

Racing through the cluster of houses, Llyat splashed in the occasional puddle from the previous night's rain. A passing stray cur caught his vision while looking for whatever scraps of food it could find. Soon he reached the small track that branched off the main dirt road and which led the short distance to the farm where he worked. The vigorous exercise amid the warmth generated by Solaris caused Llyat to sweat. The dust kicked up from the dirt track clung to the damp patches on his exposed skin and added to his discomfort as he ran on towards the farm. Soon he came towards the small gate that led through to the fields that surrounded the farm buildings of his aging employer. There Chirth Hadra stood with menace, his with arms folded and with a stern look upon his face. Llyat then knew that that he was at risk of losing his job.

"And what time do you call this?" grumbled Chirth as Llyat stopped to catch his breath.

"I'm so sorry Sir," replied Llyat panting. "It won't happen again. I'm really so sorry. I had a bad dream and overslept."

"This is becoming a bit of a habit Llyat. How do you expect to ever be useful when you can't even arrive at work on time?"

"I'm sorry sir," replied Llyat. "Just please don't tell my father."

"I'll have to think about that," added his employer while opening the gate to allow Llyat to pass. "Just make sure you don't fuck up any more today. Cleath is waiting for you in the far field. We had a couple of skyfawn attack the cattle last night. The cows that are still alive are pretty spooked and I hope you have a strong stomach lad. Three out of the nine have been slaughtered and their entrails scattered about the four corners of the meadow. Now get a move on."

Llyat did not have to be told twice. He was in enough trouble as it was. He ran along the remains of the dirt track until he found himself amid the shin high grass of the pasture. He covered the ground at speed and as he did so he started to think about the mangled flesh and bone that he would find in the field ahead. His mind became consumed by thoughts of skyfawns and the mess that they could make of something once alive.

Skyfawn were common beasts in the southern part of the Realm. They were not quite as common as the wood pigeon but were far more lethal. They were about the size of a full grown wolf with two featherless wings with which they glided short distances through the air. Each of their four legs ended in a set of five sharp talons that were strong and sharp enough to cut through bone. It was their distinctive large beak, filled with razor sharp teeth, that made them look so bird like, plus of course the feathers that covered their bodies, if not their wings. They invoked great fear upon all those unfortunate to come across them. Llyat remembered how they had found Elita Darcha when three skyfawn had attacked her. She had been sliced open across her body several times and was missing her left eye. The putrid smell of decay had been ripe in her wounds and even the healer that had come from Oakwood had been unable to save her. Her wounds had become septic and the infection had taken hold within her weakened body. She succumbed a few hours later. With the right weapons, training, and speed of thought, one of the foul creatures could be fought off, but like Elita the cattle had been unprepared and untrained. They had no doubt provided a ready meal for the ravenous pack that had descended upon them during the night.

It did not take Llyat long to traverse the green pasture which rose up over a small mound then down again on the other side. For miles around the village the landscape was the same, field after field of verdant grass. There were occasional patches of woodland at the limits of man's vision, most situated along the course of the Tiaryer. Moving through the field with Solaris rising ever higher in the morning sky, Llyat soon saw the agitated small herd of cattle close to the farmhouse barn and stable. He could also just make out the distant figure of Cleath Mark, his work colleague and mentor from the village of Ashview.

Cleath was twice Llyat's age and thirty four years old. His belly fat created an unmistakable shape which along with his short stature allowed Llyat to recognise him. Llyat had always joked about his build with the Heyn boys and even sometimes with Cleath himself. The man reminded Llyat of a small rotund pig which had learned to walk on its hind legs and developed hands instead of trotters. It didn't help that Cleath's facial features included an upturned nose and rough scaly skin which added further evidence to Llyat's evaluation. However, Cleath did not mind the jokes that came his way on the matter of his looks for he shared the same sentiments and often reinforced the taunts to which he was subjected. He liked to tell folk that he came from a great line of porkers who themselves were descended from the Boar Kings beyond the Dirmark.

Greeting Llyat with a shake of his hand Cleath was quick to show him the remains of the cattle that had fallen prey to the skyfawn.

"How many do you think were involved in the attack?" asked Llyat as he looked down at the bloody carcass of a young calf.

"It's hard to say," Cleath replied. "From my estimate it looks about three. One skyfawn to each of the slaughtered cattle. Old Chirth said he heard a noise just as the light from Solaris hit the upper part of the field. When he came out to investigate with his old sword gipped in his hand he saw these remains and the skyfawn as they fled into the distance. His arrival must have spooked them for not even skyfawn will mess with Chirth Hadra!"

With that the two friends laughed. It was what Llyat needed to break his dark mood and kick-start his day, given all the hard work ahead. After a few seconds of merriment Cleath brought Llyat back into the present and looked at him with much concern.

"So what's your excuse today?" he began. "Why are you late this time?"

"I overslept again," replied Llyat as he hung his head in shame. "I know it's a common excuse but I am trying to be the best person that I can be. The dreams that come to me in night do not help."

"Look Llyat, I'm not just your overseer, I'm your friend. So please take on board the advice I am about to give you... Try fucking harder!"

With that the pair set about their task of removing the remains of the cattle and loading them onto the back of a nearby cart, ready to be taken to the dump on the other side of the village. It was said by those who knew such things that you could not eat a skyfawn kill for their teeth poisoned the meat. That was a great pity for there were many empty stomachs that could have benefitted from a share of it.

Some hours later as Solaris was at its zenith, Llyat and Cleath began their walk across the fields towards the farm house that belonged to their employer. It was similar to all of the other buildings that made up the small villages on the banks of the Tiaryer. The walls were made from loose fitting stones gathered from the fields and above them a roof that was constructed from the wood of fallen trees and topped with loose thatch. Walking together their conversation drifted as always onto how different life must be in the Capital compared to the pathetic existence that they had to endure in the wild countryside.

"Well from what I have heard," began Cleath. "There are areas of that city where the streets are paved with gold painted stones."

"Yes," replied Llyat. "And your father was a Prince and Solaris is a ball of flaming gas."

"No I'm serious," responded Cleath as he brushed away Llyat's humour. "That bastard Denius told me all about it."

"Well, if Denius Castor says it is so, then it must true," laughed Llyat.

"No listen, please. Denius told me that Phauless Gylewu had the streets in the Capital coated with gold to mark the celebration of his fiftieth year as Sovereign Ruler."

"Denius Castor is full of shit. He's never set foot inside the Capital."

This was true. Castor was known for the tall stories that he would tell before the hearth of the Red Mare. Each night he would relate to those gathered a fresh story about his time tramping the northern parts of the Realm where he came across strange and fantastic creatures that no one else had ever heard of nor seen. All of his stories were set long before he had met Mal and his move to Maplehill which meant the bastard had no proof of any kind to support his unbelievable tales. That however didn't bother Llyat. Given his sad existence and low status within the village he was more than pleased to listen to the stories of war, knights, and amazing creatures, even if he knew Castor always lied through what little blackened teeth he had left.

"Well even if Denius is full of shit," continued Llyat. "The Capital must be worth a visit."

"Keep dreaming lad," his friend replied. "Either that or you can pray to Solaris to light your path to glory and singe the hairs on your bony arse in the process."

Llyat and Cleath approached the farmhouse door and both laughed out loud. Within seconds they passed through the heavy bolted opening of the building and entered the dim living space beyond. The familiar barking of Chirth's dog Balt greeted them and within seconds the black beast bounded over to greet the two men. Its tail wagged and it yapped with excitement.

"Okay, Balt!" exclaimed Cleath as he patted the dog in order to prevent it from jumping. "Easy does it boy!"

"Who goes there!" shouted the familiar voice from beyond one of the open doors. "Speak your business."

"Don't worry Chirth it's only us," replied Cleath. "We are back for our next task."

"Okay, pig face," came the short reply. "I'll be out in a moment."

Balt's wagging tail made its way towards the rags in the corner that served as its basket. Llyat and Cleath, as was their usual manner, began to look for any signs of change. The room was a spacious one given the size of the farmhouse. In one corner, next to the opening in the wall through which the light of Solaris entered the room, stood a large blood soaked slab. Placed upon it were tools used to butcher the farm's animals or indeed any other form of meat that should fall from the sky or wander past within reach of an arrow. A table and two chairs took up most of the central space in the room and Llyat had often wondered who the second seat was for as Chirth Hadra seldom had any visitors. That was of course apart from the people who worked for him. The floor was wooden like all the other houses in Maplehill and the walls were made of good solid stone, the pick from the fields. There was a hearth built into the wall opposite the main entrance and two other doors, one at either side of the main living space. It was through the one to their right that the old man entered.

"So have you managed to move the carcasses out of the bottom field?" he asked. "These fucking skyfawn will be the death of us all."

"I am sure they will sir," replied Cleath without emotion. "We got it done like you asked. We took it all to the dumping ground and I'm sure their remains will make a tasty feast for the rats."

Chirth looked towards the elder of the two men and grunted. Then a smile broke out on his face as he sat down at the table.

"That's good. It means we can forget your tardiness in being late this morning Llyat. Your father need never find out about this one. Just don't let it ever happen again!"

Llyat felt relieved for he had at last managed to please his employer. At least he would avoid a further reprimand from his father at the end of the day. He felt like shouting in glee but then thought the better of it. He was just about wise enough to realise that he was being let off lightly.

"After all that work I'm sure you two lads must be very thirsty," continued Chirth. "May I tempt you both to a mug of mead to cool you down after your toil under Solaris?"

"Thank you, yes indeed," replied Cleath before Llyat could even open his mouth. "We would love some."

"Good," said Chirth signalling towards the door. "You know where the barrel is Llyat. Go fetch us three mugs, all full to the brim."

Llyat did not have to be asked twice. Mead was hard to come by in this part of the Realm and even in the market that was held every day in Oakwood it was difficult to buy due to its ever rising price. Llyat was always keen to drink the amber liquid whenever he got the chance and after his toil in the heat some mead would be most refreshing. He therefore wasted no time and raced to the pantry. There he found three hand carved mugs set aside on the shelving that lined the walls of the cramped room. Moving to the small barrel in the corner he quickly poured the mead into the mugs. Then he returned to Chirth and Cleath, the latter having already occupied the vacant seat at the table. He gave each a mug before talking his rightful place on the floor next to Balt.

For several seconds he looked at the liquid, smiled, and then downed the entire mug's contents in one swift gulp. The warm, sweet, and silky texture of the mead gliding down his throat confirmed that it had to be the favourite drink of the gods. It left Llyat wondering how they ever remained sober. Perhaps they did not.

It was Chirth who broke the silence.

"So lad," he began. "Are you going to stroke that fucking dog all day? Leave it be and tell me; how are Rukave and Lyrusa? They're keeping well I hope?"

"They're fine," replied Llyat from his empty mug. "They have both gone to gather supplies from the market. They said they wouldn't be back until Solaris has set. Dad has some private business in Oakwood, whatever that could be."

The fact that Llyat did not see much of his family during each day did not bother him. With their finances being so limited they needed whatever work any of them could get. The responsibility for bringing supplies to their village had fallen to Llyat's parents. They would visit and collect provisions from Oakwood on most days and then distribute what they had obtained to others in Maplehill before retiring later to their home. This meant that Llyat seldom saw his parents but he loved them no less for that.

"Well, whatever business he has in Oakwood, it is his own and I will not pry into what does not concern me," replied the old farmer. "But with these recent skyfawn attacks I have every right to be nervous. I just hope they make it back in one piece."

"Do you think the attacks are getting more frequent?" asked Cleath, placing his mug down on the table. "I know they are common in this part of the Realm, roosting in the trees on the banks of the Tiaryer, but they don't often attack with this degree of severity unless desperate, hungry, or threatened."

"I'm not altogether sure that the attacks are getting any more frequent. It is just the sheer number of the creatures that are now nesting along the river that makes this old farmer nervous. The road to Ashview and then down to Oakwood runs by it for at least four leagues and it would be sad if the one horse in Maplehill became the next skyfawn target."

"Ah! I see" replied Cleath. "I thought for a brief moment you were showing some genuine concern for the boy's parents."

Cleath had spoken the exact words that Llyat had been thinking but the youth realised that the old man was showing the same level of respect for his parents that he gave to his employees and that was none.

"My father can protect himself and my mother from anything or anyone," shouted Llyat while jumping to his feet. "He can handle any sword that you could put before him."

Chirth sprayed out the liquid that had collected in his mouth as his laughter filled the room.

"This is your father we are talking about! He couldn't fight a worm's cock, even if his life depended on it."

"Fuck you Chirth!" shouted Llyat as the mead took control of his mouth. "My old man could fight you with both arms tied."

"That I would like to see boy," laughed the old man. "I'll have to ask if Rukave will accept your challenge for I'm sure it would be a fight the people of the three villages would pay much money to see. I'd even wager that all the Golden Knights from the Capital would come to Maplehill just to witness it. Bards would even write songs about it."

"Fuck you old man!" shouted Llyat. "No one talks about my dad like that."

"Well, he's not here to defend himself and this is my house, so I'll talk about him as I wish."

Cleath felt the tension rise such that he could cut it with a dagger, if only he had one. Llyat's face reddened as anger fermented in his blood and Cleath knew that the potent mead had gone straight to the youngster's head. The situation needed to be defused.

"Come on Chirth, you've had your bit of fun. Leave the lad alone."

"Oh I'll leave him alone," sneered the farmer. "I'll leave him alone when he turns up on time and does..."

Chirth didn't finish his words before Llyat kicked Balt who then yelped in pain at the impact of a boot so near to his bollocks. Llyat marched out of the front door and slammed it shut. The room fell silent and Cleath turned to Chirth and shook his head.

"What did you do that for?"

"The lad needs to be taught a lesson," came the curt reply. "He needs to step up and be a man. He is no longer a boy, even though he still insists on acting like one."

"Don't pick on his parents. You know how sensitive Llyat is."

Chirth took another swig of his mead, emptied his mug and then slammed it onto the table with a thunderous bang.

"Sensitive! That boy is more than fucking sensitive. He's an emotional wreck. As I said, he needs to get balls."

Cleath didn't have anything more to say. He knew deep down that Chirth was right and that he could not protect Llyat any longer. One day soon the young man would have to survive on his own and the sooner he did so then the better life would be for all.

Llyat ran through the bottom field as quickly as his legs could carry him. When he could run no further he fell to his knees and began to weep. Through the bird song that came from the nearby maples and the noise caused by the rushing water of the Tiaryer, Llyat's distress forced its way over the land. He cried as loud as he could, louder than he had ever done before. It was always the same when Chirth chastised and made fun of him. The old man was a bully and Llyat knew that one day he had to stand up to him. Yet it always ended in the same way. He could not stop his emotions from ruling his actions for they were like a black fog that clouded his thoughts and led to a tidal wave of unwanted and unneeded apprehension. It took all of Llyat's strength and inner resolve to hold himself together.

For some minutes while on his knees and with his head hung low, copious tears gushed from out of Llyat's eyes. He wiped them with the sleeve of his tunic and left damp patches amid the accumulated dirt and grime from his mornings toil. He asked himself over and over again, why could he not be brave and stand up for himself when faced with bullies like Chirth? It was not as if he liked his job and wanted to keep it. Yes, it was his mother who had found it for him, but all that Llyat wanted to do most was to kick the head of the man that caused him so much misery. That however was never going to happen for he had to bring the money home. At last he pulled himself together, stood upright and looked down across the green expanse of pasture that led towards the village below. It was now past midday and he could see the smoke that billowed out from the blacksmith's shed near to the stocks in the centre of the hamlet. He began to wonder which member of the Heyn family was working the furnace and whether or not they were content in their toil. Llyat hoped that none of them ever received the emotional torture that he was subjected to on a daily basis.

Scanning the few buildings that made up the village, his vision fell upon the weathered house that belonged to Denius and Mal Castor. He smiled as he noted the large hole in the thatched roof and realised how lucky he was to have a job, for without that work his life would be much worse. He would be like Denius Castor, close to starvation, and perhaps with a baby on the way, if he was ever lucky enough to ever get fucked. The tang of his stale breath hit his senses. He took in the aroma of stale food mixed with the sweet smell of mead. The drink he had consumed, combined with the dehydration from his mornings work, affected his thinking beyond the helpful. His emotions had been heightened and he felt very foolish. His face started to flush and he realised what an absolute arsehole he had been.

A dog barked from behind and the sound made Llyat spin. There he saw the tall slender shape of young Methladon Heyn with his brown retriever Allo at his heals. His friend walked towards him across the pasture of lush grass and away from a small copse of trees that boarded the north-eastern corner of the upper field. Llyat smiled as Methladon came ever closer. He was only a few years older and as he approached, Llyat could see that the youngest of the Heyn brothers was wearing the finest chainmail that his father had ever made. There was not a dent or a scratch upon it, nor on the sword that was slung over his left shoulder. Llyat then adopted a different demeanour. He stood tall and erect to greet his friend with as much confidence as he could muster.

"Good afternoon to you Meth," he shouted as the young man approached. "Where are you headed?"

"Afternoon to you too Llyat. How are things on the farm?"

"To be honest they could be better," replied Llyat. "Old man Chirth is still hounding me."

"You need to stand up for yourself Llyat," responded Methladon as he and Allo reached the spot where Llyat stood. "You need to tell him to stick his job up his arse. You should come and work the perimeter with me."

"My dad would never allow it," replied Llyat as his thoughts returned to his parents. "He thinks that the defence of the village should be left to you Heyns. You're the best fighters and we all know it. I would just get in the way."

"Put all your dad shit behind you Llyat. Be your own person. Come to work with us."

It was easy for Methladon to say that. He was six foot tall, well-built, and with a body that maidens from the other villages would give all that they had to have it on top of their bellies or thrusting in from behind. Llyat on the other hand was a gangly runt. He tried to force a smile in response to the complement and in recognition of their friendship but that just further messed with his emotions.

"Look Llyat," continued Meth. "I can see that you are in a bad mood right now. I don't know what old man Chirth said this time to upset you but I do have a way to get your mind off such things."

"Really!" replied Llyat as his hopes rose on the prospect of an offer.

"Don't tell anyone that I told you this, especially Catriana, but there is a bard from the Capital staying in one of her rooms at the Red Mare. He will be dinning there tonight before he travels on to the Grey Mountains in the morning."

"A bard from the Capital!" gasped Llyat, astounded that such a man would dare to visit their desolate village. "How can you be so sure?"

"Well, given his fancy clothes and the instrument strung around neck I kind of got suspicious," laughed Meth. "I saw him arrive this morning when I was over at the Red Mare."

"Bit early for your daily tipple," laughed Llyat, his mind now focused on the thought of a visitor from the Capital.

"Well I needed early morning refreshment as I could tell Solaris was going to be high and hot today. Seriously though, Catriana had a problem with a few rats that were nesting in her cellar and she offered me five groats if I could clear out the infestation for her. Business has been slow for her and it was all she could pay. She didn't want her larder to be savaged by vermin so being a gentleman I offered my assistance. It was on exiting the cellar that I came across Catriana escorting a sullen looking fellow, draped in a grey cloak and with minimal baggage. It was a man I had never seen before and even though we get the occasional visitor to Maplehill there was something about him that didn't sit right with me. I felt it my duty as one of the village protectors to find out who this man was. After introducing myself he asked me to join him for breakfast. Now I'm not that fond of Catriana's cooking but I wasn't going to decline the gift and so I joined him at the long table. It was then that he removed his cloak and I saw the finest clothes I had ever seen. What I had thought at first to be a hump on his back turned out to be a wooden lyre hung from his neck. After a brief exchange of pleasantries, I discovered his name and the reason for his presence in Maplehill. He is called Thias Calavan and as I said before, he is travelling to the Grey Mountains."

"What would a bard from the Capital be doing travelling to those peaks?"

"I don't know Llyat but you could ask him yourself tonight when you're finished with your work. I'm going to be at the Red Mare later with Fiat and Grophaldo as the bard has offered to sing us some of his many magnificent ballads."

Llyat smiled. This was indeed the best news he had in a long time. At last it was a chance to speak to somebody about life in the Capital and the world outside of Maplehill. It was an opportunity to check if Denius Castor's stories were true, fables, or just damn lies. For Llyat this was going to be a night he would remember for a long time.

The youth's thoughts were interrupted by another dog's distinctive bark. Turning in the direction of the noise and back towards the farmhouse, Llyat saw Balt approach at speed. The dog was closely followed by Cleath but there was no sign of old man Chirth and for that Llyat was pleased. With the great news that Methladon had just given him the last thing he wanted was another argument with the old man.

Balt bounded over towards Allo and as dogs do they checked each other over with their noses. They paused for a brief moment as if assessing each other's intentions and then set about chasing each other down the field. They barked and played together without an obvious care in the world. Cleath arrived soon after, joined the two friends, and jumped straight into the conversation.

"So a bard from the Capital," said Cleath. "I haven't seen one of those in years. I bet he could tell us a tale or two. Put some truth into some of Denius's stories perhaps! What do you say Llyat?"

"May be he could confirm if there are actual streets of gold," sneered Llyat.

The three men continued their discussion for a while but then as Solaris continued to descend across the cloud covered sky, Meth looked down in the direction of the village.

"Well gentleman," he began. "I must be off again. A warrior's work is never done."

The blacksmith's son parted from the group and made his way across the field. He whistled for Allo who then bounded after his master and together they made their exit through the gate and on towards the village. Llyat and Cleath began the slow walk back towards the farmhouse in order to continue with their afternoon work. Cleath tried not to chastise Llyat for the way he had spoken to Chirth earlier and the pair fell silent once they reached the farmhouse door. There the old farmer stood waiting with new instructions for the rest of the day.

The evening did not come soon enough for Llyat. Solaris dipped behind the horizon and the blue moon Mona became more visible in the darkening sky. After leaving the farmhouse together it took Llyat and Cleath only a short time to reach their place of rest, the tavern on the edge of the river Tiaryer that was known as the Red Mare. The old drinking hole was yet another single story building. Inside its sparse interior, one long table and two long benches filled the space between its stone walls. Near the central hearth several hand-made straw mats were strewn across the wooden floor, all of which were worn and frayed around their edges. A solid wooden counter spanned the length of the room in front of the far wall and from behind it the fair haired Catriana Darcha served the ale from strong oak casks. Across from the hearth and built into the opposite wall a door led into a dark corridor and on to several smaller rooms. One of these was the larder where food was stored and prepared for the few patrons that ever dared to request a meal. The other two were bedrooms, minimal sleeping facilities which consisted of a raised stone slab and sheepskin hide to keep out the chill of the night. The only other noticeable feature of these rooms was the hole in the floor in one corner where paying guests could empty their bladders and arses into the gully below. Life waste passed into a wooden open conduit that slanted ever down before entering the flowing Tiaryer as it passed the village. Such was the way of life in Maplehill. It was a shit life, the people were shit, and the river was full of shit. The place had no real prospects, just a bucketful of simple dreams. It was at times like the visit of the bard that everyone put aside whatever worries they had and tried to enjoy themselves. Tonight they would listen to tales from the greater world beyond the trees. Later while asleep they could build those stories into their dreams.

Llyat and Cleath purchased a mug of ale from Catriana and joined the Heyn brothers on the candle lit table besides the glowing hearth. The Heyns had started the evening early and were already on their fourth mug. Lost in their merriment they shared stories from their patrols around the village, fighting skyfawn, wolf, and even bear. Llyat so wished he could join in but as usual his confidence failed him and so he sat amongst the group in silence. He listened to every word spoken and wished that for once the story was about him.

In addition to the Heyn brothers and Cleath, Llyat noted others who had turned out to listen to the bard's stories. Denius and Mal Castor, along with several wandering folk from Oakwood, sat at the opposite end of the long table. They talked at an inaudible level as they waited to hear the bard's ripping yarns. Llyat wondered how Denius and Mal could afford to drink at the Red Mare since a mug of ale cost a groat and both of the Castors were at present unemployed. Perhaps it was because they were friends with so many wandering folk and offered some unknown service that provided the means to drink in Catriana's pitiful hostel.

The loutish behaviour of the Heyn brothers suddenly brought silence to the room and allowed ears to savour the sound of wood as it crackled in the hearth. Llyat's gaze then fell upon a young man, sullen of features, and dressed in the finest clothes that any from Maplehill had ever seen. A lyre hung from his neck. This was the one all had come to see, the bard called Thias Calavan. Catriana shot out from behind the counter and attempted to escort her prized customer to a wooden chair that she had dug out from the cellar and which she kept for special occasions.

"Please come this way kind sir," she said. "I have a seat reserved for you."

"No need, no need," said the bard as he raised his hand. "When I recite to such an esteemed crowd I prefer to stand and face my audience."

"Whatever pleases you sir," replied Catriana, her eyes avoiding those of her guest.

"And enough of the nice talk," he continued. "I am not of noble birth, nor am I a Knight of the Realm. There is no need to address me as sir."

"As you wish sir," replied Catriana while the stranger took centre stage by the fire.

"I understand you all desire a tale, a ballad from the Capital?" began the bard at which the Heyn brothers, Cleath, and Llyat cheered with beer fuelled delight. "So what song shall it be?"

"The Maiden and the Tower," shouted Fiat, the eldest of the brothers.

"The Sparrow and the Lark," shouted Methladon.

"Absolutely not!" exclaimed the bard.

"The Ballad of the Fall of Mighty Xenvagen and The Knight that Slew Him," shouted Cleath after which he gulped down a good part of his ale, not wishing to be outdone by any of the Heyns.

"No, no, and no," laughed the bard. "Come on, something different. One from long ago."

A thought then popped into Llyat's head. He didn't know where it had come from nor the confidence to shout it out.

"The Death of Urthanock, Lord of Fear" he shouted.

From the reaction of his friends and others, he knew that it was a song that would please all.

"The Death of Urthanock, Lord of Fear!" replied the surprised bard. "That is a tale I have not sang for many a year. It is the perfect choice for such a wonderful gathering."

Llyat could not tell if the bard was being serious or sarcastic but it did not matter. His voice had been heard for the first time in many years and for that single act of acknowledgement Llyat felt complete. He was sure that nothing else in his life could ever better that moment.

Several seconds later the bard had composed himself and in the reflected glare from the burning embers of the hearth he looked upon the faces of his attentive audience. He removed the lyre from around his neck and plucked several of the strings to make sure that the instrument was still somewhat in tune. A heartbeat later he started to play the sweetest and softest music to accompany the tale that he had to sing.

Urthanock was a giant they said,
A Lord from the realm of darkness.
He came into the world one day,
And brought despair before the Realm.

Urthanock, Urthanock, the bastard knight of old,
Most feared, most dreadful, the scourge of all mankind;
All powerful and almighty with a temper just the same,
There was no greater evil that you could ever find.

His army swept those lands of old,
Progressing slowly day by day.
Then the Realm fell to his evil ways,
As its armies turned to dust.

Urthanock, Urthanock, the bastard knight of old,
Most feared, most dreadful, the scourge of all mankind;
All powerful and almighty with a temper just the same,
There was no greater evil that you could ever find.

No mortal creature could fight that Lord,
His devastation crushed the lands.
And each he crossed, they fell in death,
While darkness marked his reign.

Urthanock, Urthanock, the bastard knight of old,
Most feared, most dreadful, the scourge of all mankind;
All powerful and almighty with a temper just the same,
There was no greater evil that you could ever find.

And as his evil swept the land,
Urthanock rode his mighty horse,
Against the Ancients of the north,
And all those who stood before.

Urthanock, Urthanock, the bastard knight of old,
Most feared, most dreadful, the scourge of all mankind;

All powerful and almighty with a temper just the same,
There was no greater evil that you could ever find.

The battles raged for many a year,
Until that fateful day.
When a Ancient's child of high descent,
Brought the evil to an end.

Urthanock, Urthanock, the bastard knight of old,
Most feared, most dreadful, the scourge of all mankind;
All powerful and almighty with a temper just the same,
There was no greater evil that you could ever find.

For that child had found his weakness,
He aimed at the great Lord's skull.
From his sling he fired a pebble,
And Urthanock fell destroyed.

Urthanock, Urthanock, the bastard knight of old,
Most feared, most dreadful, the scourge of all mankind;
All powerful and almighty with a temper just the same,
There was no greater evil that you could ever find.

The music played and words were well spoken. Llyat was transfixed by the story of the Lord of Fear. He imagined, as he often did, being a knight in some great battle, pitched against the hordes of Urthanock and the Realm of Darkness as he fought the good fight, proved his worth, and became the man that he always wanted to be. But those days were over. Urthanock had been destroyed many centuries past and the gates to Realm of Darkness had been shut tight. He had been told that the only records of that long ago time were kept within some deep, dark, crypt inside the Capital and hidden from prying eyes. As the music played and the soft voice of the bard continued, Llyat soon closed his eyes and let the sensation of calm take over his body. Soon he was sound asleep. The ballad ended but the songs continued on into the night.

Llyat woke with a start for the second time that day and he at once scanned his immediate surroundings. He was still in the spot where he had fallen asleep. The fire had died out and the other guests had left. It was not the first time Llyat had woken up in the inn when his friends had left him and he knew that it would not be the last. He moved past the ashes of the earlier fire and retrieved the spare key from under the largest of the three oak barrels. Catriana would have gone to her sparse abode next door to look after young Maria and it was her usual custom to lock the door behind her. A spare key was always left hidden in case one of the villagers fell into a stupor from an excess of ale and needed to let himself out. All those in the village understood the strict instruction to put the key under the door after locking it. Llyat would not prove an exception to this sacred ritual of Maplehill.

Keeping as quiet as he could Llyat unlocked the door to the tavern and slipped into the cool night air. He placed the key under the door and made his way past the stocks and up the hill to where his parents slept. Their horse was tethered as always beside the cart outside their pitiful excuse for a home. The day had been long and eventful and Llyat needed sleep. His bed would be his comfort and he felt reassured in the knowledge that nothing of significance ever happened in Maplehill, nothing except what came into his dreams.

2.

The bard always rose early for he believed that it was the best time of the day to catch the purest of Solaris's rays. It was the one time he could be at ease, gather his thoughts, and map out his actions in his mind. This morning was no different from any other.

On rising from his slumber, Thias found that the wench who ran the tavern had entered his room in silence before he had woken. She had left the necessary bits and pieces with which to wash and it appeared that no expense had been spared despite the impoverished state of the village. There on a stool at the foot of the granite bed she had placed a bucket of murky mud-brown river water, a block of sweet rose scented animal fat, and a dirt-grey foisty rag. Thias was most gratified that despite the dreadful poverty all around him he was being treated so well. Every member of the village had done his or her best to contribute and make sure that Thias was given the comforts that they assumed he would be used to as he made his journeys out from the Capital. However, what the inhabitants of Maplehill did not realise was that in all of his treks across the Realm, Thias had grown accustomed to the poverty that he experienced in so many of the villages and towns that he had been forced to pass through.

After a quick splash of water across his salt encrusted armpits, Thias dressed himself in the garments that passed as his day attire and then slung his lyre around his neck. His only other possessions were wrapped in the bundle attached to a long stick which lay on the floor besides the door. Having dressed and toileted he made his way out of the night cell and then down the small corridor that led into the main room of the tavern where the night before he had entertained a small crowd with songs and tales of the past.

While sat at the long table, Thias was presented with the Red Mare's standard breakfast. Catriana had procured a few strips of thinly cut rancid pork and what appeared to be some kind of beans that floated in mashed up tomatoes. There were also a couple of eggs thrown in which from their smell were way past their best. The feast was washed down by a mug of curdled cow's milk. It too was past perfection and as long as the bard held his nose and drank quickly he could tolerate it without retching. Looking at the meal before him, he calculated that such a portion would have fed a Maplehill family for several days and that thought saddened him. Before he started his meal he placed his hands together, dropped his head, and mustered his thoughts into a simple prayer.

"Under the watch of Solaris and Mona, I thank the gods for this bounty that has been provided for me this morning as I break my fast. Remember those who are your servants and deliver them to your side when their own lights are extinguished."

"Did you sleep well, sir?" said a soft voice.

Thias lifted his head and looked up into the deep blue eyes of a child of ten years. She wore simple rags, had flowing black dirt matted hair, and a carried red flush across her cheeks.

"I did child, it was a most hospitable and comfortable bed."

"My mother says you are from the Capital. Is it true the people there walk upon gold painted streets?"

"Indeed Child, they were made to celebrate the fiftieth year of the reign of our Sovereign, Phauless Gylewu IV," lied Thias as he sought to amuse the child with the common tease.

"Maria what have I told you?" shouted a voice from behind the counter. "Don't talk to the customers when they are eating."

"She is pleasant company Catriana. The child meant no harm."

The interaction between mother, daughter, and bard was kept brief. Between mouthfuls of food, Thias told Maria of his journey from the Capital, along the road that followed the course of the Tiaryer. The story however was cut short when he began to describe how he had scared off several skyfawn along the dusty track. Catriana did not want her daughter listening to stories about such creatures, not for any other reason than what they had done to her aunt Elita.

Catriana dragged her daughter away from the long table and Thias finished his breakfast. Thereafter he made his way towards the outside of the tavern, paused in the doorway, and sucked in the pungent air from his surroundings. The early morning shadows fell across the dirt track that wound its way between the few buildings that made up the village. Birds filled the air with their song and amid their chorus Thias Calavan stepped over yet another threshold. He was dressed in fine clothes, hidden beneath the cloak that protected him from chill of the morning air. His lyre hung over his back as usual and he filled his nostrils with the scent of maple and excrement. For several minutes he stood and watched the village stir and then focused his attention onto the two-story building with a workshop attached to one side. He listened to the hammering of metal upon the anvil and felt that it was an honest sound. Within moments the door to the blacksmiths building opened and he looked on as three young men walked out. They were the same jovial lads that he had seen the previous evening but they were now dressed in mail and armed with swords. The three then walked off in different directions. The one who had introduced himself as Fiat, passed the lean-to workshop and pulled the bard's gaze towards the half-naked and grime stained body of the blacksmith. Thias smiled to himself for this blacksmith was the reason for his dangerous journey to the arse end of the world.

Thias returned to the room where he had spent the night and retrieved his bundle and stick. He knelt down on the wooden floor and opened the knot that kept the bundle together. Having exposed its contents it didn't take more than a minute to find what he was looking for amongst his spare set of clothes, an opaque bottle that contained a purple liquid and a bronze pendent inlaid with an amethyst. He opened a small leather pouch that contained his money and counted the coins inside. He tried to guess if the contents were sufficient to purchase the item that he required from the blacksmith. It was a risk he was going to have to take. Leaving the confines of the tavern a second time he crossed the dirt track that separated him from his goal and he stopped for a moment as a horse and cart trundled past, driven by an old man with a scruffy beard and accompanied by the same youth who had requested 'The Death of Urthanock, Lord of Fear'. Once the cart had moved away he approached blacksmith, still hard at work at his anvil.

The workshop ceiling was supported by two large wooden struts which were situated some way from the main building. Its wooden roof was pierced by a chimney that rose up from the glowing stone furnace below. The anvil lay in the centre and on it the blacksmith hammered out the iron implement that he sought to manufacture. Next to the furnace lay the blacksmith's bellows which were mighty beasts and when used with force could produce a fire in the furnace so intense that it rivalled the dragon fire of the beast Xenvagen. Sparks generated from the striking hammer flew into the air while Thias coughed into his hand as he sought to gain the man's attention. The smith turned, placed his tools down, reached up, slapped the palms of his hands upon Thias's shoulders, and then proceeded to roar with laughter.

"Thias Calavan, you young pup," he shouted as memories flooded back.

"Vostag Heyn!" replied the bard. "You haven't changed a bit since the day I last saw you."

"I won't agree with you on that you young rascal. I am older, wiser, and as you can see, much wider around the middle."

"You've always had that belly," said Thias. "Too much of the meat and pastry I think!"

"Aye, and I hope your cock falls off at the first sign of the plague," replied the smith as he continued to laugh. "You always were full of shit young Thias."

"Yes, Vostag. I learned from the best."

"Yeah, you sure did," the smith answered, "but you never stuck around for the best part. You went to that fancy Bards Gild in Valameer and never returned. We all thought you were dead."

"I see you still like to exaggerate Vostag. That was ten years ago."

"Yes, it was, and it was enough time for me to get fat and you to grow up your own arse."

The two old friends continued to laugh while a deep smile made its home across the once sullen face of the bard.

It had indeed been ten years since Thias had last laid his eyes upon the blacksmith. He could remember the day well, the start of his journey when he had travelled with the caravan of other hopefuls along the sea road to the coastal town of Valameer where the mighty Bridge of Athuna stretched out over the crashing sea to the Towers of The Bards Guild. Thias had always meant to call on his old friend in the Capital but after the first five years of intense training in the Towers he just never got around to it. He had settled into his new life and over time the memory of his old friend had grown dim. That was of course until his recent quest began and since when Vostag Heyn had occupied almost every one of his waking thoughts. It was now impossible to dismiss his friend from his mind.

Vostag Heyn had once lived in slums that boarded the northern aspects of Parandor. Like his life in Maplehill, Vostag never knew of the greater riches to be found inside the Citadel. The City Watch never allowed slum scum inside for they were under orders from the Sovereign Advisor, Xix Blackfayer, to bar the admission of the worthless. Lowborn were not permitted to taint the elite or effect their pampered lives. Again as in Maplehill, Vostag and his wife Ruta had owned a smithy but it was just one of many throughout the Capital's slums and which provided the

City Watch with the weapons required to keep the peace. It was during that time in Vostag's life that Thias Calavan first became acquainted with the smith although he was only seven years old at the time, the same age as Vostag's youngest, Methladon.

At the height of one particular summer, during the hottest day that he had ever known, young Thias had crossed paths with the blacksmith. Thias was descended from a family of ill morals who had lived for generations in the upper slums and on that particular day he had been sent by his father to steal whatever he could on behalf of the Thieves Guild. Thias being naive in the ways of the Realm, came across the then forty three year old Vostag by the mouth of the Tiaryer. He was training his eldest and middle sons, Grophaldo and Fiat, in the art of armed combat with swords that he had fashioned out of wooden branches. Vostag had removed his upper tunic and exposed his then muscular body. He had left that item of clothing along with his belt and purse on a worn oak stump and then set about his lesson, clothed only in his boots and simple hessian trousers. Thias, so innocent and yet determined to put food on his family's table, saw the unattended valuables and realised that the purse was ripe for the taking. He was however unprepared for what happened next.

Vostag had failed to realise that his eldest son Grophaldo had started to tire and after an exchange of blows the youth lost his footing whist defending himself from his father's fierce attacks. As Grophaldo lost his balance he slipped and tumbled backwards over the oak stump where he cushioned his fall on the small child that lay beneath him. Vostag and the two Heyn boys guessed the child's true intent as he sought to hide behind the wood. Young Thias was terrified at the prospect of being turned over to the Commander of the City Watch and having his hands removed as punishment for theft. It resulted in an outflow of tears and inconsolable sobbing. Vostag then took pity on the poor boy and despite the protests of his two sons, took him back to his small workshop which doubled up as his home on the far side of the slums. There young Thias was given two purple carrots to eat. It was the only food that was spare but thereafter the friendship between the eventual bard and the blacksmith was forged. It was a heartfelt bonding that would last three years until the time that Thias was discovered to be a musical prodigy.

"I'm surprised that none of your sons recognised me," laughed Thias remembering the children of the family that had befriended him after his own father had abandoned him to his fate. "They didn't even recognise my name! I guess that's because you always referred to me as 'Runt'."

"As I said, it was ten years go," replied the blacksmith. "A lot of water has passed through the mill wheel since then. Yet when Methladon told me of the young sullen bard that had arrived at the Red Mare and gave me your name, I knew it had to be the very same young boy that I had once saved from being separated from his hands. Now look at you! Dressed in the finest of the Capital."

"I wouldn't say the finest," replied Thias. "They suit my needs and my needs are few."

"Well I hope you're staying another night. Ruta would love to see you."

"Stop the bullshit Vostag," snapped back the young bard. "I know Ruta will not have forgiven me for what happened."

"As I said before Thias, a lot of water has passed through the mill wheel since then and Ruta is not the woman that she once was. You see she was molested soon after you left the Capital and even though the perpetrator was caught and executed poor Ruta was left with a child in her belly as a reminder of that horrendous crime. She couldn't live with herself for carrying another man's spawn and she procured a tonic from a novice alchemist in order to end her life and that of the innocent unborn. Even though the unformed child fell from her innards and left her bleeding womb to become a meal for the dogs that evening, Ruta's life did not then go well. It left her scarred and barren, unable to raise her voice at any disagreement. The only solution for us all was to leave the Capital and survive out here in this desolate dump. That was the way she coped with her life. I kept up the family trade and decided to train my boys as blacksmiths, but also as the finest warriors in Maplehill."

"Yes, you must be very proud of them, but I am sorry to hear about their mother."

"Not to worry," continued Vostag "Like I said, a lot of water, and my boys help me to keep strong, even on the days when I falter."

"What are you know, sixty? Sixty five?" asked Thias attempting to change the subject and ease his old friends discomfort.

"Fuck off. I'm fifty six you cheeky young bugger," spat back the smith. "Like I said, you haven't changed at all. So what brings you to Maplehill? I know you will not have come all this way just to seek out your old friend."

Thias looked ahead as his face returned to its natural sullen state. Vostag saw that whatever Thias was about to tell him was if nothing else serious.

"There are strange things happening across the Realm," began Thias. "Small things, things that would go unnoticed to the untrained eye. A murder here and a suicide there. Things that seem unconnected and go unnoticed by the common folk that live between the Capital and the Grey Mountains."

"Cut to the chase," moaned Vostag. "I always suspected the Guild taught its students to talk in riddles and such nonsense. I see I was not wrong."

"I'm serious. The deaths that have happened of late are more than random events although I have to say that to the blind they would not seem so connected."

"So what do they have in common?"

"Death Tubaria!"

"Death Tubaria!" gasped Vostag. "The Child's Bane?"

Thias watched as the colour drained from the face and naked torso of the blacksmith. Even the glow from the furnace failed to disguise how pale his friend had become. It was as if ghosts from the past had returned to haunt the living and whatever skeletons the blacksmith had hidden deep away began to rattle and seek attention. The once quiet life of his village had been changed forever.

"None of us suspected Death Tubaria at first..."

"Not here," whispered the smith and he marched the bard out from under the workshop roof. "You don't know who may be listening and if this has got anything to do with...... well, you know..."

"I understand," nodded Thias.

"Look, meet me at the watermill when Solaris is at its highest. I have the key and we won't be disturbed there."

Thias did not have to say anything for he knew that his friend would be a man of his word. He knew he would meet with him but that did not stop him turning around to watch his tremulous and trusted old friend struggle in his attempt to return to his work. He sensed that it would be only a matter of time until the object that he had come to claim was in his grasp.

Later that day, Thias waited longer than he would have liked at the watermill as the hour of the agreed meeting slipped passed. The entrance to the old mill was obscured from the rest of the village by several large maple trees which grew around it and there the agitated bard stood and waited with his back against the door. He counted the minutes until his friend at last arrived.

"I hope you were just teasing me this morning," said a voice from the shadow of the trees.

The blacksmith, now fully clothed, moved towards the watermill. Thias noted that his old friend still looked shaken. Checking that no one had followed him, Vostag lifted a set of iron keys from his pocket and after selecting the correct one turned it inside the rusting lock. The door creaked open and exposed the darkness beyond. The watermill had not been used for a long time as was evident by the layers of dust that covered the wheels and cogs of the ancient machinery. It stood close to the edge of the Tiaryer and as a result there was clear evidence of damp and fungus that had taken hold in patches across the lower portions of the wooden support beams that held up the building. The two men moved into the gloom, lit only from two small windows. Light beams fell from the openings and lit up the hard dirt floor. Thias hear the noise of rats as they scurried about in the rafters and the occasional chirp of a nesting bird somewhere even higher. It was clear that except for the animals they were alone and given the story that Thias had to relate he felt the better for it.

"Well," began the blacksmith as he turned to the bard. "Start talking."

"It's like this," replied Thias. "The mysterious deaths in the Capital did not appear at first to be connected in anyway. Well, that was until the discovery of a small mark on the back of the head of the last victim. It was familiar to those of us who had seen it before. Do you still remember the calling card of Death Tubaria?"

"Yes I do," replied Vostag. "It's not something I will ever forget. In the three years that you were a friend to my boys and a welcome member of my family, I never saw anything more dreadful befall any living man as that cursed mark."

"Then tell me," said Thias, keeping his voice to a whisper. "What was their mark? Can you describe it?"

"The curse brand, most often found on the back of the skull. The three circle mark of their false god Kha. The same fucking mark that my boy Methladon carries under his hair. The mark that never goes away."

"Yes, that is it," replied Thias. "Try to remember the history and the lore. The Death Tubaria cult were determined to summon their ancient god from out the Underworld. Sorcerers and mages from across the realm understood at that time that the fanatics required the magical branding of twelve individuals and their subsequent deaths to make the resurrection come to pass."

"How could I forget? Those evil bastards tried to kill my youngest. They tied a twelve year old boy's limbs to four horses, intent on dismembering the poor child. It was only due to the quick thinking of the City Watch that my lad was saved and the cunts who tried to kill him put to death."

"Yes, that's what we thought at the time," replied the bard, sensing Vostag's pain. "Five bodies have turned up over the past few months. Each one having died in a different location but all in or around the Capital. It wasn't until the fifth corpse, one of the Sovereign's own household, was discovered with the brand on the back of his bald head that the first important clue surfaced. The Grand Physician was ordered to exhume the previous victims and as they too were marked we became convinced that the cult of the Death Tubaria had returned."

"Did you come all this way just to warn me?" asked Vostag after several minutes of deep thought. "That's it, you came here to tell me that Methladon's life may once again be in danger. If so, I thank you, but I'd like to see anyone try and kill him. I've trained him to be the best warrior this village has ever known and anyone who wants to get to Methladon would have to go through me first and then his two brothers. A Heyn will not be taken without great slaughter."

"Yes, I came to this shithole to warn you about the Death Tubaria. I came all this way to seek you out. As a wandering bard, I pick up many stories and whispers. During my time in the Citadel I heard mention of the cults of old. When I realised that someone was trying to resurrect this specific demon I made it my business to find you, to warn you, and retrieve the only thing I know of that could block the cult's attempts to contact the Underworld. You know what I am talking about Vostag. I have come for Kha's dagger."

"Oh! The Dagger of Kha," replied Vostag. "I was wondering when we would get round to discussing that thing. Meth found it and somehow it fucking marked him. I've always feared it and had hoped all that shit was behind us."

"Vostag, do you still have it?" probed the bard.

"Of course I still have the bloody thing," spat back the blacksmith as his temper flared. "No bugger would buy the dammed thing off me or even take it as a gift. A bad omen they called it and they were right. First the rape of my poor Ruta, then the rumours of a strange illness taking over the land and even an increase in skyfawn attacks. Elita Darcha, the poor pathetic sod, was killed by one of them. I can't even talk about it in public without fear of something happening. That dagger has only brought me bad luck and I can't even lose the fucking thing. It's forever turning up again."

"I'm glad you didn't lose it for both our sakes," replied Thias.

"Three years ago I tried throwing it over the waterfall just downstream from here but it still came back. I found our dog Allo chewing on it the next day and the thing was without a scratch or blemish."

"Well I'll be glad to take it off your hands," said Thias as he reached into his into his pocket and pulled out his small leather pouch. "I'll give you five crowns for it."

"You can put that away for a start," growled the blacksmith. "You can have it for free. I care not a shit for it."

Vostag reached down to his belt, half concealed by his tunic, and pulled out a small emerald encrusted dagger with a blade made from pure gold. Thias smiled for this was what he had come for.

"Thank you Vostag for your generous offer but I insist you take the money," said the bard, thrusting his pouch into the blacksmith's hand.

"You've done more than enough for me already," replied Vostag as he pushed it back and then handed over the dagger. "You have warned me about Death Tubaria and now you've taken their precious relic off my hands, I will not take your money. Our debts are squared."

"May I at least buy you and your wife dinner tonight at the tavern as a last gesture, a farewell offering before I continue on my travels?"

"I don't think Ruta would approve," replied Vostag, his voice full of fear.

"I thought you said that it was all water through the mill," said Thias

"As you can see lad, this mill has been fucked for years and so am I."

"I don't understand," replied Thias.

Before the bard could comment further the blacksmith turned his back and stepped outside the abandoned workings. Then he offered his parting words.

"When you leave Maplehill, never come looking for me again."

With that said Vostag strode out amid the early afternoon light. Thias was shocked by Vostag's sudden change of mood. In such situations he would have followed but this time he did not. Too much of the past had been raked up and too many memories of evil now burdened their friendship. At least he had completed the first stage of his mission.

It was early evening when Thias said goodbye to Catriana outside the door of the Red Mare. Customers had started to arrive and inside the hearth was ablaze. Its warmth would be needed now that Solaris and departed and Mona set up her night watch.

"I do hope your day was a pleasant one sir" offered Catriana. "I also hope you will stay with us again sometime in the future."

The bard looked across the dirt track to the blacksmith's building where the dim glow of the furnace highlighted the silhouette of his old friend. Thias thought for a moment that his eyes had made contact with those of Vostag Heyn but the man who worked the metal turned his head away and continued in his task of closing down his smithy for the evening. Mistaken, Thias turned his attention back to the young woman who had been his host.

"My time spent here was indeed a pleasant one, although given current circumstances I don't think I shall return."

"That's a shame," replied Catriana. "It's not often we get you city folk travelling through, but when they do, it is always a great honour and a pleasure."

"Thank you, good lady," replied Thias as he noted the blacksmith enter his house. "I shall write a ballad and sing about your hospitality in the Capital. Your beauty will be celebrated throughout eternity."

"Fuck off you flarcher," replied Catriana while trying to hide her embarrassment. "So which road are you going to take? Most of them round here can be treacherous."

"I will take the road north towards the Grey Mountains. I have business there with Lord Raorick of the Grey Keep. From there good lady, all being well, I shall journey west until I reach the town of Valameer and then return south along the coast road to the Capital."

"Oi, Catriana," thundered a voice from within tavern's interior. "Are we going to get some service in here or what?"

Thias smiled and took the woman's hand. He kissed it with a soft touch of his lips.

"Until our next meeting fair maiden, I bid thee goodbye."

Then with his stick and bundle slung over his shoulder, Thias the bard walked away down the dirt track and left the village of Maplehill.

3.

The iron blade crashed against her leather armour and threw the muscular battle hardened woman to the floor. As the heavy metal sword rose above her, ready to deliver a second blow, Tonousa Amberstone swung out her right leg and connected with the groin of her assailant. The young man fell to his knees and grabbed hold of his throbbing his balls as a bolt of agonising pain rippled through his groin. The female warrior, dressed in the standard issue armour of the City Watch of Parandor, then jumped to her feet and delivered a backward blow from her own sword. It connected against the rusty metal helmet of her opponent and knocked him senseless. Thereafter he lay motionless on the floor.

"And that my friends," began Tonousa as she removed her beaten leather helm and discarded it onto the dirt, "is not how you take out your opponent. Now can any of you tell me what master Bluehill's mistake was?"

The other four youths who had watched their instructor and fellow student face each other, hung their heads low lest their training master should catch their eye and force them to be the next to take up arms. Not one of them desired to spend the rest of the day lying on the mud soaked floor of the courtyard next to their fallen comrade. Each one had their own reason for not volunteering as all in their different ways were very scared of Tonousa Amberstone.

"Come on boys," she said. "How can you ever learn to fight if you can't face up to me, a mere woman almost twice your age? Now, what was young Bluehill's mistake?"

The four boys whispered amongst themselves for a few seconds as the woman stood before them and tapped her right foot. After a few moments deliberation and the whirling of teenage thoughts, the smallest of the four raised his arm into the air. Tonousa smiled.

"Yes Atheas?"

"He thought with his bollocks instead of his brain," offered the timid young boy with more than a hint of uncertainty in his answer.

"Indeed he did," replied Tonousa as she smiled, "and that is something we are here to correct. Now Bluehill finds himself asleep amid the mire because his intention was to take me down as soon as he could. He wanted to prove how strong he was to the rest of you. It was that male rush of power that brought about his downfall. He left that which he held most dear unprotected."

"You mean his bollocks?" sniggered another of the boys.

"Indeed I do Fillias. The best way to bring down a man is to attack his nethers. Most men trying to force themselves upon an opponent will leave that area exposed and so they can be felled with ease. Any man that thinks with his balls is easy to defeat, and that is most of you."

"What about a woman," asked the tallest of the four and as a sneer formed on his youthful face? "How should we seek to bring them down for they do not have a pleasure purse?"

"A good question," replied Tonousa. "The way to better any woman is by the use cunning and deception. That is something that takes years of practice and which most men are incapable of learning. Now who's next?"

The warrior woman rotated her sword around with her wrist and adopted her fighting stance. Then she watched as three of the four boys took a step backwards and left Atheas way out in front and alone. It was as if the young boy had been stuck across the head by an invisible hammer for his eyes rolled upwards and he fell face first into the mud. One by one each of the students laughed and then Tonousa joined in as she looked down at the limp body of the youth who had fainted out of the fear of what was to come.

"That's it boys," she laughed. "Here ends the lesson."

Tonousa looked on as the three youths left standing turned and raced across the muddy courtyard towards the barracks at its far end. She pondered whether she had been too hard on her students but then she remembered her own training under the instruction of the Commander of the City Watch, Brynn Townsforth, and how since then she had grown to become the most feared of those who served the ancient order.

From a young age Tonousa Amberstone had found more inspiration from watching the Golden Knights of the Citadel than sitting with other young girls as they learned the ways of womanhood. She had always dreamed of the day that she could pick up a sword of her own and go into battle like her father had once done. He, Mathias Amberstone, one of the Lords that sat in the Court of the Sovereign Ruler, had at first disapproved of her choice of career. *'No daughter of mine will ever serve in the City Watch,'* he often told her. Tonousa however had no interest in an arranged marriage, becoming the wife of a highborn, or bearing a succession of children one after the other. So it was that she practiced in secret and toiled hard. By chance one day her father discovered her training with a sword and was astounded by her level of skill. He then relented and signed his daughter up for a career in the City Watch.

During her ten years of intense instruction under the direction of Brynn Townsforth, long before he became Commander, Tonousa was the only female member of the Watch. She had developed her physique to such a degree that it was longer like that of a woman. Her short auburn hair, battle scarred face, and slim muscular body hid all form of femininity. She had created an image that all those who joined the Watch could rally behind. It was so powerful that the scum from the Capital's slums feared her most whenever the Watch was called to sort out disturbances.

"Training in your usual way I see!" shouted the firm but aging voice from above. "Putting the boys through their paces are you?"

Tonousa turned and looked up to where the voice had originated. She recognised at once the stern looking man who stood watching her. He too was dressed in the armour of the City Watch and stood on the wooden walkway that ran around the circumference of the stone courtyard. His position could only be reached from a set of strong wooden stairs that were built onto to the wall of the main barrack building. It was the spot he used whenever wanting to assert his authority.

"I think the younglings are going to turn into a fine set of young men," replied Tonousa, "but they need to find a sense of humour."

"You can be a little hard on them sometimes," replied the old man with a smile. "Look at young Atheas lying in the sodden soil. When he wakes, the embarrassment of what happened will take an age to forget."

"Yes it will," agreed Tonousa, "but then there is the lesson of humility that he was taught today. He will wake in the mire having learned that most important lesson. He will have a more modest opinion of himself which is a good quality to start with when shaping a warrior of the Watch."

"Ah the humility lesson!" said the old man with a smile. "It seems you have remembered all that I taught you."

"Indeed Commander," replied Tonousa with respect. "You trained me well. Out of all my tutors, you were the one who I always admired the most."

"And you were always my favourite student, not like the runts that are being sent through these days. They lack the drive and the ambition to succeed in the Watch. You however were destined to succeed."

"That I was Sir. I had my own reasons for joining and the Watch has become my family. I had, and still have today, no intention of settling down with a child in my belly. The Watch is the only life that I have ever wanted. It fulfils my desire to serve, protect the innocent, and uphold the truth."

"They are most admirable qualities and those that I will find useful over the next few days."

"Sir?" quizzed Tonousa.

"Xix Blackfayer in his role of Sovereign Advisor has sent me an order."

"That lecherous bastard!" replied Tonousa. "What does that fucker want?"

"It seems that the Court is concerned over a number of deaths that have occurred in recent months. Even your father, Lord Amberstone, is worried for his life."

"And how are all these people dying?" asked Tonousa.

"I've not been privy to the full details. An errand boy arrived this morning summoning me to an audience with Phauless Gylewu himself. The message contained minimal details but enough to indicate that an essential task had been designated to us. It is of the highest importance and so I would like you to accompany me to the Court this afternoon. We must determine what is expected of us."

"Of course sir," replied Tonousa while she bowed her head in recognition of the importance of the work ahead. Then she pointed to the two unconscious bodies in the mud behind her. "What about Bluehill and Atheas?"

"Leave them be. They'll wake up at some point. I'll meet you later by the main gate, once you have cleaned yourself and changed your garb."

"Of course sir," replied Tonousa and with that Brynn Townsforth, Lord Commander of the City Watch of Parandor, walked back along the wooden walkway towards the door that led to his quarters.

Tonousa looked down at the two bodies in the dirt and then with sword still in hand she started to make her way across the courtyard towards the entrance to the barracks. The building consisted of two distinct areas. The main component was a large stone building which housed the sleeping quarters, the wash house, the armoury, and the dining hall. Attached to it was the outer courtyard which itself was surrounded by even thicker stone wall and against which several wooden lean-to buildings had been erected. Each part had stood the ravages of time and ever since their construction they had resisted all the elements thrown against them. The main courtyard covered an area of one hundred square paces and as Tonousa made away across the mud sodden ground she passed several other small groups of warriors. Some were engaged in the art of swordplay, some in archery, and others in the basic tasks that helped the barracks continue to function.

Reaching the stone building at the far end of the courtyard Tonousa swung open the large wooden door that served as its entrance. She placed her sword in the rack of weapons by the door and then proceeded inside. There she crossed the large empty dining hall with its oak tables, wooden benches, and carried on through a door on the opposite side of the room. As she moved forward she passed a young boy who ran out to join the rest of his class of trainees, somewhere back in the open courtyard. It required deft footwork on Tonousa's part to avoid a collision. Through the next door she entered yet another room devoid of people and there stood awhile and surveyed her surroundings. In front of her stood two rows of fifteen wooden bunks, each with a solid oak chest at one end. The room was lit by a small opening at its far end which cast a little light that cut through the gloom. As she moved through the space she started to wonder what had happened within the Royal Household, the deaths and the subsequent demand for the assistance of her Commander. The Watch had not been formed to investigate the internal affairs of the Court for such dirty work was the responsibility of Xix Blackfayer and his minions. Something did not seem right.

Once she had reached a specific bunk halfway down the room to her left, Tonousa stopped and opened the chest that lay at its foot. After she had checked to see if she was alone, she began removing her armour and placing it into her chest. Next she removed her cloth shirt and covered her flat chest with folded arms in an attempt to hide her nakedness. Even though she was a trained warrior and could defend herself against any would be predator that dared attempt to deflower her, Tonousa still felt self-conscious about her body, in particular several large scars that stretched across her back, a reminder of her vulnerability. These scars were the result of past mistakes, errors of judgement that she had no intention of ever repeating. She soon left the sleeping hall though a small door at its end and locked it behind her. Standing in front of a stone bath she then turned on the tap and filled it with murky river water. Then, without hesitation, Tonousa climbed into the chilled water and uttered not the slightest hint of complaint. She was going to an audience with Phauless Gylewu and was only too well aware that she needed to wash away the smells of the day. They would be flushed down the aging sewers that ran beneath the Capital, to bathe the bravest of fish that dared to come close to the city.

Tonousa's muck ingrained cloth scrubbed away across her body, removed some dirt and most of the lice from both armpits and between her legs. It was at times like this that she knew how lucky she was to live in Parandor. It was only the privileged who had access to the plumbing systems that distributed scarce water around in lead pipes. Those outside of the walls were forced to wash in the river Tiaryer as it passed into the estuary. Most of the slum dwellers never washed at all. It was said that generations grew up and passed away without ever attempting to clean themselves. Few of the wealthy who lived inside the walls of the City had access to the water pipes and most hired young slaves to fetch it from the raging river. Plumbing was one of the few perks of the Watch and something that Tonousa much valued.

When she at last caught up with the Lord Commander, dressed in a set of clean armour she had retrieved from the armoury, the pair of warriors made their way through the training grounds of the barracks towards the Barbican. This was the most imposing of stone structures which acted as a formidable gate house, not just for the barracks, but for the inner city. The Barbican was the major gateway into the Citadel and it kept the lowborn out of both it and the barracks. The armour that now hung from Tonousa fitted to perfection. It was identical to her training suit but was clean and well presented. Even the steel helmet that covered her head was polished so well that it gleamed. Whichever armourer was on duty had taken great pride and care in his work.

They passed under the raised portcullis with the murder holes above it and then on through the mighty Barbican itself. Tonousa followed behind Townsforth as was her place in the ranks of the Watch. Soon they stepped out onto the cobbled street that led away from the control tower. They passed between the wooden buildings that lined both sides and on towards the towering battlements of the Citadel's Keep. Many of the more wealthy inhabitants were moving about the street, busy like ants on their daily tasks, but each and every one of them kept their distance from the Lord Commander and the woman who followed him. Perhaps some of the watching eyes would have seen the woman as the Commander's slave, but Tonousa was willing to follow Brynn Townsforth anywhere. After a few minutes they arrived at the final gate, one set into the high wall that guarded and encircled the Citadel's courtyard. There they were greeted by a tall knight clad in the finest steel armour that any blacksmith could forge. The coat of arms of the Sovereign Lord, a gold cross dividing a background of four equal triangles of copper-red, bronze, silver and grey, gleamed upon his left pauldron. The knight's face was obscured by the visor of his helm and as Tonousa and her Commander approached his hand fell upon the sword that hung from his belt.

"Speak your business," warned the knight as the two members of the Watch approached.

"We're here to answer a summons," replied the Commander, reaching into the leather pouch that hung at his side. He pulled out a piece of torn parchment which he then thrust into the hands of the knight. "We have been summoned by Xix Blackfayer to attend the Court of our Sovereign Lord this afternoon as Solaris falls from the sky."

The knight scanned the paper, then turned and waved towards one of the slatted windows of the gate. His voice was softer when he spoke again.

"This seems to be in order, you may pass," he said as the doors opened and the portcullis behind began its slow ascent. "Just remember to leave all weapons outside in the courtyard before you enter the presence of our Sovereign Lord."

"That is not an issue good Sir Knight," replied the Commander. "As you can see, neither my friend nor I are armed."

"That is good," replied the gate guard. "Strange things have happened in there these past few months. We need no more trouble this day."

With that the knight stood to one side and allowed the two members of the City Watch of Parandor to progress to the inner court of the Citadel. Passing under the portcullis and into the small courtyard beyond, Tonousa wondered what had been going on. Everyone, including the guards, were spooked. Whatever it was that had happened, it seemed of great concern to those stood guard and protected the rich, the privileged, and the idle elite.

Tonousa followed her Commander across the courtyard towards the large flight of stone steps that led up to the cast iron doors of the Citadel's Keep. At the top of the steps, waiting for them as if somehow warned of their arrival, stood the thin, pale, and sullen figure of the Sovereign Advisor. Both members of the Watch knew him well and all in the Realm were aware of his fearsome reputation.

"My friends," hissed Xix Blackfayer, while Tonousa looked with envy upon his fine dark velvet robes. "Welcome once again to the Royal Citadel. It is an honour to be in the presence of the Lord Commander of the City Watch and his ever faithful lap dog, the Amberstone bitch."

"And it is good to be here," responded the Commander before Tonousa could speak.

"Your presence at Court is always favoured," sneered Xix, his deep purple eyes looking Tonousa up and down with great suspicion. "Although I have to add that he company you keep is somewhat to be desired Commander. The thought of a woman in the Watch is still a most putrid one to have to endure. The City of Parandor's oldest and noblest society is tainted by its indulgence of this bitch. No wonder the stink from our once fine city grows ever fouler if this is what guards us. Come this way and do so now."

The man's comments wounded Tonousa but her well trained mind locked them away deep within her subconscious. The vile swine stretched out his arm and performed the gesture that guaranteed their entry into the Keep. If Blackfayer had been anyone other than the key member of the Royal Household then Tonousa would have hit him. Yet she was not so stupid and though she had suffered many abuses from the vile man in the past she had always remained professional, except on one specific occasion.

The two members of the Watch moved forward, pushed open the large doors that bared their way, and stepped into the vast hall that lay before them. The grandeur of the great room was a spectacle to marvel at, even for those who had seen it before. The white marble stone that made up the interior of the Keep was of the finest quality and several large pillars made of the same material held up its elegant decorated ceiling. Around the room were many doors that led to various other parts, greeting rooms, a library, and the ground floor kitchens. Tonousa followed the Commander into the interior of the hall, lit by beams of light cast through the windows cut into the stone above the height of the tallest of men. The

Court of Phauless Gylewu had filled with the many Lords, Ladies, and others bestowed with the honour of living under the same roof as their Ruler. From the multitude of highborn faces that caught her gaze, Tonousa could name only a dozen or so of the individuals gathered before her eyes. These included Sir Rayner Byddin, Lady Llys Emeny, Heward Teulu, Sir Tobye Cragtalon and several others of lesser rank. Around the edges of the walls stood the Royal Guard. Each wore the polished golden armour of the Realm and were primed to address any trouble brought before the nobility. That however seldom happened.

The Lords and Ladies stared down with fierce faces as the City Watch approached. Tonousa felt in awe and remembered the last time she had been in this situation. It was an occasion when she had lost her composure and had assaulted Blackfayer, the man that was now just a few paces behind her. On that day she had punched him after he had grabbed her between the legs in an attempt to confirm the status of her sex. It was no wonder that the Lords and Ladies of the Court stared at the two as they walked between them towards the head of the hall where the Sovereign Ruler sat upon his polished white marble throne. When she had thrown that punch, broken the nose of the Sovereign Advisor, spilt his blood on the floor in front of Lord Phauless, she had broken an unwritten rule. It was one that had been set by the Sovereign Ruler himself and stated no blood should be spilt in his presence. Any perpetrator of crimson was always arrested and evicted with force, before being flogged within an inch of their lives. That is what had happened to Tonousa after her last visit. Most of the deep scars on her back were a constant reminder of that crime and act of hot headed impulsiveness.

While pushing through the crowd of the noble Lords and Ladies gathered around the throne of the Sovereign, the Commander and Tonousa came before an odd young man dressed in motley clothes who pranced and jumped into the air while he attempted to juggle six small wooden balls. Each time his efforts ended in failure.

"And for my next trick," laughed the Fool. "I shall attempt to make all six balls disappear using similar magic to that used by our Grand Physician, Abrahamus Marus."

The crowd roared with laughter as the two members of the Watch looked on in silence.

"Fuck off Lolly," shouted one noble Lord.

"Not even you can match the skill of our Grand Physician," shouted another.

"Why don't you make yourself disappear?" shouted a third. "Climb up your own arse so that we no longer have to put with this tedious tomfoolery."

Tonousa made to laugh but somehow managed to restrain herself. Even though highborn their language was as coarse as any of that that found within the depths of the slums.

"Then maybe I shall entertain you with a song," the Fool continued. "Does anyone wish to hear the story of how Prethis shagged Mona, our goddess of the night?"

"Why don't you just slit your pox filled throat and end our misery," bellowed another Lord.

The crowd roared with laughter and even Tonousa managed a smile beneath her battle hardened exterior. The Fool also started to laugh and then proceeded to do a handstand on the floor. Nothing troubled the idiot and he ignored the torrent of abuse that came at him from all sides.

"Enough Fool," ordered a firm voice that brought immediate silence.

Tonousa looked up and focused onto the occupant of the marble throne. For a brief moment her eyes connected with those of the Sovereign Ruler, Phauless Gylewu; but then in deference she dropped them down beneath her lower lids.

"Be gone Fool, you have overstayed your welcome this morn," continued Phauless as he raised one hand to signal the quiet he now demanded. "It appears we have some visitors. Please step forward so I may look upon you further."

Tonousa and the Lord Commander moved two steps closer and then, side by side, they both fell upon bended knee and dropped their gaze to the floor.

"My Lord," said Tonousa as she knelt.

"My Lord," repeated Townsforth before adding. "I hope Solaris bestows his warmth upon you for many more years to come!"

"As it so pleases the disc," answered the Ruler. "Now stand and hear what I have to say."

"Thank you my Lord," both responded in unison.

As they rose Tonousa noted that Xix Blackfayer had joined the Sovereign upon the plinth. He stood behind the Ruler and scanned the Court with his snake like eyes.

"I thank you for coming so soon," began Phauless. "This is indeed a dark time for my Court. No doubt my trusted advisor has told you in his summons that the Citadel is facing threats far greater than our worst nightmares."

Tonousa stared at Blackfayer who sneered when their eyes met.

"The Sovereign Advisor stated in his summons that there had been a number of deaths amongst the Royal Household," began the Commander of the Watch "There were however no details, just that we were to attend Court this afternoon."

"Of course there were no details," replied Xix. "I felt it best, given the circumstances, that the reason for your presence here was not made common knowledge. The dark omens that have visited us demand the utmost secrecy."

"And yet we discuss it quite openly in Court," snorted Phauless. "No matter my friend. Those who are here present, the Lords and Ladies of my Household, are the most loyal servants of the Crown. I would trust each and every one of them with your life Blackfayer."

"Indeed my Lord," replied Xix as his gaze fell back upon the crowd before him.

There followed a brief pause as Phauless Gylewu moved a little on his throne and readjusted the position of his buttocks. Tonousa felt pleased that the old man still showed some of his legendary sense of humour. Once he was comfortable he continued with his message.

"My Lord Commander of the City Watch, my trusted servant Brynn Townsforth, as I said we are living in dangerous times. Five citizens from my Household have been found dead; in various places in and around the keep. The first appeared to be a simple suicide. Lord Tobius Faros was found hanging by his neck from the highest tower. He had lost his wife and daughter to the sweating sickness and we assumed that he just couldn't live without them, although I dare say most men would have thought it a blessing. Then there was Sir Britta Rainmark of the Royal Guard who was found face down in the Tiaryer, still in his armour, drowned yet with no signs of foul play."

"Another suicide?" questioned Tonousa, unable to hold back the thought that jumped into her mind.

"The bitch Amberstone will remain quiet until given permission to speak," ordered Blackfayer as his stare burnt into Tonousa's soul.

"Steady on Xix," snapped out the Sovereign Lord as he raised his hand to stem any further words from his henchman. "She meant no harm. She was only speaking what we were all thinking. Yes, it did look like another suicide but there was no obvious motive for Sir Britta to take his own life. According to his regiment he was in a good place, one where his merriment was at the forefront of his being."

Tonousa wanted to reply as further questions filled her head but given that she had already interrupted the Sovereign Ruler once she realised that she needed to bide her time. She could not afford to incur the wrath of Blackfayer or even her own Commander, despite the thoughts that continued to ruminate inside her head. Two suicides with no obvious connection apart from being members of the Royal Household was not much to get excited about.

"The third death of which we speak was that of a young handmaiden who worked for Lady Thinata Fullbane," continued Phauless. "She was found down in the Underkeep, in the servant's pantry, having it seemed choked on her evening meal. The Grand Physician suspected that the young woman had been poisoned with something alike to the Nightshade. There was even speculation that her lover, a servant from the kitchens, was her assassin. Yet later that same day we found his body stuffed in the spice powder store and poisoned in a similar manner."

Tonousa looked to her Commander who had remained silent the entire time. She wondered if he too was troubled by the absence of an obvious connection between two apparent suicides and the poisoning of the two young servant lovers. Still she stayed her tongue and waited to hear more.

"It was the final murder that triggered a more detailed investigation," continued Phauless. "Lord Fabius Colt, the Royal Treasurer, was then also poisoned. He was found in the Royal Vault, lying face down in a pool of his own stomach contents."

Numerous gasps from amongst the highborn behind Tonousa filled the air as the Sovereign Lord delivered this final statement. It was news to all who listened. She glanced behind and watched as several of the Ladies raced out of the hall in a state of great distress. Tonousa wanted to smile at their reactions but realised this was not the time and place. If she hadn't been so hardened from her years of service in the Watch, then perhaps she too would have felt the need to rush from the Court. However the question still remained, what linked the suicides to the apparent murders. Before she could ask that question her Commander spoke."

"So, two suicides and three murders. Forgive me my Lord Phauless, but what is the link? As far as I can see the two groups are unconnected."

"That is what we thought," interrupted Xix. "Indeed, there seemed no connection other than the two servants who were fucking each other. As our Sovereign Lord said, it was only after the death of the Royal Treasurer that we began to suspect the true depth of the darkness that has fallen upon our city."

"I do apologise Xix," replied the Commander, "but you continue to talk in riddles. You still haven't told us of the link between the suicides and the other deaths."

"Did either you know Lord Colt?" asked Phauless.

Tonousa searched through the names and faces that she had stored in her memory, people she had come into contact with through her many years of service in the Watch. As she tried to recall the highborn, the image of a short, bald, rotund man, dressed in robes of cheery red and glistening gold came to the forefront of her mind. Once again before she could move her lips, the Commander spoke.

"I remember meeting Lord Colt on several occasions. He was a stump legged barrel of a man if I am thinking of the right person."

"The oaf was a gluttonous swine and we both know it," sniggered Lord Phauless and the court laughed with him.

Even the Fool, from his position at the back of the crowd, laughed out loud and juggled his balls. Tonousa found it very hard to keep a straight face for she too then recalled the enormity of Lord Colt's gut. Then as the noise of the crowd dispersed she refocused on Phauless's lips as he continued with his story.

"It wasn't Lord Colt's weight or girth that provided the link. It was his bald head!"

"His head? I don't understand," said the Commander.

"The man was as bald as a toad's tit. The Grand Physician himself was the first to find the mark on the back of his head. It was a curse brand, the three circle mark of the false god Kha."

More gasps rose from the crowd and this time Tonousa witnessed at least one of the Ladies faint at the mention of that foul demonic name. It was a name that Tonousa was all too familiar with for the last time she had heard it she had almost lost her own life in the protection of the citizens of Parandor. Throughout the mutterings and whispers that filled the hall she heard the voice of her Commander spit out the words that were now on everyone's lips.

"The god Kha and the cult of the Death Tubaria?"

The noise echoed loudly from off the marble and reached an uncontrolled crescendo as each member of the Court started to shout out their own opinion on the issue. Some demanded an increase in protection from the Fifteen Keeps beyond the Capital, while others suggested more patrols by the City Watch. Lost in the commotion, Tonousa's thoughts focused on the past and without warning she spoke out loudly.

"How can you be sure that these events are related to Death Tubaria? What other proof do you have?"

"Silence please! Everyone be quiet!" shouted Lord Phauless as he raised his hand for the third time.

The clamour subsided, quiet returned, and the Ruler continued with his evidence.

"Tonousa Amberstone, daughter of Lord Amberstone and member of the City Watch raises a valid point. Having found one within Capital, we assumed more marked bodies would turn up if the cult of Death Tubaria had resurfaced. Our Grand Physician suggested it would be appropriate to search the skin of the others that had died under suspicious circumstances. After exhuming them all we discovered four further curse marks under the hair of those sad departed souls. They were identical to the one we found on Lord Colt."

"Do you expect there to be more deaths?" asked Tonousa as she tried to understand the full implications of what was being said.

"Indeed we do," replied Lord Phauless. "How many do we now expect Xix?"

"Another seven," replied the Sovereign Advisor without emotion.

"Seven more deaths," continued Phauless. "Another seven of my household are to be murdered to bring about the End of Days. We cannot let this happen and that is why you are here."

At last it all made sense. The Sovereign Lord, esteemed Ruler of the Capital and the surrounding Realm, was asking the City Watch to solve the mystery, to prevent further murders, and above all to scupper any attempt to resurrect the god of darkness.

"Forgive me my Lord but why ask the City Watch for help in these matters?" answered Commander Townsforth. "We keep the peace inside the Capital; that is all. Wouldn't this task be better suited to one of your Royal Household? Maybe Lord Blackfayer himself should take up the investigation."

"No need for the apology," replied Phauless. "I had thought of passing the responsibility to Blackfayer and his confidants, but if you recall eleven years ago when Death Tubaria first surfaced, it was found that some members of the Court were themselves involved in the cult's dark arts."

Malignant murmurs once again spread through the hall while Tonousa and her Commander exchanged glances. The last time the cult of Death Tubaria had gripped the Capital with fear, the investigators discovered that the previous Grand Physician, Lord Jonas Tullage, had led the conspiracy to summon Kha. Tonousa remembered how the battle between the Watch and Tullage's followers had lasted for a full night and day. The latter had swarmed through the streets of the Capital and Tonousa still suffered nightmares over all the innocents that were slaughtered.

"Do you suspect Lord Tullage again?" asked the aging Commander.

"Tullage is dead," replied Phauless. "He was sent to the dungeons of the Grey Keep under the watchful eye of my brother, Lord Raorick Gylewu. It was there that Tullage met with the sharp end of an axe, stolen and wielded by a dwarf. His body was burned along with the rest of the scum that have died there over the years."

"Then at least that is one less suspect," replied the Commander.

"So I take it you're interested then?" said Phauless.

"Of course I am my Lord."

"That pleases me although I ask for utmost discretion during your investigation. The Lords and Ladies of Parandor, along with my own Royal Guard are at your complete disposal, but I ask that matters of the Court, including these murders, are not discussed outside of the Citadel. My own personal and private investigator has been sent to the Grey Keep with instructions to search for any information regarding Lord Tullage or anything that he may have divulged to his fellow prisoners."

"Does he have a name, this secret servant of yours?" asked the Commander.

Tonousa thought it odd that Phauless Gylewu would send another to investigate the mystery in addition to calling on the services of the City Watch.

"I hope you will understand when I say his name is not for your ears," continued the Sovereign Lord. "Not even Xix knows his identity. He shall go unchecked on his journey and investigate in secret, for even though I trust you Commander Townsforth with my life, it is possible that the City Watch has been infiltrated."

Tonousa gasped at the implication that someone from within their own ranks could be party to the plot. She was however certain that whatever the truth was, the Watch would be able to apprehend the culprit. She was about to ask her Commander for his thoughts when the voice of Phauless echoed through the hall as if projected by some magical power.

"I draw this Court to an end," he bellowed as he stood up from his marble seat before directing his next words towards the two members of the Watch. "Thank you Lord Commander. I trust you will apprehend the murdering bastard without delay and report back to me in person."

As Phauless Gylewu left his throne and made his way across the hall, the members of the Court each fell to one knee and dropped their eyes down to the floor. Tonousa and her Commander followed their lead and did as expected. The only ones not to kneel as Phauless passed were the members of the Royal Guard who continued to stand to attention around the hall and Xix Blackfayer who followed behind his Lord like an obedient hound. Once the slimy Sovereign Advisor drew level with Tonousa he paused for a moment and whispered such that Tonousa alone could hear his words.

"Good luck bitch. You will need it lest you make a fool of yourself again."

The Court dispersed and the background noise of excited comments filled the void left by the Sovereign's departure. Tonousa returned to her feet first and then sought to help her creaking Commander back into an upright position. His aging joints cracked and groaned out their displeasure.

"Do you think he was serious?" she asked. "Is it possible that the Death Tubaria could be back after all this time?"

"It is not an impossible suggestion, however unlikely it seems," replied Townsforth. "It should be an interesting investigation but its best we do not to talk here. Walls listen you know! They hold many secrets."

"Indeed, they do," she replied.

Tonousa followed behind the man she so respected and soon passed a small gathering of highborn as they watched the Fool in another of his pathetic attempts to juggle his balls. It was then that she caught a glimpse of her elderly and estranged father who stood against the far wall. He had been present the whole time and his steel like gaze latched limpet-like onto his daughter face.

4.

Three nights after the bard Thias Calavan had entertained the customers of the Red Mare, young Llyat Emgar was accosted on his way home from his shit filled hours on the farm. Trundling down the dirt track he thought back to the tedium of the day, herding the cattle and mucking out old man Hadra's horse. He was exhausted and weakened to the marrow. As his weary legs approached the village a voice had called out amid the fading evening light and demanded that his eyes focus upon the entrance to the flea pit that passed as Maplehill's tavern and place of social intercourse.

"Llyat, come join me in a game of Fidchell; I have just made myself a new board and counters," yelled the seductive voice of his best friend Methladon Heyn. "I'll buy you a couple of pints of Blessed Beast if you help me break in my virgin board."

"I have never played that game on my father's instructions," declared Llyat as without any hesitation he moved towards the tavern door. "I would rather you taught me to use a sword and how to defend myself."

"You know I cannot do that for if your father found out I would thereafter walk these lands without my prized jewels," countered Methladon as he beckoned Llyat forward with his hands. "Come on in and I'll teach you the game's rules. You are the closest friend I have ever had and I would consider it the greatest honour to teach you how to play this most ancient of games; still the best in our time."

"Okay, but I can only stay to down two for my parents will be waiting with a meal on the table," replied Llyat, stepping over the threshold and following his friend into the gloom. "I hope the rules are not two difficult for I have had a hard day on old Hadra's farm and my head craves the rest of a soft pillow, not that it knows what one would feel like."

"I'm sure you'll pick it up just fine."

Llyat followed Methladon to the end of the long table where his friend had previously positioned the necessary equipment to enact the game. Seconds later they sat opposite each other as Catriana Darcha slammed two mugs of Beast upon the table. The contents of one splashed onto the metal square that separated the two youths.

"Oi!" shouted Methladon. "I've only just made this. If you do that again, I'll slap your pudding rumps."

"And I'll hit you so hard your balls will ache for a week; you cocky young bugger," replied the innkeeper as she walked away, swinging her cheeks from side to side in a show of contempt that couldn't hide her need for a fuck.

"I love it when you talk of perverted play," shouted Methladon while a great smile formed on his face. "If I play your cards well, you can have me tonight."

"Fuck off and tug on your twig!" bellowed Catriana as she left by the back door to attend to other chores.

Llyat tried not to laugh.

"You still fancy her, don't you?" he whispered as he leaned forward. "Ever since that time..."

"Shut up Llyat," stuttered Methladon as his face flushed poppy red. "Don't say such things in here of all places. She must never find out that I have told you what happened between us."

"Well I reckon you have competition," reasoned Llyat as he began an inane adolescent giggle. "Cleath would give a week's wages to take her from behind, he as good as told me so himself."

"Grow up Llyat," snapped back Methladon as he refocussed on his game and scratched the back of his neck in embarrassment. "As much as I like you as a friend, if you drop me in the shit with Catriana I swear I will stick the blade I use to defend this pestilent paradise so far up your arse that you'll be able to kiss its tip with your tonsils."

Llyat raised his mug to his mouth and emptied half of its contents in one prolonged swallow. He soon looked down upon the unusual object that formed the basis of Methladon's invitation. Then he smiled at his long-standing friend and a sensation of boyish brotherhood passed between them.

"Is this the shit that you have brought me in here to teach me to play with," exclaimed Llyat while scratching his head and looking at what lay before him. "I think you need to tell me the nature of the game before you tell me the rules. What did you say its name was?"

"I guess I do, dolt," replied Methladon while picking up the square board from the table. "The game is called Fidchell and some say it is as old as time itself. My father taught it to me years ago, but we never brought a set with us when we fled the Capital. He always reckoned it was a game that had been invented by Lugh or some other god. The idea is really simple; it's a battle of good against evil. When we start, I will play evil for its only fair that you as a novice get to play the good guys. Once you've got have hang of it then you can have a go with the dark forces."

"So, explain what these bits and pieces are and the rules of the game," suggested Llyat as he looked down once again to the collection of objects on the table.

Methladon took a long swig of his beer and began; "This large square of bronze I forged and crafted myself. I did it while my father and mother were lost in a long conversation about the bard who visited those few nights ago. It is what is called the playing board..."

"I'm sorry to interrupt Meth, but just before I had fallen asleep the other night I sensed that you half recognised the crooner. Had you ever met him before?"

"I'm not sure," pondered Methladon while attempting to smile. "There was something familiar about his face and name but if I ever had met him it was before my mind was dulled as a child; before I ever came to Maplehill."

"Did you ask your brothers or father if they knew him?" asked Llyat as he wondered why the blacksmith and his wife would be so preoccupied by a tart dresser with a lute.

"Fiat and Grophaldo were too pissed by the end of the night to even remember seeing or hearing him, let alone recognising his face. I did ask my father but he just snorted, swore, and told me to forget the fancy pants poet from Parandor. He ordered me to stick to defending the village and not lose myself amid a dung heap of nonsense."

"Oh well, I guess that's what we should do, I mean it's most improbable that we would ever meet him again," muttered Llyat before refocusing on the pieces before him. "So, you were telling me about the playing board."

Methladon laid the board back down upon the table so as to point out the markings etched onto its smooth surface. His right index finger roamed across the board as he explained its significance.

"Do you see how it is marked out into twenty-five squares, five rows containing five," the blacksmith's son began. "Now look into these two corners, the top left and the bottom right. On each there is the mark of a five-pointed star and these two squares are known as 'The Enlightenments'. The object of the game is to get one of your counters on to the enemy's Enlightenment square. Whoever should succeed in doing that first, wins the game."

"So, are these two sets of round discs the counters?" asked Llyat as he looked down to five white ones and five made from a much darker variety of wood that made them look black.

"Yes, indeed they are," responded Methladon as he placed the five black ones on squares closest to his Enlightenment yet leaving that one uncovered. "Now, you place five white discs close to you Enlightenment just as I did with my black ones... good, now we are ready to go."

"How do we move them, are there any special rules that govern that?"

At that moment the door to the tavern burst open. The interruption was followed by the dishevelled sight of Denius Castor who had called in for his nightly slurp.

"Hi Denius," the two youths shouted in unison.

"Eve...nin" drawled the tramp who, noting Catriana's absence, helped himself to a tankard of her ale. "Is that Fidchell you're playing? My old man taught me that many lives ago."

"Come and sit with us for I was part way through explaining the rules," replied Methladon.

"No, you carry on lads, I'll just watch from over here and see how many pints I can down behind Catriana's back before I have to get back to Mal."

"And you'll pay for whatever you drink you thieving twat," bellowed the landlady of the Red Mare as she reappeared through her back entrance.

"Of course I will dear sweet lady," grovelled Castor.

"As I was saying," continued Methladon. "Being good and white, you must move first. A disc can only move one square at a time, although in any direction, and you can choose the same or a different one each time it's your turn. After each of white's moves then, I as evil, will move one of my discs. Have you got that so far?"

"Of course I have, I'm not stupid."

"There are just a couple more rules to remember," continued Methladon. "First off, if any of your discs become cornered by mine and unable to move to another open adjacent square, they will be considered to have gone through the door to the Underworld. Then they must be removed from the board. Of course, the same would apply to any of mine you managed to surround but that is not likely for a beginner. The other is that you cannot reverse your previous move when it's your next turn, otherwise it ends up with counters going back and forth in a dancing stalemate. Come on, I'll get more beer and then we can start."

The two youths, the closest of friends in the valley of the Tiaryer, played on and on as time continued its relentless journey. Black mostly won. Llyat forget about going home as the beer continued to flow. The game had hooked Llyat with its spell, just as it had ensnared others since the beginning of time. When at last Llyat's legs lost the will to move and his words tripped out of his mouth without the semblance of sense, Methladon slung Llyat over his shoulder and dragged him past the stocks and up the hill to the Emgar hovel. There he left his friend on the floor before the door, much to the disgust of both Rukave and Lyrusa.

Meanwhile upon the grass covered bank of the Tiaryer, between its source in the Grey Mountains and its meeting with the sea at the Estuary of New Beginnings, a camp fire burned. Its flames cast flickering shadows upon the ground and across the trunks of the ancient oaks and maples that grew alongside the bank of the river and where roots broke through the uneven ground in many places. The sound of music that filled the night sky flowed from the wooden instrument that belonged to the bard who sat beside the fire. As he played he watched the flames and inhaled the smoke from the burning flesh of a wood pigeon placed upon a large flat stone which was balanced on columns of pebbles over the centre of the fire.

It had been three days since Thias Calavan had warned his friend Vostag Heyn about the reappearance of the cult of Death Tubaria and then set out from the tavern in Maplehill. He had followed the dirt track that meandered through fields and the woodlands of maple, ash, and oak. He had then made his way upstream on the southern bank of the murk-slow flowing water of the Tiaryer as it made its relentless passage to the distant ocean. Throughout the three day journey along the river path Solaris had been kind to Thias and kept him warm and dry. Not once did Aquaris piss down upon the travelling bard. This pleased Thias for any downpour would have no doubt slowed his progress and caused much misery as his clothes turned heavy. That was unless he expended precious magic on drying himself.

Sat cross legged with his back to a large oak tree and on a patch of bare earth devoid of flora, Thias strummed the strings of the wooden lyre that still hung from his neck. The smell of the wood pigeon filled his nostrils and the sounds of the instrument filled the still quiet of the cloudless night. The music helped Thias to think, relax, and to gather his thoughts together. He still had far to travel and walking the roads alone required a sharp and alert mind for bandits were not uncommon in this area of the Realm. Such scum were well known to prey upon the road that stretched from the Capital to the Grey Mountains and Thias was most thankful that this journey had so far been uneventful.

Music had always been part of his life since the age of eleven. He liked to sing and to entertain at any given opportunity but that was not the reason why this bard lived for music. It filled his senses with emotions seldom felt by the common folk. It was a perfect medium to relieve any tension that coursed through his body. The simple plucking and strumming of his instrument generated soothing tones and vibrations that helped him cope with all the difficulties that came his way. Thias so liked to fill his surroundings with his skilful tunes that sometimes he would do nothing else all day.

The bard's thoughts drifted back to a distant memory, the three years that he had lived with Vostag Heyn and his family. It had been just after the first rising of the Death Tubaria and a year before he left the slums to begin his journey to the Bards Guild in Valameer. It was a time of wonderful memory; of the first time that he had picked up and played a musical instrument. He remembered one specific day and a rather long one in young Thias's early life. First off he had helped Grophaldo and Fiat with their allocated chores in the blacksmiths workshop, deep within the slums of the Capital. Then when done he had been treated to a lesson in how to handle a sword by Vostag himself. Later that day Thias had found himself sat in the living space of the small blacksmith's shack, up against the wall in a corner as was usual in an evening. There he lost himself in his thoughts and made ready to drift off into a deep sleep. He had craved the rest that would rejuvenate him for an even longer list of chores the next morning.

The impoverished Heyn family owned only two chairs and they had both been taken by Vostag and his wife. He remembered his new parents had been deep talking about how members of the cult of Death Tubaria had tried to murder their youngest son. The conversation had then become heated and it had brought Ruta to tears. Thias recalled how innocent he had been in those dark times and how he had had taken hold the nearest thing he could reach to take his mind off the infighting and dark emotions that spewed out from his foster family. The object he grasped was a wooden lyre with two missing strings and yet following his instincts, having never been taught to play, he managed to pluck out the sweetest music that Vostag and his wife had ever heard. It was from that point on that Thias was no longer taught how to handle a sword but was instead nurtured and encouraged to play music that could sooth and heal the most fractured of minds. It was that very day that he started along the long road to become a bard of the Realm.

The smell of burning from the bird on the sizzling stone distracted Thias and brought him back into the present. With speed and dexterity he used a small branch to manipulate the flesh of the plucked carcass. He turned the cooked side over and allowed the remaining raw meat to feel the heat from the stone. It was during times like this that Thias wished he was back within the Great Hall of the Citadel, feasting with the Lords and Ladies of the Court, and reciting the greatest poetry and songs from across the realm for his Lord and Sovereign, Phauless Gylewu. Those were the times that he felt most alive. As the succulent aroma rose and drifted across the land the bard began to pluck the strings in earnest. In the softest voice, not much louder than a whisper, he started to recite the words to a tale that always held a special place in his heart. It was called 'The Emotions of the Lost.'

> When all were touched by the fall of Aquaris,
> And my thoughts were lost in the despair.
> With Solaris gone, lost in the shadows,
> You disappeared into cruelty and taunting,

Preying on my emotions in the darkness that appeared.

My happiness was taken, forever lost and gone,
No longer have I pleasures; not a single one.
Into the darkness you departed,
Left me shattered and broken hearted.
I am lost for you have gone forever,
Now that you have left forever.

Your beauty I remember was there to behold,
But forever still, as the years moved by.
You tried to run and you tried to hide,
But Death itself was by your side,
Leading my emotions in the darkness that appeared.

My happiness was taken, forever lost and gone,
No longer have I pleasures; not a single one.
Into the darkness you departed,
And left me shattered and broken hearted.
I am lost for you have gone forever,
Now that you have left forever.

Shades of blue and grey fill my waking thoughts,
For you left me alone to fend in the dark.
Why did you have to die and leave me here?
Now so far away, so far, far away,
Confusing my emotions in the darkness that appeared.

My happiness was taken, forever lost and gone,
No longer have I pleasures; not a single one.
Into the darkness you departed,
And left me shattered and broken hearted.
I am lost for you have gone forever,
Now that you have left forever.

Then as Thias opened his mouth to begin the final verse the sound of an approaching horse wrenched him out of his tranquillity. He listened with great intent as the noise of the hooves upon the ground grew ever louder. He wondered who would be out along the river road so late at night when bandits were known to strike. Thias realised that for his mission to succeed he would have to remain invisible to all others; he would have to hide all traces of his existence.

In a flash he removed his cloak and threw it across the fire before him. Stamping upon it, he mixed the heavy woven material with that of the fiery ground and the carcass of the wood pigeon. The fire was soon extinguished and all became invisible amongst the darkness of the river bank. He slipped his instrument from his neck and hid it under the cloak as far away from the extinguished fire as possible.

Then without wasting further time he grabbed the stick and bundle from his side and lowered himself and his belongings over the bank and into the river.

Down into the cool and murky waters of the Tiaryer he slipped without disturbing its calm. The time for eating and song was over. It was now time to disappear. He watched the dirt road from his watery hiding place amongst the reeds and bulrushes that caressed the bank and saw it to be empty save for the shadow of the trees cast upon it from Mona's radiant gaze. It didn't take long for a horse to appear, a brown and white mare with a white blaze on its long face. Upon its leather saddle sat a knight dressed in the blackest of armour. In the blink of an eye the horse and its rider passed at a gallop and gave no outward indication of having noticed the bard or even sensed his presence. Thias watched on as best he could as the knight and his steed disappeared from sight.

After several minutes had passed and amid the silence that followed, Thias placed his possessions onto the adjacent riverbank before him and with considerable care pulled himself out of the river. Lying belly down in the dirt he could no longer hear the sound of the rider's horse, only the distant hoots of an owl as it hunted for it's for its prey amongst the surrounding grasslands. Thias looked up to Mona and the constellations of stars that surrounded the goddess in the cloudless sky. Then he closed his eyes. Folding his arms across his chest he began to mutter strange words from the forgotten language; in a tongue once spoken in a far off place. Thias felt his body grow warmer. Heat generated from within his core travelled through his wet cold clothes. As that warmth traversed his being an ethereal glow shimmered off his surface and lit up the surrounding ground with a blue haze. The bard's thoughts were consumed with being dry and he focused them like light passing through bent glass. He willed it so and his mind controlled the magic that his consciousness generated. His thoughts focused the power deep within his body for this was one of the few basic spells that he knew. Thias felt the sensation of heat creep across his skin while the moisture in his clothes evaporated at an exponential rate. After just a few minutes the intense warmth began to dissipate and a few moments later the ethereal glow that had once surrounded him floated away on the breeze. He had wished to be warm and dry and that was now what he felt. Feeling comfortable once again he looked in both directions down the track. There was no sign of the horse and rider nor indeed any indication that the two had passed that way except for hoof prints embedded into the dry dirt of the ancient road.

Thias moved a few yards down the track and wondered if there could be others travelling this night. He started to question whether he would be safer off the road. The truth was that he had not hidden his presence well while passing through the three villages that sat upon the Tiaryer, nor had he covered his tracks once leaving Maplehill. He realised in that moment how foolish he had been. If it was true that the cult of Death Tubaria had returned and that if others discovered he had the Dagger of Kha in his possession, then his life could be in great danger. There would be many who would want to hunt him down and take possession of the evil artefact. Fear began to toy with his thoughts. Only Phauless Gylewu knew of his mission to the Grey Keep and not even the Sovereign knew of the Dagger of Kha. For whatever reason the horseman was on the move it could only mean that more would follow and that the road was now a most dangerous place.

Retrieving his bundle, cloak, and lyre from where he had made camp, Thias crossed the dirt road and moved into the open fields ahead. There he began to formulate a new strategy. He needed to reach the Grey Keep as soon as possible and it was still another four days journey away. Going cross country would mean a shorter distance and he reckoned that if he kept up a forced march he could make it there in three. He would need to head north east, through the wilderness and wild fields to the south of the Tiaryer until he came to the second of the three rivers that flowed from the Grey Mountains, the one known as the Valmuhsh. He would then follow that river north into the mountains and then onwards to the Grey Keep.

It took Thias several minutes to cover a sufficient distance from the river to a place where he found cover. There he rested, hidden in the dark amongst the wild vegitation and safe from those who may be seeking him. Soon he set off again and moved between clumps of scrub that gave further shelter as his journey progressed. The smell of maple faded as the bard moved at pace across the grasslands. After an hour there was nothing but open ground ahead of him and yet he could see only as far as Mona's pale silvery light allowed. He trudged on over the uneven terrain for many an hour and continued his journey in total silence. Every so often he paused to recalculate his position from the stars and the great orbed goddess in the sky.

Soon his random thoughts drifted back to the day that his thieving father had been arrested by a warrior of the City Watch and made an example of in front of the slum scum. That purveyor of the law was a sergeant who went by the name of Danisun Dain. It was a name he would never forget. The arrest had been several months before Thias had first made contact with Vostag Heyn and his sons as they had trained on the banks of the Tiaryer. It was the very same year that the deep snows of the most fearful winter in living memory had fallen upon the Capital and held it within its frozen grip for months on end. It was the very same winter that brought chaos to the Heyn household with the discovery of the curse mark upon the back of young Methladon's head.

Thias and his father Reagan Calavan, impoverished as they were and with no work passed down from the Thieves Guild, had been forced in desperation to break into a bakery within the slums in which they lived. All that they stole was a single loaf of bread with which to survive another day. Then, as Reagan had climbed out through the open stone window of the bakery with loaf in hand, and having first made sure his son had slipped away, he was spotted by the athletic sergeant of the Watch who then gave chase. It wasn't until three mornings later when Thias, ten years old at the time, came across a crowd in one of the large open areas of the slums and spotted the hangman's noose that hung from gallows that had been erected in haste. Beneath the gibbet and with the noose around his neck, Thias's father stood upon a small wooden milking stool. Then as the crowd jeered and shouted Thias pushed his way through to the front of the excited mass of lice ridden louts, just in time to see the hangman kick the stool from under his father's legs. He saw his father drop and then dance the jig before at last his limp and lifeless body came to its final rest. The corpse was left hanging there as the crowd began to move away. The throng of lowborn soon dispersed but not before all those walking past the lifeless body spat and cursed at the dead thief. Thias remembered standing there and as he had watched his father swinging in the wind he realised how much he was going to miss him. He had then been consumed by intense feelings of hatred. It was such an enormous amount of hate for one small boy to have generated. It was hate born out of being abandoned. It was hate generated by being left alone in the world. It was hate for the Watch bastard who had kicked the stool.

The sound of a twig being snapped from behind startled Thias. In an instant he turned and stretched out his right arm. As it reached full length the bard closed his eyes and shouted another word from the ancient language. From his hand came an intense explosion of light followed by a dense fierce flame. The heat did not result in any pain or even discomfort for it was generated by the bard himself. It was the Flame of Enlightenment, a secret known only to those who studied their craft at the Bards Guild of Valameer. It was pure magic.

Thias opened his eyes wide and stared through the glow cast by the flames from his hand and there he saw the cause of the sound. It was a badger, scavenging for food amongst the dirt and shrubs of the wilderness. Thias smiled and then lowered his arm. He had almost killed the poor creature with his flame and for that he felt a surge of guilt. Then he laughed for it was the first time that he had used the spell outside of his training in the Guild. The technique was one of the most basic that a bard was expected to learn. His tutor had taught him that the generation of magic was the result of manipulating the major energy centres in an individual's body. He had further been told that each one of those centres was connected to a different aspect of a person's being and learning to sense and use that energy resulted in the ability to create magic. The more one trained and focused, then the greater the development of the power. He had also been taught that the energy that flows through these centres was not of infinite supply. Physical energy depletes the more work a person undergoes throughout each day and magic behaves in a similar fashion. With each spell cast, the ability is depleted requiring both physical and mental rest to replenish it. The bard knew that he had wasted his last reserves on the badger. If he was to get into further trouble this night he would have to rely on his basic cunning and good luck, at least until his magic regenerated.

Thias lowered his hand as the flames from his palm extinguished and darkness returned. He turned and set off again on his journey through the wilderness. An hour into his march he heard the sound of screaming coming through the stillness of the night. He fell to the ground amongst the deep lush grass and in one swift motion he covered his body with his cloak and remained corpse still. He strained his eyes and looked up from his low position into the gloom. Then he began to notice flickers of light in the distance. They appeared like tiny fireflies that moved at great speed towards him. He wondered what this phenomena could be and all manner of ideas flashed through his mind. Perhaps it was a swarm of Incubi hunting for their prey. Perhaps they were will-o'-the-wisps, appearing out the wilds to lure travellers into hidden bogs. Whatever they were Thias knew to lie still. Soon he detected the sound of galloping horses and realised there were riders approaching, carrying torches, and on the hunt.

The flames grew ever nearer and a minute later Thias made out the silhouette of a man, dressed as would a farmer, who raced ahead of the horses as fast as his legs would stride. He approached Thias without any awareness of the bard's presence. The pursuing riders then came into clear focus. There were four of them, each mounted upon a strong horse and clad in the same black armour that Thias had seen earlier on the lone horseman by the river. All four carried a torch in one hand and gripped the reins of their steed with the other. Then they circled the farmer, who in a state of complete exhaustion, had fallen to his knees.

Thias wriggled forward as fast as he dared. He kept close to the ground, aided by the camouflage that his cloak provided. The mounted men continued to walk towards the farmer who shouted and pleaded for the riders listen to him.

"Please! Please! I've done nothing wrong!"

Thias watched on as the one of the riders moved up to the farmer, threw his flaming torch to the ground, and then dismounted. He then approached the peasant who in total fear screamed again and then soiled himself.

"No! Spare me! I have a wife; I have a child."

The screams did not deter the rider who looked down with contempt at the pitiful peasant. With great skill he drew his blade from the scabbard that hung at his side. It was a make of blade that Thias that never seen before, long and thin with metal that glinted even in the moonlight. The screams did not last long for in one movement the rider swung his blade outwards towards the farmer's neck. Two parts of what was once a hardworking man fell with thumps to the ground. Thias was surprised how agile the rider had been and the skill with which he had wielded his sword. He was most impressed by the powerful warrior who stood in silence over the bloody remains of his slaughter. Never had he seen such deftness by one dressed in full armour. The steel and iron types that Thias had encountered on his long journeys across the Realm had always been heavy and took the strongest of men to be able to wear and use with effect. The weight of metal armour restricted movement and for that reason that the City Watch wore the leather kind. This strange knight's armour was made of a substance that was far lighter. Whoever the riders were, they were not from the south of the Realm.

A minute later the killer remounted. As the others regrouped some distance away, and through the diminishing pool of light that was cast by the discarded torch, Thias watched the assassin raise his sword aloft and shout out into the night.

"For Avolire," his voiced boomed.

"For Avolire," replied the other three with equal gusto.

In unison the four riders took off. They rode at pace into the night, their lights soon extinguished by the darkness of the night. Once gone Thias raised himself to his feet and out from the grass cushioned ground. After dusting himself down and retrieving his few belongings he made his way towards the body of the decapitated farmer. A body lay several feet from its head and there Thias knelt down and took in the scene that met his eyes. The bloody mess that lay across the grass glinted in the nightlight and all seemed most surreal. He touched the pool of sticky fluid that collected at the stump of the farmer's neck and felt its warm and glutinous texture. Then he wiped his hand upon his tunic and wondered what the poor man could have done to have been dispatched with such brutality.

The howl of a nearby animal startled Thias and he then knew that he needed to move away. The fresh kill of the farmer would attract scavengers from out of the wilderness and encounters with such creatures were best avoided.

If Avolire was on the move, he would need to reach the safety of the Grey Keep as soon as possible. His life and the survival of the Realm would depend upon it.

5

In the late evening, just as Solaris began to descend from the heavens, Llyat Emgar and Cleath Mark headed towards the village of Maplehill as they made their way home after a long day of toil on the farm. Cleath lived in Ashview so Llyat only walked the part of the journey with his friend. He knew that it would take Cleath until Mona showed her face to reach his home in the next village. Llyat always enjoyed the company of his mentor, a man that he was proud to call his friend. It had been a strenuous day but also a good one. Between the planting of crops Llyat had tended to the cattle, those which had not been disembowelled during the recent skyfawn attack. He felt tired and had too little energy left in his bones to spend in the Red Mare, drinking with the Heyn brothers, or listening to one of Denius Castor's bullshit tales. Llyat was determined to have a night of peace and with luck, much sleep.

The two friends walked on and soon found themselves in deep discussion on the subject of dragons which fascinated them both. They knew that the creatures lived in the hills and vast plains away in the north, in an area that the map etchers and the Bards of Valameer referred to as the Dragonas. Yet over recent years the dragons had seldom ventured south. In fact for the past ten years or so, no one in the south of the Realm knew whether they had become extinct by natural means or had been hunted to destruction by the alchemists who sought out their magical properties. It was said by some that the flesh of the magnificent lizards was able to do the most remarkable things. The noble beasts that had once roamed the entire Realm at the time of the Ancients were now no longer to be seen and this saddened Llyat. Only through the songs and tales told at the long table did Llyat know anything of the wondrous beasts of the north. One particular tale, 'The Ballad of the fall of the Mighty Xenvagen and the Knight that slew him,' allowed Llyat's imagination to picture what they looked like. It was a song about one man's triumph over a fearsome creature and the vow that he then took to eliminate the rest from the surface of the Realm.

"It's such a pity that a great beast like Xenvagen had to die," said Llyat as they passed the dog Allo as it wandered up the track on the lookout for scraps of discarded food amongst the dirt.

"Yes, indeed," replied Cleath. "Xenvagen was the most fearsome beast of the Dragonas but when it killed the youngest daughter of the Mayor of Griginor it had to be destroyed."

"But not in the manner that the tale describes. Sir Belquin was a brute," added Llyat.

"There is nothing brutish about chopping off the head of such a foul creature and dragging it behind a horse. I agree that was wrong to destroy all the winged serpents of the north but Sir Belquin was just trying to protect Griginor from further destruction."

"I'm sure there could have been other ways," replied Llyat.

The youth's eyes looked to the ground and thoughts clouded his mind. He pictured himself as a knight of old, defending the dragons from great armies, cutting down his enemies with his sword while sat upon the neck of the greatest of the flying beasts. But such things did not happen to Llyat Emgar in the real world. The dragons, if they existed at all, were far away to the north, and Llyat could not even handle a sword. He was a farm yacker and not even a good one as old man Chirth reminded him every day. Llyat was a perfect living example of uselessness. He was just nobody and his passing would be missed by none; at least that is what he believed.

"Could have been another way to do what?" chipped in a familiar voice from the side.

Llyat looked towards the blacksmith's door and spotted Methladon walking towards him. Allo ran around his master's legs and craved attention.

"We were discussing Sir Belquin and the fall of Xenvagen," replied Llyat, as he stopped between the tavern and the smithy to greet his friend.

"Ha," laughed Methladon. "That's just an old child's story."

"No its not!" snapped back Llyat as his emotions flared. "Belquin the Just was a valiant knight and Xenvagen a magnificent creature."

"Don't worry Llyat," said Methladon as he put his arm around his friend and gave a reassuring hug. "I was just teasing you. Of course Xenvagen was magnificent. How I wish that I could have lived in that age."

"Never took you for a dragon lover Meth," laughed Cleath, trying to ensure he was included in the conversation.

"Not so much as a dragon lover, but a man who appreciates the magnificence of the great winged beasts," laughed Methladon as Allo continued to wag his tail and jump around. "So where are you two off to on this fine summer's evening? I guess Cleath you're heading back to Ashview but what have you planned to do this evening Llyat?"

"My bed. Every muscle in my body aches, I just want to rest tonight."

"That's a real shame. I was going to treat you to a mug of ale and a game of Fidchell. Catriana told me that your parent's brought back a barrel of some rare stuff from Oakwood. I was thinking we could sample it. Oh well, never mind, sleep if you must."

"You can treat me if you like," laughed Cleath who stepped forward with enthusiasm. "We can talk more about Sir Belquin if you like."

"Great," replied Methladon as he turned to Llyat. "Are you sure you don't want to join us?"

"Yes I'm more than sure. I need to get some rest. I don't want Chirth slinging any more shit at me by showing up late tomorrow with another hangover and feeling wasted."

"Well then young Llyat we shall not keep you," replied Methladon.

With that said he and Cleath made their way across the dirt track to the door of the Red Mare. Allo sat at Llyat's feet, rubbed his head against his legs, and demanded a stroke.

Llyat soon continued along the dirt track towards his home and bed. Once he had passed the stocks he began his ascent to the top of the rise. His thoughts and emotions however drifted back down the hill. How he wished that he could be more like his friends enjoying themselves in tavern. It was no lie that he felt tired but there was something else about the offer that troubled him. Most times Llyat would have jumped at such a chance but strange feelings had begun to plague him over recent days. A growing sensation of self-doubt gnawed away inside and day after day sought to destroy what little confidence he had left. He was forever being told by others 'to be his own person' but who that person was he had no idea. In his imagination he wanted to be like Methladon, a true warrior and defender of the village, able and willing to protect its occupants from skyfawns and wolves. He also saw Cleath Mark as someone to model himself on, except of course for his pig features as those he would not wish on anyone. His mentor was both skilful and confident; just and fair like Sir Belquin in the tale that both of them enjoyed so much. The one thing that Llyat knew for certain was that his lack of confidence held him back. He never had the courage to speak up for himself and always dwelled on any criticism that he received. He would always allow it to fester and gnaw away at his soul. This one true weakness had always been his downfall and he was desperate to understand how he could become more confident and courageous. It would be true to state that the only time that he felt good about himself was after consuming several mugs of Catriana's ale.

On reaching the top of the hill Llyat looked past the stone building that was his home, across the patches of woodland, and into vast wilderness that stretched towards the distant horizon. As the red disc of Solaris sank, rays of golden light glimmered in the darkness behind the clouds which spread across the evening sky. Llyat stood still and allowed the inspirational sight to fill his senses. There in a state of awe he muttered and prayed to any of the gods who were still awake. He demanded a new life, one in which he was in charge of his own actions; one with excitement and challenge.

"Magnificent isn't it?" said the strong deep voice of Rukave Emgar. "Sometimes I believe Solaris shows himself like this as an omen of good things to come."

"Do you really believe in that shit dad?"

While Llyat turned to face his muscular father he wiped a solitary tear from his cheek.

"I used to pray to Solaris when I was a young man," continued his father. "I can remember standing like you are now, gazing out towards a city and praying for a better life than the miserable one given to me. I prayed long and hard for luck and some fortune to come my way."

"And what happened dad?" sniffed Llyat as his emotions clouded his thoughts and forced another tear. "Did you get what you wanted?"

"Of course I didn't son. I got your mother instead!"

With that both father and son started to laugh. The one thing that Llyat knew he could count on was his father's ability to sense when he was upset. He knew that Rukave was the one person who understood him. They had their disagreements, about work on Hadra's farm, and about lessons in sword fighting from Vostag Heyn, but deep down, Llyat loved his father and his father loved him back.

After that brief moment of reflection Rukave led the way to the front of the house and Llyat followed. On entering the youth was pleased to see his mother

Lyrusa sat at the table as she peeled away at the few root vegetables that would make up part of their evening meal. The smell of roasting chicken filled Llyat's senses and as he looked to the stone hearth in the corner he saw a small plucked chicken attached to the spit. It was a meagre bird but it was enough for them to survive on. Evening was the main meal of the day for Llyat's family. They always skipped breakfast and if anything at all had a meagre slice of bread and dripping for lunch, washed down with a mug of water. Anything else that came their way was considered a bonus.

"How was your day son?" asked Lyrusa.

"It was good mother, thank you for asking."

Llyat knew that was a lie but why dredge up the bad stuff when his father had raised his spirits.

"I'm pleased to hear it," continued his mother as her attention focused on her son and away from the small pile of potato peel that lay before her. "Now be a good lad and check on the chicken."

A short while later the three members of the Emgar family sat around their one table and tucked into their evening meal. It was Llyat's favourite and one that they only had on rare occasions. Between mouthfuls, Rukave and Lyrusa told of their trip that day to the market at Oakwood. Llyat joined in the conversation when he could and mentioned the recent skyfawn attacks along the road which he said people thought were becoming more frequent. He also told his parents the latest rumour surrounding young Maria Darcha's parentage as passed to him by old man Chirth and Denius Castor. His parents then began to talk of the strange warriors they had seen in Oakwood, people the like of whom they said had never seen before. The news grabbed Llyat's attention and he listened with greater interest.

"Whoever they were," said his father. "They were looking for something or somebody. Asking everyone they met if they had seen...."

"Do you think we ought to be discussing this here," whispered his mother?

"I guess you're right," Rukave replied. "They didn't find what they were looking for anyway. It's none of our business what happens outside of this village. We keep ourselves to ourselves and we shouldn't be concerned with whatever these wandering folk are up to. Lyrusa that was one of the finest cockerels I have ever tasted."

And with that the conversation moved on. After the meal had finished and Llyat had washed the wooden plates in a bucket of river water, he retired to his allocated sleeping space. He took off his dirty clothes and threw them into their usual heap upon the floor. Then he climbed onto his wooden bed, covered himself with his sheepskin, and gazed up at the thatched roof. While he stared through blank eyes he relaxed and let his body settle onto the hard wood of the bed. His eyes grew heavy and he began to think about the strange folk that his parents had seen earlier in the day. He wondered who they could be and if they were from the Capital like the bard Thias Calavan. But he didn't think for long as his eyes soon closed and sleep took Llyat in to the realm of dreams.

The sound of raised voices and the smell of burning timber caused Llyat to shock-wake from his slumber. He did not know how long he had been asleep but he knew at once that something was wrong. He did not have long to gather his thoughts before a hand was forced over his open mouth. In panic Llyat tried to struggle and to reach out for any object that he could use as a weapon but then his eyes met those of Rukave. Llyat then stopped struggling and started to relax. Never before had his father carried out such an action. Whatever was happening, it had to be serious.

"Don't make a sound," whispered the agitated man as he removed his hand from across his son's mouth. "Be very quiet and come with me now."

Llyat didn't wait to ask questions. He jumped out of bed and put on the tunic that he snatched from the floor. Then he followed his father into the main room of their house.

"What's going on dad?" demanded Llyat in a whisper. "Whose were those voices? Where is mother?"

"I have no time to explain Llyat. I need you to stay quiet and get into the space beneath the house. Your mother is there already. We must not be seen. Just do what I say. Now!"

Llyat moved over to the corner of the room. He kept as low as possible to avoid his movements being seen through the open window. As quick as he could he approached the area near the hearth where the wooden floor boards had just been lifted to reveal a small hole. Below it was the store space which was just deep enough to take a grown man standing. There he waited and held his breath for just a brief moment. The smell of burning filled his nostrils and he realised that a fire was raging somewhere outside. Without hesitation and with the smell of smoke fuelling his fear, Llyat peered through the window that looked down the hill towards the village. What he saw startled him for it was the last thing he would have expected to have seen.

Outside the Red Mare he saw Catriana screaming in terror. Her livelihood was on fire and the flames burned and crackled high into the night sky. Dense smoke lingered around the surrounding area and blanketed the village. The young woman was then joined by two men who Llyat recognised from their distinctive silhouettes. It was the two eldest Heyn brothers but the youngest of the three was nowhere to be seen. The men pointed towards Chirth's farm on the opposite side of the village which Llyat then noticed was also on fire. In that that same direction he saw four horsemen riding towards the village and away from the burning farm. He could just make out that the riders wore armour and carried burning torches in their hands. However before he could witness anything more he was wrenched backwards by a pair of strong hands and then pulled to the floor.

"I thought I told you to get below. We have no time to waste," whispered his father with great urgency to his voice. "Get the fuck in there now."

Llyat didn't wait to be told a second time and down he jumped. Within seconds of hitting the damp earth a second pair of hands grabbed him and pulled him deep into the darkness. From within the gloom Llyat watched the floorboards being replaced one by one as his father concealed his son and wife beneath their house. The only light then visible was that which crept through the cracks of the wood. This was the first time that the secret space had been used in such a way. Something dreadful was happening in Maplehill and although he did not know what, Llyat somehow knew it meant death and destruction.

"Mother," he whispered, hoping that she could hear him above the screaming and panic that came ever closer to their home. "What's going on?"

"It's those men from Oakwood," began his mother. "They were looking for someone. One who they call the 'Marked'. Your father sent them away saying that there was no one of that description living in the three villages. They said they would return with more of their friends, and that if Maplehill, Ashview and Oakwood did not surrender this Marked they would pay a heavy price."

"Who did?" he said. "Who are they?"

"Soldiers. Knights in black armour," replied Lyrusa

Before Llyat could ask any more questions a loud hammering echoed from the door to their home. His mother gasped, released her grip, and allowed Llyat to move within the confines of the darkened space. He peered through the wooden floor boards into the room above and watched his father pace the room. Then a second and louder series of knocks rattled on the door which caused Rukave to stand still. A deep voice bellowed out once the hammering ceased.

"Open up in the name of Avolire! Open the door before we knock it fucking down."

Llyat watched on through a crack while his father rushed to the wooden portal and with one swift motion flipped the bolt and opened it wide. In the next instant, four large knights in black armour and with swords drawn stepped inside. They then proceeded in great haste to search the two rooms. Rukave stood helpless, saddened that his minimal possessions were being destroyed by the intruders. It was evident that the strangers were searching for someone or something that they believed was hiding in the rustic hovel.

"I told you before," shouted Rukave, "We have never heard of the Marked. Why can't you just leave us in peace?"

Standing and fearing to move, Llyat and his mother continued to follow the events as they played out above. They dared not make a sound lest they were discovered. Llyat attempted to stretch his body, to move closer to the room above, to listen and to see what was happening. Then without warning a fifth figure burst through the door and joined the four burly knights and his father. Although Llyat could not make out the facial features of this new intruder, he could just see enough to note a dark cloak that covered a full suite of armour. Upon this man's head, instead of the same helmet that covered the faces of the other four, sat a white skull of human origin, hollowed out and fixed to the front of the stranger's helm.

"Not you again!" exclaimed Rukave. "I told you this morning in Oakwood. The Marked is not here. How many times do I have to tell you?"

The Marked and Avolire were names Llyat had not heard before. He wanted to ask his mother what she knew about them but he also understood the seriousness of their predicament and so held his tongue. In that moment Llyat was grateful that his father had placed them in the hiding space for he had without doubt saved their lives. However, before he could think further the stranger began to speak.

"Look friend," he growled with a deep and penetrating voice. "We have good reason to believe that the 'Marked' lives within one of the three villages that lie upon this stretch of Tiaryer and that in all probability it is this shit hole called Maplehill. One of you peasants is hiding what we search for and we will kill you all one by one until someone hands him over."

"I'm telling you for the last time," snapped Rukave "There is no fucking marked one here."

Before Llyat's father could protest further one of the other four black knights marched back into the main room from the sleeping space and tapped his right fist across his chest. Standing tall he saluted his Commander.

"My Lord, we have searched the house. There is no sign of the boy."

Llyat gasped. It seemed that these knights were searching for him. Surely they couldn't be. He was so insignificant. He was just a dirty dishevelled nob, an irritating arse grape at the edge of a bum hole.

"Where is your son?" spoke the Commander as Llyat tried to process the information.

"I don't have a son."

"Do not lie to me. Where is he?"

"I'm telling you, I don't have a son," shouted Rukave, his voice reflecting a level of anxiety that Llyat had never heard before. "Now leave my house at once!"

Without warning and as Llyat and his mother watched on in horror, the Commander of the knights raised his right arm and pointed his finger at Rukave. In the next moment Llyat's father was flung across the room where he collided with the table in the corner and fell to a heap upon the floor. Llyat was stunned for it appeared that the knight had used magic. At that moment he wanted to burst out from under the floorboards and attack but he knew there would be little sense in doing so. If these people were indeed looking for him then his best course of action was to remain hidden. That is what his father would expect of him. Should he act on impulse and reveal himself then he would put his mother in danger. Llyat decided to bide his time and continue to watch from below.

The stranger walked the length of the room and stood above his father who lay in obvious distress upon the floor. Then the Commander placed one of his solid black boots upon the outstretched hand of his victim and pushed down with all his weight. Rukave screamed in pain and once again Llyat felt the need to jump out from his place of hiding.

"We've got to do something," he whispered as he looked back towards his mother

The terrified woman shook with fear and Llyat realised that it would be only a matter of time until she screamed and gave their position away. Somehow they had to remain quiet; he had to save her.

Before Llyat could whisper instructions, the Commander spoke with menace.

"This is your last chance my friend. Where is the 'Marked'?"

"Go fuck yourself!" screamed Rukave as he spat blood from his mouth.

"Kill him!" ordered the Commander.

With that said the skull knight turned and marched out of the door while the others advanced on Llyat's father. The young farm boy realised to his horror that they going to execute his dad. The four knights drew their long thin swords and before Rukave could react they hacked and sliced away at the honest man who lay before them. The screams diminished with each stroke of their blades and blood splattered in arched patterns across the walls. Llyat so wanted to cry out but he focused all his energy in preventing his mother from giving their position away. The frantic woman tried to scramble from Llyat's grip but he threw her to the ground and thrust his hand across her mouth to stifle her screams. He then looked up to the carnage above and felt something drip onto his forehead. With his free hand he wiped the sticky liquid from his face and looked at his reddened palm. Rukave's life force was dripping through the floorboards and onto his family.

"Burn it down," shouted one of the knights and with that the four marched out of the house and into the night.

Llyat's breath started to labour as a great anxiety took hold. He struggled to understand why these men had killed his father and what they wanted with him. Nor could he make sense of the word Avolire and its connection to someone who was marked. So many questions raced through his mind but they would have to wait for he still had to save his mother. He removed his hand from her mouth and whispered.

"We need to be very quiet. We need to get out of here right now."

His mother nodded in recognition of his words. Llyat then helped her to her feet and pulled her in close. There would be another time for tears but the priority now was to escape and find help. Llyat moved to loosen the floor boards that had been placed over the entrance to their secret hideaway but they would not move. He looked up through the gap in the floor and saw to his horror that in ransacking his home the knights had pushed one of the family's two cupboards over and that it now lay over their only means of exit.

"Shit!" shouted Llyat as he realised the seriousness of the situation.

"What is it?" asked his mother as the tears ran down her cheeks and left tracks through the dirt that covered them.

"The cupboard is blocking the way," replied Llyat "We need to get out before we burn."

His mother joined him and side by side they tried to push upwards with all their strength, to free themselves from what was now their prison. Then to add to his terror Llyat began to hear the sounds of wood burning. Seconds later the pungent smell of smoke filled the air for the thatch on the roof had started to burn. Mother and son's actions became evermore frantic and desperate. Within moments the entire roof was alight, crackling and forming black acrid smoke that sought to fill every available space of the basic cottage. Llyat knew in that instant that their hiding place would be their tomb if they did not at once find a way to break free.

Then as if the gods had answered his prayers one of the oak beams that supported the thatch came crashing down amongst the flames. It smashed through the wooden floor boards and brought sections of burning roof material along with it. Both Llyat and his mother shielded their eyes as the beam penetrated the floor but it had created the escape route that they both so needed. Llyat was first to act. In no time at all he clambered up the burning wood, ignoring the blistering of his hands as he raced upwards. All the while he inhaled the thick black smoke from the fire although he began to cough with a violence he had never before experienced. He reached the floor above and in a heightened state of awareness then lay down upon it and sought to grab his mother's arm. The young man surprised himself with the strength that he found and soon he began to pull his mother out from the pit. In that moment he sensed his body had been possessed by some hero of a time long ago. As he strained to lift his mother, Llyat's gaze fell upon his father's mutilated body and two eyes devoid of life. He swore he would live on. Rukave must not have died for nothing.

Without warning a second beam crashed down and brought with it further burning debris. Llyat was covered in the fiery material which hit his back with great force. He felt his grip on his mother loosen and so he tried to gasp hold with his other hand. Lyrusa fell back into the pit and Llyat screamed out loud. Burning debris covered her and thereafter there was no further sign of movement.

"Mum!" shouted Llyat through his tears as the fire raged around him.

No reply came back. Lyrusa Emgar was gone, buried beneath the oak beams and thatch that had once formed the roof of her home. For a brief moment Llyat froze and looked down at where he knew his mother lay. Tears welled in his eyes as he tried to come to terms with the loss of both his parents. He contemplated lying there to be consumed by the fire so that he too would join them in the Underworld but then something else took hold. He had crossed a threshold and there would be no turning back. He cursed and vowed to kill the man with the skull helmet, even if it took him until the end of time.

Llyat jumped to his feet and made his way through the dense black smoke that filled the room. He then threw himself through the open door of the house and into the night air beyond. There he rolled over on the ground to extinguish the fire that had taken hold on the clothes on his back. At last he stood up and looked down the hill where what his eyes then saw shocked him to his core. All the buildings that made up the small village of Maplehill were on fire. They lit up the night sky with an orange hue and cast a blanket of nose and stinging smoke across the land. It was if Llyat's whole existence was being destroyed in a single moment when the forces of the Underworld had descended upon his village. He scanned the scene before him and sought the location of the man responsible for the murder of his parents. His eyes picked out various figures fighting in different parts of the village as the few inhabitants sought to repel the fearsome black knights that had taken their village by storm. At the base of the hill, just before the stocks and in the midst of the inferno, Llyat made out the fallen body of Denius Castor. The teller of tall tales lay motionless and with a blade still in his hand.

Insanity overtook Llyat and consumed by his desire for revenge he ran as fast as he could toward the fallen body of his neighbour. As he did so he tripped, slid through the dirt, and came to a rest besides Castor. Scrambling back to his feet amid the unfolding chaos Llyat heard the screams of a woman. He ripped the blade from the corpse's hand and noted it felt lighter than he had expected. With a mind consumed by rage he turned around to scan the road and through the falling ash he saw the bodies of Catarina and Fiat Heyn lying face down in the dirt. The murdering

Knights who had slain them were walking away towards the Red Mare and the Darcha house further up the track. Without conscious thought Llyat raced across the road to the stone walls of the ruined house that had belonged to the Castors. Parts of the roof were still ablaze and its glow lit up the maple trees beyond the village.

There Llyat leaned against the hot wall of the house and for a brief moment tried to decide on what he should do next. He wanted so much to fight but his mind told him to flee. He held up the sword and studied it. He had always been forbidden to touch such weapons and had not been trained in their use. For a second he wondered how hard it would be to kill someone.

Suddenly from around the side of the house one of the Black Knights spotted Llyat against the stone wall. The youth felt warm liquid flow from under his tunic as the enemy sprang forward, blade raised high into the air and primed to kill. Llyat closed his eyes for he knew that it would all be soon over and yet still death did not come for him. To his surprise as his eyes opened he saw that the knight had been felled. A severed head lay a short distance away in an expanding pool of sticky red. While trying to ascertain what had happened he became aware of the young man that stood by his side, busy wiping the blade of his sword against the material of his own trousers. Llyat grinned for he had never been so pleased to see Methladon Heyn.

"Are you okay Llyat?" shouted Methladon as he lowered his sword to his side. "What the fuck is going on?"

"I don't know," lied Llyat, thinking that it would be best not to tell his friend that the knights were in fact looking for him. "They just turned up and started torching the houses. They have killed my mum and dad."

"Shit! They are slaughtering everyone. They've already killed Catriana and my brother who was trying to protect her, and young Maria.

"What do the bastards want?" demanded Llyat. "What happened to Maria?"

"They struck her mother down and then dragged her towards Chirth's farm. Grophaldo chased after them thinking they would be raped."

More shouts sounded from behind as several Black Knights raced down the road. Methladon pushed Llyat back into the still burning building and flattened them both up against the wall. Two further knights ran past the gap between the Castor house and the blacksmiths but neither of them saw the two friends. The sound of a dog barking was followed by a high pitched yelp as it was forever silenced.

"What shall we do?" cried Llyat.

"My mother has escaped to the mill along with Mal Castor. My father and Denius stayed to hold off a couple of the Knights but I think Denius got taken down. I haven't seen either them for a while."

"Denius Castor is dead," replied Llyat. "He's lying down by the stocks. This is his sword."

"They must have gone to warn you and your family. I'm sorry they didn't get to you in time."

Llyat thought about the events of the night but he couldn't bring himself to admit that the carnage was all because of him.

"Listen to me, this is what is going to happen," continued Methladon. "You're going to make for the watermill. Go there and stay safe. I'm going to see if I can find dad and if I can rescue Maria."

"But Meth..."

"No arguments Llyat. This isn't time to play the hero. Get to the watermill and hide."

With that said Methladon Heyn left the cover of the Castor building and raced off towards the farm in the distance. He moved behind the back of the Heyn house to save time but also to avoid being seen. Llyat took a deep breath and closed his eyes. From somewhere deep inside Llyat found a morsel of courage and set off running once again. He raced through the gap between the two buildings and soon reached the road. It was the same spot where earlier that evening he had parted ways with Cleath and he wondered if his mentor had left Maplehill before the fighting had started. Perhaps he too was lying dead somewhere within the burning village. Between the blacksmith's and the tavern Llyat stopped for ahead of him Methladon fought with one of the knights. Llyat wanted to charge in and give aid his friend but the coward inside took over and instead he fled. His excuse was to follow orders for it was Methladon who was responsible for protecting the village. For a brief moment he stood and stared in awe at his friend's swordsmanship but then his attention moved beyond the two warriors to the knight with the skull helmet. The Commander of the raiding party sat on his black steed and watched the fight unfold. Llyat felt his anger grow and a black veil of hatred clouded his mind. He raised the sword, charged forward along the road.

"For Maplehill!" he screamed.

"Llyat, get the fuck out of here!" shouted Methladon.

The knight's blade hammered down and dropped the blacksmith's son to the floor. Llyat knew that the blow had been a fatal one for Methladon lay still and showed no sign of life. His best friend, just like his parents, had left for the Underworld. Llyat froze at the furthest edge of the Darcha house. He stared at the large knight that had felled his friend as he walked towards him. The need to flee returned and Llyat turned and ran. Soon he veered off to the right and on towards the old watermill. Approaching the banks of the river he saw Vostag and Grophaldo engaged in a fierce sword fight with yet another of the knights. Both father and son fought with the same style and Llyat stopped to watch despite his terror. Vostag was the first to fall as he defended his son from a heavy blow. The knight's blade struck down through the old blacksmith's shoulder and sliced deep into his torso. Grophaldo then moved to attack, his sword raised high as it glinted in Mona's light. With several swings and thrusts, some of which were deflected by the knight, Grophaldo knocked his assailant to the floor and with his sword held high made ready to deliver a fatal blow. The knight swung out his blade without warning and removed both of Grophaldo's lower limbs. Llyat stood frozen in terror as the knight rose his feet and then drove his sword downwards into the body of his writhing friend. Grophaldo's suffering ended at once.

"You bastard!" screamed Llyat as he readied his sword to attack.

Llyat no longer feared the knight for his body felt on fire. The raiders had destroyed everything precious to him and now he had nothing left to lose. He covered the short distance to the knight in no time at all. Insensitive to the pain from his blistered hands he brought his blade crashing down upon the knight's armour with all the force he could generate. The weapon just bounced off the metal plate without leaving as much as a scratch. In one swift movement the knight disarmed the bold but naïve youth. Llyat's sword fell to the floor and once again he froze for his swordsmanship had proved to be shite. He stood and cowered as if rooted to the ground. The knight then grabbed him by the throat, lifted him into the air, and then searched his head for a mark. When nothing was found the brute spoke.

"I want this to be the last voice you hear before you die."

Wasting no further effort the knight tossed Llyat into the raging river. As everything went black Llyat's last thoughts were of his family and friends. All were now dead, most had been incinerated, but Llyat's life would have a watery end.

6.

The river named the Valmuhsh differed in many aspects from its sisters, the Tiaryer and the Awyth. Unlike its more sedentary siblings its upper reaches contained surging torrents and rapids that pushed its waters at a greater speed down to the ocean in the south. From its source it followed a great gash, a narrow channel that caused it to rip and tear through the rock of the wild lands. The Valmuhsh was an unstoppable force and it prevented anyone from crossing it by natural means. Those throughout history who had been foolish enough to try were lost forever amongst the foam of the surging channel.

Loud the river crashed and although he could hear its noise it was as yet invisible to Thias Calavan as he walked amongst the grass of the adjacent flatlands. Out of the land ahead a mist began to form and spew upwards from the hidden rush of water. In its midst multiple rainbows came and went as if teasing the eyes that dared to look upon the vapours. It had been two days since the bard had witnessed the murder of the old farmer by the knights clad in the strange black armour; those who had wielded the lightest of swords and displayed an agility the likes of which Thias had never seen before. He had made his way at speed across the wilderness that lay between the Tiaryer and Valmuhsh and had stopped only to sleep and to drink from several small lakes that he had passed along the way. He had survived off berries that grew from coarse shrubs that he found scattered across the land.

During the first night of this latest chapter of his journey he had turned around to look back from where he had started. A red glow in the distant night's sky, beyond the oaks, ash, and maples far in the distance could only mean one thing. There was a great fire burning somewhere and whatever was alight produced a most disconcerting sight upon the horizon. Thias wondered if the murder he had witnessed was somehow connected to the false sunset which competed with Mona to light up the distant lands.

Now on this second day, Thias at last came across a small gully that sloped down through the rock towards the channel that contained the swollen torrent of the Valmuhsh. It provided a route down into the canyon and he was grateful for its presence. This more gradual path to the side of the river enabled him to avoid the risk of an otherwise impossible descent. Once down at the water's edge he hoped that he was hidden from those who might be looking for him. And so he moved alongside the rocky bank and travelled onwards ever north. He was careful to watch each step that he made for one false move would result in a fall into the swollen river. The ancient path that he now travelled was narrow and treacherous and should he stumble from it he would have no hope of survival. His body would be dashed against the rocks, flung and tossed about by the surging foam before being spat out into the far distant ocean. It was essential that he made it to the Grey Keep as soon as possible and to the protection provided by Lord Raorick Gylewu, the brother of the Sovereign. Thias trudged across the rugged ground and as he did so his thoughts fluctuated between that of his own safety and the resurgence of the cult of Death Tubaria, the underlying reason for this most dangerous journey.

It had been some twelve years previous that Death Tubaria had first surfaced and caused so much suffering throughout Parandor. Though Thias Calavan was but a boy of eleven at the time he remembered it well. Just like recent events in the Royal Court of Phauless Gylewu, the chaos of eleven years past began with the apparent suicide of a person who was found marked with the three circle curse upon his head. Over the days that had followed more citizens of Parandor had died, either by apparent suicide, murder, or accident. It later transpired that not one of them had died from natural causes and each bore the same brand on the back of their heads which then became known as the Mark of Kha. It had brought fear across the Realm and at first even those who led the City Watch and the Guild of Magic could not understand the true nature of its appearance. It was only after one of the Royal Guard's became suspicious that a detailed enquiry began. The investigators focused their enquiries on a specific member of the Royal Court, a physician called Jonas Tullage. In the rooms of that Lord a young chambermaid found a strange book, written in the lost language of the ancients. She later reported the find to a guard after whom she lusted.

Hidden within the books dusty sleeves lay the Lore of the Dead, including the incantation that legend said was to be used to bring about the resurrection of Kha. Lord Tullage was taken away for questioning by the Royal Guard and under an inquisition led by Sovereign Advisor, Xix Blackfayer, Tullage revealed the plans of the gang of nine who were then sentenced to death by Phauless himself. Thias had been told that one of the artefacts, the Dagger of Kha that was now in his possession and which a young Methladon Heyn had once found abandoned in the mud in the estuary of the Tiaryer, had been responsible for the appearance of the magical brands on the heads of the victims as well as that on the scalp of young Methladon himself. It was that cursed blemish that had led to the attempt on Methladon's life and it would scar the youth both physically and mentally for the rest of his teenage years. As a young boy Thias could never understand why his adopted father had kept hold of the evil relic given all that had happened to his youngest son. But fear and grief does the strangest things to a person, especially when a family member is condemned to a lifetime of danger.

Of the nine individuals that had belonged to the cult, only Jonas Tullage was spared a public beheading at the hands of the Royal Executioner, Sir Richemanus of the Nightfall. Phauless Gylewu had allowed Tullage to live because of the many years of exceptional service that the Lord had hitherto devoted to the Royal Household. The bastard needed to suffer much torture before being permitted to die. The other eight were taken to the Richemanus Folly and in front of a crowd that had gathered from across all corners of the Capital each lost their heads within the same hour.

Thias paused for a moment upon a small rocky outcrop that jutted out over the surging river. In the quiet stillness he stood and watched the water bubble while lost in his thoughts. Several large salmon jumped out from the torrent as they tried in vain to climb the rapids on their journey towards their place of their birth, intent on giving life to young of their own. After that brief moment of reflective calm Thias continued his trek north. Soon his thoughts turned to the one issue that he feared most, the city that lay in ruins far beyond the Grey Mountains at the edge of the Dragonas; the ancient metropolis of Avolire. During his studies at the Bards Guild, Thias had learned about that once prosperous city from one of his tutors. In fact it was the Head of the Guild himself, Grand Musician Owasorin Fusepelt, who had imparted the knowledge. A thousand years ago when the great dragons held dominion over all the Realm, it was said that Avolire was the most beautiful place for any eye to behold. The multi-tiered city with its great stone viaducts and spires that reached up to the heavens had once been the capital of the Realm. It had also once been a place full of life with streets brimmed with markets and a population that reflected the vast diversity of the region and beyond. Traders would travel to Avolire from lands far and wide just to visit the grand markets and trade their wares. You could purchase anything there it was said, from exotic foods from across the great oceans to magnificent jewels from the dwarf settlements of the Dirmark. After the great wars that were fought across the Realm, a conflict started by Urthanock the Lord of Fear, Avolire fell into ruin. Its population had been slaughtered and its prosperity destroyed. The few survivors who left its walls went on to found the new Capital of Parandor. Avolire was left to fall into ruin. Within its decaying walls and empty streets evil was allowed to go unchecked. There the Army of Avolire was formed, made up from nomads of an ancient order and many renegades from long lost battles. All were opposed the rule of the House of Gylewu and claimed Avolire as their own.

A noise from above brought Thias back into the present. He looked up from the bottom of the gorge to the edge of the wasteland and then jumped to his right as a large boulder fell from the rocks to the very spot he had just occupied. It landed with a thump, rebounded into the surging river, and sprayed a plume of water high into the air which then fell as a shower of rain. From his position, prostrated on the ground, Thias looked up at the spot from where the boulder had detached and searched for signs that might account for its displacement. Other than the briefest hint of moving shadows there was nothing to be seen. He decided it had been a natural event and yet he was still unsure. The bard was troubled for he couldn't get it out of his head that he was being followed. He scanned the ridge again and looked for others who could be monitoring his progress or intent on ending his life. Given the recent death of the wretched farmer, visions of evil stretched his paranoia to breaking point. The thought that Death Tubaria was stalking him caused beads of sweat to form on his brow and upper lip. The quicker he made it to the safety of the Grey Keep, then the sooner he would be able to relax. Thias recovered his composure as best he could and continued on the rock strewn bank as Solaris descended into the west and cast black shadows over the depths of the chasm. In that bleak darkness the bard's thoughts once again returned to the Knights of Avolire.

There had been several occasions during the years before his birth when an army from the ruins of Avolire had sought fit to march across the Realm and take what they could for their own needs. Stories that he had picked up during his training and later travels talked of what happened when the Knights reached a town or village. It was always just a matter of hours before that settlement was levelled and reduced to ash. The woman were all raped and their husbands and children murdered. The Knights seldom took prisoners and when they did they were transported back to their city as slaves to be sent into the mines that stretched deep below its ruins. In such dark times when the Knights marched unopposed across parts of the Realm, the world had seemed at its lowest ebb. It made the events of the first rising of the Death Tubaria seem tame in comparison. Thias recalled that it was some six years earlier that the armies of Parandor, under the banner of Sir Britta Rainmark, finished off the last of Avolire's army, or so it then seemed. There were however rumours that survivors of that war still lived within the ruins of the city to the east of the Dragonas. If the knights that Thias had seen slaughter the old farmer had indeed come from Avolire, then a great evil was once again on the move. The bard sensed a growing presence to challenge the House of Gylewu, and it all seemed linked to his reason for visiting the Grey Keep.

The difficult journey along the bank of the swollen river took another two days but at least they passed without further incident. As the torrent grew narrower, the channel that Thias traversed started to rise almost vertically through the rock. The strenuous climb into the Grey Mountains had begun. The craggy peaks that now stood before the bard were magnificent to behold, their snow-capped tops stood out against the dark foreboding clouds that massed in the distance. Sheer cliff faces rose high and created natural sculptures out of stone to either side of the gorge. Thias continued up alongside the ever shrinking waterway and on the fourth day after he had left the wastelands he came upon a well-travelled track. It was the road that led from the Capital along the Tiaryer and it now snaked its way through the tall mountain peaks.

The ancient pack horse route was unerringly quiet for the time of year. During the spring months the roads were often busy, at least during the daylight hours. Yet there was no sign of anyone, not a single passing trader, hire-sword, or even evidence of the fabled creatures said to descend from the high passes and attack the caravans that passed along the road. Amid this unnatural solitude Thias felt vulnerable and alone.

After several leagues of struggle through the craggy slopes of the desolate mountains Thias reached a fork in the road. Here the immense granite walls cut off most of the light of Solaris and hid any dangers that lay ahead. At this intimidating junction stood a large wooden structure about the height of twenty men. At various points from its edge, strong wooden side-arms jutted out into the cold mountain air. At the end of each a metal chain had been bolted to the wood and from them dangled metal cages. Each was large enough to fit a grown man and they swung in the wind that blew across the mountain tops. Thias knew that this diabolical contraption belonged to the Grey Keep. Anyone sent here and locked inside a cage would be left without food or water, abandoned to die in misery, their corpses left to feed any creatures that chose to dine off their rotting flesh. A few contained the bleached skeletal remains of the sad unfortunates who had been incarcerated there. Several others contained more recent kills. The rotting and putrefying flesh left a stink that soiled the air and caused Thias to retch. It was then that he spotted something alive. Sat upon one of the cages was a bird that pecked and tore at some mutilated human remains. The black vulture gnawed away with no regard for the human eyes that watched it. At last the bird acknowledged the bard's presence and uttered a warning cry. It was a mixture of a rasp and a hiss and it spooked the bard. These birds were renowned for their silence and its cry encouraged the bard to keep moving. With one last look at the bird he took a deep breath and set off into the dark shadows.

The pass began to narrow and the mountain walls encroached ever closer. It seemed that at any moment they could topple and crush the bard. Then the light from Solaris disappeared altogether. Thias closed his eyes before holding out his palm and muttering a word from a long forgotten language. He focused all of his energy into the palm of his hand which then burst into flame and lit the way forward with a new ethereal light. Thias continued along the trail for several miles while watching the play of the light against the stone. Step by step he scanned the surface of the rock walls, wary that some creature could be lying in wait amongst one of the many crevices. At last the narrow pass opened out into the small barren valley where the Grey Keep had been built many generations earlier. The foreboding edifice stood directly ahead with its four mighty towers that seemed as tall as the surrounding mountain peaks. Once in the open the flames that had burned bright on Thias's hand faded away and allowed the soft glow from Solaris to bathe the majestic structure.

Between the towers of stone sat the main halls of the Grey Keep. The building was a large and ugly construction with no major distinguishing features save for the strong iron doors that bared its entrance. Numerous arrow-slit windows lay at regular intervals across the main body of the walls and intimidated all who dared approach. Above the solitary door and blowing gently in the light wind flew the Royal Coat of Arms. The presence of a single white horse, tethered to the wall outside that main door, filled Thias with unease. With care he began his approach. Soon he began to make out the shapes of bodies which lay scattered across the valley floor. Moving closer he saw that most were the fortress guards who ought to be manning the gates and walls of the Keep. Scattered amongst the dead however were other creatures, ugly, dirty, and scaly beasts. They were clad in the simplest of chainmail that seemed to have been forged from any waste metal had just happened to be available to its makers. Thias knew what these creatures were for he had encountered one of their kind before. They were the Lizardmen of the Eastern Marsh.

Thias bent down to examine one of the fallen guards that lay in his path. The man had a small axe embedded in his head, soaked in bloody crimson and splattered with globules of brain. Death stench crept into his nose. The man's pale face was etched with a great fear and it was obvious that he was beyond saving. No amount of magic from a bard of the Guild or indeed from any wizard, mage, physician, or sorcerer could ever restore life to his shell. Thias picked up the fallen guard's sword and claimed it for his own. He made his way in silence across the open ground towards the granite steps before the iron doors of the Keep. Soon he stood amongst and examined the bodies of the dead that lay at the base of the stone stairs. There to his great surprise he found that the two doors to the Keep had been left open, just wide enough to allow a thin man to pass through them. He climbed the steps without making a sound, all the while concerned over what he would find beyond the thick heavy doors. Moving through them and into the darkness beyond, he saw more signs of battle. Having stepped over many more bodies he began to tingle with trepidation. There was something unholy and un-nerving about the Grey Keep, something deep within the structure of the building itself that kept Thias on edge. The dark passageways that were devoid of flame and the carved stone grotesques above each wooden door fed his sense of dread. Combined with the remains of the mass slaughter, the pools of clotted crimson, the heaps of gore, and the stench of death, the stony silence of the Keep sought to crush his courage.

The bard moved forward and soon found himself in a large but roofless space which though open to the heavens was barely illuminated by the setting of Solaris. Around its perimeter had been built a small covered walk space, the roof of which was supported by large grey stone pillars wrapped in vines. He stepped into the space with his sword raised, his senses on full alert lest he be attacked. Lightly his feet stepped over yet more bodies and amid the corpses he noted the remains of a man he had once seen before in the Court of Phauless Gylewu. Underneath the armour he made out the pale and lifeless form of a once noble Lord. There, wrapped in his entrails and with his eyes in a fixed stare lay Lord Raorick, the man he had been sent to find.

A sudden scream made Thias jump. Startled, he turned around to see an aged knight in armour charging to towards him. Thias dropped his bundle and raised his weapon high into the air. The dual handed sword of his assailant came crashing down towards Thias's head but with a subtle deflection from his own blade the bard pushed it aside. He then swung his own sword in a continuous circular motion and sought to connect with his assailant. The crazed man dodged Thias's attack and thrust his sword forward once again. For a second time the bard was skilful enough to avoid his opponents steel.

"Who the hell are you?" shouted the stranger as he prepared to renew his attack.

"And who the fuck are you?" answered Thias.

Then with all of his guile the bard initiated a series of well-practised moves. He swept and swung his sword in quick succession and pushed his foe backwards towards the dark recesses from where he had emerged just seconds earlier. With one final flick of his blade, a trick he had picked up from Vostag Heyn, Thias disarmed his opponent.

"Now I will repeat my question," he said as he pointed his blade into the soft flesh of his opponent's neck and pushed him back against the wall. "Tell me who you are and what has happened here?"

"I'm Sir Cristofre Randle," spluttered the man in fear of imminent death. "I am Head of the Royal Guard that is garrisoned here to protect Lord Raorick Gylewu and to keep the prisoners secure."

"Tell me all that happened here!" demanded the bard as he pushed the blade further into the man's neck.

"Only when you tell me who you are."

The words caused Thias to push the blade in deeper and this time the point drew blood.

"Wait, wait, I'll tell you," screamed the man. "But please first lower your sword."

"I will Sir, but I warn you, do not try anything foolish for it will be the last thing you ever do!"

"It's like this," the knight sobbed. "Last night the Lizardmen appeared out of the mountain pass as if from nowhere. They came in force and they took us all by surprise. They killed anyone who resisted or who tried to escape. A group of us, including Lord Raorick, managed to hold up here but there were too many of them and we were soon overrun. I somehow managed to escape with my life and so I hid. But the others...."

Thias thrust his sword back at the coward that stood before him.

"Do you mean to tell me that you left your Lord to face these creatures while you saved your own worthless skin?"

"I had no choice. I had to escape. I had to warn people," sobbed the man.

"And yet you are still here?"

"I was too scared to leave," continued the man as his eyes filled with tears. "The Lizardmen butchered all of my men. They could have been waiting outside for me. I didn't want to die. I was just going to wait until they all left or until help arrived."

Thias punched the man in the face. The knight recoiled and spat a broken tooth upon the dirt.

"Pull yourself together. You are a knight of the Royal Guard. Stop your snivelling and tell me what they wanted. Were they looking for something or someone in particular?"

"They didn't take anything but they went through the Keep and killed everyone, even the prisoners."

"Why the prisoners?" questioned Thias for he had never heard of Lizardmen killing condemned men before. "Show me!"

It took several minutes for Thias to persuade Sir Cristofre to accompany him down into to the lowest part of the Keep, the place where the traitors and the most hardened criminals were kept. He even had to punch him a second time but after that he had the full cooperation of the treacherous coward. The knight led on as the bard followed through the darkened corridors of the Grey Keep and through one continuous scene of slaughter. The bodies of Royal Guards and Lizardmen were everywhere. It was obvious that the battle had not long finished for the pools of crimson on the floor were still sticky. Yet there was something else that troubled Thias. He began to suspect that he could be walking into a trap but he pushed his paranoia aside for he had no alternative course of action.

Deep beneath the Grey Keep, down dark corridors from which the prison cells branched, lit by the glow from one solitary burning torch, Thias saw that Sir Cristofre had told the truth. In every cell the prisoners lay dead, their flea infested rags soaked in blood as they remained chained to the wall by their ankles. Each had been pierced by several arrows through the chest and from which wounds their life blood had drained away. Thias could not make sense of all that he saw and one particular observation troubled him. He pushed the thought aside as he approached the last of the cells. Leaning on the wood the door creaked open. Its occupant had gone and the manacles on the floor were unlocked.

"Sir Cristofre, tell me who occupied this cell; was it a dwarf?" demanded Thias.

"I think so but I cannot be sure. We had so many prisoners."

"It is important that you think clearly and remember, for our lives may depend upon his whereabouts."

Thias turned to the knight behind him and looked to the blade that the knight carried in his hand. Something else had distracted the man.

"Sir Cristofre, are you listening to me?" demanded Thias. "I was sent here by Phauless Gylewu on a mission to question a dwarf that you had in your keeping. When I arrived I found the Royal Guard had been slaughtered, including Lord Raorick. The only one left alive is you, a snivelling coward. Then there is the horse tethered up outside the great door. You told me that the Lizardmen killed all the prisoners and yet there is evidence that one managed to escape. Now you must tell me the truth, did a dwarf occupy this cell?"

Thais stopped to gather his breath for he had lost all patience with Sir Cristofre. He wanted to punch the man again but the knight had somehow rearmed.

"Sir Cristofre, are you listening to me," he bellowed into the gloom.

"The dwarf is out of your reach now bard," said the knight.

"I'm sorry. What did you...?"

In that instant the bard knew that he had made a grave mistake. He had failed to ask the most important question.

"Whose horse is tethered up outside the Keep?" he shouted but he received no answer.

"So be it" continued the bard as he raised his sword again and sought to anticipate the knight's next move. "Given I may die in this hell hole then tell me this. Who are you really and what have you done with the dwarf."

The knight smiled and began to laugh; not a joyful one, rather the kind designed to instil fear in whoever heard it. Randle's skin then started to ripple as if it had a life of its own. The knight of the Realm started to melt away and left behind a skinless amorphous shape. Then as quickly as the creature had shed its skin a new one replaced its covering of cheap metal and leather. It was all over in less than two seconds. A scaly shape had reformed and when the tail began to grow from out from the creature's back Thias realised the extent of the deception.

"Fuck you! So you're from the Marshes too. You're a Lizard man, one of their foul shape-shifters."

"Correct!" hissed the creature as it stood rooted to the ground.

"So what does the dwarf have that you want?" continued Thias "I demand that you tell me!"

"The dwarf holds the arcane knowledge needed to bring about the resurrection of Kha."

"So you're the swine behind the resurgence of the cult of Death Tubaria?" gasped Thias.

The words slammed through the bard's head.

"Wrong on so many levels," laughed the Lizardman.

"If you're not Death Tubaria, then what are you?"

"The House of Gylewu will fall from within and our armies will sweep across the Realm. The race of man shall be extinguished and only those loyal to our Marsh will be permitted to survive."

"What do you mean, will fall from within? Is there a traitor in the Royal Court?"

"Enough of this," hissed the creature.

"You have forgotten something very important," Thias shouted as he inched forward.

"And what is that?" hissed back the creature.

"Never fuck with a bard!"

Thias focused his energy through the palms of his hands and his sword ignited in flame. Having thus distracted his opponent Thias thrust his weapon forward and into the belly of the creature. The Lizardman spontaneously ignited, thrashed, and screamed in a hideous reptilian manner before falling limp to the floor. The flames about bard's sword then dissipated and left only a few charred remains of the once hideous lump of scale. Thias stood thinking for several seconds and realised how foolish he had been. He had walked like a blind worm into a trap, oblivious to all the dangers that the enemy had set. With his sword pointing forward he returned to the open space where he had fought the shapeshifter the first time. All was silent and the fading beams of Solaris failed to add light to his darkness.

The bard retrieved his bundle, checked if the contents had been damaged, and half smiled when he saw all were intact. He made his way across the hall and soon came back to the fallen corpse of Raorick Gylewu. He stared at the dead Lord for some minutes while wondering how the next page of his journey through life would be written. As far as Thias could tell he now had two choices. Whichever he decided upon would shape, if not decide, his fortune. The first would be to return to the Capital and report to his Sovereign Lord, inform him of the death of his brother, the Lizardmens' attack on the Keep, and their abduction of the dwarf that he had been sent to question. The other would be to track the Lizardmen and discover their true role in the events that were playing out across the Realm. Thias could not help but think that everything that had happened to him since he had left the Capital was in some way connected. The Death Tubaria, the Knights of Avolire, and now the attack on the Grey Keep by the reptiles of the Eastern Marsh. Something, somewhere, deep within the workings of the bard's complex mind, tried to draw lines of connection.

As the thoughts in his head grew ever darker Thias realised that the problem was far too complex to make sense of alone. He would need help and returning to the Capital seemed a pointless exercise. The briefing of his Sovereign Lord would have to wait. He decided that he needed a greater understanding of what the reptile race was up to. He would track the Lizardman and locate the dwarf but to do that he would require assistance. Such help could only come from the one great place of knowledge at the western outreach of the Grey Mountains. He would make for the town of Valameer and seek help from those who never turned away one of their own. He would hurry on as planned to the Bards Guild.

7

In her solar, reclined upon a velvet upholstered chaise longue that was positioned against an open window, and with her silhouette emphasised by the rising sun, the grotesque figure of Lady Thinata Fullbane rested on her more than ample backside. Her platted red hair fell upon her portly face which in turn sat upon an even rounder body. Her legs looked like two bags of whale meat, bursting at the seams as they positioned themselves to her side. As the great obese Lady munched on the enormous sprig of grapes that hung above her mouth, Tonousa Amberstone sat on a wooden ornate chair opposite and sought to control her feelings of disgust. The gross woman reminded Tonousa of a mother bird as it stuffed itself in readiness to feed its young, stocking up on its daily source of food to ensure that a thousand offspring got their fill. It was as if she no idea of where the next morsel would come from but food was not in short supply for the infamous Lady Fullbane.

Tonousa and a colleague from the City Watch sat opposite the whale and endured with some difficulty the piggery of the woman at her breakfast. In front of her mountain of flesh were many plates piled high. There were mounds of the sweetest oranges, apples, grapes, apples and figs. Then besides the fruit there were plates of bacon, sausage, chicken legs, loaves of freshly baked bread, cake, and to top all that off, several bronze flagons of sweet red cinnamon wine. It was a feast that could feed a household from the slums of Parandor for a year and yet one very fat lady for a day. As the monstrous mathulath took bites at whatever food came within close proximity of her lips, Tonousa watched and retched as crumbs, mixed in with sticky globules of saliva, dripped onto the Lady's cavernous cleavage. The falling waste dropped down the great crevice between two mountainous breasts that poked out through the semi-transparent silk negligee that she somehow deemed appropriate to wear for breakfast. Beneath the material, part covered by the growing pile of waste, three red objects sought to gain the attention of any onlooker; two saucer sized nipples and a small red jewel attached to a golden chain.

Tonousa felt ever more uncomfortable by the minute at having to look upon the enormous woman who seemed so reluctant to dress for the coming day's activities despite the fact that there were several in her diary. While watching Lady Fullbane sink her carious teeth into a second cornucopia of grapes, forced in between great mouthfuls of wine, Tonousa wondered if her companion sat to her right, a colleague from the City Watch called Irabo Basequin, felt the same feelings of revulsion. She glanced to the side and noted the man's youthful features. He was some ten years younger than Tonousa and he too showed signs of severe discomfort. Given the expression on his face Tonousa prayed he would not throw up inside the Lady's solar.

Then as Tonousa and Irabo waited, Lady Fullbane lifted a hand high into the air. She made a small gesture with her wrist and from the side of the room a small boy with olive coloured skin, no younger than twelve years and dressed in simple serving clothes of red and black, raced over to her table. He had stood to attention by the servant's door but following the signal began to move the table away from the Lady to a position equal in distance between herself and the two members of the Watch. On the bottom of each table leg was a small wheel which made the task possible for one so small. The boy then pushed the table through the servant's door and away into the Lady's private apartments. Fullbane would no doubt finish off the feast later in the day. The largest of her kind at last broke the silence that had hung over her sumptuous repast.

"He's such a wonderful boy," she gasped as she used all of her available energy to swing her legs from off the chaise longue and onto to the floor. "I wouldn't know what I would do without him now that fate has robbed me of young Golda. But to business my friends. How may I help you this fine morning when once again Solaris deems it fit to bestow his warmth upon us?"

"I am so pleased that you could see us both at such short notice my Lady," began Tonousa. "I'm sorry that we had to interrupt your breakfast and that we had to sit with you while you ate it."

Layers of blubber rippled under the woman's transparent night attire and mesmerised the four eyes of the Watch.

"Don't be so ridiculous," laughed Lady Fullbane. "It's not every day I get company so early in the morning. Why it must be almost eleven by the hour. Not since my dear departed husband Lord Enguerrand Fullbane used to rest his head in my chambers have I had such esteemed company. This opportunity, given your fresh faces and good nature, is an offer that I just could not refuse. Now please tell me how I may assist you Tonousa, and your very attractive assistant."

Lady Fullbane winked at Irabo but the young man remained expressionless and without as much as a twitch. He was determined to act in a manner that reflected his position as a member of the City Watch.

"My Lady, young Irabo here is not my assistant, but shares the same rank as I do," continued Tonousa while maintaining an official tone.

"Such a pity. I like to have boys running around after me. You never know what favours they may consent to carry out, if you follow my drift."

Without a hint of shame she looked the young man up and down, undressed him with her eyes, and imagined how his body would work for her

"Lady Fullbane," coughed out Irabo. "We are here to talk about the apparent murder of your serving girl and her lover by the hands of persons unknown. We have reason to believe that the killer's intention is to recreate the ritual which will bring about the resurrection of the god Kha."

"So forceful!" flirted Lady Fullbane. "Such a prime specimen of manhood. You would have been able to give my Enguerrand a run for my bed young man...."

"Lady Fullbane," interrupted Tonousa. "Please may we keep to the subject of the murders? That is all we are here to talk about."

"Yes of course, but I don't know what I can tell you that I haven't already told Lord Blackfayer?"

Lady Fullbane sank back onto her chaise longue. Having failed to lift her feet from off the ground she flashed her unsightly privates before the shocked eyes of Irabo.

"So you've spoken to Xix Blackfayer already?" asked Tonousa as she raised an eyebrow. "I thought our Sovereign Lord had passed the investigation to the City Watch?"

"Now I can't help you there. I haven't been to the Court, well, not since the passing of my husband and..."

"What did you tell Lord Blackfayer?" interrupted Tonousa.

"Well it's like this you see. I told him that it was my young servant boy Ourri that found poor Golda's body lying there, pale as a sheet and void of any life. I had sent him to find the sweet girl as it was time for me to rise from my bed. It was her job to help me into my clothes each morning and I thought it was odd that the youngling would be late for such an important task. So, young Ourri alerted one of the Royal Guards stationed outside my private chambers. Now ..., erm..., what was his name? Oh yes, Sir Digory Berthellemy. Well Sir Digory alerted old Abrahamus Marus who arrived and examined the body there and then. They closed off the whole servants quarters that day and tried to work out what had killed the poor girl. It didn't take them long to find the cause. It was in her food you see. A bowl of soup, spilt over the floor by the side of her head. What was it they called it? Oh yes, Nightshade. That was the poison they suspected and I guess you've heard of it."

The fat woman's patronising tone did not sit well with Tonousa. She saw that Irabo also felt uncomfortable as the colour of the skin of his forehead and cheeks had turned cherry red. Of course they had heard of the poison. It was squeezed from the 'bonny woman' plant that grew in abundance across whole the Realm and was used by the members of the City Watch to coat the tips of their arrows. Tonousa also knew from her use of the poison that it could paralyze and in a large enough dose even cause death.

"We do indeed know of that poison," replied Tonousa, desperate to finish interrogation.

Lady Fullbane somehow managed to get one leg up onto the chaise longue and continued.

"Well, old Abrahamus Marus did something with his potions, his mystical ramblings and such stuff. He found poison within the remains of the soup that Golda had been eating. I paid the Grand Physician and Sir Digory good money to keep this matter from reaching the Royal Court. I even sent one of my own household to find poor Golda's lover for he worked in the kitchens and would have had access to many herbs and spices and assisted in the preparation of food. You see, I believed that he was the one responsible for the horrendous crime. I made it my purpose to turn the boy over to the City Watch but then the Royal Guard found his body stuffed inside the spice powder store, down in the cellars of the Underkeep."

"Is there anything else you can remember?" asked Tonousa. "Perhaps something that you told Lord Blackfayer that might help us with our investigation? Anything that Golda may have confided in you?"

"I'm sorry that I'm not being more helpful," replied the Lady as she managed to wriggle her second leg upon the chaise longue. "That's all I know of this dreadful business. To think that it happened right in my very private quarters! What would my Enguerrand have said?"

"He would have told you that you have been very helpful to our enquiry," replied Tonousa, unable to prevent herself from smiling. "What more can you tell me about Webb, the kitchen boy, Golda's lover?"

"I always told young Golda that nothing good would ever come of that boy. She was such a nice girl and was clearly led astray. *'Golda'* I said, *'there are plenty of other handsome men in the Capital; men of fine upbringing, and there you are having this secret tryst with the bastard son of one those harbour trash?'* Now, let me think. What was his last name? Ah yes, Underscroft."

"Underscroft?" gasped Tonousa for the name was familiar to her.

"Yes, Webb Underscroft. Do you know of them?"

"Sadly yes," she replied. "We have had our run-ins with that family over the years."

"Well if anyone's got anything to do with this dark magic, this Death Tubaria stuff, then I'd start by talking to them," added Lady Fullbane.

Tonousa closed her eyes for a brief moment. Indeed Lady Thinata Fullbane was right. The Underscrofts who lived out by the Estuary of New Beginnings were a family to be reckoned with. She recalled several occasions when she had arrested one of their many children for one petty crime or another. Tonousa would have locked up all of the robbing shites if it wasn't for the fact that the Underscrofts, though nothing had ever been proven, were the supposed gate keepers of the Guild of Thieves that was located somewhere within the walls of Parandor. Tonousa had always been cautious not to cross that most dangerous of Guilds; not for any other reason than for a fair price the Guild would supply the Watch with information regarding the city's criminal activity, other than of course the thievery that they specialised in. Such was the way of life in the dark underbelly of Parandor.

"Well, I must say, it has been an absolute delight to have entertained you," added Lady Fullbane, dragging Tonousa out of her private musing. "But you must excuse me for I have sat here in my scant attire for far too long and it's time I had a bath."

With that she clapped her hands twice in the air. Tonousa and Irabo watched as a dozen muscular men, dressed in similar clothes to the olive skinned boy they had seen earlier, entered the room and proceeded to try and lift the chaise longue on which the Lady rested. Each bent their backs as they strained to control the weight. Tonousa was most surprised at their success and they appeared well practiced in their art. At any moment she expected some servants would drop their end causing the great lump of womanhood to crash in a rippling heap upon the solar floor. Tonousa smiled.

"You're welcome to come and join me in my bath," said Lady Fullbane as she winked and teased Irabo. "I feel the need of another pair of strong hands to scrub my crevices clean and lather up my treasures."

"With respect I think I'll pass on that offer if you don't mind my Lady," replied Irabo with hint of revulsion. "We have important business to take care of just now; a matter most urgent."

"Oh well, suit yourself. Please see yourself out."

With those last words said the removal men continued on in their struggle. With great effort and substantial difficulty they carried the chaise longue out of the room and with it the monstrous figure of Lady Thinata Fullbane.

"What a horrible woman," said Irabo once the two Watch members were alone.

"I'm surprised how you managed to stay in control," laughed Tonousa. "From the look on your face, I thought you were going to puke."

"Oh don't please," replied Irabo.

The young warrior's face contorted with disgust. Imagining being seduced by her more than ample flesh made his legs weaken.

"I'm just glad I hadn't had anything to eat this morning. Has she always been like that?"

As Irabo asked his question, both he and Tonousa left the solar and walked into the corridor beyond. They made their way through the Royal apartments, descended the grand staircase and passed through a door into the courtyard of the Citadel. Both were relieved to leave the Court and as they walked on Tonousa answered the question that her young colleague had put to her a minute earlier.

"There have been many theories about that Lady's weight. Some say that she was born large but there are others who say that she was born stick thin and only put on all that lard as she grew older. As you saw for yourself she does enjoy her food and idle luxuries. So the opinion whispered in Court, and indeed the wider populous, is that she just eats for pleasure. Even her husband before he died said that she was becoming a monstrosity. It is said his death hit her hard and it caused her to eat even more. Food was the one comfort that she could find solace in, apart from her 'young boys' of course."

"What happened to Lord Fullbane?" asked Irabo. "How did he die?"

"Rumour has it that the old duffer fell sleep following a night of passion and never woke up. He was suffocated according to Abrahamus Marus. The bed servants recorded that the Lord was deep in the realm of dreams when his soporific wife rolled on top and crushed him under her mountains of flesh."

"That's disgusting," choked Irabo as he imagined the horror of such a demise. "It's horrible beyond words. Please don't tell me anymore."

Tonousa turned to look at her friend. She saw that she had disturbed him and therefore sealed her lips. The pair passed on through the courtyard of the Citadel which that morning was in a state of chaos. The square was filled with the Royal Guard, all busy in their training. Most were without their armour and wearing training pads that resembled those that Tonousa used. There were also many members of the Court present, some in pairs and others in groups of four or more, all going about their daily routine as they moved from building to building. Solaris was now high in the sky and cast short shadows down upon the dirt. The voices of the noble Lords and Ladies were joyous as to a one they basked in the glorious brightness of Solaris. Tonousa and Irabo felt a darker presence as they made their way on towards the Barbican. There the conversation changed to more serious matters.

"So now what," asked Irabo?

"We're going to have to ask the Underscrofts a few questions about their son.

"Is it possible that the Thieves Guild has a connection to Death Tubaria?"

"I don't know. I wouldn't want to speculate just yet. We need to be cautious in how we approach this. The last thing we want is for the Thieves Guild to loosen its ties with the Watch."

The portcullis that bared the way into the streets beyond rose slowly by the inch and after some minutes allowed passage beneath its teeth of iron. The warriors continued on into the dark guts the Capital's underbelly where Tonousa was grateful not to be claustrophobic for the streets they walked through were most narrow. The wooden houses with their thatched roofs were small timber framed buildings and had been constructed so as to fit as close together as possible. The upper floors of the buildings projected out over those on the ground such that houses on opposite sides of the street almost met in the middle and created a man-made tunnel that blocked out most of the light from Solaris. It was always eerie and dark amongst the City streets and the smell of shit and pestilence filled the nostrils of all who walked them. Tonousa knew, as did every inhabitant of Parandor, to be extra careful when traversing the close packed buildings for it was not uncommon that a window would be thrown open and the contents of a piss pot tossed out into the street. For this reason Tonousa always walked with one eye looking up.

On the pair marched while Tonousa began to question herself as to how well she knew the man by her side. Irabo had been ordered to accompany her by Commander Townsforth and she wondered why he had chosen this particular officer out of the many others that she knew better. It had been her duty sometime past to help train Irabo although she remembered little of that experience. She then realised that she did not know much at all about this young warrior.

"Tell me about yourself."

"Ma'am?"

"Tell me a little bit about yourself Irabo. Where in the Realm do you originate from? Who were your parents? You know, tell me about you."

"Well, what is there to tell," began Irabo. "I was born in the village of Falahorn, north of the coastal town of Valameer, beyond the Ivory Pass and on the western edge of the Dragonas. My parents were simple farmers who scratched a living off the land and traded their wares such that we might eat. I had two twin sisters but they both died in their second year. When I was twelve my parents were taken by the plague and I had to fend for myself. So I decided to journey south, taking whatever work I could find and..."

A voice then screamed out 'Shite away!'

The sudden sound interrupted the Irabo's story and while the pair stood motionless the contents of a pot fell from an open window on high. As the ripe smelling turds hit the floor they splashed up onto Tonousa's legs. In that instant and amid her disgust she prayed for the god Aquarius to rain down and wash the excrement away into the Tiaryer. Gathering her thoughts Tonousa stepped over the steaming pile as Irabo continued with his tale.

"As I said, I journeyed south, taking whatever work I could find between Valameer and the Capital. I arrived here desperate for food and shelter and I came across a talk given by our Man-at-Arms, Danisun Dain. He was seeking to recruit people into the Watch and told me that by joining I would get to see the world. And so here I am, stuck inside the walls of Parandor."

"Yes indeed!" said Tonousa. "Danisun does talk nonsense much of the time."

With that both started to laugh. On they continued until they came across a beggar who lay against the wall amongst the mud. The wretch held a wooden bowl between his emaciated thighs beyond which the rest of his legs were missing.

"Spare a groat good sir," cried the beggar as he held out his bowl.

Tonousa watched as her young friend produced a silver coin from beneath his leather tunic and tossed it into the receptacle before him.

"Here you go," said Irabo, his voice full of cheer. "Your next ale is on me."

"May the gods look down on you with great favour my friend," replied the beggar.

Tonousa thought hard about the display of humanity that her young colleague had shown to the wretched man. Any other person would have walked past and not cast a care towards the poor unfortunate soul with only a wall for company. There was something about Irabo that made her feel proud to be in his company. It felt good to see aid given to the destitute and those forced to exist in abject poverty. Tonousa then started to think about their encounter with Lady Fullbane and she struggled with the obscene unfairness of life in Parandor. How unjust it seemed that people like Fullbane were allowed to gorge themselves on expensive foods from far across the Realm and beyond while others were starving just outside the gates of the Citadel. It was at times like these that Tonousa became angry. She hoped that one day, those such as Fullbane would be made to redress the gap between the greedy elite who controlled everything and the rest who survived on their scraps.

Their journey soon came to an end and as the gap between the houses widened out they approached the Southern Gatehouse, an imposing redoubt built into the thick stone wall that surrounded the city. The four main gates, all identical in construction, led out into even more pitiful slums. Each was manned by a rotation of two members of the Watch yet as the two warriors approached Tonousa could only see one at his post. She knew from experience that his colleague would be on the other side of the gate but the one ahead she knew very well. He went by the name of Lolye Throissler.

"Good Morning Tonousa; morning Irabo," called the guard from out of the shadows.

"Morning Lolye," replied Tonousa. "Who is with you today?"

"Young Karkis Snouth. So what brings you to the Southern Gate?"

"We're heading to the docks. We have business there on order of our Lord Commander."

"Well in that case, I shall let you pass," smiled Lolye.

With that said Lolye wandered over to the large iron doors that bared their way. On reaching them he grabbed hold of one of the brass rings that were attached to it at chest height and with great effort pulled one of the doors open. Tonousa and Irabo passed through and soon left the young guard behind. They walked under the arch of the Gatehouse and into the buildings beyond having acknowledged Karkis Snouth as they passed his position. In just a few minutes

Tonousa and Irabo found themselves in the decrepit slum that stretched south of the City between its walls and the docks at the mouth of the Tiaryer. The buildings, if you could call them such, were composed of small wooden shacks, some of which were lucky to have a door. Most relied on a gap in the thin wooden panels to act as the point of entry into their innermost recesses. The smell of decay, effluent, and burning horse dung became ever more oppressive. The scum of the slums beyond the wall lived in a state far worse than poverty, if such a one could be imagined. All those forced to live beyond the stone looked gaunt and were covered from head to toe in filth that had accumulated over lifetimes. What little clothes they had were in tatters and the majority resorted to begging as the only means of obtaining sustenance. Tonousa, as grateful as she was that she lived inside the walls, nevertheless felt much pity and a deep sorrow for each outsider that she passed. Sadly Irabo would not have sufficient coin for all who approached for alms.

"Life is so unfair," groaned Irabo as he gave his fourth and last coin away. "You have people like Fullbane who have never had to graft for a crumb and then the poor wretches out here who are dying from the moment they are born. I just wish something could be done about it. All that ever seeps down from Blackfayer is that these impoverished souls are but scrounger scum that he deems unfit to even clean his arse."

Tonousa could only agree with this observation. Deep down she knew there was enough gold and silver in the Realm for everyone to live a comfortable life if only it was shared amongst all. She despised those who wielded the power and had always been driven by greed. There were but a few honourable individuals like Irabo Basequin who gave hope for the survival of humanity.

"I agree with you," said Tonousa. "Life is shit at the best of times and ever more so for these poor souls that live out here. You worked your way into the city as did I and yet there are those who have never known pay for a day's labour. People like Fullbane deserve a sharp lesson. Even Phauless Gylewu sees her as an embarrassment and is pleased that she no longer attends Court."

"I now understand why she doesn't appear there," added Irabo. "Having that monstrosity in his presence must make our Sovereign want to vomit. No wonder she tried to keep the business of the Death Tubaria from him."

"We don't know her real reasons for that action Irabo," said Tonousa. "That's why we are investigating this matter. Come on now, Solaris is high and we have questions to put to the Underscrofts."

Several minutes passed before the smell of fish and sea salt began to drift on the breeze and displace the city's stench. The two warriors of the Watch then found themselves standing within the docks of Parandor, a cluster of wooden buildings that sat upon the mouth of the Tiaryer where it joined the ocean after its long journey from the Grey Mountains. A wooden pier had been built into the estuary bank and it protruded a small distance out into the water. Moored up against its rotting planks was the Royal Barge, 'The Mermaids Tail', a large oak vessel with two masts. The ship's sails were all wrapped and secured but at the top of the highest mast the Royal Standard blew in the gentle wind that came in off the ocean. The only sign of life by this most impressive of vessels was a member of the Royal

Guard who stood at the head of its gangplank and prevented any uninvited entry. Tonousa walked onto the wooden boards of the dock and her eyes focused on a fishing ketch called 'The Master's Catch'. It was at its usual resting place for this time of day having returned earlier that morning from the ocean with its catch of fish. The fruits of the sea had long been sold at the market and sent to the kitchens of the Citadel to be served to the elite. Once again the inequality of life burned inside Tonousa's heart. She knew that none of the oceans gifts would ever reach the tables of those that inhabited the slums, not that any of them had tables. The docks were quiet with few people skulking amongst the shadows. Some fifty paces later the two warriors arrived at their destination, the shack that belonged to the Underscrofts.

Tonousa hammered upon the wooden door and then stepped back to await an answer. Irabo stood guard by her side. She glanced up at the wooden sign that hung above the door, held aloft by rusted chains as it dangled from a wooden post. The words 'Dead Collector' were etched into the sign and they reflected the Underscroft's occupation. The dead collectors of Parandor would take their cart round the Capital each morning, remove the bodies of the deceased and the almost dead from when they were dumped in the streets and then dispose of them into one of several large pits that were constantly being dug outside of the city walls. Tonousa had long suspected that this was the route and method used by members of the Thieves Guild to enter and exit the city. The door was thrust open and from within a middle-aged man with one leg limped forward, his wizen frame supported by a wooden crutch that was wedged under one arm. He looked with suspicion at the two warriors through his one eye. The other was missing but its empty socket fixed on Tonousa's presence.

"What the fuck do you two want?" shouted the man.

"You are Underscroft I presume?" snapped back Tonousa.

"Aye, I'm Cassius Underscroft. What do you fuckers want?"

"My name is Tonousa Amberstone and this is Irabo Basequin of the City Watch. We're here to ask some questions regarding the death of your boy Webb."

"That little shit got what he deserved. Always fucking off to that bitch of his and abandoning his family when he had jobs to do."

"I thought he worked in the kitchens of the Citadel," added Tonousa.

"Yeah he did," replied Underscroft as his temper wilted somewhat. "But I can't tell you anything more than I told that other fellow who came asking questions."

Tonousa raised an eyebrow. "Other fellow?"

"Yeah. Some gangly bloke. Said he was also investigating young Webb's involvement in some crime or other."

"Did he give a name?" asked Irabo.

"No he didn't... said he was snooping on behalf of gormless Gylewu. Started asking questions about young Webb's nocturnal activities. As if I'd know what the little bugger got up to at night. Suggested he was part of some dark cult or something."

"Death Tubaria?" asked Tonousa.

"Yeah, that's the one. Said something about dark magic being involved in the young lad's death. Wanted permission to exhume the body. I told him he was wasting his time as Webb was buried amongst the other corpses for that day but the fucker was insistent."

Tonousa's mind raced on in overload. She could only assume that this other had been sent by the Sovereign Ruler.

"Do you mind if we come inside?" she asked, realising that they were being watched by an ever increasing number of eyes on the surrounding dockside. "We don't want you to get any unnecessary attention."

"Unnecessary attention!" snarled Underscroft. "Because of young Webb's death we've had every fucking Guild under Solaris poking their noses into our business. Even the Wizards sent an odd looking twat to discuss the magical marking on my sons head. I thought this messy business had been well and truly buried along with Webb. Now you two show up and start asking questions again. So in answer to your request. No you can't come inside. In fact you can both just fuck off."

With that Cassius Underscroft attempted to slam the door to his hovel but Tonousa was one step ahead and placed her foot between the rickety door and its frame. As the wood failed to close, Cassius looked down at what blocked his doorway and then back up to its owner.

"You have ten seconds to remove your foot before I call one of my boys to do it for you."

The action failed to intimidate Tonousa who continued with her questions.

"Underscroft, we need to hear everything that you know. It is obvious that you are hiding something, no doubt because it connects you to the Thieves Guild. Tell me what else you know or I'll be forced to arrest you and take you to the dungeons"

There followed a brief pause during which the tension hovered in the breeze. Tonousa watched as the dead collector mulled his options. After a moment of deliberation Cassius spoke again.

"Look," he whispered. "It was like this. From what he told me, Webb had gotten himself into trouble with someone who was smuggling various poisons into the city. From what I then gathered, Webb had been helping to peddle these poisons in order to pay off a debt to someone he knew in the Citadel."

"Did Webb give you a name?" asked Tonousa.

"No he didn't. No name was given. He just said that it was someone in a high and trusted position. He hinted that this individual had infiltrated the Court in order to bring it down from within. Well we would all like to do that would we not? Webb told me that the supplier of poisons had a far greater plan in mind and that it only began with the fall of the Capital. Webb had tried to get the Thieves Guild involved in the plot but the Head of the Order refused. Said it was too dangerous. Now what were the words that he used? Oh yes, that was it. He said that his people were thieves not associates of the Guild of Assassins."

"Guild of Assassins!" gasped Irabo. "Shudder the thought."

"Aye lad," continued Cassius. "It would indeed be hard times if assassins ran a Guild."

"Did you tell anyone else these facts?" demanded Tonousa. "Does anyone else know about the invitation made to the Thieves Guild?"

"No," Cassius replied as he scratched away at his crotch with his free hand. "I didn't tell anyone one about it. Apart from our regulars, only the City Watch know about my family's connections to the Thieves Guild. We sometimes send out the odd rumour here and there when our folk need work but apart from that, no one knows of this link, not even that fellow that came asking about young Webb, the one I told you about."

"Do you think that your son met this conspirator through his employment at Court?"

"Aye, I think so."

"Thank you Underscroft," said Tonousa as she frowned. "Thank you for your time."

"Sure," replied Cassius. "Anything to help the City Watch! Now if you don't mind I have things that I need to do. So just fuck off."

With that Cassius slammed the door in the faces of the two members of the City Watch and this time Tonousa did not try to prevent its closure.

"Well that was interesting," said Irabo.

"Indeed it was," Tonousa replied as both turned and began to walk away. "It seems to me that young Webb Underscroft was using his relationship with Golda Flintwind and his employment in the kitchens to act as a cover for his malignant activities inside the Citadel. I wager that whoever is responsible for the recent series of deaths is a key member of the Court."

"So what do we do next? We can't just arrest them all."

"I realise that Irabo. I am not so dull of mind! No, we must figure out a way to trap this conspirator without alerting his attention. One false move and we could lose the man. He could just melt away and disappear."

"But if he disappeared then wouldn't that mean we would have him?"

"Perhaps," continued Tonousa. "It would indeed point the way but we would be no closer to catching him or stopping the ritual. I'm just glad that we haven't had more bodies turn up."

"Do you think there will be more?"

"Yes I do Irabo. The urgency given to this matter by Xix Blackfayer and our Sovereign Lord is such that they, like me, believe that it is just a matter of time before the next murder. I will wager that another corpse will soon turn up with a brand of three circles on the back of its head.

The two warriors moved away from the dead collector's building and crossed the open ground towards the bank where the river Tiaryer joined with the estuary. Standing at the edge of the water they looked across the mouth of the river to the old stone beacon that had long stood upon the opposite bank. Everyone who visited the docks knew the purpose of this device. It was to be lit on nights when the winds and sea threatened to destroy any vessel trying to make it to the Capital. Tonousa had known days when thunderous Hamthor had cast storms so great that the waters of the ocean surged up, only to then crash down upon the docks and destroy its buildings. The one thing that had saved The Master's Catch on one particular night was the fire of the beacon as it guided the ship home. While the two warriors looked out across the water Tonousa noticed something bobbing around in the swell.

"What is that?" she cried while pointing in the direction of the object.

"I've no idea, "replied Irabo. "Whatever it is, it's drifting this way."

The two stood in silence until it became apparent as to what they were looking at. A large branch of a tree came floating down through the mouth of the river on the outgoing tide. Slumped over it was the body of a young man who showed no obvious signs of life.

"Shit!" shouted Irabo "There's a man on top of it."

Before Tonousa could respond Irabo removed his leather armour and in nothing but his flimsy tunic dived head first into the river. After a few seconds beneath the surface he at last re-emerged. Tonousa had at first feared that her colleague had drowned and was much relieved when he surfaced and began his swim towards the fallen branch and the young man that lay upon it. With her gaze fixed on the action she watched Irabo reach his goal. The fit young warrior dragged the man off the log and pulled him through the water with one hand under his chin and while trying to keep them both afloat.

Tonousa was ready once Irabo reached the edge of the dock and she helped pull both out of the cold water. She knew then that Irabo was selfless and generous in all aspects of his essence. She had witnessed a side of her companion that she never knew existed and a feeling of great pride seeped into her chest.

8

The road east beyond the Grey Mountains was a most treacherous one. Having traversed through the rock crevasses, shale screes, and the desolate but daunting snow covered peaks, the Eastern Road wound out of the high range and down onto flat and stagnant marsh land. Both sides of the road sloped into the stinking putrid ground where thick weeds and bog plants grew in abundance from out of steep banks before the deeper water curtailed their growth. Water reeds flourished with such proliferation that they gave the impression of more solid land rather than the swamp that lay beneath their foliage. A strong dense fog covered the poor road and limited the view of those that travelled along its course. It made it dangerous to deviate from the firm dirt surface while the putrid egg smell lingered in the air, forced its way up nostrils, and induced a great nausea in most who inhaled it.

Along this road travelled a caravan comprised of black armoured knights and their mighty steeds. At the slowest of walks, step by careful step, they plodded down the trail. Within that caravan a large wooden cage, mounted upon an oak chassis, which in turn was attached to two solid wheels, trundled forward on its unending journey. The cage was tethered to the back of several brown horses that pulled the mobile prison cell through the steaming stench. Inside the cage three people slept, despite the difficulty induced by such a confined space. Of the three, the young female child had found the journey the most difficult. Every time the caravan had stopped the child had cried for her mother and each time received a blow to the face from one of the black knights' gauntlets.

Two adults, a young man and a pregnant woman, had at first tried to defend the child against their abusers but then they too were punished for resisting and soon learned not to protest. It was self-preservation that forced their silence and yet their hearts wept. At least they were given water and stale bread whenever the cage stopped. For some reason they were needed alive and even though they wanted so much to survive, death at times seemed preferable to the continuous torment that they were forced to endure.

"Who do you think they are?" had asked the pregnant woman on the first day of their journey. "What do you think they want with us?"

"I don't know," the young man had told her. "During the attack on Maplehill, I heard them cry out for Avolire, wherever or whatever that is."

It had been six days since their abduction and the slaughter that had taken place in their village. The young man and the pregnant woman, between attempts to comfort the child, had tried to map out the course of their journey. Now they had given up as the caravan moved forward through the dense fog that spewed up from the waters of the marsh and hid any point of reference in the landscape. They had travelled, or so they believed, along the Eastern Road and through Oakwood and Ashview. Unlike Maplehill, no survivors had been taken when their communities had been put to the sword. Each of the villages had been burned to the ground and their terrified inhabitants slaughtered without mercy or compassion. At each of the hamlets the knights had made it known that they were looking for a youth whom they called the 'Marked'. From the three villages the caravan had journeyed towards the Grey Mountains and crossed the Tiaryer as it disappeared underground towards its source. Soon after it took the fork that led off to the Grey Keep. For another day and night the caravan had travelled along the same road before it reached the edge of the mountain range and then began it's decent into the Eastern Marsh. During their six days of confinement the man and woman delved deep within their thoughts and tried to find a valid reason for their abduction. Both were unable to come up with an answer, or at least one that made any sense. It was during his ruminations on the sixth day of the journey that the youth heard the name of the man who led the group of knights, the one with the skull fashioned helmet.

"They all seem to be following the orders of that bastard with the death head," the young man had told his fellow captors. "I heard one of them talking and he called him Commander Rhaizen."

This beast led the way forward, always at the head of the caravan while sat upon his black steed. Its colour was in clear contrast to the brown coats of the all the others that travelled behind it. Rhaizen's coal black cape draped around his shoulders and covered his armour. Often it blew outwards in the gusts of wind that came in from the marshlands and gave the impression of a giant bat on the wing. It was on the seventh morning that the caravan paused for a prolonged rest. The young man figured that this was to allow time for the horses and their riders to recover from their long trek. Whenever his captors approached the cage he tried to listen into their words but most of the time conversations were held far away and he had difficulty in picking up what was said.

Once again the child began to cry and the pregnant woman tried to comfort her as best she could. Yet the soothing words of her soft voice had no significant effect.

"Shush child," whispered the woman. "They will hear you."

It was no use. The young girl's cries turned to howls and she screamed out aloud.

"I want my mother. Mother please save me!"

The man and woman watched the murmurings of the knights in black and realised the seriousness of their situation. As the child's screams built to a crescendo the man held her on the floor of the cage. Later she tried to squeeze her frail body out from between the narrow bars but still her screams continued. Even when the woman placed her hands across the child's mouth, the girl continued to wail. She bit the hand and the woman did not try again. Then without warning the door to the cage was forced opened and the terrified captives cowered as one of the knights climbed inside and snatched the young child by the hair. Neither of the adults could have prevented what happened next for the knight whipped out a knife from within his armour, lifted it high, and shouted:

"I'll give you something to fucking scream about."

With that the knight plunged the dagger deep into the chest of the young innocent. The child's crimson fluids gushed onto the floor of the cage. Then she coughed and passed into unconsciousness. The knight, still holding the girl by the hair, then dragged her limp body out of the cage and threw it to the ground.

"You evil bastard," screamed the woman as she stood and tried to grab the hold of the body. "She was just a child."

The murderous brute turned on the spot to face the woman, watched all the time by his fellow knights and Commander. He pointed his knife in the direction of the two remaining captives.

"One more word bitch, and I'll cut that fucking runt out of your belly."

"Captain Nictis," shouted Commander Rhaizen. "Leave our prisoners alone. You have had enough sport for one day."

"Yes Sir. As you command."

The Captain saluted his Commander and walked away to join his comrades. The woman sat down and as she did so found it hard to control her emotions and the deep grief that crushed her heart. The male captive put his arm around her and hugged with enough reassurance to keep her sane.

"They killed her," sobbed the woman. "They killed Maria."

"I know, I know. She'll be with her parents now, perhaps up in the heavens in the care of Solaris; at peace within her mother's arms," replied the man.

"I pray she has been reunited with Elita."

"What do you mean?" quizzed the man. "Her mother was Catriana. Elita was her aunt."

"Oh come off it! Everyone knows the true story of Catriana and Elita Darcha. It was Elita who produced Maria. The father was one of the Red Mare's passing sots and Catriana took Maria as her own in order to prevent the shame of delivering a bastard falling upon her sister. I am sure that you remember the insults that my husband had to live with."

"Of course I do Mal," he replied. "Denius was a good man and didn't deserve the shit flung his way. He may have been a teller of tall tales but he didn't deserve to be shunned by the three villages."

"I thank you for your support," replied Mal as her tears flowed. "You've always been such a caring boy. Your family always had much praise for you even though they may not have told it to you straight. Families should always stick together. Maybe that's why Elita left Catriana the Red Mare in her will, as a thank you for bringing up her child."

The young man shook his head. There were no words that he could say that would make the situation better. All he could do was to offer Mal Castor his support. He couldn't bear the thought of another of his friends, the last surviving member of their village, being killed in front of his eyes. Before he could say anything further, Mal winced in pain, and then clutched at her belly.

"Are you okay? Is something going wrong inside?" he asked.

"I'm fine," she replied as she took a deep breath and attempted to focus through the discomfort. "It's just the baby kicking, though given our current terrors I'm surprised it has survived this long."

"Don't talk like that Mal."

"I'll talk how I like," she snapped back. "I wish Lord Solaris would take me now and free me from this torture."

Before the young man could reply, Nictis walked past the cage where the captives sat. The foul murderer looked in and glared at the two young villagers. Pure evil stared through the slit in his helm and the woman and man kept silent.

"We're moving out now," barked Nictis.

The brute then turned and kicked the lifeless body of Maria Darcha over the bank of the road and into the marsh land as if disposing of a sack of rotten turnips. Then he mounted his horse and the caravan set off once again into the night. It was a long and dreadful darkness and neither the young man nor the pregnant woman were able to snatch a single minute of sleep.

On the eighth day the caravan was suddenly joined by several armoured Lizardmen who appeared out of the fog. Behind them the creatures dragged a naked and long haired dwarf, bound at the wrists, and with a metal chain secured around his neck. The young man watched from the cage as the interaction between the two parties began and his ears strained hard in an attempt to capture the conversation. The exchange of words was led by Commander Rhaizen and the largest of the Lizardmen who without doubt was the creatures' leader.

"You took your damned time," snarled Rhaizen.

"We encountered strong resistance," the Lizardman replied. "We stormed the Keep as requested but their numbers were many and they fought to the death."

"At least I see that you were successful," said Rhaizen as he pointed to the dwarf. "Did he resist? I hear that dwarves can be ferocious fighters."

"There was indeed resistance but nothing we couldn't handle. We soon over powered him. One dwarf on its own was no match for my warriors."

"Yet you are few in number" laughed Rhaizen. "I congratulate you on your success. Tell me, what of the Guard at the Grey Keep? Will they follow us and attempt to retrieve their prisoner?"

"Only if a necromancer was to resurrect their corpses," hissed the creature. "We left no one alive, lost many of my kind, but we shall not be followed. Our shape changer was left there to divert anyone that would try to follow. Even the best of trackers couldn't now pick up our trail."

"That pleases me Sslashnash. Now put your prisoner in the cart with the others."

The young man in the cage moved away from his position against the bars. He tried to avoid his captors eyes should they realise he had been listening to the words that had passed between them. Then he put his arms around Mal and held her close and vowed to protect her no matter what happened next. As two of the Lizardmen dragged the naked dwarf towards the cage the young man noted the weapons that hung at their sides. Both carried scimitar like swords and leather handled whips which divided into many separate individual barbed strands. Realising that the creatures were formidable opponents he hoped he would not have to face one down in battle, at least not just yet.

The cage was then forced open while the dwarf struggled to break free. A blow to the back of its head stunned it for a brief moment which allowed time for two Lizardmen to remove the metal chain from around the pitiful creature's neck.

They then bundled the dwarf into the cage where it landed with a thud at the feet of the man and woman. Once the cage was closed and locked the two reptilians made their way to the front of the caravan and joined the rest of their raiding party which continued to emerge from out the marsh.

"Time to move out!" shouted Commander Rhaizen.

Following his command the caravan started to move forward again through the swirling mists of the swamp. It had doubled in size and together the mounted knights and the scale covered foot soldiers created a substantial fighting force. It would be madness for any others to engage them on the narrow road that was surrounded by fog and swamp. While the cage lurched forward the young man moved over to the dwarf who lay without moving on the floor. After untying the ropes that bound its wrists he helped the creature up onto its knees.

"Are you badly hurt?" asked the man.

A most unexpected response crawled out from the dwarf's mouth. It was a mixture of slurs and snorts that neither of the prisoners could understand.

"Are hurt?" he asked again before pointing to himself. "Me friend."

Through the vast amount of hair that covered the dwarf's face, eyes looked out with great suspicion. Once again the dwarf opened his mouth to respond and uttered a further mix of the slurs and snorts that was its own strange language.

"Can you understand me?" asked the young man, ever hopeful of a positive response and desperate to make any sense of what had happened. "Do you follow anything of what I am saying?"

This time the dwarf pointed to its chest. It was obvious that the little creature was trying to communicate something important.

"Grovrouk!" spoke the dwarf. "Grovrouk!"

"Grovrouk?" repeated the young man. "Is that your name?"

"Grovrouk!" said the dwarf and once again the action was repeated.

"Well Grovrouk, this is Mal," said the young man as he pointed to the woman next to him. "I am Methladon, Methladon Heyn. I don't suppose you know what is going on?"

Once again the dwarf spoke in its strange language. The stunted being's body language became more animated and the tone of its voice implied more anger than fear. Methladon didn't bother trying to communicate with the dwarf again. It appeared more human than animal although it was clear it, or he, could not speak the common language of the Realm.

In the early morning light of the ninth day as Solaris tried to penetrate the thick fog, the caravan reached the first reptilian settlement the prisoners had seen along the road. As Methladon Heyn looked out from the cage he saw houses made from mud and bundles of cut reeds. There were no more than about fifteen of these small huts and amongst them Methladon saw more of the Lizardmen, each dressed in the same tattered brown rags that looked of considerable age. He noted the differences between these reptiles and those that had joined the caravan on the road. With no other clues to go off, Methladon presumed that the new ones were the poorer end of their race, unlike the warrior elite that had no doubt ventured out from some hidden city buried deep within the marshland. The caravan continued to roll forward until it had entered the centre of the settlement and there Methladon was forced to shield himself and Mal from a flurry of small stones thrown at them by filth smeared offspring. Once the barrage had ceased he tried to survey his surroundings and look for any opportunity to escape. It was then that he spotted the focal point of the village, a large sacrificial alter decorated with the bones of human victims and other varied creatures. This stone slab was covered in blood, smeared over its surface and decorative sides. The vison sent a shiver down Methladon's spine for it was before this place of butchery that the caravan came to a halt.

Rhaizen dropped down from his horse and stepped towards the largest of the adjacent buildings. A portly Lizardman with a frog like appearance stepped out from its interior. This new creature was dressed in ceremonial robes with a crude crown made from bone and feathers upon its warty head. This toady beast was flanked by more Lizardmen who wore the same mixture of cheap armour that Methladon had seen on the other warriors.

"Hail Mighty Ssonsh, High Priest of the Eastern Marsh," shouted Commander Rhaizen. "We the Knights of Avolire seek passage through the Rift."

"The god's of the marsh will demand a sacrifice," replied the frog priest. "I see you have prisoners. Just one of them will suffice. Spill some blood and the Rift will open for you."

The word sacrifice stunned both Methladon and Mal. The two began to scream and protest but the dwarf remained silent and looked out of the cage towards his captors, his face devoid of any emotion.

"Shut the fuck up!" bellowed Nictis.

No sooner had the prisoners protest begun than it ended. Methladon and Mal fell silent as both somehow managed to hold back their terror. Neither wanted to inflame the wrath the evil Captain.

"Thank you Nictis," grumbled Rhaizen before turning back towards the High Priest. "Yes, we have three prisoners. A man, a woman and a dwarf. The dwarf is essential property of Avolire, but you can choose either of the others."

Ssonsh moved forward towards the cage and began to inspect its occupants. The frog creature looked through the gaps between the bars and studied each of the occupants in turn, including the silent dwarf. There followed a heavy silence as the priest sought to decide which one of the two young adults would make the most appropriate sacrifice. Then as the face of the Ssonsh pushed closer to the cage, Methladon saw two bloodshot eyes search for imperfections in the captive pair. After a few moments of deliberation, the High Priest of the Eastern Marsh turned to face Rhaizen.

"I'll take the boy," croaked the beast as it signalled to two of the armoured Lizardman. "He will do well."

Within seconds of the order being issued the cage door was forced open and despite the struggles of the young man and the screams of the woman who tried to protect him, the sacrificial offering was extracted. One of the Lizardmen took hold of Methladon by the neck and threw him out of the cage and on to the marshy ground. At the same time Mal was knocked backwards against the dwarf which caused both to collapse against the sides of the cage. Through Mal's screams and his own resurgent protests Methladon was pulled to his feet. The two

Lizardmen then dragged him towards the blood soaked alter. Mustering all of his strength, Methladon span around in a tight circle and somehow freed himself from the grasp of the Lizardman who had held him by his right hand. He reached down and drew the weapon that hung at his captor's side. The scimitar was wielded at speed and Methladon decapitated the creature before the other could move.

Within seconds all the Knights of Avolire had their weapons drawn and made ready to protect their Commander and the High Priest. Those Lizardmen who were armed also drew their blades while those without swords ran into their mud huts and hid. Nictis was the first to move forward and within seconds he and Methladon were locked in a fierce combat. Behind them in the cage the dwarf watched and Mal cried tears for her doomed friend, certain that his life was about to end.

"Meth, don't give in, die fighting," she bellowed. "Don't give the swamp shits the satisfaction of a sacrifice."

Her cries were lost between the cheering of the Knights, the hissing of the Lizardmen, and the crash of metal upon metal. Methladon Heyn fought hard and long for his life.

Without warning Methladon was pulled from his feet and he landed face down in the mud. Having lost his grip on his sword it was kicked away by the towering shape of Captain Nictis. The youth looked towards his legs and through the pain that surged through his body he became aware of the reason for his collapse. A barbed whip had entwined itself around his ankles. He let his eyes follow the tort cable towards its end, held by one of the Lizardmen that flanked the High Priest. Nictis moved closer and stood over him with his sword pointed downwards. For the first time on the journey from Maplehill, the Captain removed his helmet and Methladon's eyes gazed upon the pale and sunken features of a white haired old man.

"I want this to be the last voice that you hear before you die boy," barked the Captain as he raised his sword into the air and made ready to strike.

"Enough!" shouted Commander Rhaizen and the Captain lowered his sword.

"Meth!" screamed Mal and in the midst of her fear she wet herself.

"Good. Very good!" hissed the High Priest as he sniffed the air. "The woman's fear is perfect. I can smell it in her piss. She will do much better and be well appreciated by the Rift."

"What! No you can't," shouted Methladon from down in the mud.

"A sacrifice to the Rift demands fear," began the frog creature as it grabbed the young man's face with one of its scale covered hands. "The Mighty Rift will only open when the fear of an innocent is ripe. The woman stinks of it but you showed nothing but foolish courage. That lack of terror has spared your life, at least for now."

"Go to whatever fucking hell you believe in," shouted Methladon as he tried to wriggle free from the creatures grasp.

Two of the larger Lizardmen grabbed the youth and lifted him back on to his feet. Then they forced him down to his knees and held him in place such that he could watch events unfold. Sslashnash and another of the many Lizardmen opened the cage and began to drag Mal Castor from within its stinking confines. Without warning the Grovrouk pounced on Sslashnash and tried to protect the screaming woman from further harm but his actions were futile and he was beaten unconscious within seconds. Once the naked dwarf had slumped to the floor there was no one left to save Mal from the reptiles' evil machinations.

After being thrown from the cage, Mal was dragged kicking and screaming towards the sacrificial alter. Methladon could only watch with despair at the imminent demise of his last friend. Any further attempt to free himself would have ended his own life and he wasn't yet ready to die. He vowed in that moment to live long enough to avenge all those that had died at the hands of the Knights of Avolire. Forced to look on he watched the pregnant woman as she was held down upon the hard stone where her final struggle took place. The Lizardmen tied her limbs to the ancient alter and soon the screams and struggles of the young woman began to fall away. Methladon realised that Mal Castor had given up her fight to survive. She would at last realise her wish to be taken to her gods.

The High and Mighty Ssonsh took his place behind the slaughter stone and looked down at the helpless woman before him. Methladon heard the incantation leave the priest's mouth although he didn't recognise or understand any of the words spoken. For a brief second he was reminded of the strange language that Grovrouk spoke but this one was somehow different. It was a combination of hissing noises, each uttered at a different pitch. They would be the last words his friend would ever hear.

The fog that once had previously engulfed the settlement began to shrink back across the swampland. It allowed Methladon to see into the marsh beyond and to glimpse the darkening sky. The air began to cool and water vapour showed on his breath as he exhaled. Above the hissing of the incantation, he began to hear the faint sounds of crackling, not the kind generated by the burning of timber, but a different one, the likes of which he had never heard before. As he continued to watch from the mud, the young blacksmith saw the high priest remove a stone dagger from on top of the sacrificial alter. It was then raised high up into the air and without pause it stuck down into the heart of the pregnant woman. Mal and her unborn infant were released from the Realm.

"No!" shouted Methladon into the black of the night.

The scream of woe was silenced in an instant as an explosion of pale light formed in the air. It cracked, snapped, and then opened outwards to create a large ring of blue flame. All around him the remnants of the fog sank back into the marsh. The sky was covered in gathering storm clouds, head heavy and ebony black. The burning circle of blue flame continued to grow outward and only stopped when it connected with the marshy ground. From the dark clouds Aquaris pissed his waters across the marsh in the form of a heavy drizzle. Amid the falling water the High Priest croaked again.

"The Rift has been opened. Behold the way forward."

"For Avolire!" shouted the knights as one.

"For Avolire!" hissed the Lizardmen as they joined in with the salute and the gentle rain turned into a downpour.

Knelt on the ground, held firm by two knights, Methladon felt compelled to look at the strange phenomena that rippled in the air. Despite burning brightly it gave off no heat. It was then that Nictis moved forward, grabbed Methladon's hair, and yanked it with sufficient force to cause the youth to scream out in pain.

"What about this little cunt," yelled the Captain? "What shall we do with him?"

"He comes with us," replied Rhaizen laughing. "He will be of use to us in the mines. Toss him back into the cage."

"My pleasure," replied the Captain after which he pulled young Methladon across the ground by his locks and dragged him through the now deep mud of the marsh.

Any thoughts the young man had were pushed to the back of his mind by the searing pain that shot through his head. Each time he tried to free his hair Nictis gripped harder and no amount of struggling brought release from the sadist's grip. Within moments the cage door was open and Methladon Heyn found himself flying into the back of it. He landed in a heap upon the naked body of the unconscious dwarf.

"You bastards!" shouted Methladon as he regained his feet and attempted to rush the cage door. "You fucking murdering bastards."

The door slammed shut and the youth fell backwards. Then, after his next attempt to stand, Methladon looked out towards the sacrificial alter and the lifeless corpse of Mal Castor. Tears flowed for his departed friend and her unborn child that never had the opportunity to see the light of Solaris. Whatever happened to him now seemed of little consequence. All hope was lost for he no longer had anyone left in the world to love or protect. He slumped to the floor, brought his knees up to his chest, wrapped his arms around them, and sobbed as if there was no tomorrow.

"Now we enter the Rift," bellowed the Commander.

Despite his distress Methladon heard the caravan begin to move forward. Before he could react further to the movement of the cage he felt the shock of a sudden blinding flash that consumed his essence and sent a surge of pain throughout his body. It seemed as if his guts were being spun on a spindle into a fine thread before being reconstituted into the mush which lay beneath the marsh. Methladon Heyn drifted into nothingness.

9.

The bright light of Solaris fell upon soft lids and caused the youth to open his eyes. Globes then scanned unfamiliar surroundings. Several feet above his head he noted a ceiling of painted planks, of a wood and of a type that he had never seen before. Llyat Emgar sat upright and he felt both shocked and disorientated. He lay in the middle of a large bed upon a straw filled mattress, covered in sheets of material that felt soft against his skin. The bed head lay adjacent to a grey stone wall and its foot pointed towards the centre of the room. A single door provided the only exit out of the chamber and into places unknown. A lone three legged stool stood near to the bed, lit by a beam of light from Solaris that poured in through a solitary window. Llyat looked around for other features that would give clues as to his location and then his gaze fell upon one of the great stone walls. There he noted what appeared to be a golden rope and a huge woven tapestry that depicted some great war in a long forgotten time.

Once he had managed to orientate himself Llyat realised that he no longer wore the filthy clothes that he had worn every day of his working life. He found himself dressed in a white material similar to that of the bed sheets. Embarrassed by his semi-nakedness he jumped out of the bed and onto the cold stone floor where some clothes had been left. On inspection they appeared to be a little too big but he decided that he had no option but to make do with them. The top that he pulled on fell down over his knees but yet where his arms passed through the sleeves it seemed to fit quite well. Next he looked around for trousers but found none. Whoever had thought to leave him this strange and oversized garment had forgotten to provide him with something to cover his lower half. A wisp of a breeze sneaked in through the open window and he felt vulnerable as the cool air played upon his privates.

While examining the clothes further he noticed something quite remarkable. There was an absence of the smells that used to torment his nose, sweat, pig shit, and skyfawn carcase that always followed him around. He looked at his fingers, then his skin, and then he touched his face and hair. To his amazement Llyat realised that for the first time in his life he was clean. Not a single speck of dirt was to be found upon him, nor any lice between his legs or under his arms. And so it was that he then started to piece together what had happened to him. Although there were many blanks in his memory he recalled being held aloft by a knight in black armour who had then cried, *'I want this to be the last voice you hear before you die boy.'* Those words he would never forget. The knight had then cursed him and with great force had thrown him into the flowing waters of the Tiaryer. It was then that Llyat's memory failed him. He couldn't remember anything else save for a brief moment when he had regained consciousness in the river and had tried to find something that would support his weight. After that it was all black.

Llyat's thoughts were interrupted as the door to the room opened. He jumped backwards, ready to defend himself against whatever or whoever came through its opening. A bearded man dressed in fine clothes entered at pace. Llyat grabbed the three legged stool from besides the bed and held it forward to fend off the approach of the old man who just stopped in the centre of the room and laughed.

"Ah, so you're awake at last?" he chuckled. "It's about bloody time."

Llyat looked back with disbelief and concern. He tried to work out who this man with a white beard could be. There was something about him, something in his demeanour, which gave out messages that spoke friend not foe. Llyat sensed that he had no option but to trust the stranger and he prayed that there was no evil afoot.

"Where am I?" he demanded, fixed to the spot yet primed to fight or run. "Who are you? Where are my clothes? What the fuck is going on?"

"Ah, with that sort of colourful language you will feel right at home here young man," reassured the stranger as he stepped forward to offer a hand of friendship. "I can understand your concern, waking up in such strange surroundings; so allow me to introduce myself. I am Lord Abrahamus Marus, Grand Physician to our Sovereign Lord Phauless Gylewu IV. These are my private chambers within the Royal Citadel. You are in one of my rooms, deep within the heart of the City of Parandor."

Llyat's mouth dropped open. He was astounded and could not believe what the old man had said. If he was in the Capital it would be truly amazing.

"It looks like you've been through some tough times lad," began the physician.

"Llyat," the youth muttered while lowering the stool to the floor. "And where are my clothes?"

"Llyat?" quizzed the old man. "I'm guessing that's your name."

"Yeah! Llyat Emgar."

"Well Llyat Emgar, I am pleased we have managed to establish who you are and where you are at this moment in time. As for your clothes, I do not know of their whereabouts. Three handmaidens that I borrowed from Lady Calendrial Lorst stripped you, then scrubbed you clean before tending to your wounds. I would start by asking them. As to 'what the fuck is going on', well, I was hoping that you could shed some light on that matter. It's not every day that the City Watch find someone floating in the river who is still alive."

Once again thoughts ran through Llyat's mind as he tried to make sense of all that had happened during and after the attack on Maplehill. Everything from the time that he had hit the water still remained a blur and eluded his powers of recall. Through this torment he attempted to work out why he could still make no sense of it all. Then he imagined being stripped naked by three handmaidens which brought a smile to his face and a rush of blood to his cock.

"The only part of the story that we understand..." continued the old man "....is that young Irabo Basequin and Tonousa Amberstone, daughter of Lord Amberstone, recently brought you to the Citadel. You were waterlogged and they carried you between them like rag doll from a bath."

"Why didn't they just leave me in the river and let me drown?"

"Well it's like this you see Llyat," mumbled the old man as he manoeuvred himself forward and sat on the end of the bed. "Young Basequin has always been a bit of a soft touch, always prepared to help a fellow soul in need. He's one of those… err… what you call them… err… 'Holy Happy Helpers'. Unlike the rest of us he is always willing to support the lowborn in their time of need. I guess it was fate that had Aquaris bring you all the way to the Capital and to drop you in Irabo's lap. Either that or just plain fortune."

Llyat wasn't sure if it had all been down to luck. He sensed that someone was playing a cruel joke and that he would wake up again amid the maple scented woods that surrounded his home. It had to be just another dream and he would let it play out to its end.

"After he rescued you," continued the old man. "Basequin brought you here. I owe him a debt you see for something that happened long ago. I offered to take you in and look after you until you recovered your strength and that allowed me to settle my account with him. So are you going to tell me how you ended up in the river or am I going to grow even older while waiting for the truth to emerge?"

Llyat looked at the old man and then around the room. He wondered what to say but in the end all he could think of was to tell the old man the few facts that he knew to be true.

During the recounting of his tale Llyat sat on the three legged stool and faced the physician who now reclined on the bed, listened intently. Llyat described the attack on Maplehill by the knights in the black armour and their leader, the man with the skull adorned helmet. He told of how his parents had met their end and how he had witnessed the slaughter of several close friends during the destruction of his village. Llyat then described how the blacksmith and one of his son's, his best friend Methladon, had been cut down. He told, with a little licence and embellishment, of his heroic fight with one particular knight and how he had ended up in the river. He recounted the beast's last words to him, *'I want this to be the last voice you hear before you die boy'*. The one thing that Llyat omitted to tell the old man was that the knights had been looking for him and had referred to him as 'The Marked'.

"An interesting tale" said Abrahamus the Physician after a few seconds stroking of his beard. "Do you have any idea what these strange knights wanted or where they came from?"

"I have no idea," lied Llyat, thinking it best not to divulge too much. "There was one word that they said that seemed important. I think it was a name of a place?"

"What was that word?"

"I can't remember, but I would know it again if I heard it."

Llyat hung his head low as tears formed in his eyes. Visions returned, those of knights butchering his father while he and his mother looked on.

Before Abrahamus could question Llyat further a loud tapping sound attracted their attention. Llyat jumped up from the milking stool and turned to face the door which then opened wide. In walked a young girl of a similar age to Llyat, if not a little older, with her long blonde hair tied in a plat and slung over her left shoulder. Her dress of blue and white had seen better days but in it she still looked a beauty. Its quality was not however as impressive as the old man's clothes and reminded him of the style that that his mother would wear. Whoever she was, to Llyat's eyes she was a stunner. His cock thought so too.

"Ah, Heliana, please come in," ordered the physician as he beckoned the young woman forward. He pointed to Llyat and continued. "Allow me to introduce our guest. Heliana meet Llyat, err…. what was your last name again, no don't tell me… Llyat, Llyat Emgar. Well young Llyat this is my handmaiden, Heliana Pulchra."

"Pleased to meet you," giggled the young woman and she held out her hand in friendship.

"Likewise," he replied.

Llyat shook the beauty's hand before moving both of his own back across the front of his strange tunic. He pushed back against his erection which, with its mind of its own, attempted to turn the garment into something that resembled a field tent.

"What may I do for you my girl?" interrupted Abrahamus.

Llyat flushed with embarrassment and sought to control his unruly and substantial manhood.

"I'm so sorry for the interruption my Lord," began Heliana, turning to face her master and away from her new focus of interest. "Your presence is required by Xix Blackfayer. Sir Jasper Redglade of the Royal Guard is waiting outside to escort you to the scene."

"The scene?" questioned Abrahamus as he stood up from the bed. "You make it sound like there has been another murder."

"I don't know any more my Lord," she replied. "Sir Redglade didn't say anything except that your expertise was required and that no one else would do. He is ordered to take you to Lord Blackfayer by force if necessary."

"Oh really!" said Abrahamus before he turned to Llyat and smiled. "We never seem to get a minute's peace in this place. You'll learn about that soon enough. Fate dictates that we will have to continue our talk later when you can then finish your fascinating story. Just try and remember the name of the place that those knight's spoke of."

Llyat did not know if the old man was being sarcastic or in fact serious about talking further. He so hoped that he was dreaming, to be left alone in his fantasies, in the arms of the girl in the blue dress.

"Heliana, would you be kind and fetch young Llyat here some fresh clothes. Get him out of that ridiculous nightshirt of mine and take him to the Grand Hall. Then get him something to eat."

"Of course sir," replied the young woman as she curtsied to her master.

With that both Llyat and Heliana watched as the physician walked off with a spring in his step. He showed no signs of disease, the limp of age, nor any lack of fitness. To Llyat it was further evidence that he had to be dreaming.

As the door closed behind the Grand Physician, the room fell silent save for some birds that chirped out love songs beyond the open window. After a few moments of awkwardness Heliana spoke and a strange sensation ensnared Llyat. The feeling was unlike any he had ever experienced before. It was as if he had eaten some bizarre creature that wriggled around his belly as it tried to eat its way out.

"Okay Emgar," she began. "Let's see if we can get you something more suitable to wear."

"Llyat," he whispered.

"Sorry. I didn't catch that?"

"Llyat," he replied "My name is Llyat."

"Well Llyat, we will need to find you something more suitable if you are going to be dinning in the Grand Hall in the company of Lords and Ladies."

With that the girl turned to the door and left. As she departed Llyat watched her bottom sway through her dress and thought to himself; 'Please let me dream for ever.'

It didn't take long for Heliana to return. She carried a set of clothes which she then placed with care upon the bed. The white and brown gambeson with a golden yellow trim was of particular interest to Llyat and he stood for some time and admired it. Then he picked up a pair of black leather breeches and brown boots which he also caressed. While admiring the clothes Llyat became aware that Heliana was watching him with her arms folded.

"Come on then big boy," he heard her say. "We haven't got all day and I have already seen you're cock when you first arrived."

Llyat's face turned red and his manhood wilted somewhat. He tried to suppress his embarrassment at the thought that the girl had already seen him naked and wanted to do so again."

"Well if you're so shy I don't mind turning around," she said.

"Please," pleaded Llyat.

Llyat watched as Heliana turned to face the wooden door. As quick as a flash he removed the nightshirt and pulled on the breeches. He struggled for some seconds to pull them up over his engorged manhood. Then in a rush he put on the gambeson and laced it up as best he could. After that he turned his attention to the leather boots and in no time at all he looked presentable.

"You can turn around now," he said, no longer so embarrassed.

Heliana span on her toes and faced Llyat. A smile formed on her lips. She moved forward and adjusted the gambeson around his neck line and then stepped back to admire the torso adorned in fine new clothes.

"Well, it all looks perfect. You could now pass for one of the Court."

"Thanks," replied Llyat, not knowing how else to respond.

It was as if everything that he had become in his short life had been rubbed clean and rewritten in an instant. He no longer felt like a farm boy and somehow sensed that he was in a place that he belonged. Then from out of nowhere he felt he could accomplish anything life threw at him.

Heliana brought Llyat out of his daydream.

"Having been out of this world for a several days you must be famished."

"Yes I am," replied Llyat as his stomach rumbled.

"Well, as my master instructed, I am to take you to the Great Hall and get something inside you. So if you would like that, please follow me now."

With that said Heliana turned to the door and beckoned Llyat to follow. Within seconds she was through it and into the next room. Llyat followed like a young pup behind a bitch with milk.

The new room was of similar design to that of the bed chamber with solid walls and a cold bare floor. The main difference was that there were two other doors in the opposite wall and instead of a bed there was a large wooden desk filled with many strange objects that were all new to Llyat. Against one of the walls, and next to the only window, was a large bookshelf upon which sat more unusual objects and leather bound tomes of different shades; each one just as worn as the next. The musty smell of the room lingered in his nostrils despite the fresh air that came in through the open window.

"What is all this stuff?" asked Llyat as he moved through the room, unable to control his eyes.

"Don't ask me to explain what they are," replied Heliana. "As much as I like and respect Lord Marus, I leave him to his work and I don't ask questions. I am sure if you get the chance to talk to him again he would be pleased to explain all to you, being male and all that."

Llyat followed the maiden out of the door to their right and found himself in a long stone walled corridor with many similar doors to the one he had passed through. There were no windows to allow the ingress of Solaris but instead at regular intervals there were metal bowls that contained burning oil. These provided the lengthy conduit with an eerie glow and illuminated the various tapestries that sat between them. Llyat wondered which poor sod had the job of replenishing the oil. He wanted to ask Heliana but there were so many other questions that flooded through his thoughts that he decided that it was one that he could leave until later.

He began once again to consider the possibility that this was all a dream. Perhaps he had died when he had been thrown into the river. It was possible that he could be amongst the gods and this was what it was like in the afterlife. Then he became aware of other people moving through the corridor. Some were dressed in fine clothes, similar to that of the Grand Physician, whereas others looked like servants busy running errands. The male help wore red and black whereas the women were in blue and white dresses similar to that worn by Heliana. All the faces that he passed looked at him through uncertain and questioning eyes but Llyat somehow hoped he was assumed to be another young Lord who had just arrived at Court. Beginning a new fantasy he imagined he had come from some distant town to pay homage to the Sovereign Ruler and to marry some beautiful and wealthy highborn girl. Llyat felt important for the first time in his life. He wished that old man Chirth could see him but then with a gut-tearing sadness he remembered that Hadra was dead, just like his parents and everyone else from Maplehill.

"This is the Royal Corridor of the Blessed," began Heliana as she broke into Llyat's daydream. "Each of these doors opens into chambers that have been designated to one or other of the Royal Household."

"And what about you?" asked Llyat, "Where do you sleep?"

"The servants have their own rooms in the Underkeep. There are many of us sharing them so we work in rotation. Some of us work the day hours and some at night and our bed places are always occupied. Yet this life of servitude is the only one we have ever known and so we are happy with the arrangement. You must understand and realise that this is the only life we will ever be allowed to know. At least the beds are always warm, even in the depths of the coldest of winters."

Soon the pair reached the end of the corridor and came before a large flight of stairs that passed down to a small landing before descending once again. On the break in the stairs and set into the wall, Llyat gazed upon a large stained glass window, coloured vermillion, golden yellow, and river blue. The pattern of glass pieces depicted the image of an ancient knight while slaying what appeared to be a strange shadow like creature. Llyat became lost in the moment as he stared at the beautiful yet haunting image, lit from the outside by the light of Solaris.

"Awesome!" he gasped as he stopped and gawped at the stunning sight.

"It's magnificent, isn't it?" said Heliana, as she stood by his side. "I could look at it for hours. The detail is so amazing. Whenever I feel sad, I just stand here and gaze at this beautiful yet scary image and it reminds me that we do live in safe times, far removed from those evil days of darkness."

"Who is the one in the glass?" asked Llyat.

"You don't know? By the gods, your brain is as dense as your cock is long young Llyat. It shows the slaying of the mighty Urthanock, the Lord of Fear, at the hands of Sir Raulyn the Grand and his mighty battle axe, Fortune's Edge."

"Really! I always thought that Urthanock was killed by a child with a slingshot and pebble. At least that is what Denius Castor and the songs of the travelling bards always said."

"Slingshot and a pebble!" said Heliana laughing. "I am guessing you're referring to the bard's ditty, 'Rejoice at the Death of Urthanock', set to the music of a lyre. No Llyat, as with all stories that the bards concoct, there is but a small element of the truth in them. They are embellished to such an extent that they become new stories and what actually happened is lost."

"I had no idea," replied Llyat, his thoughts clouded and confused. "All these years I was lead to believe something different, that even an insignificant youth could accomplish anything. Now I find that it was all an untruth. I feel betrayed and lost."

The cogs inside Llyat's head clunked against each other. It was as if Fatumai herself teased him, the goddess said to dictate the fate of man. She had plucked him from the waters and given him in a new life, one where he would have to adapt and survive on his instincts or else pay with his life.

Heliana didn't say anything in reply but began to move down the stairs at the foot of the window. Llyat stood motionless while a solitary tear ran down his cheek. Then as he pulled himself together, he wiped his face clean with the sleeve of his new clothes and followed the girl down the stairs. After descending to the landing, then down the second set of stone steps, Llyat found himself on a similar corridor to the long one he had just left. He didn't have chance to take great note of his new surroundings before Heliana passed through one of the wooden doors on her left and into yet another small passage beyond. A faint light came through a small window where Solaris fought to make its presence felt.

After reaching the end of this short corridor, Heliana stepped through yet another door. Llyat followed and then found himself in a large space which reminded him of the Red Mare tavern yet much larger and grander. There were three long tables and benches that stood upon the stone floor and spanned the entire length of the hall. Raised above the floor at the far end was a small wooden platform where yet another table had been placed. The chairs placed behind it faced outwards towards the long tables below. The seats were of simple design and made from wood, apart from the one in the middle. This one was much more impressive, forged of metal with padding of red velvet. It was a chair fit for Royalty. Against one of the walls and almost spanning its height, Llyat noticed a huge ornate hearth, the opening of which was surrounded by the mouth of a huge dragon carved into the stone. A heap of burnt wood and grey ash lay in the void, left over from the fire that had occupied it the previous night. At regular intervals in the room's side walls were doors that led off to places unknown.

"Well young stud," said Heliana as she walked forward towards the three long tables. "Here we are. Please make yourself comfortable while I go and find you something to eat. Solaris is almost high so the Lords and Ladies of the Court will arrive soon for their midday meal. Did you noticed that you were already getting quite a lot of attention as we made our way here? They must have heard tell of the size of your cock!"

With that said, Heliana winked, turned, and walked away. She left the hall through the furthest door on the opposite side of the room. Once gone from view Llyat began to find the room creepy and haunting. His eyes moved down its centre between the two of the long tables and towards the metal chair. Looking up he scanned the great tapestry above the platform as it hung from the wooden beams that supported the roof. The wondrous woven fabric moved gently as a stiff breeze entered the hall through gaps in the rafters. This majestic tapestry depicted a golden cross that divided the background into four equal parts of copper-red, bronze, silver and grey. Suddenly Llyat worked out its relevance. He was looking at the Royal Coat of Arms, and the mighty chair before him belonged to the Sovereign Ruler, Phauless Gylewu. Now he knew that he was not as dense as he had so often been told. If only Heliana was there to marvel at his insight.

Llyat's appreciation of the coat of arms was soon interrupted as a door opened and closed behind him. He turned with the expectation of seeing Heliana but instead he gazed into the eyes of a several new faces, members of the Court of Parandor who had turned up to eat. Llyat's attention was drawn to one in particular, a most odd buffoon who had dressed in strange clothes.

"Well good morrow to you young sir,"

So began the Fool as he moved forward and pranced around Llyat in strange rhythmic movements that bewildered the young farmhand. As he danced, bells on the ends of his clothes jingled and irritated Llyat's eardrums. He looked the youth up and down and then opened his mouth again.

"And what prey be your title? Be you a young Lord or a bum boy from Valameer? Speak thee at once, for I know not who you are?"

"Err, I'm neither," replied Llyat, unsure as to what to make of the strange fellow or his bizarre way of speaking. "I'm just a farm boy."

"A farmer's boy! He be a farmer's boy. A boy of the farm. And does thou have a name pig chaser?"

"Llyat. Llyat Emgar."

"Oooo! Llyat Emgar, boy of the farm," continued the Fool as he stopped his merry jig and placed his left arm on Llyat's shoulders to support his weight. "Sir Llyat the Swineherd perhaps?"

"No, just Llyat,"

"Okay, just Llyat it will be. I be known as Lolly the Lune, but my friends just call me Lolly."

The Fool removed his arm from Llyat's shoulder and performed an exaggerated bow.

"I hate to think what your enemies call you," replied Llyat as he smiled.

"I answer to most names, clown, idiot, tosspot, and the like. For I am the one and only Fool in this Court of our Sovereign Lord, Phauless Gylewu. It is my purpose to entertain and bring merriment to all. But you young sir, your face tells of a sad and shit filled existence. So do speak to me, what be your story?"

With that the Fool moved Llyat towards one of the benches where he forced him to sit down. As the farm boy wondered what would happen next Lolly climbed up onto the adjacent long table and sat upon it. He crossed his legs, faced Llyat head on, and with his chin rested upon both of his hands he stared with an unnerving intensity.

"Look Lolly," said Llyat. "I don't mean to be rude, but could I politely ask you to fuck off. I have had a shit of a morning, woke up in a strange bed to the memory of my parents murder, and then to cap it all my cock tried to force itself on a servant girl who belongs to someone important."

All was suddenly silent as Llyat stared at the gurning Fool. Lolly tried his best to contort his face one way and then another until at last he settled for an expression like a frown but with his bottom lip stuck out in mockery of the situation. The last thing that Llyat wanted was an idiot making fun of him. He felt an urge to punch the face before him, release his frustrations and beat the Fool into a pulp. Llyat so wanted to let out all the anger that had built up since the destruction of his village by the knights who wore black. With heavy tears in his eyes he began to sob. The Fool then jumped off the table, put his arm around Llyat, and attempted to comfort the distraught youth.

"I am sorry, oh true and just Llyat," he began. "I meant no disrespect."

"That's fine then Lolly," replied Llyat between snivels as he stemmed the flow of tears with the sleeve of his gambeson. "My emotions are not good today. It's been a very strange morning.

"Then allow me to cheer you up with a song of my own creation," cried out Lolly.

With one great leap the Fool jumped upright onto the table which managed to bring a half-smile to Llyat's face. Then he turned to address the few members of the highborn present.

"My Lord and Ladies of the Court, may I present for your pleasure a little tale I like to call 'Our Drunken Friend of the Keep.' He did not wait for a response and just launched himself into song. His hands clapped out a rhythm as he pranced on top of the table.

Our friend sat down and drank some ale,
Drank some ale, drank some ale.
Our friend sat down and he drank some ale.
Along with you and me.
He drank a yard of Blessed Beast,

Blessed Beast, Blessed Beast.
He drank a yard of Blessed Beast,
And then had two or three.
Drank some ale, Drank some ale.
Blessed Beast, Blessed Beast.
And so we joined his drinking song.
Tra la la la la.

He drank along with Lolly the Fool.
Lolly the Fool, Lolly the Fool.
He drank along with Lolly the Fool.
A friend to Llyat and me.
Our new friend to cheer you up.
Cheer you up, cheer you up.
Your new friend to cheer you up.
A friend for all to see.
Drink some ale, drink some ale.
Blessed Beast. Blessed Beast.
Lolly the Fool, Lolly the Fool.
Cheer you up, Cheer you up.
And so we joined his drinking song.
Tra la la la la.

And on it continued, repeated again several times. At the songs end the fool jumped down from the table, landed with a thud on the floor and then fell backwards. Llyat could not help but laugh at the idiotic man and at the atrocious song that the he had just sung.

"You made that up on the spot didn't you?" giggled Llyat as he stood up from the bench in order to help Lolly from the floor.

"No! Oh, well, maybe I did, but it served its purpose young master Llyat. See, you're happy again."

It wasn't long before Heliana returned and interrupted the merry discourse between the two new friends. The Fool soon made his excuses and left. Llyat described the song that Lolly had just performed and Heliana sneered for she had heard a similar version on numerous other occasions. She presented Llyat with a plate of food the likes of which he had never seen but which he wolfed down in great gulps.

"So what do you think of city food Llyat?" she asked as Llyat used his tongue to lick the last morsels from off his plate.

"It was amazing. I never knew food could taste that way. It was awesome. What was it?"

"Well, the paler meat was swan and the wine red meat was venison. The sauce, if we are to believe what the cook said, was a mixture of sunflower oil and blackberries plus some cabbage that had been soaked in salt and vinegar."

"Wow, that was delicious," continued Llyat. "My mouth is still on fire from all those strange flavours."

"My master gave instructions that you were to be looked after during your stay here in the Citadel so I can offer you the best that we have. The food you have just eaten was fit for enough for Lord Gylewu himself. Now young Llyat, if you were able to do anything you desire right now, what would it be?"

Llyat thought for a moment and was reminded of the last sunset he had witnessed with his father, how the reds and yellows had mixed as they had swirled across the evening sky behind the cover of the maples. He knew then how to answer.

"I want to see Solaris," he began. "I want to climb to the highest tower you have so that I can see all the lands between the Grey Mountains in the north and the ocean to the west. I want to gaze upon the vastness of the Realm and appreciate its full glory."

"You don't ask for much do you Llyat Emgar," laughed Heliana. "Sure, I can take you to the highest tower and show you the wonders of the Realm, but you will owe me a favour if I do this for you."

"Then I thank you very much kind maiden," said Llyat as a smile spread across his face.

"You must close your eyes and take my hand," she whispered into his ear.

The trust that Llyat felt grew ever stronger. He stood still, held out his right hand and gripped Heliana's left. Squeezing it gently in recognition for all that she had done for him the young woman sensed the gratitude seep out through his rough skinned digits. In all of Llyat's brief life, no one except his family and his friend Methladon had ever treated him with such kindness. Although he felt a little embarrassed having been cared for, naked and unconscious, by this girl and others, the day was turning out to be the best so far. Llyat somehow knew that Heliana would never seek to harm him and that he could indeed trust her with his life. With his eyes closed he was led forward at a run and in an unknown direction. Heliana let her game play out and continued to pull Llyat through the dark. He listened to the shouts of people as the couple weaved in and out and often changed direction. Yet still he kept his eyes shut tight. Then without warning Heliana stopped and spoke. Llyat wanted to open his eyes but he knew he had to wait for her permission.

"Ahead are a series of steps," he heard her say. "Put your left hand out and touch the wall. There you go. They are quite steep and they spiral upwards. Be careful with your footing Llyat. I don't want to explain any new injuries to my master."

"Understood," replied Llyat as he stuck out his left hand to touch the curved wall at his side.

With his eyes still closed Llyat edged forward. He felt his foot collide with the first step and then he began to climb. He could hear his own heart beating amid the excitement of the moment. The only other sound came from Heliana, the softness of her breathing brought on by light exertion as she moved ahead. After a few minutes of steady climbing Llyat felt the coolness of a light breeze blow across his face. The steps levelled out on to a flat surface and Llyat realised that he was outside and exposed to the elements.

"Llyat, you are now standing on the top of highest tower of the Royal Citadel. I have placed you facing west towards the ocean. I want you to take several steps forward and reach up with both hands. Then hold on to the wall in front of you, but don't open your eyes until I tell you to do so."

Llyat obeyed and inched forward. Soon his fingers reached the cold stone. He could sense the different aromas of the city below and it seemed to him that his sense of smell was heightened now that he was blind to the world. Soon he then became aware of the warmth of Solaris on his skin, caressing him with a gentle touch as its warmth broke through clouds.

"Now Llyat," ordered Heliana into his ear. "Open your eyes."

Llyat did as he was told and lifted his lids. What he saw before him was both awesome and inspiring. On the distant horizon he saw the Bay of New Beginnings as it stretched far and wide towards the Great Ocean beyond. The light of Solaris glinted on the water and made it shine like molten silver. Llyat then focused his gaze towards the city below. Between the port and the stone walls that marked the outer perimeter of the Royal Citadel, he looked upon the ram shackled buildings as they formed part of the dense slums of the Capital. He then moved around to the north side of the tower and looked over the battlements. There he saw, far off in the distant horizon, the snow covered peaks of the Grey Mountains and the verdant grasslands that filled the land between them and the Capital. That was when Llyat knew that he was looking in the direction of Maplehill. A mixture of intense emotions engulfed his soul. Even though the awe inspiring vista brought with it great wonderment and exhilaration, he felt a deep sadness for the destruction of his village and all that he had ever known and cared for. His skin sensed a gentle touch as Heliana held his right hand for a second time. He turned his head and smiled at the girl who had been so generous and kind. With a little hesitation he opened his mouth to speak as his free hand pointed out into the distance.

"My family were murdered out there," he began. "Strange and evil horsemen came in the night and destroyed my entire village."

Heliana turned her head and in her eyes Llyat saw that she mirrored his own deep sadness.

"I don't know what to say," she said in the softest of voices.

"There's nothing you can say," replied Llyat. "Unless you know of an incantation that can raise the dead and turn back time."

"Unfortunately I do not. Not even my master would know of such a spell."

A brief silence hung over the top of the Citadel's highest tower as Llyat once again became lost in his thoughts. The image of the knight in the skull adorned helmet dominated them but then Heliana's voice dragged him back.

"I am going to talk to my master about you," she began. "He has long been looking for an apprentice to help him with his work and I can put in a good word for you. Just remember that you are not on your own Llyat Emgar. There are many here with similar tragic stories. One day I am sure that you will find justice for your family but until then you will at least have my support."

Heliana squeezed Llyat's hand and together they stared out to the horizon. In that brief moment in time Llyat felt that he was no longer alone in the world. He now had another who would give his life meaning and purpose.

10

Tonousa Amberstone stood and scanned the corpse that she had been summoned to investigate. The body was beyond recognition for the man's head had been obliterated by a large heavy boulder that still lay at the head of the torso. Its lower surface was covered in blood, bone, and brain matter which had also splattered far and wide across the accumulated dirt and horse dung that covered floor of the Royal Stables of Parandor. Irabo stood by Tonousa's side and fought to hold onto the contents of his stomach. The gruesome sight was so horrific that even Tonousa was forced to fight the waves of nausea that rippled snake like through her gut. Amid the shadows hovered a ghost-pale man who had not been as successful. Traces of breakfast coated his rugged stubble covered chin and added to the smell of his pustulent gum rot. The master of the stables, Edwardis Treveyn, had spewed until there was nothing left in his belly.

"So who was he?" asked Tonousa as she searched for clues.

"Mikus Danbury," replied the Stable Master after which he wiped his chin. "He was my assistant, a simple lad of little sense. Never did anybody any harm. Always followed orders without cursing; yet now this."

"Who found him?"

"Me. I heard a disturbance early this morn, just as Mona was about to disappear, her rump chased by Solaris. My sleeping pit overlooks the stables and it was unusual to hear such excited sounds from the horses at that time of the morning. The snorts and whinnies and woke me from my slumber and when I then got down here, I found young Danbury lying in the dung with that fucking great boulder having crushed his head and all the horses gone."

Tonousa looked around and noted that fact to be true. Not a single animal was to be seen. Before she could ask the obvious question as to who would have dared steal seven horses, Irabo introduced a new line of enquiry.

"How can you be sure that it is Mikus Danbury? The face is way beyond recognition."

"It is without doubt him sir. Look to the scar on the back of his hand," replied Edwardis. "I gave him that wound, by accident of course. I tried to close the stable door one day and Danbury's hand got in the way."

Tonousa bent on one knee while her eyes scanned the corpse. As she examined the boy's left hand she noted the scar as described. There was however something that seemed out of place and her mind sought to make sense of it all.

"When I found the body lying as you see it, I first summoned one of the Royal Guards," continued the Stable Master. "He then alerted the City Watch. I understand you are already investigating the recent murders that have occurred about the Citadel."

"How did you know that?" asked Irabo. "Your stables lie outside the Citadel. Only members of the Court knew that Lord Phauless had instructed the Watch to investigate those murders. Who told you about them? What else do you know?"

"I know nothing else I swear it," continued Treveyn while his tone indicated he spoke the truth. "There has been much gossip amongst the servants.

Lolly the twitter-twat was unable to stop blabbering about your work and all of us servants know of your investigation."

"He talks too much," muttered Irabo. "We will deal with him in due course."

Knelt in the dirt beside the corpse, Tonousa listened to what the Stable Master had to say yet still sensed something wrong about this particular crime. The event was a first, something that she had never encountered in all her days in the Watch. Even during her training she had never encountered such a strange death, a young boy's head crushed by a boulder. The scene did not sit well and she began to wonder if it could also be connected to Death Tubaria.

"Please excuse me," said the Stable Master. "I must inform your father that his prized stallion has gone."

With that said the keeper of horses turned and left the two members of the Watch alone with the body of the young stable boy.

Tonousa raised herself up from the dirt. Both warriors then stared at the bloody mess.

"Tell me Irabo," she began. "What do you see? What do you believe happened?"

"To be blunt, it's a bit obvious. I think that someone crushed the boy's head with a boulder. He no doubt disturbed those who came to steal the horses and they turned on him and killed him before he could summon the Watch or the Royal Guard."

"Do you find any of this odd? Can you not see anything strange?"

Tonousa watched her colleague shrug his shoulders. She had just realised what had been bothering her and sought confirmation of her new theory.

"I don't think so," continued Irabo as he tried to second guess what Tonousa had seen. "To me everything appears to make sense. The boy was killed by the blow to his skull."

"Yes, but look at the size of it," said Tonousa. "That boulder is massive and I doubt that a single person could lift it beyond their knees, let alone high enough and with the force needed to bring down upon the young lad's head. It is most odd. I'll wager this is no ordinary death."

"It does look rather suspicious, doesn't it?" snarled a voice from behind.

Tonousa and Irabo turned to the stable door. Light flooded through the opening but there was no mistaking the silhouette of the figure who stood before it. The gangly snake-like Xix Blackfayer, flanked by two members of the Royal Guard, stood and observed with menace. Tonousa recognised the others at once for Sir Digory Berthellemy and Sir Horace Mandleworth were well known throughout Parandor.

"I am surprised to see that the Amberstone bitch can read the clues," sneered Xix.

Tonousa ignored the insult as the Royal Advisor stepped forward into the stables. She was determined not to rise to his bait.

"What are you doing here Xix?" demanded Tonousa as the Sovereign Advisor looked down at the corpse. "This is out of your jurisdiction and we seldom see you outside of the Citadel."

"Any death that occurs within the walls of Parandor and is believed to be connected in some way to the Citadel is always within my remit. I try not to visit such shit holes but when the Realm is threatened, needs must..."

"I refuse to exchange insults with you Xix," replied Tonousa as her anger began to cloud her judgement. "We are both here to do a job, so let's just get on with it."

"Yes, let's get back to the examination," ordered Irabo. "This is a most terrible crime and it will not be solved by bickering. We must work together. "

"I'm glad to see that at least one of the City Watch has sense," continued Xix. "Even if he does take orders from the Amberstone bitch."

"Lord Blackfayer!" shouted Irabo with a level of authority that surprised Tonousa. "Either you tell us what your purpose for being here is or fuck off and leave us to do our job."

Tonousa was astounded. Never before had she seen Irabo behave in such a manner and yet she agreed with his sentiments. Blackfayer made her skin crawl as if infested with a legion of fattening maggots. The very presence of the man caused her blood to heat and her bladder to leak. Poor Irabo was caught in a long history of enmity between Tonousa and the Ruler's vile serpent. He was out of his depth but as he had bluntly pointed out, the Watch were there to do a job and the presence of the Royal Advisor was in danger of obstructing the investigation. Tonousa would remember to report this interference to her Commander.

"So tell us then esteemed sage, what is your take on this matter?" demanded Tonousa as she turned to face the man she so despised. "What do you think happened here?"

"As much as it unsettles my bile," began the Royal Advisor "I would have to agree with your conclusions. We are looking at something most strange and unnatural. When Sir Mandleworth alerted me to the nature of the young man's death and then described what he had seen in detail, I suspected there was but one thing that could have been responsible. It had be due to some form of magic."

"You've got to be fucking joking!" laughed Irabo.

"Now who's being unprofessional?" sneered Xix. "Yes, magic. There is no man alive who could have lifted that boulder on his own. It looks like whoever stole your father's stallion, and the other horses, knew the ways of magic. I think that the murderer brought the boulder into existence with some sort of spell and with the sole purpose of adding to our confusion."

"Lord Blackfayer, do you see a connection to the cult of the Death Tubaria?" asked Irabo.

"There is no reason to think so. Apart from the obvious fact that the boy was associated with the Royal Household through his work here, there is nothing else to underpin such an assumption. Any signs of the three circle brand would have been crushed underneath the boulder, if indeed such shit had formed on the back of his head."

"So stripping this back to its core," concluded Tonousa. "We have no way of knowing if this young man is connected to any of the previous murders and that..."

Tonousa did not have chance to finish before being interrupted. The voice of Grand Physician, Abrahamus Marus, echoed from out of the doorway.

"No connection! I'll be the judge of that, if you don't mind."

The physician entered into the stables alongside the diminutive Jasper Redglade. "

"I'm so pleased you could find the time to join us," sneered Xix as the old man made his way forward and pushed between Sir Berthellemy and Sir Mandleworth.

As the physician approached the corpse Xix added, "You took your time getting here."

"Look you slime encrusted turd, I am here to help you as a favour to our Sovereign Lord. I did not appreciate you sending short arse Redglade to escort me here by force. I am the Grand Physician of Parandor and not some mare's wazzock that you can order around as you see fit."

Tonousa smiled at the exchange of words. She hoped Blackfayer would now leave and allow them to conclude their examination of the crime scene.

"I am so pleased you could join us Lord Marus," began Irabo. "Your opinion on this case will be much appreciated and if magic was involved then the City Watch would be most pleased to hear your theories and conclusions."

"Once again I am in debt to you master Basequin; now let me see what we have here," replied the physician.

Tonousa looked on as the old man moved forward with ease and knelt down upon the dirt floor. She noticed that he carried a leather satchel which hung around his neck and was held across his chest by a solid leather strap. Within moments examining the body the old man reached into his satchel and removed various dried leaves and roots which he then rubbed together in his hands. He ground them into a powder and sprinkled the mixture onto the body of the stable boy. Old lips muttered several strange words in a long forgotten language which Tonousa assumed to be an incantation. An ethereal glow then surrounded the corpse but as quickly as it had formed it disappeared. The experiment, if it could be called such, lasted mere seconds, but the expression that appeared on the Grand Physician's face indicated that it had been sufficient time for him to have made his diagnosis.

"Well!" demanded Xix before anyone else could speak. "What have you found?"

"If Lord Blackfayer would allow me a moment to gather my thoughts then I will be able to tell you… It would appear that as you suspected, magic was indeed used in this crime. There is a certain aura that appears around a person whenever they come into contact with charms and such. The light that you just witnessed surrounding the boy was confirmation that a spell was used. It is something those who have been trained in the art of spell casting call the Kundalish Aura. Now I must ask you all, has anyone touched the body since it was first discovered?"

Tonousa looked to those present and watched as all shook their heads and confirmed that the body had not been disturbed. She wondered if he had found something that would link the crime to the cult of Death Tubaria.

"I will however need to conduct a full examination of the body. I need it to be taken to my workshop in the Underkeep. Sir Berthellemy and Sir Mandleworth, you both look strong enough; if you wouldn't mind doing this for me."

The two knights that flanked Xix Blackfayer looked to each other before turning to the Royal Advisor for instructions. Xix signalled the two men forward. Tonousa knew of Mandleworth's strength for he had demonstrated his prowess during his time as a member of the Watch, long before his knighthood and promotion to the Royal Guard. She also knew that Sir Berthellemy had equal power from the stories that she had heard of his exploits in battle. The two moved to opposite ends of the stable boy and one took hold of the feet while the other gripped the corpse's hands. The two men lifted the remains of the young boy from the floor but they had only taken two steps towards the door when something most unexpected happened. As Berthellemy lost his grip on the blood soaked hands of the deceased he released the body which then fell to the floor. This caused Mandleworth to lose his balance. Danbury's clothes caught around his armour and pulled the unfortunate Knight on top of the dead lump. Tonousa wanted to laugh but somehow she held back for she did not want to inflame the situation further. With some difficulty Berthellemy then tried to help Mandleworth rise from the floor. Sir Redglade moved over to help but he too slipped in the gore and brought Berthellemy back down with him. The three great Knights clunked around like fresh caught fish on the deck of the Masters Catch. Tonousa began to laugh for the display was far funnier than anything that even Lolly could have orchestrated. As the farce played out she noticed a section of the stable boy's bare belly that protruded from under the cotton tunic that had been ripped away by Sir Mandleworth's armour.

"What's that on his skin?" she shouted.

Her right index finger pointed to the bare flesh and the mark now revealed on boy's torso. In haste the Grand Physician bent down to examine the body a second time. He lifted the cotton shirt to expose the full extent of stable boy's trunk. Sir Redglade vomited with the shock of what he saw while Tonousa noted the looks of horror on the faces of all others present. Signs of deep concern formed on the wizen features of the Grand Physician for carved into the chest and stomach, were a series of deep wounds. Below the ragged cuts were three circles.

"And there Lord Blackfayer is your proof," said the tremulous physician.

"So this too is the work of Death Tubaria; that makes six," said the Sovereign Adviser.

"What about the other markings," threw in Irabo as he pointed to the deep lacerations above the three circles? "The curse mark is obvious, but what about those? What are they and what do they mean?"

The Grand Physician looked back at the body with even greater concern for the Realm.

"Well?" sneered Xix. "What are they?"

"They look like runes. The written form of the forgotten language of the Ancients."

"Do you know what they say?" asked Tonousa.

"At this moment in time I have no idea for I cannot read them just like that," replied the old man as he returned his feet. "….but, I will decipher this message given time. I need to get to my books and potions as soon as possible. I'm sure they will all be needed!"

"We are at your service," announced Tonousa as she bowed in respect.

"Thank you Tonousa Amberstone. Your help will be most appreciated given that the Royal Guard cannot carry the dead."

Great shame showed in the knight's eyes and their flushed faces beneath their helms. She felt a sense of justice that compensated for the way that Blackfayer treated her. Then Tonousa took charge and signalled to Irabo to take hold of Danbury's legs while she in turn took hold of his arms. Between the two they managed to lift the dead boy's body from the ground and began their journey towards the stable door. As she came level with Xix, Tonousa could not help but smile.

"We'll leave you to clean up!" she sneered.

With Irabo, the corpse, and the Grand Physician in tow, Tonousa left the confines of the stables. Xix snarled, turned to his Knights, and bellowed out another order.

"Sort this fucking mess out!"

Within no time at all Tonousa and Irabo had carried the headless body from the stables, around the outer walls of the Citadel, through its East Gate, and on into the courtyard that surrounded the Keep. The warriors walked at double quick pace and the old man followed as best he could, his aging joints creaking and groaning at the forced exertion. As they made their way across the courtyard, several knights, their squires, and numerous servants, eyed the Watch with interest. All stared at the headless corpse that was carried in procession before them.

"I think we need to take him to the rear of the Citadel and in through the dungeons," whispered the Grand Physician.

"I agree," answered Tonousa. "If we take this body in through the main entrance we will attract far too much attention. It's still oozing from the neck and the last thing we need is to leave a crimson trail across the marble floor.

The group changed direction and soon came to small flight of steps that led down to the base of the Citadel. At is far end a solid iron door with a small window in its middle barred their way. Just before they began their descent the Grand Physician pulled a large ring of keys from out of his satchel and searched for the one that would open the lock. Tonousa and Irabo then moved with care down the stairs so as not to drop or damage the corpse. At last made they moved through the door and into the musty corridor beyond. Once the portal had closed the troop made their way deep into the Underkeep and entered the maze of tunnel that branched in every direction. The way was lit by flaming baskets, identical to those that illuminated the windowless corridors of the upper floors of the Keep. Flames flickered in a light draft and cast dancing shadows on the walls. The screams of the incarcerated mixed with those of scuttling rats and echoed off the walls. After several long minutes the Physician led them into a room off the main tunnel, its interior lit by four wooden torches that hung in the middle of each of the walls. All had spontaneously burst into flames as the door had opened.

"Welcome to my laboratory," said the Grand Physician. "Please put the body on the slab."

The marble plinth was the most striking feature of the cold stone clad room. Along each of the walls were fixed shelves of books and strange metal instruments, some of which could have been mistaken for the tools of the torturer. A wooden cupboard stood large in one corner and next to it, supported on a wooden stand with each component wired together, was a full male skeleton. Having placed the corpse upon the slab Tonousa continued to scan the contents of the strange room. She noticed several large drawings that depicted symbols of alchemy and which were fixed to the wall with nails. The site of this strange paraphernalia stirred Tonousa's apprehension and the longer she stayed the greater became her desire to leave. She wondered if her friend was also feeling uncomfortable but then remembered that Irabo was already an acquaintance of the Grand Physician. He had no doubt been here before on numerous occasions and this sudden insight was insufficient to prevent battle hardened Tonousa from submitting to her fears.

"I must thank you both," said the Grand Physician "I wouldn't have got him here if I'd had to depend on Xix's morons."

"No problem!" replied Irabo. "I'm just glad we were of service."

"You're a good lad Irabo. Always willing to help in any way you see fit."

"It's my mission in life, to conduct acts of random kindness wherever the opportunity arises."

"Speaking of good deeds," continued the Physician. "That boy you fished out of the Tiaryer two days ago has woken at last. He opened his eyes this morning just before I was dragged down to the stables by Sir Redglade."

"That is indeed good news," replied the warrior.

"Of course," continued the Physician. "One thing that worries me is the story of how he came to end up in the river. The lad said there were knights in strange black armour that came and destroyed his village. They were laying waste to the lands between the Capital and the Grey Mountains."

"That's all we need" mumbled Tonousa. "When the youth has recovered and can talk sense, I will come and discuss all he has told you. Meanwhile I'll have words with the Commander to see if he will agree to send out riders to scout the wild lands. It will be interesting to see if they find anything."

"That sounds a good plan. Now if you don't mind I have some important work to do, so please excuse me."

It did not take long for Tonousa and Irabo to return to the surface along the narrow tunnels of the Underkeep. Once in the courtyard she made her excuses and left it to Irabo to return to the barracks and report back on the events of the day. Tonousa then made her way across the open space towards a small partition that jutted out from the main perimeter wall. Once there she sat upon the stonework and watched a young boy being taught how to fire a longbow. She then started to consider the evidence that been unearthed during her investigation and tried to join it all together. It was clear that someone from within the Citadel was responsible for the murders and the magic brands found on each of the victims. From her conversations with Lady Fullbane and with Cassius Underscroft it seemed someone was peddling poisons to members of the Royal Court and that at least one of them, and maybe more, must know the identity of the murderer. She tried to think who would have had access to poisons such as Nightshade and soon her thoughts turned to the Grand Physician. It was hard for her to believe that he was the one she sought, despite his predecessor's leadership of Death Tubaria.

The young archer missed the centre of the target and suffered the immediate displeasure of his instructor. Tonousa refocused on the events of the morning. It was clear that the stable boy Mikus Danbury had disturbed whoever was responsible for the recent murders but she struggled to understand why the killer had stolen the horses. She thought perhaps it was just an accident that the boy had been chosen as a sacrifice to Kha. Once again her suspicions pointed to Abrahamus Marus for he had been very quick to confirm the use of magic. And yet the involvement of the Grand Physician seemed far too simple a solution. Surely the murderer would have made himself less conspicuous.

"I thought I'd find you here," said the familiar voice of her father. "I can remember you as a child, sitting in this exact spot, watching all the knights in training while dreaming that someday you too would be a great warrior.

"And I can remember your disparaging remarks," replied Tonousa as her father brushed dust off the small partition and sat beside her. "You never wanted me to become a warrior. You always said that you were going to make a lady out of me, even if it meant sending me out of the Realm."

"Aye that I did. It wasn't until I witnessed your talents in action that I understood your true calling. Do not forget that it was I who signed you up to the Watch and allowed you to follow your passion."

"It must still be hard for you father, watching your only daughter putting herself in peril every day and not knowing if she will make it through to the next morning."

"Indeed it is my girl. It gets harder each day that passes; that plus the knowledge that I shall never see any grandchildren. But after all this time I have got used to it, even though it pains me still. There was no point pushing my desire to see you wedded and gentile for as they say 'put a lady on pig's back and they will still ride to a midden.'"

At that the conversation paused and Tonousa wondered what her father's purpose was in seeking her out this day. She knew that it would not be to rake up the past but there was something about the way he talked that made Tonousa convinced this was not just idle conversation. As she watched the young archer at last hit the centre of the target and receive much praise from his instructor, Tonousa turned to her father.

"I know you didn't come here to talk old times. What are you up to?"

"That's my Tonousa!" laughed old Amberstone and as he rocked on the partition and almost lost his balance. "Direct as always. To be honest, the real reason for my presence is to pass on a little information, something that I think may help your investigation."

"Really!" exclaimed Tonousa, loud enough for the archer to hear. "Go on, I'm listening!"

"As long as I have your word not to repeat what I am about to say. Have I your promise?"

"Of course father. It will be a secret that I will take to the grave."

"Good. It's regarding the death of Jonas Tullage."

"I already know about that. He died at the Grey Keep at the hands of a..."

"Tonousa, please listen, this is important. I know that you know about his involvement when the cult of the Death Tubaria first attempted to resurrect Kha. I also know that you were told several days ago by the Lord Sovereign himself that Tullage was killed by a dwarf of the Dirmark, a prisoner who goes by the name of Grovrouk the Despoiler. What you don't know is that the book that implicated Lord Tullage and which led to a riot by his followers against the..."

"The Lore of the Dead?"

"Yes, that's the one; the Lore of the Dead. I'm glad you can remember the name and..."

"Father, please. The information!" interrupted Tonousa, frustrated by pace that her father's story was unfolding.

"Sorry, yes. That evil book was lost some years ago, presumed stolen from the Royal Archives."

"Stolen?" gasped Tonousa as once again her voice rose. "Why was the City Watch not informed? That may have been vital evidence. It could have led us to any surviving practitioners of the cult. Perhaps we could have prevented all these recent deaths."

"The theft of the Lore of the Dead from the Grand Library was never considered to be of high importance. Tullage was in captivity and so were his followers. We chose to ignore the theft and prayed to the gods that there wouldn't be a repeat of the events that happened eleven years ago. By the crypts of god's spleens, we were so wrong."

"So who was involved in this cover-up father? You need to tell me everything that you know."

"If I speak names then only the gods will ever know what happened to me when I disappear."

"Tell me, NOW!" shouted Tonousa as her father jumped up from his seat with the intention of walking away.

"If you don't give me names I will drag you before Phauless Gylewu myself and see what he has to say about the matter," screamed Tonousa as she grabbed her father's shoulder and turned him around. "Who ordered the cover-up of the theft?

"Quiet...Please, I beg of you!" whispered Lord Amberstone as he managed to free himself from his daughters grip. "There were two of us."

"Father, give me the name of the other," barked Tonousa as her anger grew with each second that he stalled. "Just give me a fucking name."

"Xix... Xix Blackfayer."

"Blackfayer!" gasped Tonousa.

Perhaps she had not heard her father correctly. She lowered her voice in order to deflect the attention of onlookers. "Did that bastard really know about the theft? Tell me that you are joking."

"I wish I was child and I have said too much already. You must understand this my daughter..."

"Don't you 'my daughter me'," snarled Tonousa as she grabbed him by the arm to prevent him leaving the courtyard. "If you are so scared to tell me the truth about that snake Blackfayer, why then did you bring me this information?"

"You don't understand Tonousa. There is more to the story. The missing Lore of the Dead isn't the only source of the incantations. We have strong reason to believe that Lord Tullage, during his incarceration at the Grey Keep, relayed the words he had learned by memory to his cell mate. It was the very same dwarf that later murdered him, Grovrouk the Despoiler."

"So you're saying that there are two copies of the incantations. One that was stolen with the Lore of the Dead and one that is locked in the mind of a prisoner in the Grey Keep?"

"No. The pages that contained the incantation to summon up Kha were removed and burnt by Xix. He didn't wish the cursed lines to fall into the wrong hands and take the Capital back into the depths of despair. Both of us thought it best to forget about the tome, well that was until it was stolen two years ago."

"You may have just redeemed yourself there, father," replied Tonousa. "So you are telling me that whoever is behind this series of murders, has spoken to the dwarf?"

"More than likely yes... or even the dwarf himself could be to blame."

"I thought he is locked up in the dungeons of the Grey Keep?" said Tonousa.

"Indeed he is, or at least I hope so, given what I have been told."

"What have you been told? What are you getting at?"

"Three days ago we sent a carrier bird to Lord Raorick wishing him all the best in his upcoming marriage to Lady Flurdiana of Valameer but there has been no answer from the Grey Keep. All is silent along the Eastern Road to the marshlands. I just hope the dwarf has not escaped. Phauless did send another in secret to the Grey Keep, long before the bird was sent, to question the dwarf and find out what he knows. He hasn't yet sent word of his arrival."

"So father, if I understand what you are trying to tell me; Grovrouk the Despoiler, the only person in possession of the details of the ritual, could have escaped from his cell?"

"Exactly, but I have said too much already."

With that the old man broke away from Tonousa and made his way across the courtyard. As he did so he interrupted the young archer's lesson by walking across his line of fire. Lord Amberstone then continued up the stone stairs that led into the Citadel.

After watching her father scuttle back inside the Keep, Tonousa sat back onto the stone. Her thoughts raced with the information that her father had imparted. She tried to somehow link Blackfayer's intervention with the Lore of the Dead, the passing of knowledge to the dwarf, with what was now happening in the

Capital. She at least agreed with her father's interpretation. If the incantation to raise Kha had indeed been taken out of the Lore and burned, then its future use would be dependent solely on the dwarf. She began to question if her father had told her everything and perhaps the incantations had not been burned by Blackfayer after all. Whatever the truth was she was determined to get to the bottom of it.

11

It had been two long days since Llyat Emgar had been found floating in the river Tiaryer. True to her word the servant girl Heliana had found Llyat employment within the Royal Citadel. She had spent many long minutes persuading the Grand Physician that he needed an assistant. Actually, in the end, it did not require much analysis. Abrahamus Marus had jumped at the chance to have an extra pair of hands for the Grand Physician was showing no signs of slowing down and Heliana was already working to full capacity. Llyat was humbled and most grateful for this opportunity to work for someone of importance. In addition to finding him work, Heliana had procured a place for Llyat to sleep amongst the servant's quarters, down in the Underkeep. There he could retire during rest breaks and as Heliana had already explained, it would be a room he would share with others. He was most grateful for the kindness that both Heliana and the physician had bestowed on him since his arrival in the Capital. With the trauma of all that had happened in Maplehill still ripe in his mind, Llyat had snatched at the opportunity to rebuild his life. One immediate task that he set himself was to seek out the man who had fished him from the river. Despite his new duties he would somehow find the time to locate Irabo Basequin and thank him for saving his life.

On his first day of work Heliana described his responsibilities; helping her with the cleaning, the laundry, and indeed any other household chores that their master required of them. That is all except the nightly bed rituals which Heliana would continue to do alone. She also spoke of the room their master had in the Underkeep and where he spent several hours of each day. There the old man worked hard harvesting herbs, extracting their active juices for medicinal use. Gnarled fingers studied the anatomy of the deceased to find out how they functioned and in some cases their cause of death. The Grand Physician had decided that the future of the healing arts should take a more intellectual approach rather than a reliance on magic and spell casts. Heliana suggest Llyat take on responsibility for any work that was needed in the laboratory as the place made her feel cold and uneasy at the best of times. One day when she had been alone in the strange room she had felt as if some crone like spectral form had manifested itself within the laboratory's walls and walked right through her. It had left its icy presence in the very soul of her body and she never wanted to experience the sensation again.

Heliana informed Llyat that during the evenings when food was served in the Great Hall to the Lords and Ladies of the Court, he would attend his master there while she ensured that his chambers were ready for his return. In particular she would turn down his bed down and ensure that his piss pot was clean and empty. It was normal practice at the evening feast for servants to dedicate themselves to their own Lord or Lady despite the efficiencies that could have been made had the work been better organised. On the sounding of the horn Llyat would need to move forward and present his master with a bowl and water filled ewer for the ritual washing of hands before the feasting could commence. He would then act as a cup-bearer to his master ensuring that his goblet was never, ever, empty of wine. All the servants of the Royal Citadel knew that an empty cup meant an angry master and that even the kindest Lords would punish them if their vessel ran dry. The standard penalty was a day in the stocks, pelted by rotten fruit if lucky, but more likely dung from off the streets. During the explanation of his duties Llyat asked if the serving of the food was also one of his tasks but Heliana pointed out that there were kitchen servants who would bring the feast to the table. It would be Llyat's job however to ensure that the plates and eating implements were ready for each of the many courses as they arrived. Heliana had also managed to find Llyat some serving clothes so not to damage the new gambeson and breeches that the young man had become so fond of. These would also ensure that he was recognised as hired help and not highborn.

During Llyat's first two days of work he was confined to the chambers of the Physician and was able to familiarise himself with his new master's routine. It was on the night of this second day that Heliana took Llyat down to the Great Hall where the evening banquets were held and stayed for a short while instruct him further. At the appropriate time Llyat followed Heliana and his new master down to the refectory. As they made to enter the hall, the senior steward on duty announced that this particular evening's feast was to be dedicated to the purpose of 'Lightening the Darkness'. The dark referred to was the feeling of unease that had surrounded the Court after the recent cluster of suspicious deaths. While waiting to enter Heliana told Llyat that two of her closest friends, both members of the serving staff, Golda Flintwind and her lover Webb, had been amongst the six recently found dead, most probably murdered, and who it seemed had died in bizarre circumstances. When Llyat had questioned her on what she had meant by 'bizarre', she dismissed his question saying it was best not to ask. She said he would find out in due course, but not from her.

Once he had been checked out by the steward and at last permitted to enter, Llyat found that the vast room already occupied by the majority of the highborn who resided in the Court. The privileged idlers immersed themselves in deep conversations and as they bellowed at each other they created a vast cacophony of sound. All waited in anticipation for the arrival of Phauless Gylewu who was always the last to enter. Music from several instruments struck up and danced through the air, created by players stationed near the huge hearth. Lolly the Fool skipped around the drinking revellers and chased a young servant girl with a bell covered stick, thrusting it between her buttocks at every opportunity and shouting out 'dickdangel' every time he succeeded. Llyat had been told that drinking was always allowed before the arrival of the Sovereign Lord, but anyone caught eating before he did would be sentenced to a month in the Citadel's small space located deep within the dungeons, and with only scraps of mould covered bread and mugs of river water on which to survive. It was for this reason that the kitchen servants never brought out food until Phauless Gylewu had placed his ample rump upon his robust chair, the reciting of the banqueting prayer had been delivered, and then at last and as if by force of habit and great gusto, the Sovereign let out air in respect for his bowels.

Abrahamus Marus thrutched in his seat on the raised partition at the far end of the hall. It was one of the six chairs that faced the gathered highborn. The other five seats were filled with senior members of the Court, either side of the velvet padded chair that would soon be occupied by the Sovereign Lord himself. As their master sought to find comfort for his arse, Heliana filled the goblet in front of him from the large pitcher on the table. It contained the sweetest wine that Llyat had ever smelt and in no way could it be compared to the vinegary shite that used to be served up in the Red Mare. Standing behind their master the young girl began to whisper and identify each of the Lord and Ladies of the Council of Parandor that sat at the top table. To the right of the Royal chair and their master Abrahamus sat the Court Judge, Lady Llys Emeny, and the loud and boisterous whiskered Royal Chamberlin, Gilebin Ystafell. One the three chairs to the left of the throne, the one closest to where their Sovereign Lord would sit, remained empty. Heliana told Llyat that it was reserved for Xix Blackfayer. The remaining two seats were taken by Heward Teulu, High Priest of the Court, who according to Heliana had refused the title of 'Lord' in order to follow the strict doctrine of his order. Next to him sat the large muscular form of Sir Rayner Byddin, Head of the Royal Guard and the Armies of Parandor, dressed in his ceremonial bronze armour. An eye patch covered his left eye and his presence was more than menacing.

"So you're the boy that the City Watch fished out of the Tiaryer?" shouted Sir Byddin

The knight looked Llyat up and down and then downed the contents of his goblet. Having then belched he signalled for Arfon, one of the four other cup-bearers, to refill his cup. Heliana whispered again and told Llyat that for some reason Sir Byddin did not have his own servants but with agreement of his peers, shared theirs.

"Yes Sir," replied Llyat, not knowing if he was permitted to make eye contact. "I owe my life to those that you command, the great warriors of the City Watch."

"Ha, ha!" laughed Sir Byddin. "Me! Command the Watch! Now there's something I don't hear often. I'm sorry lad but you have been misinformed. I am in charge of the Royal Army and am the sworn protector of our Sovereign Ruler and the Capital. The Watch is something different. They are more of a rabble and are led by one called Brynn Townsforth. Their primary role is to keep the scum in order and ensure the peace amongst the common folk. On rare occasions Lord Gylewu will require their services here in the Royal Citadel, but only if he is desperate, if you understand my meaning boy."

"Thank you for correcting me sir," replied Llyat. "It was an honour and privilege to receive such knowledge from one so important."

"Ha, ha," laughed Sir Byddin and as wine sprayed from his mouth like a fountain unblocked. "Dogs bollocks, you have a lot to learn boy. You may be naught but a wazzock but there is no need to kiss my arse with such pride!"

Noticing how Llyat was struggling with the conversation, Heliana pulled the youth away from Sir Byddin and began to introduce him to the other cup-bearers who stood behind their Lords. There he met young Arfon, servant to the absent Lord Blackfayer, the rotund and rosy cheeked Mervrig who served the priest, the tall yet scrawny red-haired Wil who served Lord Ystafell, and the short of stature

Tecwyn who served the Lady Emeny. Llyat heard Heliana ask Mervrig and Arfon to look after Llyat while she went to prepare for her master's nocturnal activities.

Within moments of Heliana leaving the Great Hall and despite the riotous cacophony of noise that came from within its candle lit space, Llyat heard the sounding horn play out by the main doors. The blast from the blower, Sir Watcyn Dustfury, signalled the immediate washing of the hands. Mervrig showed Llyat the side chamber where he would find his master's bowl and ewer. The feasting implements that belonged to those who sat upon the royal table were kept separate from those of the lower Lord and Ladies of the Court and this made them easier to find by the busy servers. Llyat filled his allocated ewer with water from the pump in the side room and returned with haste to his new master. There he poured the water from the ewer into the bowl. Abrahamus Marus began the ritual of removing the day's dirt.

After the cleansing, which Llyat found most strange for he never washed his own hands before eating and could not understand the reason for removing the dirt and grime which only added flavour to the food, he fetched a clean cloth for his master. No sooner had Llyat removed the dirty water bowl from the table and poured its contents it into the designated barrel in the corner of the room than a second blast of Sir Dustfury's horn signalled the arrival of the Phauless Gylewu. The highest born of all Lords entered through the back of the hall, flanked by two Knights of the Royal Guard. He moved at speed through the crowd which had stood in respect and on towards his most impressive chair.

In the quietening that followed, Llyat watched as Phauless Gylewu took his seat and signalled for the rest of the gathered to do likewise. As they did so, just one remained standing, Heward Teulu. The priest waited in total silence for a signal from his Sovereign Lord. As quiet fell Phauless turned his head and nodded towards the priest whereupon the holy man opened his palms in the direction of the sky, closed his eyes, and began to speak.

"Under the watchful presence of Solaris. Thank you for the bounty you are about to bestow upon us. Remember those who are your best servants and deliver them to your side when their own lights are extinguished. Look over our Sovereign Lord and guide him in the judgements that he must make this and every day."

"Praise be Solaris!" echoed throughout the hall. "And to the House of Gylewu!"

With that Heward Teulu sat beside Sir Byddin and bowed in acknowledgement to his Sovereign.

"Now let the feast begin," shouted Phauless as he raised his hand and signalled to the servants to bring in food.

The music returned and Llyat watched as the kitchen staff left the hall through one of the side doors and returned moments later with plates piled high with the finest dishes that Llyat had ever seen. There were miniature pastries filled with beef marrow, eels in a thick spiced and pureed sauce, loach and lamprey in a cold green gravy flavoured with sage and various other herbs. There were large cuts of roast lamb, beef and pork along with several plates of large fish that Llyat presumed were salmon. He had heard tales of such beasts but had never seen one until now. The smell of a bacon broth filled Llyat's nostrils as it wafted past and he drooled at the sight of the large meat pile, formed of pieces of chicken and veal, sautéed and served in a sauce of pounded crayfish tails, almonds, and toasted bread. The site of the strange and exotic coloured jellies filled Llyat with an intense feeling of hunger. He watched with envy as the feast was devoured and he knew that he would have to control his desires. Only when the highborn had retired for the night would he and the rest of the servants be allowed to finish any scraps that remained from the banquet. Despite his salivation and hunger pains Llyat became aware that he too was being watched, not by any of the Lords and Ladies that pigged out on the feast, but by the two members of the Royal Guard who stood behind Phauless Gylewu. The knights stared out with suspicious eyes.

"That's Sir Wesmin Lightmain and Sir Tobye Cragtalon," whispered Mervrig at an opportune moment when both refilled their flagons with wine. "They are the sworn protectors and the personal bodyguards to Lord Gylewu. Wherever he goes Lightmain and Cragtalon are not too far away. Oh, you may not see them at first, but if you dared to try and harm their Lord they would strike you down before you could so much as blink. That is how lethal the Royal Guard are..... Sorry Llyat, it looks like you are being summoned by your master."

Llyat looked up and noted that Lord Marus was trying to make eye contact with him. Then with a small gesture from his right hand the physician beckoned Llyat over. The youth moved quickly yet without attracting attention despite at one point having to avoid Lolly who sought to waylay him. Pushing the Fool aside, he made his way across the hall and jumped upon the platform on which his master sat.

"You seem to be fitting in well young Emgar," whispered the Grand Physician as he turned to face Llyat. "If you would be as so good to refill my goblet, I appear to have let its content run dry."

"Oh shit, of course Sir," replied Llyat as he snatched the goblet off the table and filled it to the brim from the flagon in his other hand.

"Thank you Llyat, but don't let it run dry again," continued the Grand Physician between mouthfuls of food, wine, and raised eyebrows. "How are you finding your new life in the Capital? Is it everything you could have hoped for?"

"If it pleases you sir, it is everything I could have hoped for and more; although I wish I had arrived under different circumstances. Not many from the villages of Maplehill, Oakwood, and Ashview have ever been to the Capital. The only real contact we have is from either with the wandering folk or the travelling bards who share their stories with us."

"And what stories have you heard?"

"Just that there are streets in the Capital that are paved with gold. The usual shit!"

"Now isn't that an interesting story," replied the old man as he laughed. "There is an old child's tale about a young boy who came to Parandor to seek his fortune where the streets were paved with gold, reached the highest of positions and served the Sovereign Lord. Ha, ha! I'm sorry to tell you Llyat that the truth of the matter is there are no golden streets. Shit yes, there is a lot of that, but definitely not gold. I am afraid it is just a nonsense story we tell to children and simple bastards so that they can aspire to accomplish something with their pathetic and wretched lives. It sounds to me that someone has been playing this very game with you."

Llyat thought for a moment about the first time he and Methladon Heyn had heard that story from Denius Castor. With a wave of sadness ripping through his soul he realised he would never get the chance to tell them the truth about Parandor's stinking thoroughfares.

"So what about these knights of yours," continued the old man while breaking Llyat's chain of thought? "Have you managed to remember that word you were struggling to recall? The strange place name that you said was spoken by that man in…… how did you describe it as? Oh yes, the skull helmet."

"I'm sorry sir, no, I haven't. It's as if the word doesn't exist in my head any more. No matter how hard I try to remember the more I feel that it is trying to avoid me."

"That's a pity," replied Abrahamus. "Though I must tell you that Townsforth of the City Watch has sent riders out along the Tiaryer in the direction of your village. They will seek out the facts about these black knights and their Commander, if of course they ever existed outside of your imagination."

Before Llyat could respond, the music stopped as did the many voices of those who feasted at the tables. Silence descended on the Great Hall for Phauless Gylewu had risen from his seat and had begun to address the room.

"My friends," he bellowed. "Lords and Ladies of the Court. Tonight we have gathered, not just for merriment and frivolity, but to stand together against the great fear that has gripped our Capital. As most of you are aware there have been several murders within our midst. Six in total."

"Pssst, Abrahamus," whispered Lord Ystafell to Llyat's master. "Where is Xix? Phauless never makes a speech without Blackfayer by his side. I wonder what could have happened to the rat."

"You may listen to me now and think that each and every one of you is protected here within my walls," continued Phauless. "But I tell you this, none us are safe from the dark forces that are being manipulated by the cult of Death Tubaria. I speak now to you all in the absence of my Sovereign Advisor, for he would advise me to lie in order to protect you from the truth. Yet I feel the need to be as honest as I can for I hold you all so dear to my heart. Please everyone, be extra vigilant. Lock your doors and do not trust anyone that you do not know. Beware of all strangers for there could be those who seek to infiltrate our community, dressed perhaps as servants, or others of such ilk that we take for granted. Look in particular for those whose clothes look new or strange."

Llyat was convinced that the Sovereign was talking about him. He was just about to call out and say that he had never done anything wrong when he remembered that once in days past a man had been put in the Maplehill stocks and left to rot there for just interrupting one of the Sovereign Lord's travelling news tellers. He dreaded to think what punishment would befall him if he dared to speak one word in the presence of the Great Gylewu. The Sovereign Lord then talked in some detail of how much the cult was a serious threat to the Citadel. He informed everyone that the City Watch had been tasked to investigate the murders but he also let slip that he had sent his own most trusted spy out into the Realm to discover who was behind these terrible crimes. Llyat however was far too distracted to hear the words of the Sovereign for he had tuned in on a whispered conversation between his own master and the Lord Chamberlin.

"You do have to question why Blackfayer absented himself from tonight's feast," said Lord Ystafell, his voice so quiet that only Lord Marus and Llyat could hear it.

"You'd best hold your tongue," ordered the Grand Physician. "Should Sir Wesmin or Sir Tobye hear you, or worse still Phauless himself, then it will be more than the stocks for you. We will be eating your spiced balls for breakfast, and it will be bits of your cock that will stick between our teeth!"

"Once again," bellowed Phauless, oblivious to the many side conversations that had started in the room. "I do beseech you all to stay safe and to trust no one."

With that he lowered himself back to his seat and signalled for the musicians to recommence their well-practiced and melodious tunes. Even though the merry music filled the hall Llyat could not but help notice the concern on the Sovereign's face.

The feast continued long into the night with Llyat always on hand to refill his master's goblet. He had let it go empty once and vowed it would never happen again. Phauless did not attempt to interrupt the feast a second time. Some considerable time later when the very last morsel of food had been consumed and the scraps taken away to the kitchen, the Sovereign Lord rose a second time and brought the room to silence. Once on his feet and without any desire to speak further he was escorted out of the room by his bodyguards. As the other Lords and Ladies followed his lead and began to exit the hall, Llyat said his farewells to the other cup-bearers and then escorted his new master out of the vast chamber and along the dim corridors of the Citadel. The fires of the wall beacons waned as the two very different souls travelled ever closer to the Physician's rooms.

"I will be able to make it alone from here Llyat," said the Grand Physician as he stifled a small yawn. "Heliana will have warmed my bed and will assist me in getting off to sleep. Then as always she will dress me and bring me my breakfast on the morrow. I want you to come and meet me down in the Underkeep around midmorning for I have decided to teach you the basic skills that you will need to assist me in my work. Would you like that Llyat?"

"Yes indeed sir, I would love to acquire much of your knowledge and wisdom."

"Then till the morning," the old man replied with a wry smile.

With that said the Physician entered through the door to his chambers and left Llyat to walk alone down the long corridor and on towards the Underkeep.

The next morning, Llyat rose late from his slumber and donned his servant attire. He had considering wearing the new gambeson and breeches but thought better of it as he did not want them soiled by his work. After he had finished munching leftovers he left the confines of the dank servant's quarters and made his way along the network of tunnels to his master's laboratory. He saw no sign of Heliana that morning and wondered what late night duties his master had required of her and whether she had managed to get much sleep. He was keen to tell her about his experience at his first feast and all that had transpired there. On he walked on through the semi darkness while the flames from the fires on the walls cast sinister shadows upon the dirt covered floor. Soon he began to reflect on some of the conversations that he had heard during his cup-bearing duties of the previous evening. The one that stood out most was the speculation as to why Xix Blackfayer had missed the feast and the Sovereign's speech. He wondered if he dare ask his master about it but that would give away the fact that he had listened in to a highborn conversation. For that he expected to be punished and therefore decided in the end that it was best to keep silent. The last thing he wanted was to risk losing his new position in the Grand Physician's household

Llyat passed two other servants that he had seen at the feast and after acknowledging them he followed a beanpole of a man with a sulked face and purple robes. At last Llyat arrived at a wooden door that he recognised. It led into his master's laboratory. He had never been inside it but its location had been revealed to him by Heliana on his first walk around the Citadel. After knocking several times and hearing no answer Llyat pushed the door open and stepped into the dark.

In an instant numerous torches fixed to the walls fired up. Amongst the flickering light Llyat began to move around as a great curiosity overtook him. He looked at the strange markings and drawings upon the papers that lay scattered on the floor and at some which were fixed to the walls. His eyes scanned the weird instruments upon the shelves and they reminded him of similar objects in his master's study. Then he focused his attention on the naked and headless torso that lay stinking on a stone slab. Shocked by the sight of the man's privates, exposed in their full glory to the musty air of the room, he reflected on how small they looked in comparison to his own. As he stared closer, Llyat saw strange marks carved into the skin of the corpse, recently slashed for they were still angry and inflamed. He had no idea what the strange marks were but one reminded him of the birthmark that Methladon Heyn had upon the back of his head. He began to think about what could have taken away the man's head so completely. A strong urge to reach out and touch dead skin began to grow but just before his hand could connect with the body the distinctive voice of his master made him jump.

"Interesting, isn't it? Young master Danbury here appears to be another victim in the series of murders that trouble the Capital."

"I beg your pardon sir," replied Llyat. "Are these the same murders that Lord Gylewu was talking of last night?"

"That is correct Llyat and I have been tasked to find out how and why this young man died."

"Pardon my impertinence sir, but wouldn't the removal of the head be the obvious cause?"

"Ha, ha!" laughed the physician as he moved towards the slab and stood beside Llyat. "Indeed that would be a logical explanation... yes it would. However the facts are like this. The young man was found lying in the stables outside the walls of the Citadel. His head had been crushed by a large stone boulder. Everyone else seemed to want to put it all down to an accident yet there was nowhere that the bolder could have fallen from and no indication how it got there. No man or woman that I have ever known could have picked it up due to its sheer size and weight. It was therefore my belief that magic had to have been employed in the slaying of the poor lad."

"Magic!" gasped Llyat, wondering if the old man meant the trickery of wizards and sorcerers, or something more sinister of which he had no understanding. "Do you mean spells and stuff?"

"Yes lad, I do. Just like the enchantments of light upon the torches that burst into flames as you entered this room. I am sure you must have wondered at their remarkable sudden combustion?"

"Yes, for a brief moment. Well, until I saw the body."

"Once I suspected that magic was involved, I carried out a small test at the scene of the crime. Have you ever heard of the Kundalish Aura?"

The Grand Physician then walked around to the other side of the slab and as he did so he continued to look at the body that lay upon it. Llyat scanned his memory to see if he could recognise the words but as usual his mind was blank.

"No sir, I haven't"

The Grand Physician smiled, turned away, and made his way over towards the wooden cupboard next to the skeleton. Within a matter of seconds he returned with a dusty leather bound book and a small jar of what appeared to be powdered herbs. The jar was placed into Llyat's hands.

"I always use the fresh stuff when I am out on location but I have a small preserved supply down here and also some in my study. This stuff is called Masslewort. It is a mixture of wolfs-bane, witch-hazel, bluebell, and fire flower. Oh, and a few spells and incantations placed over it to hold the mixture together."

"Do you mean you can do magic sir?"

"Just a few basic spells my young friend," replied the old man as he once again returned to the slab "Just the casting of fire, the gift of healing small wounds, and a small levitation spell."

Llyat smiled to himself for he had always wanted to meet someone who could do the magic mentioned in so many of Denius Castor's stories. He held the small jar a little higher and looked down into its contents. A strange sensation rippled through his fingers but it lasted no more than a second. Llyat looked ever deeper into the Masslewort while Abrahamus Marus thumbed through the pages of the leather bound book. After finding the one he was looking for he placed the tome down upon the headless body on the slab.

"Here, look at this," shouted the old man. "Can take it you can read?"

"Just a little, I never had time to learn well, but I can understand a few of the simple words."

"Oh dear," continued the physician. "That's just something else I'm going to have to teach you, if you would like me to of course."

"Sure I do," replied Llyat as another great opportunity dropped into his lap.

"But for now, I shall just explain this page of text to you," he mumbled as he beckoned Llyat closer so that he could see what was written on the pages.

Llyat placed the jar of Masslewort upon the stone slab and looked down at the strange marks upon the book, the things that he knew were called words. His gaze was soon drawn to a picture that took up the whole of the right hand page. It depicted a featureless person with their arms and legs pointing away from the centre. Upon the body were seven circles of different faded colours stacked one on top of each other. They started at the head and ended around the bollocks.

"As you can see here, Llyat," began Abrahamus. "There are seven pools of magic in our bodies and with practice and knowhow we can learn to tap into them. All you need is self-control and mental focus. Each centre is connected to a different aspect of a spell caster's being and each depletes its energy throughout the day and recharges during sleep or rest time. The Kundalish Aura is produced when an outside magic interacts with a person's pools and is magnified by the application of the mixture in the jar. You see, even though the aura is invisible to the naked eye, there are ways of forcing it to show itself. The use of Masslewort, long ago developed by the Wizard's Guild, is one of the two ways that you can get to see it."

"What is the other way?"

"Oh that's even more interesting," replied the old man with a sly smile. "There are said to be a few individuals whose aura is so powerful that after exposure to magic that they give off a spontaneous glow without the need of Masslewort. The owner displays a fiery essence they say but it very rarely happens and I have never seen it."

Llyat looked down at the corpse. Its wound marks were significantly different to those in the book. He tried to make sense of all that he had been told for it was weird stuff that his master sought to explain. Yet before he could ask further questions the physician closed the book, picked up the stone jar, and returned both to a shelf inside the wooden cupboard. Then he re-joined Llyat by the side of the slab.

"Listen lad," he began. "There is so much more I can teach you, but right now we need to make a start on deciphering the runes carved into the young man's chest. I am guessing that you have noticed them?"

"Yes... Yes sir, I have."

"Well young Llyat, as you can see, the final one of these strange runes is the curse mark of the cult of Death Tubaria. I made a guess that if young Danbury was killed by the cult then I would find the mark elsewhere since his head was destroyed beyond recognition."

"What do the other markings say sir?" asked Llyat with much curiosity.

"A good question lad, and I am so pleased that you asked it. Do you recall the conversation I had with Lord Amberstone, our Royal Librarian, as we left the Great Hall last night?"

"Yes I do," replied Llyat. "You were asking after a book. I think you called it 'Arcane Knowledge' or something like that."

"Indeed I did. Within that text there is a chapter on runes and their meaning. I asked Lord Amberstone find that book last night so that together, you and I, could translate the signs morning. I was going to try and do it yesterday before the feast but I was called to fix a blockage in Lady Fullbane's bowels. That woman is intolerable and nothing less than a pig heaver. I hope you never have to meet her lad for she would eat you for sure. Anyway Llyat, what I want you to do now is to run off the Royal Library, a large room just off to the side of the Marble Court. There you must seek out Lord Amberstone. He should have found that book for me by now and I need you to bring it back as soon as possible. Do you understand your task?"

"Yes Sir. I've to go to the library and get the book from Lord Amberstone."

With a quick bow to his master Llyat turned and ran out into the corridor beyond the door. It didn't take him long to find his way through the twisting tunnels of the Underkeep and up onto the ground floor of the Citadel. After asking directions to the Marble Court from a young olive skinned servant named Ourri, Llyat resumed his dash through the corridors until he found himself in front of the empty throne. He stopped for a brief moment to admire the impressive marble seat but then hastened on towards his intended destination. He barged past several disgruntled members of the Court who cursed him as he passed. Seconds later he ran out through a set of double doors and into the library.

To Llyat the library was the second most impressive room in the Citadel. The long, tall, and cavernous room, was crammed wall to wall with books and scrolls of varying shades of brown, green, and black; all stacked high upon tall wooden dust covered shelves. The scene filled Llyat with a sense of shock and awe. Light from Solaris burst in through long arched windows set high into the walls. Bright shafts highlighted the myriad of dust speckles that floated on the air. At several wooden desks scribes sat copying books, each one as silent as the next. The same intense quiet seeped out from several courtiers as they busied themselves amongst the stacks of books and scrolls. The one exception to the quiet came from the raised voices of two men at the far end of the library, both hidden from Llyat's view by a very large pile of books.

Llyat wandered through the musty space as he sought out Lord Amberstone but in the end he could no longer avoid approaching the raised voices. He passed around the great pile of tomes and came before the commotion. Llyat recognised Lord Amberstone first. The other was the tall man he had followed in the corridors of the Underkeep earlier that morning.

"I don't care what you say Xix, I know now why you were not at the feast last night," insisted Lord Amberstone. "You need to talk to the Watch and inform them of the theft of the Lore of the Dead. They must be made aware of what you have just told me."

"The Watch has nothing to do with this Mathias. If you think I am going to let your daughter take charge of something that is beyond her capabilities to comprehend then you are much mistaken. I know that you spoke with her in the courtyard two days ago and told her about the missing book. My spies overheard your conversation as they do all others. You have seen the signs and read the messages from the north, the east, and across the marshes. Yet still you persist. His resurrection is..."

The conversation continued until Xix Blackfayer noticed Llyat's presence. The gangly man turned his back on Amberstone and pushed past Llyat as he stormed away. As soon as the Sovereign Adviser disappeared around the great book pile Llyat moved towards the man he had been sent to find. He was shocked at how pale the Royal Librarian looked.

"Are you feeling unwell my Lord?" he asked.

"That's none of your fucking business lad," snapped back Lord Amberstone as he attempted to follow in the footsteps of Blackfayer.

Llyat knew that he had to act at once.

"My master, the Grand Physician, sent me to find you sir," he stuttered and as he hoped he had not caused further offence. "He said you would have a book for me."

"Ah yes, a book on Arcane Knowledge, written in the language of the Ancients," mumbled Amberstone to himself as he stopped in his tracks.

The aging librarian then then changed his demeanour and escorted Llyat to an unoccupied section of the library. There from out of a dust piled shelf he retrieved a large coal-black leather bound book upon which two golden keys had been embossed.

"Here you go lad," he whispered as he handed over the tome. "I would appreciate it if you didn't tell Marus about my disagreement with Blackfayer. It would just complicate matters and I sense you wouldn't want to be left to rot in the oubliette. Do you understand what I am saying? Keep your trap shut if you would like to see the year out."

Growling once again the Librarian then scuttled off and left Llyat alone with the book he had been sent to retrieve. For a brief moment Llyat wondered what an oubliette was and thought about asking the closest of the scribes, but then he felt better of it. This thought was then followed by one most deep and worrying. Perhaps the two Lords who plotted in the library were responsible for the murders that his master had been ordered to investigate. It wasn't his place to ask questions and yet he felt uneasy and confused and so he decided to talk to Heliana about it when next he saw her. Llyat returned to the laboratory at a slower pace and on his arrival saw that his master had transcribed the strange runes from the chest of the stable boy onto several sheets of parchment. The documents had been arranged in line upon the stone floor. He looked on as the physician cut open the Danbury's chest with a sharp instrument. It left a trail of blood and entrails over the floor but having seen what skyfawn could do, the gore did not bother Llyat one bit.

"Ah, so you're back," said old Marus as he took hold of a cloth from off the slab and wiped his hands. "Did you manage to get me the book I need?"

"I did sir. Here it is."

"Good, very good," replied the Physician as he began to thumb through the pages while intermittently looking at the line of parchments upon the floor.

Llyat was more interested in the gore and guts. A memory returned. It was one from some years past, a day he had been out hunting for game with Fiat and Methladon Heyn. The three friends had come across an overturned carriage by the side the Eastern Road and which had been travelling to the Capital. The occupants of the carriage, along with their horses, had been slaughtered by a group of bandits that were known to hide in woods around the Tiaryer. Llyat then recalled that both Methladon and Fiat had been disturbed by the vision of the dead Lord and Lady who had been dragged with force from the overturned carriage and eviscerated by the roadside. Their guts and entrails had hung out of their bellies, slit from nape of neck to nethers and left for the skyfawn to chew upon. Yet, apart from a brief feeling of sorrow for the loss of innocent lives, Llyat had not been troubled by any sensations of nausea or disgust. It had only been when Methladon and Fiat had expelled their stomach contents upon the dirt that he had thought anything of it. Even though Vostag had trained the brothers to be warriors, the sight of the slaughter had been too much for his two friends. As the image of Methladon's puke grew evermore vivid in his mind, a sudden gasp of air from the Grand Physician brought Llyat back into the present.

"Oh fuck!" exclaimed the old man as his pallor waned.

"Sir, are you ill?" asked Llyat as he raced to his master's side.

"It's worse than I could have imagined Llyat. Far worse."

"What do you mean sir? What is wrong?"

"Tell me Llyat, have you ever heard of the ruined city of Avolire?"

12

Mighty waves crashed upon a great outcrop of land that rose from the deep ocean. They sprayed foaming water and a salt leaden mist against the jagged rocks that made up the barren island. The inhabitants of the imposing and eerie edifice who stood in wondrous solidity upon the highest point of the primal land were at one with the ever present surge of water that that broke upon the rocks below its sturdy walls. The high towers with their Realmgoth spires, inset with arched stained glass windows, pointed up towards the black pendulous storm clouds. Behind the glass it was the candlelight that provided a reassuring sense of security to the students and masters of the Bards Guild. Yet at the same time the imposing building created a sense of fear and foreboding to all those who looked upon it from the nearby bay, encircled as it almost was by enormous jet-black volcanic cliffs. The small coastal town of Valameer with its contrasting white marble buildings sat at their base and faced towards the west and the awesome Guild. The outcrop upon which the Guild sat was forever surrounded by a boiling sea that had destroyed many a ship over time. So many souls had drowned there, all sunk deep and washed out into the vast expanse of the great ocean, only to be devoured by the scale covered scavengers that waited with jaws at the ready.

Aquaris and his lover Bycphy the goddess of the sea, revelled in the destructive power they could wield. Those who managed to make a successful landing upon the island would then face a steep and dangerous path up the sheer cliffs until reaching the seemingly tenuous foothold of the Guild. There was however a much safer way to approach the ancient building. A second mighty structure had been built long ago with much hard labour and a little magic. It spanned the gap between the island and the mainland. Over the surging waves below the incredible Bridge of Athuna provided the preferred route into the Guild. Like the sturdy stone walls and towers of the Bards Guild, the Bridge of Athuna was the best preserved example of ancient Realmgoth architecture. The towers and walls featured many pointed arches with grotesques carved into centre of each point. The imposing stone battlements that lined the bridge reached out from the mainland to grab hold of the island rock like the fingers of a giant's hand. It was as if those stone digits were frightened to loosen their grip lest their catch fall into the surging torrent of the sea. Upon this mighty bridge, perched upon a white steed, Thias Calavan forced his horse at a gallop.

As the grey storm clouds opened and Aquaris pissed down rain, pools of water began to form upon the stone surface of the bridge. Ploughing through the deluge without obvious concern for his mount, the bard at last reached the thick stone walls that surrounded the Guild. There he came to a halt before the enormous tower that housed the portcullis that bared his way forward. Thias dismounted but held onto the reins to prevent the horse from galloping back over the bridge if spooked by the storm. He then pulled his mount forward as he walked through the lashing rain to base of the imposing portcullis and sought out the gatekeeper in order to gain entry into the dry and warm interior of the Guild. Moments later a voice shouted down from one of the murder holes in the overhanging stone of the gatehouse tower.

"Who goes there at this time of night amid this deluge of the gods?" bellowed a gruff voice.

"I am Thias Calavan," the bard shouted back as he looked up through a torrent of water that poured through the murder hole. "I am the appointed bard to our Sovereign Lord Phauless Gylewu IV and friend to this Guild. I have travelled for several days from the Grey Keep of Lord Raorick and I need to speak to Grand Musician Fusepelt on a matter of great importance."

After a few minutes of silence, save for the smashing of water against stone, the portcullis began to rise. It groaned and creaked under its massive weight but soon Thias moved forward into an inner stone walled courtyard. His gaze fixed upon the distant wall and the large iron entrance doors to the Guild's main building. Before this portal stood a young man, dressed in a red doublet lined with golden embroidery, and who then ran forward into the downpour to greet Thias the bard.

"I am glad to see you again my old friend," said the man. "Let me take the horse from you?"

"Of course and I thank you most humbly Dayis," replied Thias as he handed over the reins of the chalk white horse. "He will need food and water and a warm dry stable. I hope you can find a place for him."

"He will be well looked after here, do not worry young bard," replied Dayis.

After he had lifted Thias's belongings from behind the saddle Dayis led the horse away. Thias turned and made his way through the rain towards the iron doors and on into the cavernous hall beyond. Compared to the foul external weather the instant warmth gave Thias the feeling of having landed inside a house of the gods. Like the great architecture of its exterior the inside of the Guild offered much of the same. The great Realmgoth pillars and arches were vast, lit by burning fires embedded in wrought iron cradles fixed upon the walls and from large chandeliers that hung suspended from the highest of ceilings. As Thias walked forward into the vast hall the water that had soaked his cloak dripped upon the red and gold carpet that spanned the length of its floor. Ultimately this magnificent carpet led up a wide stairway which split off at each level in two directions forming balconies at multiple levels on either side of the main body of the hall. Squelching forward over the intricate weave Thias could not help but revel in the sounds of the celestial voices that sang out in melodious octaves, mixed with tones of the delicately plucked strings of harps and bows that flashed across a multitude of strings.

There were several others that wandered through the hall and then in and out of the various doors that lead off deeper into the Guild. Thias knew by their doublets that they were students for he too had once worn identical garb during his studies in the confines of the Guildschool. The bard scanned the fresh faces of the students and recalled the time of his own studies. Another minute passed and he arrived at the foot of the stairs. On either side of the great stone steps, two Knights in bronze armour stood guard. Upon their left pauldrons they bore the sigil of the Bards Guild, a golden lyre upon a black background and surrounded by burning flames. Both stood to attention and were armed with intimidating metal pikes. Thias picked his way between the two sentries and began the climb up the stairs. At the top he turned to the right and then followed another set of spiralling steps towards the uppermost of the balconies. There he pushed through the first door that he came to and walked on into the long corridor beyond its wood. This passageway was in many ways similar to the vast hall he had left behind although the ceiling was much lower. On he marched down this empty corridor towards the thick oak door at its end. He knocked four times upon the grain and waited for a response. Standing in silence Thias then focused his thoughts to the centre of his being, generated internal heat and within seconds both he and his clothes were dry. After the click of a lock the door was opened by a middle aged man with long black hair and a beard to match. His flowing robes were of a rich dark mauve material and were an indication of his high status. The man looked at Thias for some moments with a deep suspicion as he tried to work out who it was before him. Then he smiled and held out his hand.

"Thias Calavan, What brings you back to the Guild?"

"Master Peaceore," replied Thias. "I didn't expect you to be one to open the doors to the chambers of Grand Musician Fusepelt. I need to speak to the old man at once for I bring disturbing news from the Capital and the Grey Mountains. I am in urgent need of his assistance."

"Then enter at once," replied Peaceore as he moved away from the door. "You are always welcome within these walls, young Thias."

The bard followed Master Peaceore into the chambers of the Grand Musician and then on into a large room in which one wall was taken up by a large stained glass window. Along the sides of the other three walls stood several ornate wooden cupboards. At the far end of the candle lit space, in front of the window that revealed the ever growing storm, sat an old man. Over the parchment on which he painstakingly wrote with a quilled pen, sat the coiled body of Owasorin Fusepelt. On noting Thias's presence the ancient sage placed down his quill, stood with great effort, and then staggered forward in obvious discomfort. Supported by a gnarled wooden staff he took care not to catch his feet in the trailing hem of his heavy robes. As the Grand Musician and the bard approached each other the old man raised his arms in order to embrace one of his flock.

"You haven't even grown a wrinkle since you left for the Citadel," croaked the old man.

"Neither have you master. You are still the same old man that welcomed me to this college some ten years ago, although I must admit you do seem to be moving slower than before."

Thias tried to break from the embrace, fearful that the lyre still strung around his body would be crushed.

"Yes my dear friend. Age is remorseless and takes no captives. But still, one hundred and five is a good age to reach, given all the years I have had to deal with the stress of teaching know-alls and upstarts like you Thias. But where are my manners? Master Peaceore would you be so kind as to fetch our young bard a chair on which to rest his bony arse."

"Of course," responded Peaceore, "faster than you can hum your scales!"

Then with a swift bow he left the room and closed the door behind him.

"So tell me, how are things in the Citadel of Parandor?" began the old man as he made his way back around his desk. "How is our Lord and Sovereign Phauless Gylewu? Is he still being manipulated by that snivelling snake Xix Blackfayer?"

"Our Lord Phauless is in good health, Grand Musician. As for Blackfayer, I would rather let my arse speak for him."

"Please, enough of the Grand Musician title. You are no longer a student of mine. You have earned the right to call me by my birth name, just as it should be."

"As you wish Owasorin," replied Thias as he smiled. "As I began, our Sovereign Ruler is in good health, although I believe that you will in all probability outlive him. He is still the same man that you knew from many years ago, sober, fair and just. Blackfayer still wields a high degree of control over the Royal Court yet most of us believe that if he had wanted to seize the throne then he would have done so long ago."

Thias paused at the sound of a knock and the door opened without further delay. In strode Peaceore with a chair in his arms which he passed over to the young bard. After he had sat down Thias watched Peaceore manoeuvre around the desk and stand at the side of the Grand Musician, an indication of his position of power. The travelling bard then allowed his weary body to sink into the fabric of the chair and permit his tension to roll off his limbs and down through the floor.

"Thank you Master Peaceore," he then said to the black haired man. "I am most grateful for the opportunity to sit a while."

"So what brings young Thias Calavan all the way back to us in Valameer?" began the Grand Musician. "I cannot believe that life in the Capital is so bad that you come and visit us here?"

"I seek your advice and assistance my friend, for as I informed Master Peaceore upon my arrival, I bring bad tidings from both Parandor, the Grey Mountains, and the Grey Keep."

"Ah the cold dark prison, the place of 'death while yet alive'. I have not thought on the Grey Keep for many a year. Is it still under the watchful eye of Raorick Gylewu, our Sovereign's brother? Am I correct Master Peaceore?"

"Yes Master, that is indeed correct."

"Tell me then Thias," continued the old man as he looked to the bundle on Thias's lap. "What ominous tidings do you bring from Lord Raorick? Has he finally decided against the challenge of penetrating the Lady Flurdiana?"

"He's dead," replied Thias bluntly as he saw no point in delaying the truth.

"Dead?" interrupted Peaceore before Thias could continue. "How?"

"If you don't mind Alfrabra, please let him finish his story," ordered the Grand Musician "Don't mind Peaceore young Thias. He is acting as my personal assistant here in the Guild and he has taken over many duties that I can no longer manage myself or those I feel better fit his many talents. Sometimes however he forgets himself and the fact that I am in still in charge. Do continue."

The old man chuckled. Peaceore's cheeks turned cherry red and created a striking clash of colour with the mauve of his high status robes. The bard knew that he had an important story to tell and one that would require their full concentration.

"Where to begin?" spoke Thias. "There have been five murders in the Citadel. Each one of the deceased bore an identical curse brand. It was the mark of the three circles and the calling card of the cult of the Death Tubaria. Lord Phauless Gylewu himself sent me in secret along the Eastern Road to the Grey Keep with instructions to question a dwarf known as Grovrouk the Despoiler who was locked away in the dungeons of the great stone stronghold. In my time here at the Guild I had learned the rudiments of the language of the Dirmark which would help in my interrogation. Along my journey I encountered horsemen wearing the strangest armour that I had ever seen. They wielded unusual weapons that could cut through a man with little apparent force. These black knights forced me to take an alternative route through the wilderness until at last I made it to the Grey Keep. Upon my arrival, instead of the open fires and feasting that I would have expected from the brother of our Sovereign Lord, I found myself amidst a massacre. All who had once dwelt there were dead, including the prisoners. All that is except one."

"Let me guess," interrupted Peaceore. "The dwarf called Grovrouk."

"That is correct. I found one survivor at the Grey Keep, Sir Cristofre Randle of the Royal Guard. But I failed at first to notice the trap that I had walked into. You see the man that I thought was Sir Randle was in fact a changeling, one of the Lizardmen shaman that live in the Eastern Marsh. I had to kill the creature once its true identity had been revealed and I have done much thinking about it ever since. I believe that the dwarf has been taken into the marshes as a prisoner but I fear something much more sinister is going on. I hesitate to say this but I believe there could be a spy in the Citadel, another one of their shape changing shamans, and that no one in the Court has any idea of its presence. It could be in the guise of any who walk its hallowed halls."

"So the Lizardmen have left the Marsh," muttered the Grand Musician. "I was wondering when they would have enough courage to cross the Grey Mountains and venture south."

"A thought I also have pondered on," continued Thias. "But the apparent capture of the dwarf causes me great concern."

"In what sense," questioned the old man? "Why worry about a dwarf? For all you know he could be dead."

"The creature was believed to have had significant knowledge passed to him by Lord Jonas Tullage. I'm sure you remember his name, Owasorin.

"Indeed I do. The once Grand Physician of the Royal Court and secret priest to the cult of the Death Tubaria."

The old musician glanced sideways at Peaceore who mirrored his master's surprise. Thias knew at once from the look on their faces that both men remembered past events with equal concern.

"It is suspected that the dwarf had been given knowledge relating to specific passages and incantations from the Lore of the Dead. The actual book is however under lock and key within the Royal Library. With the resurfacing of Death Tubaria in Parandor, and with Lord Gylewu suspecting that some of his own Court could be murderers, he turned to me as one of the few that he felt he could still trust. As I can speak the dark tongue of dwarves I offered my services and agreed to question Grovrouk in order to see what he knew. If possible I was to find out from him the names of any who were plotting against our Sovereign Lord. If there was a traitor amid the Court I was ordered to do anything I saw fit to find out who he, she, or they were. However, the assault on the Grey Keep complicates matters. If the dwarf, now free from his cell, has passed on his knowledge of the passages from the Lore then who knows what may result from it. It could embolden the Lizardmen. They may even dare rise up and march upon the Capital."

A flash of lightening filled the room with an intense blue light and it was followed a second later by a crash of thunder so loud that the room shook with unprecedented violence. It took a good minute for those present to collect themselves as the gloom returned to the dim candle lit room.

"And then there is this!" continued Thias as he opened his bundle and pulled out the emerald encrusted golden dagger.

"The Dagger of Kha!" gasped the old man. "How did you come by this evil relic?"

"A friend of mine has a son who carries the curse mark. It dates from the last time that the cult tried to become all powerful. But I must be honest with you, the boy is the son of my foster father to whom I will always be indebted although we had lost contact when I joined the Guild in order to train as a bard. The boy, despite the years that forced our distancing, I also hold close to my heart like a true brother. The brand first appeared on his skin after he had found this dagger lying in the mud in the Tiaryer. After the cult had been thwarted my adopted father for some unbeknown reason held on to the accursed blade. It was either by luck or the divine intervention of Fatumai that I stumbled across Vostag Heyn and his three sons in the small village of Maplehill, a hamlet lost in the middle of nowhere. That was where I obtained this relic."

After a further pause the Grand Musician and the music master looked to each other and nodded in recognition village's name. This did not go unnoticed by the bard.

"So you have heard of it Owasorin?" asked Thias with much curiosity.

"Of course I have heard of it. The name troubles me a great deal," replied the old man.

"Tell the young bard about the prophecy," interrupted Peaceore.

"What prophecy is that," replied Thias?

No answer came but Thias could see that both elderly bards looked troubled. Whatever they knew and were hiding, it was clear it had something to do with his investigation.

"We cannot explain it here," responded the Grand Musician as he stood up slowly. "We need to go to the Orrery in the high tower. I will attempt to explain everything to you once we are there."

It took Thias far longer than he had expected to follow the Grand Musician and Peaceore through the corridors of the Bards Guild and up numerous stone stairways. This was in part due to the slowness of the old man who continued on with remarkable perseverance given his majestic age. It was also a consequence of Peaceore's insistence in stopping to talk to most other Guild Masters that he passed on his way to the Orrery. He told all of their destination and where they were to be found if they were needed. Eventually the three arrived at the foot of the last of the spiral steps that led up to the Tower of Insight and the Great Orrery built into its highest point. The progress up was as slow as Thias could move without standing still. The Grand Musician led the way but he struggled with each and every step as if climbing the highest of mountains. If not supported from behind by Peaceore the old man would have no doubt fallen. Throughout the long journey Thias reflected on what the Grand Musician had meant by a prophecy and what it had to do with the Dagger of Kha and the cult of the Death Tubaria. Soon he would have answers and that made the long climb more bearable.

At last the stairs widened out into the highest room of the tower, one that commanded the best view of the Guild's buildings and the town of Valameer beyond the bay. Within the confines of the tower's chamber, lit by the torches that lined its curved walls was a sight that Thias had seen just once before when he had first enrolled as a student. There before him stood the most impressive of mechanical contraptions, ticking away as it always had done with the turning of a thousand cogs. Sounds clicked and echoed throughout the otherwise empty room. Upon arms that stuck out from the mighty machine were many orbs of different colours and sizes, each spinning upon its own axis and turning at different and almost unperceivably slow rates. This was the Orrery of Anyle Belanore, named after the greatest of the philosophers of the Ancients; the man who believed that everything in the heavens was connected through vibrating living filaments or 'twisted strings' as he called them. Belanore also believed, although he could never prove it, that it was the frequency of the vibrations of these silky strings that governed all living things and dictated their destiny just as they did the fate of men. He called the planets and the stars the 'Moirai Marionettes' although no one else knew why.

"Are you going to tell me about the prophecy?" said Thias once all three had finished looking up in wonder at the great orbs that moved in their endless dance.

The Grand Musician turned to face the bard while supporting his senile skeleton with his staff. He then pointed to the fourteen orbs that circled high above his head.

"As you can see by the line of these celestial bodies Thias, we are approaching the alignment of Enderdetag, the unique rare occurrence when the fourteen known orbs of the heavens move into one straight line."

Thias furrowed his brow as he had limited knowledge of the stars.

"I am sorry sir, I was not good with star casting and fate telling. I always favoured the arts, music, and the sword."

"It is known as the 'Alignment of the End of Days,'" interjected Master Peaceore. "It is during this very heavenly configuration that the prophecy will come to pass and a great evil descend upon the land. Yes indeed young bard, when these planets create a linear conjunction the predictions of the Ancients will be enacted."

"You speak of a prophecy that I have never heard of, one that has not been taught," replied Thias. "Please explain the meaning behind your message."

Before the young bard could speak again the Grand Musician lifted his hands above his head. Still with his staff in his right hand he rolled his eyes up inside his head. Without pausing he began to recite the haunting words of an ancient prophecy.

> When the Marked is found amongst the Maples,
> And the armies of the East shall walk again,
> With the Enderdetag alignment in the heavens,
> Then shall be the end of good men.
>
> When the Oracles crypt shall be opened,
> And the choices we make must thrive,
> The Powers of Evil shall be woken,
> And no one alive shall survive.
>
> From the innocent the savoir shall waken,
> To the Bards he shall appear,
> To reunite the Gems of Thamous,
> And destroy the Lord of Fear.

As the old man finished Thias began to search his memories for clues as to the true meaning behind the words that had been spoken. 'The Marked' could mean many things. He tried to recall his recent visit to Maplehill and his conversations with its inhabitants, an event that seemed so long ago and yet was only two weeks in the past. Could it be that the one that the prophecy called the 'Marked' was his foster brother Methladon Heyn and that his curse brand was the reason for this title. The 'Oracle that shall be woken' and the other strange words that he had heard did not make any sense. He knew would have to push for answers before he left to hunt for the dwarf and the Lizardmen of the Eastern Marsh. But how to begin.

"For those like me who don't speak prophecy tongue," he began, seeking to compete with the whirring noises of the machine "What the fuck does all that shit mean?"

"It seems the chatter in the Royal Court has rubbed off on you young Thias," laughed the old man. "Such colourful prose could have only come from there. But yes, I do understand your question. What indeed does all of this mean? Who or what is 'The Marked'? What are the evils that the prophecy speaks of and what about these Gems of Thamous? Where do you think they are hidden; I don't suppose you know"

"You make it sound like you already know where these gems are," replied Thias "What are they? I have never heard of them."

"The Gems of Thamous are five unique cut gem stones that when reunited in the right place, under specific circumstances and incantations, give the wielder enough power to vanquish darkness from the Realm."

Fusepelt paused long enough for Thias to realise his task was not so straight forward.

"But in the wrong hands they can open a doorway to the Underworld, release the forces of darkness, and set them loose amongst us."

"Are you talking about Kha?" asked the bard. "Is this the true purpose of the Death Tubaria?"

"I think this extends much deeper and further that that misinformed cult. Even with their curse marks and relics there is no way to open the concealed portal into the underworld. It can only be done with the power of the five. The cult already had possession of one without knowing it. However, given the timing of its resurgence, I am sure that the true purpose behind the recent murders that you are charged to investigate is linked to the Enderdetag Prophecy."

Thias listened to the words of the Grand Musician and in that moment they all seemed to come together in his mind. Something much bigger was at play, something far more sinister than he had hitherto contemplated.

"I can see you are deep thinking young Thias and yet the answer is so simple. The cult once held one of the jewels but now you have it and you have brought it with you to the Guild. It is the very one that you acquired in Maplehill."

"You don't mean..?"

"I do indeed. It is cursed of all their relics, The Dagger of Kha."

It took a few moments for Thias to assimilate the information and begin to understand the implications of this turn of events. He thought about the goddess Fatumai and if he was now her servant, the one chosen to deliver the dagger with its emerald to Valameer?

"So this Death Tubaria stuff, is it all a ruse? Something to make us look in the wrong direction? From what you have just told me, the cult will not accomplish anything by the curse branding of innocents so long as the portal to the Underworld remains sealed. To open it you must possess the Gems of....what did you call them again?"

"The Gems of Thamous," replied Peaceore. "It is said they were named after the Great Sorcerer Thamous who sealed the door to the Underworld and trapped its evil deep within the foulest of the dimensions."

"If the doors are sealed and the gems hidden across the Realm then that is good is it not?" asked Thias. "To me the most important questions are; where are the rest of the gems hidden and are they safe; what do they have to do with 'the Marked'; if this marked person is indeed the saviour that the Prophecy speaks of, then who and where is he now? How much danger is he in?"

"As the Prophecy says, he will make himself known to us bards," continued the Grand Musician. "Until then we will have to bide our time and wait."

"Wait!" gasped Thias as the statement hit him like an axe to the helm. "Why do we have to wait? If the Lizardmen are behind the resurgence of the cult's activities and for some reason require the incantations of the Lore of the Dead, then wouldn't it be best to take the fight to them rather than have them compound and confuse what's going on? And what of the other four gems? They can't remain hidden for ever. We need to find them before whoever else is looking for them gets his sullied hands there first."

"And where would you have us start looking?" added Peaceore. "Please remember that it was by pure chance and good fortune that you brought the dagger here with you."

"But if this is all true and the alignment of Enderdetag is upon us, then we must act at once?" said Thias as he pointed to orbs above his head.

"Indeed we must," continued the old man. "The Marked will show himself sooner rather than later and maybe then we can solve these riddles that you have brought to our door."

Thias thought for a moment. He found it hard to comprehend all that he had been through since he had left the Capital. There had been the retrieval of the dagger, the strange knights upon the road and now reference to a marked one who would reveal himself to the bards. Although some thoughts seemed to be falling into place, with each question answered another took its place. The abduction of the dwarf Grovrouk from the Grey Keep still troubled Thias for he did not know what information the dwarf carried. It was possible that the little man had he already passed on his knowledge but it was impossible to guess who that recipient could be. Yet he was determined not to give up. Somehow he had to find a way to tie up the loose ends and put his mind at rest. While the Orrery above moved ever on Thias turned to the Grand Musician and relayed his decision.

"Now I know what I must do. With or without your permission, and on my own if I must, I will journey into the Eastern Marsh and locate the dwarf myself. I cannot leave any loose ends. If the stump knows the incantations, the passages of the Lore of the Dead, and for what purpose they are to be used, then I too must discover the truth. That is my duty to our Sovereign Lord."

"It is a most brave but still foolish quest," answered old Fusepelt. "But if you must, then you must, and it is your decision alone Thias Calavan. We bards never turn anyone away who is in need of our help. You shall not be alone on your journey."

"For that I am most grateful," replied Thias as he dropped his head in deference.

"You are most welcome Thias, but I beseech you to stay a couple of days. Rest yourself and clear your mind. Allow your horse to recover if nothing else. I can get Master Ulthirn to make a chamber available for you and ask one of the students to find you something warm to eat."

"Once again I am most grateful," responded Thias as a wave of weariness swept through his body.

With that the three men turned and made their way back down the spiral steps and away from the giant mechanism. Its ticking was replaced by the claps of thunder and the lashing of rain upon the window panes.

13

"Llyat, tell the Lord Commander exactly what you told me earlier," ordered the old man.

The youth sat at the wooden desk in the rooms of his master, the Grand Physician of the Citadel of Parandor, and his pulse quickened. He felt unnerved and yet at the same time he was pleased he could remember the word that the knights who had murdered his father had shouted on that fateful night. In those few hours of darkness everything that had meant security in his life had ended but now a new chapter of hope had begun. The word 'Avolire' was fixed at the front of his thoughts. Then as his master paused and waited, Llyat looked towards the others present; the stern looking athletic old man dressed in the armour of the City Watch and his two subordinates; a man-like woman and a warrior much younger who emitted a quiet yet powerful presence.

"Llyat," began the Commander of the Watch. "Please tell us all that you know. You are not in any trouble lad. There is no need to be worried."

Llyat laughed to himself. The last person to say that to him was Chirth Hadra when he had found out Llyat had planted the turnips before the hard frosts had ceased. He had asked his old employer not to tell his father for fear of another scolding and the farmer had promised that everything would be just fine. Unfortunately for Llyat, Chirth had told many others of the mistake and his father had exploded in another of his rages. Llyat no longer believed anyone who told him 'No need to be worried'. The Grand Physician then placed a reassuring hand upon his shoulder. Llyat lifted his face and looked into the eyes of the three members of the Watch who awaited his answer.

"Where would like me to begin?"

"Start at the beginning Llyat, that's always the best place," replied Brynn Townsforth. "Tell us everything, how it happened, and how you saw it."

"Well, it's was a bit like this," answered Llyat, despite memories of that fateful Maplehill night being clouded in a mist of uncertainty. "I was woken by the sounds of shouting from outside my house, from somewhere down the hill in the village. My father bundled my mother and me into the hidden space beneath our house and no sooner were we in there then the men in the black armour arrived and shouted 'Open in the name of Avolire'. They were looking for something or someone. Through the gaps in the floor I watched an argument rage between my father and the man who wore the skull helmet."

"Skull helmet!" said the masculine woman. "Did the others give him a name or rank?"

"Easy now Tonousa, let the boy finish," said Townsforth.

"No" said Llyat as he looked to the woman and continued. "They didn't give him a name but the men that followed him referred to him as Commander, just like Commander Townsforth. It was when my father stood up to them that they used magic against him."

"Magic, are you sure?" asked Townsforth with curiosity and surprise.

"Yes it was magic alright. The man with the skull used some form of enchantment that threw my father across the room without touching him. The bastard then ordered his men to kill my dad."

Painful emotions returned as Llyat yet again relived the moments of his parents death. His eyes filled with tears of despair and his voice began to whimper. Despite this pain he felt compelled to finish his story.

"They set fire to our house and yet somehow I escaped with my life. My mother was killed when burning roof timbers crashed down on her. I chased after the skull man intending to kill him but I couldn't keep up. If it hadn't been for one of the other villagers, my best friend who was later struck down, then I would never had made it to the river and escaped. On my way to the Tiaryer I lost control of my senses for a moment and tried to fight back, taking on one of the black knights. The scrap did not go well for me and the last thing I remember before hitting the water was the fucker's words as he growled at me through his helmet. He wanted me to know that his voice would be the last that I ever heard and that seemed to give him great pleasure."

The room fell into a chilled silence. Llyat looked in turn to each of the four who had followed his every word. He wondered if the Watch believed his tale. Perhaps if they did they would deliver vengeance for the devastation wrought upon the village of Maplehill. He pondered what he could say next that would encourage them to take up arms against those that had killed his parents and friends. Once again he felt the reassuring hand of the Grand Physician on his shoulder.

"So there you have it Lord Commander. This is proof that the Knights of Avolire are on the move again. Given the state of young master Danbury when we found him in the stables with those runes carved into his chest, it seems the Knights have forged a connection with the cult of the Death Tubaria."

"I beg your pardon for interrupting sir," uttered the youngest warrior who had so far remained silent. "In your summons you didn't reveal what the runes spelled out. Please tell us the meaning of their message."

"Young Irabo makes a good point Abrahamus," said the Lord Commander. "What did the markings say to you?"

Once again there followed a brief silence before Llyat's master spoke. During that hiatus Llyat realised who the other man was. It was the very same person who had pulled him from the waters of Tiaryer. Llyat's grief was replaced with deep gratitude for the man who had saved his life.

"From the translation I made using the book of Arcane Knowledge that I managed to procure from your father Tonousa, I did come to some basic conclusions. The runes appear to be a threat, demanding the unconditional abdication of Phauless Gylewu from the throne so that he can be replaced by one of their own. If this simple demand is not complied with, whoever is responsible will continue evoking the ritual of Kha and release unimaginable evil across the land."

"So the Realm is being blackmailed by a bunch of murderous scum from beyond the Grey Mountains," snarled Tonousa.

"It does appear so," continued the Grand Physician. "But at least that explains the motive behind the six murders."

"It may explain the motive but apart from knowing that the Knights of Avolire are sponsors of these crimes we are still no closer to finding the perpetrator," added the Commander. "The Knights of Avolire are the turds of the Realm. They are a bunch of devious shits that would stop at nothing to bring down Parandor and the rule of our Sovereign Lord. But there are many others who also carry grudge and hatred against us. There are thieves and mercenaries for hire throughout the city. This place is a cesspit of intrigue and into that pile of excrement we must now add these bastards from Avolire."

"You do indeed speak the truth Lord Commander," added the Grand Physician. "I stand corrected; there are many that would seek to bring us down."

Llyat continued to sit in silence and listen to his master. Everything that had happened to him since the death of his parents all seem connected with the work that his master was charged to conduct. This pleased Llyat for he too was a crucial part of that investigation, a witness to the horrors that the Knights of Avolire had begun amid the lands that boarded the Tiaryer. His thoughts were broken when talk returned to events that had played out in Maplehill.

"And what of the riders you sent out Brynn?" asked the Grand Physician. "Did they manage to uncover anything of significance along the Eastern Road and surrounding lands?"

"We sent many men out. One to each of the fortifications between the ocean and the grey Mountains, along the Eastern Road towards Maplehill and the other outlying villages. None however have returned as yet," replied Tonousa. "Danisun Dain, our fastest rider and Man-at-Arms, was amongst them. If there is anything untoward happening between here and the mountains then he will be the one to uncover it."

"But what about here in the Capital," added Irabo, unable to constrain his concern? "The City Watch is a mere one hundred strong. We cannot protect the Capital against all that Avolire could throw at us."

"Have you informed Lord Gylewu and Sir Byddin about this?" asked the Commander. "Maybe it is time for our Sovereign Lord and the Head of our Armies to call in those who have pledged their loyalty and banners to the defence of the Realm? Then there is the Guild of Wizards. If dark magic is being invoked to bring about the destruction of the Capital then perhaps they would be willing to come to our aid.

"Lord Gylewu is of the opinion that one within the Royal Household has manipulated events," replied the Grand Physician. "If this is true then once our forces begin to gather and prepare to move on Avolire their spy in the Court would warn our enemies. They would lie in wait to ambush us. As of this moment, only those here present know of the connection between Avolire and the cult of the Death Tubaria. Until we have more evidence to put to the Sovereign then I think it should remain that way. As for the Wizards, I would rather not get them involved. They are greedy and self-centred buggers and would want to gain more influence and power within the Citadel. I recommend that we avoid them unless we become desperate."

"But we must not let this dark magic go unchecked," snapped back the Commander. "If these threats ever become common knowledge amongst the slum dwellers there will be riots. We cannot afford to have infighting at a time like this. I say we need magic on our side."

"I would in part agree with you Lord Commander," replied the Grand Physician. "But I don't think that the wizards should be the first choice. In the light of what we know, there is another option available to us. I suggest that we ask the Bards Guild of Valameer for their assistance in this matter."

"But Valameer is at least five days away," added Tonousa Amberstone. "Even if you sent a carrier bird it would take several days to receive a response. That method is not secure for birds can be intercepted. If events move as quickly as I fear they may, then there may not be sufficient time to wait."

"Then I must set off for Valameer as soon as possible," replied the Grand Physician while once again placing his hand upon Llyat's shoulder. "I will take young Emgar with me and he can tell them his story and how he fits into our investigation."

"But if the roads are being watched by the spies of Avolire then our plans would soon be discovered," suggested Irabo. "You cannot risk travelling to Valameer on the open road and being captured by our enemies. The Watch could not allow it."

"I will do what whatever I want to young man," snapped back the Grand Physician as the force of the response caused Llyat to jump.

"Let us be calm Abrahamus," said Townsforth as he glared at his young subordinate. "Irabo meant no disrespect."

"Truly sir, I did not," said the young warrior. "What I meant to say was that we cannot let you go alone along the open road. With all the dangers between here and Valameer you will need someone to protect you and I volunteer to be that person."

"In that case, I would be glad of your service," continued old Marus. "Though the open road however is not how I would choose to travel. No, I think that if we are to reach Valameer in secret then we need to approach the town by other means."

"What do you suggest then?" asked the Commander.

"I propose that we sail up the coast on board one of the vessels that are docked in Parandor's harbour. With a fair wind it would take us perhaps four days to reach Valameer that way and if we can arrive there in secret then all the better."

Llyat's eyes lit up. While the four others continued to talk across him the thought of travelling on a boat for the first time in his life excited his senses. The positive images that such a journey conjured up pushed back against his grief and caused him to smile. The pain that had consumed his mind for days vanished as a wisp of smoke on the wind. His heart began to pound at the prospect of a journey upon the waters of the Great Ocean. For once in his short life he felt good.

"What chance is there that the City Watch could procure a vessel for this journey?" asked Llyat's master.

"I'm sure we can find one that would suit your needs," replied Townsforth. "If young Irabo is to accompany you to Valameer, then he shall not be alone in his task. I hope you will consent Tonousa to go with these brave souls on their journey across the waters. Be assured that I will continue the investigation here in your absence and will have answers for you upon your return."

"If that is your wish Lord Commander, then it shall be so," replied Tonousa without emotion.

"Good," continued the Grand Physician. "However we must not mention the link between the Knights of Avolire and cult of the Death Tubaria in any conversations from this moment forward. We need to act in secret for we cannot afford to instil panic across the Realm. I too will do my part and inform the High Council that I received a carrier bird summoning me to Valameer. I will say its content concerned the death of an old friend and that my presence is required for the reading of his will. With a bit of luck that will be enough to stop Blackfayer asking too many questions."

"Then it is settled," replied Townsforth. "We will sort out your transportation. I'm sure there will be someone willing to take you up the coast for a good price. Come Irabo and Tonousa, let us begin our preparations."

With that the Lord Commander of the City Watch bowed and left through the chamber door. Irabo and Tonousa followed in his wake. However, before he took his final step through the portal, Irabo turned back, smiled, and said;

"I am pleased to see you have recovered young man."

Then as he turned again he bumped into Heliana who entered through the door in the opposite direction

"And it's nice to see you too!" shouted Heliana after Irabo disappeared from view.

"That lot seemed to be in a bit of a rush. Have I missed something?" she added.

"No, not at all Heliana," replied Grand Physician Marus. "Just listen my dear and press your lips together for a moment. We are about to embark on a sea trip to Valameer but you must not speak of this to anyone. I will need clothes and my usual personal essentials for such a voyage. Take young Llyat here and ready my things. I shall return to the Underkeep to collect some specific items needed for the journey. That is where I will be if you need me. Oh yes, I also need to arrange for the dead collector to come and take young master Danbury's corpse away and throw it into the pits."

"Of course sir, whatever your desires I fulfil... as always," the girl replied with a knowing smile before turning towards Llyat and adding; "Come on Emgar, shift your scrawny arse, we have much work to do."

Llyat stood up from behind his master's desk and like an obedient pet followed Heliana across the room and out into the physician's bedchamber.

The room was adjacent to the one in which he had woken on his unexpected arrival in the Capital. This one differed in that were two large wooden chests, one at the foot of the bed and one up against the wall next to a large ornate wardrobe. Light from Solaris cut through the gloom and illuminated the room's contents. Llyat felt a little uneasy for there was something strange about the place, something he could not work out nor understand. It was now the fourth day since he had been reborn amid the Capital and yet it was the first time that he had ever been in his master's bedroom. Heliana had always taken full responsibility for dressing the old man and preparing his most private of chambers and a dark thought entered Llyat's head. For the next few seconds he was consumed by ideas on what additional duties Heliana carried out while he was busy elsewhere.

Llyat made his way into the centre of the room and looked towards the red woollen bed cover over which a wolf skin lay. From there he noticed a portrait that hung above the head of the four poster bed and beneath its canopy. It depicted an image of a young woman with the fairest of hair, set against the background of mighty cliff tops and a surging sea. A vast bridge spanned out across the water to a fortress built upon a rocky outcrop.

"Who is she?" he asked Heliana. "Who is this maiden so beautiful and fair?"

"That Llyat is the Lady Rakasha Marus. She is our master's late wife," replied the girl.

"She's beautiful," gasped Llyat as his gaze remained fixed on the portrait.

"Yes, she was. Our master loved her very much but we never talk about her to him. It brings up memories that he would rather remain locked in the depths of his underkeep. They are memories of betrayal so treacherous that it pains him to talk about them, even to me his most trusted confident and despite all the years that I have served him and looked to his needs."

"What happened to her?" asked Llyat. "How did she pass over?"

"They say that it was poison. An extract perhaps of the spiky fruit of the jimsonweed but I'm not sure on that. It slowed her breathing and stopped her heart. They say it was an accident and that the poison was meant for her brother Lord Selwyn Taith of Griginor but there were those who suspected that she had been murdered by her brother. There was never any evidence found to support that theory. Our master felt a great sadness at the loss of his of his wife, but an even greater anger at not being able to tie Lord Taith down to the crime. It's been many years since her death and he still hasn't moved on. I've often heard him at night after I have finished my work. He tosses and turns in his sleep, cries out her name, and then ends up waking with his sheets covered in sweat. No one ever talks to him about his loss and you should abide by that rule or else live to regret it. I should have told you sooner Llyat, if only to save you from the risk of embarrassing yourself. Now come on, we have a lot of work to do if the master is to set off on a voyage to Valameer."

Llyat helped Heliana to pack their masters chest with the various clothes that he would need at sea. There were linen shirts and woollen tunics along with several pairs of breeches that Heliana folded and then placed inside the wooden chest. Three pairs of leather boots were inserted alongside the clothes but of most interest to Llyat was the short sword in a leather scabbard that Heliana next placed amongst the shirts and tunics.

"He calls it Destiny's Song," she said once the sword had been secured inside the chest. "No one in the court knows that he still carries this family heirloom with him whenever he leaves the Citadel."

"It looks impressive," said Llyat as he admired the blade before it was finally covered by even more clothes. "Why is it called Destiny's Song?"

"Even our master doesn't know the reason behind its name. It was called that when he was given the sword by his father and it is the same name used throughout time by his many ancestors. He told me once that there was an essence of fate embedded within the sword and that he believed it was meant for some greater purpose and not just for hiding in his cupboard."

"Do mean the blade has never been wielded in anger?" asked Llyat as Heliana placed several furs inside the chest, each skinned from a different animal.

"As far as I know, it hasn't," she replied. "The old man isn't much into fighting. He may act stubborn at times but when it comes to a scrap our master has others do it for him. He prefers a battle of wits over brawn. In all of my years of service I've yet to see anyone that has been able to beat him with knowledge alone."

As the pair talked about their master, Llyat realised that he knew very little about the young woman who had cared for him and introduced him to life in the Citadel. She had become his closest and most intimate of friends in what seemed like no time at all. Others he had been able to call close, the Heyn brothers, Cleath Mark, and to some extent even Denius Castor, were now all dead. Then another feeling stirred inside. There was something about the way that Heliana smiled at him and the way that she walked, her arse swaying with each step, which made Llyat feel a deep internal warmth. It was a new sensation and one that he had never felt for any of his friends before. It was something very different and it left him feeling confused.

"Heliana, I've just realised that I know so little about you. We've been so busy working together to please our master that I have forgotten to ask you things like how old are you, where do you come from, are your parents still alive, when did you start working for Abrahamus and...?"

"Steady on Llyat!" snapped back Heliana as she interrupted the flow of questions. "For fuck's sake take a breath. I don't want you passing out on me, not when must prepare for our master's journey."

"I'm sorry. I'll try not collapse although I know that I would be in safe hands."

Llyat could not understand why he had spoken without thinking. It was as if someone sought to control his words, to make him look as dumb as the fool called Lolly. His cheeks grew rosy with embarrassment and he felt the rush of blood as it spread through his face. Before he could say more the girl smiled and closed the lid of the chest.

"It's a girl's right never to talk about her age," she said with a giggle and as she moved over to her master's bed and sat. "But because it is you, I will make an exception. I am twenty two years old and was born in the middle of winter when the snow covers the lower half of the Realm and the frost causes even the Tiaryer to freeze. I was born in the Capital, though not within the city walls. My parents died of the sweating sickness ten years ago and ever since I have been looked after by the Grand Physician. I started serving him as repayment for the care he showed me through my younger years and have been by his side ever since. And you Llyat Emgar; what about you? I know you come from Maplehill, a shit hole along the Eastern Road and that your parents were murdered by unknown assailants..."

"Avolire." replied Llyat at once. "They were the Knights of Avolire."

"Avolire? Right!" continued Heliana without a pause. "Well, I hope you can repay my answers to your questions by answering some of mine. How old are you Llyat and what did you do before you came into our lives? You seem rather shy so I'll wager that you were either a blacksmith's apprentice or a farm boy. My guess is on the latter."

"Yeah, I was a muck spreader," replied Llyat with a degree of embarrassment. "I'm seventeen years old and was born in the middle of the summer. I used to work for Chirth Hadra who owned the largest farm between Maplehill and Ashview. I tended to the cattle, planted the crops, and cleaned up the skyfawn mess after they attacked our animals."

"Well, you'll be pleased to know that there are no skyfawn in the Citadel although you may have to catch rats if asked too, especially the big fat buggers down in the Underkeep."

Heliana smiled, tapped the area of bed next to her thighs and indicated that Llyat should join her on it. Llyat understood the command and so made his way over. Within seconds of sitting upon the red woollen cover Heliana inched towards him until there was no space between the two young adults. Llyat felt fearful but it did not stop the hardness that grew within his pants.

"Do you mind if I kiss you Llyat?" asked Heliana as she turned her head and smiled.

"Err…." stuttered Llyat, unable the think.

"I've never kissed a young boy before. I used to peck my father upon his cheek whenever I said goodnight but I've never locked lips with a boy properly, you know, like a man and woman like to do; sharing tongues and the like. I am drawn to you in so many ways Llyat Emgar. Every time I see you my stomach twists and turns. It is the most strange of sensations."

"And I think ….. I feel the same Heliana," replied Llyat as his heart pounded.

"So may I kiss you?"

"Sure, but I may not be any good at it for I have never done it either. I never even kissed my parents. Kissing was not done in Maplehill."

With that said, Llyat and Heliana turned their heads towards each other and despite his intense nervousness Llyat tilted his head and leaned forwards. His lips pouted and from somewhere that he could not explain he found the courage to savour the young woman's soft ruby lips. As their mouths locked the door to the room burst open and caused both to jump up from the bed.

"Ah, Heliana I forgot to ask you……." began old Marus. "I shall be needing my books and recent notes on this journey. We will need all the knowledge of the Ancients to hand if we are going to solve this mystery of the Knights of Avolire."

After a thoughtful glance the Grand Physician looked at the couple through increasingly suspicious eyes. Llyat's thoughts began to drift again, this time to the possible consequences for himself and Heliana had they be caught flirting on their master's bed. Sensations of panic begin to surface and a sudden intense need to confess hammered away inside his head. It was perhaps good that Heliana had more control over her wits.

"Yes sir. We'll be right on it and you'll be ready to travel in no time at all."

"Good, I am so glad to hear it!" replied the old man. "Once you have finished packing my essentials, return to the servants' quarters and pack your own things Heliana for you are coming with Llyat and me on this journey. Once we are all ready and I have confirmation from the Watch that they have procured a ship, we will get Stable Master Treveyn to take us down to the docks in his horse and cart, if there are any mares left. I don't fancy dragging our belongings through piles of shit just to get to the boat."

"Of cause sir," replied Heliana as she lifted her eyes to catch her master wink.

"Oh and Llyat, one more thing..." he chunnered before leaving.

"Yes Sir?" said Llyat, hoping that the growth in his breeches was not too obvious.

"If you are going to take advantage of young Heliana, do not do it on my bed. Do it somewhere else for the last thing I want is to lie on stained sheets or wake with a hair from your groin between my teeth!"

"Of course sir," stammered Llyat without thinking.

The image was not lost on either of the couple who blushed plum red as the Grand Physician left the room. Llyat and Heliana then stood and stared at each other with their jaws wide open. Both soon burst into spontaneous laughter.

"So where were we...?" Heliana began.

The girl took hold of Llyat's hand and pulled him towards her. "Oh yes that's right. We were just about here."

Llyat's cock twitched.

14

Tonousa strode with vigour as she made for the Southern Gate. During her short journey she dodged many buckets of festering slop thrown from high above. With some difficulty she also avoided the most of the slum folk that passed her, all unwashed and with a uniform pervasive pit stink that lingered long after their passing. Her intended destination, close to the southern aspect of the City Wall, was the infamous tavern that went by the name of The Murdered Wolf. It was known by all as the place to go if you needed the assistance of the nadir of Parandor's lowlife. There it was possible to employ without questions being asked an endless supply of cutthroats and thieves, all willing to carry out any request in secret and in silence. It didn't matter what the job entailed as long as the price was right. Everything and anything could be bought from within that timber framed hovel.

Having reached the door to the evil place Tonousa heard the drunken roar that forced its way out from the flea pit. She filled her air sacks before pushing the door open and entering into the gloom beyond. After several paces into the interior Tonousa stopped to ajust her eyes amid a foreboding darkness lit by traces of light that seeped in through a couple of small dirt stained windows. The hubbub of noise fell to corpse like silence as all present, including Isambard Hotch the barkeep, turned their heads as one towards Tonousa. To a one they glared with intense intimidation as they sought to determine who had dared to enter their private den of deceit and villainy. Once her eyes had accommodated to the dark Tonousa inhaled again, summoned up all of her courage and began to return the stare of those that still chose to look upon her. Soon the scum of the Realm returned to their drinking and the level of their conversations rose once again. The muscular woman from the City Watch then made her way forward through the crowd and as she did so she scanned each and every wrinkle and eyeball as she sought out the one who could provide a sea going vessel for her use. Tonousa knew all present, some better than others, and many that she would rather not have known at all. An arm wrapped around her shoulder. Having dropped her hand to her sword Tonousa looked up to her side to see a half-naked girl of no more than nineteen summers, her head topped with golden hair, caked with dirt and grime, and missing most of her teeth. She leaned into Tonousa's body for she was barely able to stand given the vast amount of cheap spirit she that she had already consumed. The smell of her breath was enough to make even the most life hardened sailor stagger.

"Looking for a good shag..." whispered the girl who then hesitated as she realised that her hoped for customer was in fact a woman.

"No thank you," replied Tonousa as she brushed the young girls arm from her shoulder and continued with her search.

Tonousa knew from past experience that within a few seconds the unfortunate whore would soon find another willing customer. She also knew that once the low life had drank a sufficient fill they would need little persuasion to take the girl into the straw covered rooms at the rear of the tavern and take it in turns to release their pent up frustrations into all the orifices their bleary eyes could locate. It was common knowledge throughout the Capital that Isambard Hotch employed girls who were so desperate that they would carry out any sexual service to any depraved deviant at a fraction of the cost of any other establishment. The Murdered Wolf was just about as bad as a place could get. Tonousa passed the open fireplace where a small dragon like skull hung over the hearth. The glow and roar of the fire and the smell of burning wood were the only endearing features of the worst shithole in Parandor. She stood for a while next to the hearth and soon noticed Cassius Underscroft and two of his sons, both elder brothers to the murdered kitchen boy Webb. She nodded her head towards Cassius in a gesture of recognition and as the dead collector returned it Tonousa noted that the Underscroft family didn't seem to be at all bothered by the recent death of their youngest son. She smiled to herself for this was the true life of the Capital. Despite all the darkness and despair of the underclass, no one ever dwelt in the past for they knew it never helped to do so. Neither did they think about the future for it was very difficult for any of them to imagine that they had one. Each day passed as the one reality they would ever know; a present from the present.

Tonousa pushed her way through the throng and over to the solid wooden block that acted as the serving counter. It was also as the main barrier that prevented customers from helping themselves to the large casks of Blessed Beast, recycled vinegar wines, and home distilled firewater stored behind it. Once there she looked over the divide towards the bulk of a very large man. The hulk was the lump of lard that Tonousa was keen to speak with. He was built from the mould of Thinata Fullbane although much smaller by comparison. After a few minutes Tonousa managed to make eye contact with Hotch who then acknowledged her request to join her in a private discourse to their mutual advantage. The flash of a coin helped seduce the man who reeked of ale.

"We don't often get your likes in here. I don't want any trouble."

"If there is any trouble then it won't come from me," snapped back Tonousa as she sought to get that key message across. "We members of the City Watch are entrusted to uphold the peace and the laws of the Capital. We do not go around provoking trouble. It tends to seek us out."

"That is good to hear," continued Hotch. "I'm glad we spit in the same pot but I can remember the last time the City Watch called in on my business for it turned into a blood bath. Look over there, I still have the stains on the wall to show it."

Hotch sniffed with gusto, swallowed a great bolus of mucoid catarrh and at the same time pointed towards a section of the stone wall in the corner of the room. Tonousa smiled for at least The Murdered Wolf had something to remind its patrons that the City Watch were a force to be reckoned with.

"So what may I do to assist the Watch?" demanded Hotch. "Would the warrior wish for a tankard of Blessed Beast or perhaps a bottle of the finest re-bladdered wine from Valameer?"

"I'm on duty," she snarled. "What I need is information?"

"What kind do you seek? We do not sell the secrets of others to the Watch."

"I'm looking for..."

"Oi! Isambard," shouted a fierce voice from the opposite end of the counter. "How about some service down this end. My throats as dry as your mother's snatch."

Tonousa turned her head and noted that the sound had passed through the ranks of rotten teeth that belonged to a one-armed brute of a man who also carried a deep scar across his face.

I'll be with you in a minute and I'm busy just now; so fuck off," shouted Hotch after which he turned his attention back to Tonousa. "Sorry about that. I am not so well off as to be able pick and choose the scum that I let in here to drink themselves senseless."

"So I see. As I said before we were interrupted, I need information. I am seeking Ligart Highroar, the Captain of the Banshees Wail."

"I've not seen or heard from that cunt for a very long time," snapped back the barkeep

Tonousa was not convinced and sensed he was lying.

"Are you sure of that?" she challenged. "As we agreed, I do not want to want to cause any trouble for you. I could search your establishment if you do not wish to help me and then who knows what else I might find."

"I don't know where he is," stuttered the lardy lump. "I can tell you news of a band of ogre slavers lurking in the ruins of Barad Elestor, or that there is a mad hermit living in the Howling Hills. I could even tell you that there are still many undiscovered treasure filled chambers in the Barrow of Harico, but of Ligart Highroar, I haven't a fucking clue. In fact I have not seen him in months."

"Look, cut the shit," barked back Tonousa. "Either you tell me where he is or I will put more than a sprinkling of blood upon your walls. I know you spew lies out of that festering hole you call your mouth. Speak the truth before I stick one of your precious ale barrels up that great fat arse of yours."

"Look, I don't want any trouble. He made me swear not to let slip where he had made for. He threatened me with the wrath of his men and even you must be aware of the reputation of the murdering bastards that crew the Banshees Wail. Beware his First Mate; that's what they all say."

"That is the reason why I require your services," shouted Tonousa. "From the look on your face and your shifting eyes you have as good as confirmed that Ligart Highroar is somewhere inside your shit hole of a tavern. Now for the last time, tell me where the fucker is."

Tonousa watched the fat man trembled with fear for he did not know what woman from City Watch would do next. She would not have been surprised to have learned that he had already soiled his pants. As she continued to stare the man out, his eyes flickered and she followed his gaze with her own. The fearful globes had looked towards a small corridor that led off from the main hall. It was where the bug bunks and the lice infested straw mattresses lay in dismal small chambers that passed as the shagging sheds for those with a groat to spare.

"Thank you Isambard," said Tonousa as she smiled. "You have told me all that I need to know."

She turned and pushed her way through the crowd. Then as she made her way towards the corridor she heard Hotch call out and plead with her not to cause trouble. Tonousa crept into the dismal passageway and soon heard the bestial sounds of frantic copulation that came from within one of the rooms to her left. She put her ear against its wood and tuned into the grunts and expletives of the man that she had come to find, the fearsome Ligart Highroar. A warriors boot kicked open the door and Tonousa entered. A startled couple who lay on the stinking mattress decoupled in a moment of frustration. The whore grabbed at the grimy single bed sheet and attempted to cover her nakedness, after all, who ever had entered had not yet paid to look upon her quim. The man jumped to his feet and attempted to grab hold of the nearest object that he could defend himself with. Grime encrusted paws reached out to a rickety old chair and thrust it forward with no apparent concern for the naked vulnerability of his mucous smeared cock and dangling sack. Tonousa drew her sword from her side and pointed it in the direction of the man's gruesome bits.

"Ligart Highroar!"

Tonousa's voice rose above the screams of the startled whore and the protests of the man.

"What the fuck do you want?" demanded the Captain. "There had better be good reason for your intrusion. Since when has it been against the law to pay for a good fuck?"

"I need to speak to you on a matter most urgent."

"Urgent!" spat back Highroar as the as the whore continued to scream. "It had better be fucking urgent. I paid good money for this bitch and you are wasting the little time I have left with her. My balls are full to the brim and my sack will bust if you don't piss off right now."

"Finish off then, but empty your load as quick as you can," ordered Tonousa. "I'll give you two minutes to get dressed and meet me back in the tavern. Any longer and I will drag you out by your pathetic cock. Never before have I had to gaze upon such a lazy lob. It will no doubt give great amusement to all those piss heads out in the tavern to gaze down you're your inadequacies. I'm sure that you wouldn't want others to see its woeful length."

Ligart thought for a brief moment then dropped the chair that he held. He then covered his privates with both of his hands as his face flushed with embarrassment. His cock withered away to nothingness as he turned to the wailing whore beneath the sheet.

"Shut the fuck up and clear off Jaylin. I have lost my desire," bellowed Highroar.

At that insult the whore jumped off the bed and raced out of the door and into the corridor. Her more than ample bare arse bounced as if with a will of its own as she grabbed her few clothes from the floor on the way. Then Ligart Highroar turned towards Tonousa with intense rage still evident on his face.

"This had better be good," he barked. "Whore's don't come cheap."

"Get dressed and meet me outside," ordered Tonousa with authority.

The warrior of the Watch turned and walked out of the fuck pit. All the while she prayed she had avoided picking up more lice.

It did not take long for Ligart Highroar to join Tonousa in the main part of the tavern, anger at the intrusion into his debauched affairs still evident on his face. After clearing several of the customers from around a table which she commandeered for official business, Tonousa scowled into the eyes of the Captain of the Banshees Wail.

"So what does the Watch want that is so important as to drag me away from the pleasuring the hairiest whore in Parandor?" whispered Ligart so low that only Tonousa heard his words.

"I am here on a specific order from Commander Townsforth. I was sent to find you in order to procure the immediate use of your vessel. I need to take several passengers to Valameer in secret. Do not ask any questions about them for no answers will be given."

"You want to hire me to sail you to Valameer!" snarled Ligart with a great show of contempt. "You disturbed my fuck with Jaylin, one of the finest trollops Hotch has on offer, just to ask me to take you to up the coast. Could that not have waited, bitch of the Watch?"

"No, it could not," shouted back Tonousa expecting the Captain to turn nasty. "We need a ship to get to Valameer in secret and as soon as possible. You have helped the City Watch with much discretion in the past and we expect more of the same."

"And the cargo?" rasped Highroar's throat. "What of them? Who are they? I will not accept the work unless I know who I am carrying. That rule is not up for negotiation."

Tonousa for once thought before she answered.

"You will be carrying the Grand Physician of Parandor, his two servants, myself and another of my colleagues from the Watch. But as I said, this must be a watertight secret. No one must know of our journey."

"Then it's going to cost you double. Plus the price of the whore you deprived me of."

"Double?" gasped Tonousa.

This response did not come as a great surprise for secrecy always came at a cost. Tonousa pretended to deliberate for several minutes but reckoned that she would not get a better offer if she stayed and argued for hours. Finally she held out her right hand to the Captain.

"You would rob your own father if you ever managed to find out who he was. It's a deal. Let us agree on it now."

As Tonousa shook the sea swine's hand she knew that she been ripped off and had no doubt submitted to his price far too soon. Who she wondered had manipulated who in the contract that they had just agreed? She understood that she needed to pay hush money for the crew of the Banshees Wail but she also felt anxious that her Commander would balk at the deal given his limited financial reserves. But what was done was done and she had to move on. Having turned away from the Captain she failed to notice the influx of new customers that had entered the gloomy tavern.

"You will get your payment upon our safe arrival in Valameer," added Tonousa.

"You drive a hard bargain Amberstone but you have always honoured your contracts in the past. I will deliver, but just make sure you stick to your promise of coin."

"And you make sure that you do not double cross me," responded Tonousa as her voice rose to compete with the ruckus from a table in the corner; one that had just been occupied by three rough looking ne'er-do-wells.

"When are you wanting to set sail?" asked the Captain.

"Tomorrow morning at the latest. The mission we are undertaking is most urgent and we cannot delay. We must get the Physician to Valameer as soon as possible."

"We can just about get ready to set sail by tomorrow," confirmed the Captain. "Make sure all your belongings are brought down to the docks before the end of this day."

An explosion of noise forced Tonousa to take note of the commotion around the table in the corner. The largest of three cutthroats that sat and cursed was a dark haired brute that Tonousa knew only too well. Nedes Karoly was a blacksmith who also sold his services to the Thieves Guild. He was in the process of forcing the face of the ugliest of the tavern sluts onto his exposed private parts. The scab faced whore was having none of it and screamed and cursed as she sought to extricate herself from the drunkard's firm grip. Having watched the drama unfold for a minute or so, Tonousa returned her attention back to the Captain.

"I'm sorry," she said "You were saying?"

"I said," grumbled Highroar, "I will ensure that my vessel is ready to set sail tomorrow at first light. You just need to see that the others who intend to travel with you are there on time and ready to go. I cannot leave the Banshees Wail at readiness to sail too long before prying eyes begin to suspect that something is afoot. There is also the question of the tide and that will wait for no one. Because you above all others in the Watch have always honoured your price I am willing to sail with you and keep your secret, but just this once. Should you not uphold your end of the bargain then I will ensure your most precious part is pierced by every one of my crew."

"Thank you Captain for you kind thoughts," sneered Tonousa. "I will inform the Grand Physician that..."

Tonousa did not have time to finish her sentence as screams of help cut through the background noise. She turned towards Nedes Karoly while her eyes focused on the whore's distress. The sad woman bellowed to be let free from Karoly's hand which, thrust up her skirt, was attempting to pull out hairs. Somehow the sellsnatch managed to break free from the excruciating assault and span around to face her assailant. A bony fist struck the man hard on his evil and deep pock marked face. The brute fell silent as his laughter died. Tonousa wasn't the only one in the tavern to have witnessed the slut's assault on Karoly and all focused on what would happen next. Karoly rose to full height and towered over the shaking harlot.

"No one strikes me across the fucking face and lives, especially a scank faced skirt scum that's not even fit to suck my cock."

"Oh go fuck yourself you bastard! You weren't my customer," spat back the whore. "I don't give freebies to pigs like you."

Nedes reached out, grabbed the young woman by the throat, and began to squeeze the life from out of her body. Tonousa was quick to stand for she could not witness the murder of a whore and do nothing to try and prevent it for her presence was known to most still drinking in the tavern.

"Put the girl down Nedes," shouted Tonousa from across the room.

Karoly turned his head.

"Tonousa Amberstone!" he sneered. "Keep your nose out of my affairs. The issue is between me, the whore, and no one else."

"Let her go Nedes," shouted Tonousa as she transferred her hand to her sword and stood up from behind her table. "This is your last warning. Let her go."

The command had no immediate effect. Karoly stood unmoved and challenged Tonousa's authority. The brute then released his grip upon the young woman's throat which allowed her to drop to the floor and gasp for air. A second later she picked herself up and ran. Karoly then took a two paces forward and shouted for all to hear.

"Listen well you collection of bilge rats. This bitch from the Watch thinks that she can give me orders! How fucking sweet! Maybe she intends to take the whore's place beneath my cock. I'd give her a shag she would never forget. Maybe it will be the first and last she'll ever get."

"I am ordering you to stand down Nedes. This is your last warning," growled Tonousa.

"Ooh, I'm quaking in fear," laughed Karoly, as he walked forward and shouted to the watchful crowd. "What are you going to do bitch, arrest me? I'd like to see you fucking try."

"I thought you said there wasn't going to be any trouble," howled Hotch from behind his counter.

"Fret not Isambard," shouted back Tonousa. "Karoly will stand down or I will put him down."

"Ha fucking ha!" shouted the blacksmith through fat cracked lips. "What this bitch is forgetting Hotch, is that she is just a woman and I could drop her with one hand tied to my cock."

"I'm warning you Nedes..."

Tonousa forced herself to stand tall while she assessed Nedes capabilities, given his consumption of ale. She knew the man did not stand a chance against her well-honed fighting skills but it was also one of the rules of the City Watch never to reveal your true potential unless forced to do so. Keep your strengths hidden until the right moment was how she had been instructed and the words of her teacher ran loud through her memory. *'The second that your opponent is at his most confident is the time when he is most vulnerable.'* She noted that the one obvious weapon available to her nemesis was his anvil hammer, tucked in between his leather belt and tunic. But before Tonousa could say or do more, Karoly began to rant and fired off his venom towards anyone who would listen.

"All these fucking warnings! Either fight me now or piss off. Be the man you have always wanted to be. Oh, sorry, I forgot. You don't have a cock or balls where it counts, do you, slit arse?"

As quick as a flash, Tonousa unsheathed her sword and with one swift motion swung it around in a short circular movement that brought its point to rest against Karoly's throat. The sudden action had the desired effect and it stopped the brute's forward momentum. The bully fell silent.

"Now, as I was saying; you will stand down and leave this place before I cut off the friend that you are so fond of playing with. Then I will feed it to the dogs. Do you understand me?"

As no reply came Tonousa looked around the silent room and then back into the eyes of the swine before her. All she saw was the fear of a scared and simple blaggard. She smelt the strong odour of piss that came from the steaming pool around his feet and then noted the wetness at the front of his clothes. 'Fear does strange things to men, especially those with a full bladder' she thought.

"Do you understand that I mean what I say?" Tonousa barked out and she thrust the point of her sword forwards a short distance.

"Yes, yes I do," whimpered the bully who quivered with fear.

"Good. Now this is what we are going to do. We..."

Tonousa did not have time to finish her sentence before being attacked from one side. With a kind of sixth sense she span around to see one of Karoly's companions jumping towards her with his knife ready to strike. In an instant she swung out with her sword and removed the assailant's hand above the wrist. Then she whipped her blade back onto Karoly's neck. The would-be assassin fell to his knees in agony. The rustic dullard cursed every foul name that he could think of at the woman who had just parted him from his hand. With his one remaining set of fingers he clutched at his bloody stump. Pulses of crimson sprayed out from between the grime covered digits.

"Right then you bag of turds!" shouted Tonousa. "Does anyone else fancy having a go?"

In the silence that followed Tonousa looked to each and every one of the dumb struck customers of the tavern. Not one of them opened their mouths to reply. All sat or stood still and not the smallest of muscles twitched. Even the southerner, Falaz Al Hizdor, one whom Tonousa had arrested on several occasions for provoking the Watch, failed to utter a single word.

"Good, very good," she snarled over a resurgence of screams from the bleeding man. "Your friend is in a bad way. Now either you can either follow me out of this tavern and finish this in the open, or you can go and stick your friend's hand in the fire over there and seal off the wound. It's your call."

Karoly looked towards his friend, then along the blade of the sword, and back into Tonousa's eyes. Her instinct told her what the man was thinking. It would be impossible to save his friend and also fight. She was therefore not at all surprised when Karoly backed away and rushed to the aid of his comrade. There he was joined by the third of their group, the man who had sat and said nothing throughout the attack. Having paused for several seconds Tonousa then returned to her seat at the far end of the room and sheathed her sword. The chair next to her was empty. Sometime during the fracas Ligart Highroar had left the tavern. With a feeling of great frustration she made her way through the crowd of inebriates and fornicators who all moved aside as she passed. Once level with the tavern's counter where

Isambard Hotch stood rooted to the spot, she pulled a small leather pouch from out of her tunic and tossed it into his hands.

"For your trouble," she added with a wry smile as she left the gobsmacked lump behind and exited into the street.

Once outside the tavern Tonousa sighed into the bottom of her boots. Then she looked up and down the street and sought any sign of the man with whom she had just struck a contract. There was not even a sniff of the swine whose help she so needed. She could only hope and pray that the Captain would keep to his word and have the Banshees Wail ready to sail the next morning.

"Looking for someone?" asked a familiar voice from behind.

Tonousa jumped in her skin and span on her toes. There before her was Irabo Basequin leaning against the wall under the sign of the tavern.

"Fuck you Irabo! You scared me shitless. Considering what just happened to me in there I'm surprised you were foolish enough to try and spook me like that."

"I'm sorry Tonousa, I meant no harm."

"Arsehole! I could have taken your fucking head off and for what ends? Then where would we be? I would have a lot of explaining to do, that's for sure. Did you know I was involved with that scumbag Nedes Karoly?"

"Sure I did, the whole street did. So what set Nedes off this time?" asked Irabo as Tonousa tried to compose herself. "What did you do to provoke him today?"

"He was just acting like his arse ruled his head again. I'm guessing he still harbours a grudge against me for kicking him out of the City Watch. Do you recall the event? The time that he insulted the Lord Commander."

"Yes, I remember that day well," replied Irabo, "and I seem to recall he left you with great scar across your back."

It was in fact common knowledge that Nedes Karoly had left his mark and Tonousa was reminded of it every time she took her shirt off in the presence of others. None could resist commenting on the scars. Long ago she had made the mistake in reacting to words that had come from out from the swine's mouth. It had been during a particular training session that Karoly, then a City Watch trainee, had called the Commander 'a lecherous old fucker'. Tonousa had not stopped to ask why he had said it but had shouted that she would not tolerate such an insult against the most senior and respected member of the Watch. Karoly did not back down and had continued to throw out insults. Something within Tonousa then snapped and it pushed her to make her error. In her bravado she had challenged Karoly to settle the issue by combat, with real swords and without shields. The loser would, by agreement, leave the City Watch forever. During the beginning of the clash of swords the two combatants had appeared well matched but then Karoly decided to fight dirty. He grabbed a handful of gravel and flung it into Tonousa's eyes. It blinded her for a brief moment during which he swung his sword around and connected with her back. The force of the blow knocked her to the ground and left her with a deep wound in her back. It took three other trainees and Irabo to prevent Karoly from landing a second blow, one that no doubt would have been fatal. A priest who knew a little magic helped heel her wounds over time. Karoly had been arrested for breaking the strict rules of combat and once recovered, Tonousa ensured that he was evicted from the Watch. He had never set foot in the barracks again although did find work in providing a constant supply of weapons, many of which were of poor quality. Tonousa broke from her daydream.

"How long have you been standing there," she asked?

"Oh not long, just long enough to hear the shit coming from you and Karoly."

"You could have come so my aid you bastard," sneered Tonousa.

"It sounded like you had everything under control. I didn't want to spoil your sport."

After another quick scan of the street Tonousa then asked;

"Did you see Ligart Highroar leave?"

"No, sorry!" replied Irabo. "I have seen no one leave since I arrived. So you did find him then?"

"Yes, although I did have some resistance. Hotch was covering for Highroar while he was with one of his whores. I later found him and managed to procure the Banshees Wail even though I had to pay double."

"Double!" gasped Irabo "I hope the old physician has enough money to repay the City Watch."

"Me too, for all our sakes."

"Since the death of Fabius Colt, why does the City Watch have to act as the money lender? I can't see why the Royal Citadel can't put up the money?"

"You heard what the Grand Physician said," replied Tonousa. "Someone in the Court is responsible for these murders and they have a connection with the Knights of Avolire. That being the case, our journey may be of critical importance and no one must know of our plans. Come, we have much to do."

15

The caravan of knights in strange black armour, led by the one called Rhaizen, and accompanied by a number of Lizardmen, delivered the moving cage to Avolire. Methladon Heyn, captive inside its square of iron bars, had only Grovrouk the dwarf to break his isolation. All had materialised out of the blue sparking causeway known as the Rift and into the ruins of a decaying city. Spires of crumbling stone reached far into the sky and the partial remains of once mighty viaducts rose high above the ground. A thick overgrowth of vegetation covered many areas the city having commandeered the once impressive stone structures that made up the ancient metropolis. As the cage was pulled through the desolation, Methladon looked on as the inhabitants of this strange place gathered together to watch the caravan pass. There were a mixture of races from all across the Realm and the lands beyond the seas; yet all had three things in common. They were impoverished, malnourished, and beyond filthy. Amongst these pitiful folk, dressed in clothes that time had long given up on, wandered the Lizardmen of the Eastern Marsh. Methladon knew that wherever he was it was a long way from Maplehill. A woman greeted the caravan. With the most piercing ice blue eyes and pale skin she had draped herself in magnificent robes of blue and green. The flowing material clung to her slender figure and caressed the youthful body which it delighted to adorn. Upon her head she wore a circlet of white stones with the depiction of an eye where they met at her forehead. The procession stopped before the steps of the derelict church on which the woman stood. Commander Rhaizen approached her presence, fell to his knees, and dropped his gaze to the floor. From within the cage Methladon listened to the exchange of greetings between the knight and woman who outranked him.

"My Lady," he said. "We have returned."

"That I can see! Now rise my Commander and tell me, what news of the Marked of Maplehill? Did you find the traitor Rukave?"

Methladon watched in disbelief as Rhaizen rose from his knees to address the woman in charge. He struggled to understand what the words 'the Marked of Maplehill' could mean, what these people could want Rukave Emgar, the father of his best friend, and why they thought him a traitor.

"The devious Emgar has been disposed of," continued Rhaizen. "No one in Maplehill was left alive. If the Marked was amongst the fallen then he too perished along with the rest of the scum. I have brought you a sole survivor from their village, a blacksmiths son who fought well and will make an excellent slave. He may also be able to shed light on what happened to the Marked for he is the nearest we found that could fit the description of the one we sought."

"That much pleases me Commander but some confirmation of the Marked's destruction would have been more reassuring," she replied before making her way down the stone staircase to the caravan below. "And what of the Grey Keep? Does our way to the south stand unopposed?"

"My Lady," hissed the Lizardman Sslashnash as he stepped forward. "The Grey Keep of Raorick Gylewu fell as you had predicted. The pass through the Grey Mountains to Parandor now lies unguarded and is at your mercy. Our forces in the

Marsh are growing larger by the day and we will soon be ready to make an assault upon the Capital. We just wait upon your command."

"Excellent!"

The woman moved towards the centre of the caravan. Reaching the cage she looked upon its occupants with her intense blue eyes seeking out the vulnerable as an eagle would its prey.

"I am pleased to see you have also brought me the dwarf."

By the time a week had passed Methladon had become numb to his suffering. Each time the whip cracked across his back an intense pain shattered any resurgent resilience. All such times he had he screamed out in paroxysms of agony. He had felt that same pain every day since he had arrived in the deep dark caverns under a godforsaken city in the remotest region of the Realm. Each time he tried to escape or slowed the blows of his mattock upon the hard rock face, Methladon had been thrown down to the ground by the Lizardman slave master that stood watch. The whips frequent use had long since shredded his shirt and what remained of it hug precariously from his shoulders. Caked from head to toe with sweat and grime he struggled to survive within the confines of the deep mine. He had lost all track of time since arriving at his place of torture. The absence Solaris frustrated his attempts to estimate the passage of days. Life now consisted of facing the granite rock that crowded around his soul within in the low roofed caverns beneath the world of the living. His new home was lit by burning torches, scattered at random throughout the excavated tunnels and it was the most dark and dismal place in which any man could end his days. As best as he could make out he had slept seven times since the beginning of his forced labour. Each time he had been wakened by the slave master called Ssnakash. This evil reptile was in charge of a gang of seven of the many prisoners that worked the rock and who smashed away at the stone until they dropped. Ssnakash had been ordered to watch over Methladon above all others and was an exemplar of scale scum. The creature performed its duty with great relish. According to Fines Lockmeer, one of the six other prisoners who had sought to befriend Methladon on his first day in the mine, Ssnakash was just about the worst imaginable. The creature was so sadistic that it was even feared amongst its own race.

As another lash cut deep into Methladon's back he heard the beast hiss out orders to the other prisoners in his charge who had been forced to watch the flogging.

"Learn from this lesson scum or you will receive the same. You two shits, take him to his cell."

Methladon heard the others approach and was barely conscious when they lifted him from the ground and began to carry him further into the depths of the mine. Through his part closed eyes he noted the identity of two who had come to his aid. One was the dark skinned Tycus Thork and the other, a once hire sword called Lancet Dark. The pair proceed to drag the blacksmith's son through the tunnels towards a large stone construction that had been built into the rock face in order to house the prisoners. They passed a shaft that contained a wooden cage, ropes, and pulleys. The contraption provided the only means of transit in and out of the mine and its workings reminded Methladon of the Maplehill watermill. After some minutes had passed he felt the burning pain in his back begin to subside which in turn allowed what little energy he had left to return. Meth, as his fellow inmates had learned to call him, then became aware of other harrowing screams that echoed throughout the cavernous complex. They came from others being punished by the slave masters. He felt sorrow for them all but also knew that each and every one was better off than he, for they were not under the care of Ssnakash, the swine of the swamps.

Methladon's confused thoughts drifted to memories of the hairy dwarf called Grovrouk. When the cage had arrived in the city, the dwarf had been dragged away with brutal force by the bastard Nictis who had then set about beating the little creature senseless. He had thought about the dwarf often and always he wondered if it were possible that the little man had survived. Dropped to the ground within the stone workers cells Methladon winced as Lancet and Tycus pinned him to the floor, rubbed his flesh against the gavel strewn surface and inflicted further wounds upon his back. Amid the darkness of this hell, the anguished youth looked up at the haggard emaciated faces of the two prisoners who stood over him. Through his swirled confusion he heard the gruff voice of Lancet bare down upon his eardrums.

"Why did you have to answer back you fucking idiot? We've warned you many times not to cross these slave masters, so what did you go and do? Your attempt to stop young Carlia's beating was crazy, even dumber than the shits of Fallguard could ever come up with. Now we will all pay the price for your stupidity."

"Leave it be Lancet," said the one called Tycus. "The boy was just doing what we cowards would not. Be grateful that Ssnakash didn't kill the young girl."

"But why should the rest of us suffer when none of us are at fault. I say let the lad take the pain for all of us."

"Come Lancet, have you no warmth in your heart?" replied Tycus. "Have some compassion for just once in your self driven life. Your time in this hole has destroyed what little soul you were born with. The boy saved Carlia from a most savage beating that would have cost the child her life. Try and think more about others than just your own worthless hide."

"I am!" shouted Lancet. "I'm trying to keep us all alive. If it hadn't been for this dumb fuck then Crekas might still be with us. I'm pissed off with him and all the shit that his actions have dropped on us these past days. So help me Solaris, one of us is going to have to sort him out once and for all."

"Look, the poor bastard is awake and can hear you."

Through his confused and foggy thoughts Methladon felt the need to rise from the floor. An intense pain shot through his body as he attempted to roll to his right and caused him to collapse back down. He felt a burning dryness lining his throat; one so severe that it forced him to wake.

"Water!" he gasped.

"Steady lad," said Tycus. "What are you waiting for Lancet, get him some fucking water."

Methladon felt strong arms drag him upright as Lancet's footfall receded. While Tycus propped Methladon up against the wall the blacksmith's son felt yet another searing pain course though his back. Fighting hard he somehow managed to stay conscious.

"Carlia," he muttered. "Is she okay, did she live?"

"A broken arm that is all," replied Tycus while he knelt to prevent Methladon from sliding back onto the hard stone floor. "Fines has taken her to his cell and is trying to comfort the poor wretch as best he can. What were you thinking of lad?"

"I couldn't stand by and let them kill another child," said Methladon as he thought back to Maria Darcha's murder and the evil Nictis. "I had to stop them. She couldn't have survived another beating."

"I know that Meth but you may have condemned us all to march to the grave pit. None who incur the wrath of the slave masters ever survive more than a few days."

Before Methladon could say anything further the sound of approaching feet crept through the opening to his cell. He tilted his head to one side and looked to Lancet. The other had returned with a wooden cup that was full of water and which he then passed down.

"Here you go boy," grunted Lancet. "Though it's more than you fucking deserve."

"Lancet!" bellowed Tycus. "If you've nothing useful to say then keep your foul mouth shut."

The man who had once made his living selling his sword did not speak again and in that moment Methladon sensed the thoughts behind Lancet's eyes. The man would bide his time and wait for an opportunity to strike a fatal blow. Methladon stared down at the cup in his hands and the murky fluid at the bottom of the vessel. He took a gulp of the soiled liquid in the hope it had not been poisoned. He felt each and every drop trickle down his throat yet as bad as the water was it refreshed him. Once again he attempted to move. The pain from the lash marks on his back had lessened and this time Methladon managed to stand up and lean against the cold wall of the cell.

"I thank you both with all my essence," he croaked through cracked lips and across a swollen tongue. "I could never have made it back here without you. I thought I was gone for sure this time."

"We were just following Ssnakash's orders," sneered back Lancet from the room's far wall. "By the end of this day you'll wish that your miserable life had ended back there."

"Stop it Lancet," shouted Tycus. "The boy has suffered enough. We've got to get him fit enough to return to work on the rock face otherwise they will kill him for sure."

"Best put him out of his misery right now," snarled Lancet.

"Shut your mouth. I don't want to listen to any more of your shit. We need to keep focused if we are to survive whatever Ssnakash has planned for the seven of us," shouted back Tycus.

Once on his feet Methladon began to focus on the extent of his plight. It felt so much longer than the seven days that had passed since he had arrived in this most desolate of nightmares. He tried to work out how he had survived given his repeated attempts at escape and the number of subsequent and savage beatings he had received. Taking a deep breath he began to stagger towards the arched entrance to the cell, each step a little easier as his waddle turned into a slow walk. Pain passed across his back with every twist of his spine but that was not going to stop him. He vowed to remain alive as long as possible for he was determined to destroy both the Commander and the Captain of the Black Knights who had destroyed his village.

"And where do you think you're going?" snapped out Lancet as Methladon passed him.

"Back to the rock face. I'll show those scaly fuckers what a Heyn is made of."

"How many times do I have to tell you," barked the mercenary. "You are going to get us killed."

"I am not going to be crushed by them," snapped back Methladon and he stood still and turned his anger towards Lancet. "Even if I die trying I am going to get out of this shithole and I swear that I will kill anyone who tries to stop me."

"Look Meth," responded Tycus as he moved to Methladon's side and placed a hand upon his shoulder. "You haven't seen the job that Ssnakash did to your back. It's truly horrendous. Another beating like that and you will die for sure. Just keep you head down and do whatever he asks."

"And let the bastard win?" snapped Methladon. "No, never. Not while I ever breathe."

"The Lady of the Silverwynn will never let you leave Avolire."

"I have no intention of leaving," he replied. "Not while the men who slaughtered my family are still alive."

Methladon felt another surge of anger course through his body. It was a feeling the likes of which he had never felt before. Amid this intense fury the skin around the three circled mark on the back of his head burned with a great ferocity. The pain at least masked that which came from his back and all he wanted was to kill Rhaizen. He was determined to end the life of each and every one of the knights who had destroyed his life, but most of all he was consumed with the need to destroy Nictis, the man who had murdered young Maria Darcha for just crying. That bastard would be first on his list. The force of his anger would have continued to bubble up had he not been brought to his senses by Tycus who gripped his shoulder and turned him around.

"Don't be a fucking martyr lad! You will have your time for revenge. By Solaris and Mona, I promise that you will have your reckoning with the Knights of Avolire but only if you stop acting like a fool. You must bide your time and keep your head down."

"If the boy wants to go up against them then why stop him?" questioned Lancet. "At least it will be an end to his torment, after they have buggered him and then burned him alive."

"Lancet," snarled Tycus as his dark skin blanched with anger. "What did I tell you, keep your mouth shut? Leave him be. I will not allow Meth to kill himself, not while he still has strength and energy to help us in our own plans."

"If you think this dumb shit is going to help to get us out of here then you're more of a tosser than I thought."

The idea that the two were planning to use him in some way made Methladon feel uneasy. He struggled to contemplate what devious scheme they could be fermenting in their desperate minds. However, before Methladon could respond, Tycus began to expound his views.

"Look! You know the rumours are as well as I do. The Lady of the Silverwynn intends to fulfil the Enderdetag Prophecy. She seeks the one from Maplehill as well as the stones. She has gathered us here to dig for one of the lost Gems of Thamous, the Seer's Diamond, rumoured by the great Thamous to be buried deep beneath the ruins of Avolire. This lad said he came from Maplehill and I want to believe, as do others of my creed, that he could be the one foretold in the Prophecy, the one who is to lead us to our freedom."

"You cannot be fucking serious Tycus," snapped back Lancet. "That prophecy it is just a story; something to frighten small children."

"And yet the Lady of the Silverwynn searches for the Gems of Thamous," added Tycus. "Yes, Meth, I believe that you may be the one destined to bring an end to the evil that has gripped this Realm in its iron fist."

"You talk bollocks," spluttered Methladon. "I'm just a blacksmith's son. I'm nobody from nowhere. I have no power, no knowledge of spells or incantations. I'm just me."

"You are wrong Meth. I sense a strength in you that will steer us through the darkness..."

Tycus did not have the time to finish his sentence before the arrival another wretched slave who went by the name of Tansil.

"Quick, follow me," he shouted. "Sslondart's team have found something. The Lady and the Commander are coming down into the mines. Whatever they have discovered has got the Lady all lathered up."

Methladon knew that the Lady of the Silverwynn seldom visited the mines and that she always send her orders via intermediaries. There were no prisoners left alive who had ever cast eyes upon her powerful presence, except of course himself. Tansil turned and ran off and Methladon set off in pursuit as fast as his abused body would permit. Tycus and Lancet followed close behind and pushed Methladon forward whenever his pace slowed. The struggling threesome left the stone corridors and soon entered the vast rocky caverns and tunnels of the subterranean labyrinth. Methladon was struck by the frenzied excitement of the pitiful souls who worked the mines as the rumour of the discovery of something special swept through the living hell. Prisoners, slaves of all race and colour, began to shout and move towards a gully at the far end of the main cavern. Some ran forwards and others just wandered without aim in their shared belief that something significant had begun. Methladon too was desperate to understand what it was that Sslondart's slaves had found amongst the stone.

Several minutes after he had crossed the uneven floor of the cavern, lit by the flickering light of excavation torches, Methladon approached a gathering of slaves and masters. He knew at once that this was where the discovery had been made. Using his elbows to punch a hole through the collection of emaciated and foul smelling wretches he pushed his way to the edge of a deep gully and looked down into the shadows. His gaze fell upon the striking form of the Lady, flanked on one side by Commander Rhaizen and on the other by a knight that he did not recognise. The Lady was in deep conversation with a slave master and Methladon presumed it to be Sslondart. Hints of the conversation drifted up towards his ears and soon he tuned into what was being said.

"Is it true? Have they found it?" asked the Lady with affected excitement.

"Yes my Lady. The Sceptre of Urthanock has been unearthed," hissed Sslondart. "And the Seer's diamond along with it."

"Bring it to me at once," she replied.

Methladon watched from the front of the growing crowd as the Lizardman moved across to a small crevasse in the gully, reached down with his long elongated fingers and picked up something from within its dark recess. Within a matter of seconds Sslondart was upright once again and he turned to face the Lady of the Silverwynn with what passed as a reptilian smile. His hand stretched forward and he presented the Lady with a mud encrusted ornamental staff with hints of gold that glinted from underneath the grime. At the head of the sceptre Methladon could just make out a jewel that was the size of a man's fist. The Lady took the sceptre in her hands and held it high into the air. She admired it from every angle while a sinister expression formed on her face. The excited crowd was then stilled and the vast cavern fell into silence. After a minute of death like quiet during which Methladon could hear nothing but his breath as it passed over his lips, the Lady shouted aloud.

"For Avolire!" she cried as she raised the sceptre aloft into the stagnant air.

"For Avolire!" answered Rhaizen.

After another brief pause the crowd behind Methladon began to chant in unison. It started softly, in the throat of one individual, then increased in volume as each of the slaves joined in. They repeated the words of the Lady of the Silverwynn and soon the chant filled the vast cavern and echoed around its walls with an ever increasing intensity.

"For Avolire......For Avolire......For Avolire..."

As the words pounded in his ears, Methladon turned and fought his way out the mass of decrepit souls until he found Tycus and Lancet. Neither had joined in with the chant.

"Well?" asked Tycus. "What have they found?"

"You were right," said Methladon. "They have their foul hands on what they were looking for."

"You mean..."

"I do," interrupted Methladon. "The Lady herself confirms that they have found the Seers stone. Perhaps the prophecy you spoke of is real and about to be enacted."

"I take it that you're going to help us get out of here," said Lancet

"I will try," replied Methladon, "although I cannot promise anything. I may be from Maplehill but I refuse to believe I am the one mentioned in your prophecy. The first thing we should recognise is that if the Lady has found what she was looking for then she won't need slaves anymore. We must execute an escape before it is too late."

16

The pitch and roll of the Banshees Wail, tossed by the turbulent ocean swell, forced Llyat to his knees and triggered the emptying of the contents of his stomach across the main deck the aging vessel. The Banshees Wail was not a military ship, it was a caravel; a small boat built for trading across the high seas and the passage of cargo between the port towns along the length of the Realmcoast. Those who had seen the mighty vessel had always marvelled at the splendour of this maiden of the waves. Her vast wooden hull with her two strong masts from which grey canvas sails collected and held the wind was as grand as any that ventured out to sea. At the front of the ship, carved into the wood as it supported the bow sprit above, rested the imposing figure of a banshee from which the vessel had been named. The foaming waters of the ocean crashed upon the underbelly of the naked figurehead and sprayed plumes of salt water high up into the air.

While he continued to retch out the contents of his stomach Llyat's thoughts were not focused on his dreadful nausea, nor his embarrassment in front of his fellow travellers, but on the girl Heliana who just five days earlier he had fucked on the floor of his master's bedchamber. That same young woman now saw Llyat in a different light as she tried to comfort him while watching his breakfast slide over the deck and into the crashing waters below. The taste in Llyat's mouth was so rank that that he found it hard to believe that his new found love would ever want to kiss and share tongues with him again. Ligart Highroar, the Captain of the ship, had told Llyat on the second day that such sickness was quite normal for first time voyagers. He had further commented that as a young cabin boy he too had suffered from the pukes to a similar extent; but after a few days it had left him and so it would be with Llyat. It was now the fourth day at sea and Llyat did not feel any better.

Throughout the journey Highroar had spent most of his time confined in his cabin at the aft of the ship. The commands and orders to the thirteen man crew of the vessel had been shouted out by the muscular dark skinned First Mate who went by the name of Theoplous Danmar. The experienced mariner's face was as haggard and rough as the layer of barnacles that clung to the hull of the wooden vessel. This unusual man cut a dash in his crimson shirt and the half-mast yellow trousers that covered his legs. Like all sailors he did not wear shoes and this seemed somewhat strange to Llyat for he had always done so whenever his father could afford them. Despite the First Mate's sober presence Llyat could tell from the way the crew responded that Theoplous Danmar was feared by them all. Between his expulsive involuntary retching and as his head rolled from side to side across the wooden boards, Llyat observed this commanding figure who stood firm on the deck at the stern. Theoplous's feet stood directly above the Captain's quarters and were positioned behind the distinctive whale bone wheel that controlled the vessel as it crashed and forced its way through the ocean.

From his low position on the main deck and as he looked over the side of the boat Llyat tuned into the sounds of other members of the crew who sought to remain in control of the ship that seemed at the mercy of the turbulent sea. Above the noise of the crew and the crashing of the waves against the sides of the hull,

Llyat heard the sounds of metal upon metal. They were accompanied by the voices of the woman Tonousa and that of Irabo, the young man who had saved his life. Llyat turned his head to see both engaged in combat play while their blades flashed and slashed through the air. The sparing between the two members of the City Watch of Parandor had occurred each day of the sea voyage and despite his constant and intense nausea Llyat had watched the two in awe. Their movement and skills reminded him of the three Heyn brothers and in particular his once great friend Methladon. He had often watched with envy as those three youths had partaken of the training that their father insisted was necessary in order to protect their village. If Llyat hadn't felt so ill he would have asked his new acquaintances to teach him the art of the sword; it was something that he realised he would need to master if he was ever going to take revenge upon the beast who wore the skull helmet.

Another crash into the waves followed by a rapid downward pitch brought the sickness back into Llyat's stomach. His belly knotted as the retching began all over again. There was now nothing left of his breakfast in his stomach, just copious quantities of saliva that also went over the side through holes in the bulwark. This time however he felt the gentle touch of Heliana's soft hand upon his shoulder. She had stayed by his side and attempted to reassure him that all would be well. Even in the short time that he had known her he sensed there was another side to her gentle personality.

"Holy fuck Llyat," she began. "How much more shite is there in that stomach of yours?"

"Go away and leave me alone," he whimpered as he wiped traces of puke from his mouth.

"Look Llyat, you are such a twat," continued Heliana. "I'm trying to help you if you would but let me. Like the Captain said, this is a feeling that will soon pass, though I must say stuffing your face each morning with milky oats isn't going to help your guts cope."

The thought of food once again tightened Llyat's stomach. Combined with the rocking of the Banshees Wail he began to heave but this time nothing came up his gullet. His stomach was empty, his saliva had dried up, yet still his body tried to expel anything that remained inside.

"Do you want me to see if our master has any potions that could settle your innards?" Heliana asked while with a light touch she rubbed Llyat on his shoulder. "I'm sure he has some lemon, ginger, and peppermint in one of his travelling chests."

"Oh yes please, if you think that will help. I will try anything," replied Llyat as he tried to focus on one stationary point on the horizon and ignore the rolling motion of the boat.

"I'm sure it will. I saw him give those herbs to Phauless Gylewu one time in order to help him over a sickness caused by a surfeit of green lamb pie. It may do the trick."

"Yes anything; the sickness is worse than ever today!"

Then Llyat turned to face Heliana, slumped backwards onto the wooden deck and leaned against the side of the boat.

"I thank you from the pit of my gizzard."

"I'll see what I can do then," she replied. "I'm not promising that we can cure your sea pukes, but I'm sure our master will give it his best shot. Anything is better than having to watch you make such a cock of yourself."

Heliana walked away towards the cabin at the front of the boat where their master had taken up residence ever since their voyage had begun. Like Highroar, the Grand Physician had spent most of his time inside its cramped space, reading through his books and the lore. The old man had not required the services of his two servants often; only in fact when they had helped him get him ready in the mornings and when Heliana assisted him into bed each evening. Ever since Llyat had told his master and the City Watch of the destruction of Maplehill by the Knights of Avolire, he had seen a change in his master's demeanour. The old man now treated him more as a friend than a servant and gave him a degree of respect which no one had ever offered before. Despite this new and unexpected upturn in his relationship with the Grand Physician, Llyat felt compelled to continue to serve his master with total subservience. It was after all he, along with Irabo, who had changed his life for the better.

Switching his gaze from Heliana's rear, Llyat began to observe the sparring on the deck. His thoughts continued to wander. He began to think more about his master and what Heliana had told him of the Grand Physician's investigation into the death of his own wife, said to have been murdered by his brother-in-law, Selwyn Taith. In that moment Llyat felt a great sadness for his master and he compared it to his own loss. He wondered if he should approach old Marus and offer to talk with him for he too was no doubt experiencing similar pain. However, before he could think on it further, a shadow fell over him and a looming figure blocked out the rays of Solaris. Llyat eyes looked up to the imposing figure of Irabo.

"Are you surviving this day lad?" asked the young warrior.

"Yeah, I feel fucking great," sneered Llyat. "I have never been better!"

"Well, tell that to your face, it looks like shit warmed up."

"Just leave me alone," said Llyat as he felt the sickness return to his belly.

"Not until you give me your hands Llyat."

"What for?"

"You're just going to have to trust me," replied Irabo smiling.

Llyat felt unsure of the young warrior's intentions but given the motion of the boat and the waves of nausea that continued to sweep through him he felt he had no choice other than to comply. Holding his arms towards Irabo he put his trust in the hands of the young man who had pulled him out of the Tiaryer. He felt the warrior take hold of his arms above the wrists. The pressure mounted between the two bones of both of his forearms. Irabo pressed in with his thumbs while he gripped the youth's wrists with the rest of his fingers. As the discomfort grew Llyat attempted to pull back but the more he struggled the harder the warrior pressed.

"Ow!" screamed Llyat while several members of the crew turned their heads. "You're fucking hurting me."

Before Llyat could lash out with his legs Irabo loosened his grip and allowed Llyat to pull his arms back into his torso. There he cradled them across his chest while he looked at Irabo with malice. Then, before he could curse, Llyat noticed that the feelings of sickness that had plagued him for the past four days had disappeared. No longer did he want to expel his stomach contents over the side of the vessel. His belly felt settled and his head no longer spun. An expression of intense curiosity formed upon his face.

"You see Llyat," said Irabo smiling. "I told you to trust me."

"What the fuck did you do?" gasped Llyat, unable to understand what had taken place. "Don't tell me that you too can do magic too."

"I wouldn't call it magic," laughed Irabo. "It's just a little something that I was once taught. No spells or incantations, just the application of force to the sweet spots above your wrists."

"I don't know what to say! Once again I am indebted to you?"

"There isn't anything to say," continued Irabo as he then sat down with his back up against the side of the boat. "I was shown the technique by one of Heward Teulu's priests, those who serve Fatumai. He said it would be a useful skill to know if I was ever to go out to sea. He was right and here we are."

"Indeed," replied Llyat as he smiled for the first time since the voyage began. "Did he tell you that for nothing or did you have to pay a price? What did you have to give a priest in return for gaining such a skill, or should I not ask? My father often told me to beware the vices of the holy huggers."

"If you're suggesting that I allowed the old fool to bugger me then you are very much mistaken," snapped back Irabo. "Heward Teulu is not like most of the other priests in the Realm. If you must know, I gained this knowledge about three years ago. There had been many cases of a strange plague that arose in the slums surrounding the Capital. As part of the duties of the City Watch it was my job, along with two others, to help prevent any infected individuals from crossing through the western gate and into the Capital. During one particular day in the midst of the driest summer we had known for many years, and just after I had arrived on my watch, I found an old man lying slumped against the gates, caked in dirt, mud, and blood. He begged me to help and assist him in his hour of need. Upon closer inspection I saw that that the old man had been most savagely beaten and left for dead. I had to stop Karkis Snouth, the man I was paired with that morning, from finishing the old man there and then with his blade. So I made a snap decision, one that I am still proud of to this day. Instead of letting the man die from his injuries I went against the orders of Commander Townsforth and dragged him to safety behind the walls of the Capital. After a heated argument I managed to get the reluctant Karkis to assist me and we carried the old man to the Temple of Fatumai and to the care of the priests within its walls. In such times of need I would have called upon the Grand Physician for assistance but he'd gone missing and so the priests of Fatumai were the most obvious alternative choice. On our arrival they took over the care of the beaten man and helped him into their innermost sanctum where they nursed him back to health. It was for my selfless act that day that Heward Teulu asked one of his priests to reward me with something that would one day be of great use. I declined their generosity at first but the guardians of the temple would not let me leave until a gift from Fatumai had been bestowed upon me. The trick that I just used was my reward for saving the old man's life."

"And the old man?" asked Llyat. "What happened to him?"

"Ah yes, the old man," continued Irabo, "He was cleaned, his wounds dressed, and returned to full health. The day I received word that he had recovered was the same one that Grand Physician Abrahamus Marus returned to the Sovereign Keep. A feast was held that night to celebrate the last of the cases of plague and the excellent job that the City Watch had done in preventing its spread into the Capital. During the celebrations the Grand Physician announced to the Court that he had a story to tell. It transpired that the man that I had saved from death was none other than our own Abrahamus Marus. Due to his wounds, the mud that covered him, and his blood ravaged appearance, I had failed to recognise him. So it was that we became good friends. He owed me his life and he vowed to fulfil any debt that I would in the future bring before him; that is where you come in."

"What do you mean?" asked Llyat unable to put the pieces together. "I don't understand?"

"When I found you that day as you clung to a branch that floated in the Tiaryer, I couldn't just let you drown in its cold waters. After I had fished you out of the river, landed my catch, thumped upon your chest to make you breathe again, I decided that you would be the debt that old Marus would repay. In the greater plans of the goddess Fatumai, the fate of our Grand Physician was in that moment tied to your survival. There are those who say that there is no such thing as fate and that we control all our actions, but that requires no element of faith. I believe that we are all born into this Realm with the opportunity to fulfil a much higher purpose, a life course that has been predetermined. Fatumai asks us to commit to the incredible journey of life and test ourselves to our limits. Whatever our eventual fate, I am certain that it was my goddess that brought you to Parandor."

"I have never thought of such things before," replied Llyat, somewhat confused by the nature of Irabo's ideas.

However before he could think more about them the light from Solaris was blocked by second silhouette and this time a female voice rang out.

"Oh no, not that same old holy crap Irabo!" said Tonousa. "You are so deluded my friend. Fate does not control us. I am in change of my own actions and I am not governed by the whims of phantoms. My future has not been written out by make-believe gods that are best kept for children."

"See what I mean Llyat," said Irabo. "Tonousa is one of those people who are without faith. Faithless Tonousa, the forger of her own fortune!"

"I have faith," insisted Tonousa. "I just don't have the same kind of faith as you. I have faith in the City Watch and in my friends, I have faith in my own ability to make the right choices in life. I alone dictate my path and I will have none of your infantile nonsense."

"Hmmm, very interesting," said Irabo as he laughed. "I see we will need to debate this further in due course."

"Well are you going to stand here all day?" demanded Tonousa. "Solaris will not remain high for much longer and we need finish our training for the day."

"Sounds good to me but this time I have an even better idea to keep us sharp."

"What do you suggest?"

"I say we let Llyat show us how good he is with a sword," replied Irabo while nudging Llyat in the ribs with his elbow. "What do you say to that Llyat?"

"Err..."

Llyat did not know what to say. He had been taken aback by the kindness and generosity that Irabo had shown him but this last suggestion had stunned him into silence. Even though he had grown up in the shadow of the blacksmith's sons and longed to be as good a fighter as Fiat, Grophaldo and Methladon Heyn, Llyat knew the truth; he had rarely handled a sword in his life and had no skill whatsoever in using one. He had been denied the opportunity to train by his father and with such failings in the forefront of his mind all Llyat could do was blush.

"Well?" began Irabo as he turned his head to the youth. "Do you want to give it a try?"

"I suck at sword fighting," replied Llyat. "I couldn't even save my family from being murdered, that's how useless I am with weapons."

"Don't worry Llyat," said Irabo as he jumped up, a feat that was not easy given the leather armour that he wore. "The one thing I have noticed over these past few days is that you worry far too much. That is why you are so under confident. You have very little belief in your own abilities and you don't like yourself enough."

Once again Llyat's face flushed crimson. His mind raced and he thought perhaps the young warrior had another special talent, the ability to read minds.

"You concern yourself far too much about what others think of you and that's why you have as much confidence as a gnat, but don't worry lad we, will soon sort that out. Every novice has to take the first step to whatever challenge fate has chosen to put before them. Believe me, I too was once nobody, but then I learned from the best. Now come on, I insist you give it a go?"

Irabo held out an arm and helped Llyat up to his feet.

"Sure, why not," replied the quaking youth.

As Llyat stood and regained his balance on the rolling deck he closed his eyes to check that his sickness had gone. He looked out over the ocean to the landmass that passed in the east and examined it for several seconds. There he realised that over the passing of days the land had dramatically changed the further north the Banshees Wail had sailed. No longer were there flat verdant fields with patches of dense woodland scattered amongst them. Now in its place was a very different terrain. Upon and over mighty cliffs, the rock strewn harsh lands stretched upwards towards the foot of the Grey Mountains; snow-capped pinnacles that towered high up into the sky. The jagged peaks reminded Llyat of a set of teeth from the jaws of a skyfawn that he had seen once seen and inspected with a stick.

"Wow!" he gasped as the vision unfolded before him. "The mountains, they're beautiful."

"You haven't seen anything yet lad," said Irabo as he turned to face the black cliffs of the coast. "Wait until you see the Bridge of Athuna. Then you will see something truly magnificent."

"The Bridge of Athuna? What is that?"

"It's what connects the mainland to the Bards Guild...."

"I'm sorry to interrupt you two amid your sweet talk but I thought we agreed to train young Llyat in sword craft," interjected Tonousa. "Irabo, give him your blade. You are far too much of a romantic. One day it'll be the death of you."

Llyat watched as Irabo moved across the deck to the wooden structure that surrounded the main mast and where he had left his sword before initiating the cure for the ocean sickness. As the warrior moved away, Llyat's emotions surfed back in on a wave of anxiety. His thoughts were drawn to the dreadful night in Maplehill and the black Knight that had thrown him into the Tiaryer. He remembered how Denius Castor's sword had bounced off the strange armour of his opponent without leaving a scratch. Perhaps if he had been trained on how to handle such a weapon he would have made his first kill but more likely he would have died fighting. If Fatumai did dictate the fate of men as Irabo had suggested then it seems she hadn't planned his death on that night of horrendous slaughter. Llyat took the blade from Irabo and was surprised on how light it felt in his hands. He glanced up and saw that Tonousa had placed a beaten old leather helm on her head. She waited for him with her sword in her right hand, her feet spread wide and fixed as if in tar.

"Right Llyat," she began. "I want you to attack me the best way that you can. Don't worry about hurting me. The blade is of the training type, blunt and dull, but yet still useful to practice with."

Llyat looked and saw that the edges of his blade were indeed blunt. He ran his left index finger over the tip and found it devoid of a point. He then looked to his opponent who appeared ready for whatever he would do next. Llyat gripped the hilt of the sword with two hands and prepared for his first attack.

"I hope you are ready," shouted Llyat with a hint of uncertainty to his voice.

With all of the strength he could muster, Llyat charged at Tonousa. His swung his weapon up over his right shoulder and brought it down towards her head. With a fierce clash of metal Llyat felt his sword fly out of his hands. Before he could register what had happened he felt a sudden blow from the flat surface of his opponent's sword strike his back. The impact had been sufficient to knock him down onto to the deck and before he could move further he felt the dull point of Tonousa's blade push between the notches of his spine. Even though the point had been dulled it created sufficient discomfort to cause him to yield. Had it not been but a lesson he would have been dead before he had time to think. Lay face down on the salty planks he heard the laughter of the ship's crew but the person who laughed loudest was Irabo.

"Llyat!" shouted the young warrior while trying to contain his mirth. "You have without doubt failed your first lesson."

Llyat felt the sword tip lift from his back after which a hand grabbed him by the scruff of his tunic and dragged him back up to his feet. He dusted himself down while trying to hide his embarrassment. Irabo retrieved the sword from the deck and passed it back after which Llyat turned to face Tonousa. The powerful woman rotated her sword in her right hand and smiled back.

"Is that all you have lad?" she shouted while trying to provoke his anger. "I've seen children wield a sword better than that."

Llyat felt the heat of his blood and once again he readied his weapon. This time he held the sword in one hand only and moved with stealth towards Tonousa. He watched and waited for her to move first for he did not want to be so easily disarmed a second time.

"Come on, hit me!" she shouted. "We haven't got all day."

Llyat made eye contact and with a sudden jump he employed a new tactic. His blade stabbed forward in a straight line. Tonousa parried his strike but this time Llyat held onto his weapon as the steel collided. Although he was thrown off balance and fell back against the side of the boat, Llyat moved forward again and resumed his attack. This time he aimed at Tonousa's head with a wide arced swing. The warrior ducked under the blade as it passed an inch above her head and before Llyat could react Tonousa jumped to full height and kicked out. Her right boot landed on Llyat's chest and its force sent the youth sprawling onto the deck of the boat. Llyat opened his eyes as Tonousa placed the tip of her blade on his throat and pressed down. The discomfort was far worse than when the sword had trust into his back.

"Tell me lad," she began. "What are you are thinking at this moment? Don't hold back, just speak the truth."

"How much I want to hurt you and make you suffer for humiliating me," replied Llyat as the pain stung his throat, back, and chest. "I want you to feel the same agony that I now endure."

"Just as it was did all the others who have gone before you. I offer you this advice young Llyat Emgar; you think too much when you're fighting. Your first thought was to damage me, to inflict as much pain as you could on my person, prove to others how great you would be if you could take me down. It was those thoughts of power that were your downfall. You need to develop more awareness of your opponent and take time before you rush to strike. Try and work out their weakness first and above all remember that you will never be invincible. Have you got that?"

"Yeah," replied Llyat. "I think so. I need to take my time, get to know my enemy, and avoid acting out of anger."

"Exactly, you cannot be angry and conscious at the same time. Are you ready to try again?"

Tonousa removed her sword from Llyat's throat and then offered him her hand in order to prolong the lesson. The caravel ploughed forward along the coast while Llyat's training continued. Although it had only been a short session thus far, it seemed like a lifetime to Llyat. He had spent most of the time on his back looking up at the blue sky and yet his skill with the sword had much improved as time passed. After fifteen minutes he was able to stay on his feet without being forced to the deck.

"Good, good," shouted Tonousa as Llyat had managed to lay his first blow on her body. "You seem to be getting the hang of it at last."

Llyat smiled for even he appreciated the rapid improvements he was making. He also knew that he was still far from the level needed if he were to call himself a warrior. He sensed that if he applied himself to regular training and developed some self-belief, then his confidence would grow; he would then be able to face anything that his enemies threw at him. So it was that he readied himself for his next attack but now he had two to fight. Irabo had joined with Tonousa and they were both ready for their student's next move. Llyat imagined himself a knight from one of the many stories that he knew so well. He saw himself clad in the finest armour, up against a mighty foe; one twice as fierce as the dragon Xenvagen. A shout from Tonousa forced him out of his daydream and he refocused on the two warriors before him who stood in eager anticipation and ready to strike him down. Before Llyat could advance, all three were startled by a loud cough that came from the front of the boat. Llyat turned and saw Heliana behind him, her arms folded as her right foot tapped with force on the weathered oak planks. Her expression it said all and she was clearly pissed off. Then Llyat noted the vial of green liquid clutched in her left hand.

"So you're feeling better now are you?" sneered Heliana. "Or were you just pretending to be sick in order to distance yourself from me?"

"No, you have got it all wrong," protested Llyat as he realised how his sudden recovery must have looked. "I was sick, honest. Irabo knows a special trick and cured me."

"That is true fair Heliana," added Irabo. "I helped him with his sickness and then offered to..."

"Keep out of this..." snapped back Heliana "And throughout all of this play fighting did it ever occur to you to tell me that you were feeling better?"

"Of course you are right," replied the timid youth, unable to conceal his embarrassment. "I'm sorry. I should have come and found you."

"Indeed you fucking should," snapped back Heliana as she stepped forward to confront Llyat.

"I'm so very sorry. I didn't mean any offence."

"Apology accepted although I ought to slap your face for scorning me Llyat Emgar but it looks like these two have given you enough of a beating already so I will spare you the force of my hand."

Llyat attempted a weak smile and then uttered a nervous laugh. He knew he had erred and would have to try harder if he wanted to retain access to Heliana's fruits.

"I can only apologise once again," he grovelled. "I intended to come to you but I just got lost in the moment."

"Lost in the moment!" bellowed Heliana, her voice oozing venom. "Lost in the fucking moment! Don't talk such claptrap. Get your head out of the clouds and come back down to shit reality. I don't know what sort of rubbish these City Watch arseholes have filled your head with so just remember you are nought but a simple peasant from Maplehill; one who hasn't got a fucking clue about anything in life."

Before Llyat could respond to her rant, Heliana turned and flounced off towards the ladder that led to the forward updeck of the Banshees Wail.

"What was all that about?" said Llyat as he turned to Irabo and Tonousa. "What did I do?"

"Nothing my young friend," replied Tonousa while she stifled her laughter. "You did nothing wrong. Nothing at all."

"Then why did Heliana react so?"

"It is obvious that you know nothing about women," giggled Irabo. "Where they are concerned the game goes like this. You need to let your woman know that she is always right and that you are always in the wrong. There is no point trying logic for they just don't get it. Just let them have their way or your access to the sweet pot will dry up. Never try and blame a women for anything, isn't that so Tonousa?"

"Should I go after her?" asked Llyat, still at a loss as what to do next.

"Of course," said Tonousa. "Go and apologise and show her how sorry you are. Tell her how special she is to you. Even if she doesn't believe you, the fact that you say it will help. "

"I think I understand but this is fucking harder than fighting."

Llyat followed in Heliana's path over the deck of the boat and on towards the ladder that would lead him to the upper reaches of the vessel. He made his way forward past several of the crew who continued to fight to keep the Banshees Wail on its northern course. To a man they all smiled as Llyat passed and this caused his face flush again. Once on the updeck he found Heliana where the bow sprit joined the hull. She was lost in her thoughts and she looked down upon the figurehead as it crashed in and out of the waves. Llyat sensed she was crying but as soon as he stood by her side she stopped, lifted her right arm, and dried her face with the sleeve of her tunic.

"I Love you!" said Llyat as attempted to place his arm around her.

"You really have no fucking idea, do you?" she snapped back while shrugging Llyat's arm from her shoulders. "You men are all the same. Steal a girl's heart and then piss on it at the first opportunity."

"Heliana, what's your problem?" growled Llyat as his confusion turned to anger.

"Like I said, you have no idea." she replied.

"Then tell me!"

Heliana turned and as she did so Llyat softened at the sight of her eyes, still red from the tears she had just shed. When Heliana spoke there was no trace of anger in her voice, just sadness.

"Do you remember what I told you about never having been kissed by a man?"

"I think so," he replied Llyat without conviction.

Llyat tracked through his memories, back to the afternoon when he had first kissed Heliana and then taken her on his master's floor. "Yes, I remember now. You said that you had never been kissed before and that you wanted to kiss me so much."

"No Llyat," replied Heliana as she switched her gaze to the ocean. "I said I had never kissed a man before."

"You mean… you hadn't kissed a man but you had kissed a …."

"That's right Llyat, well done. Her name was Ailith. She was handmaiden to Lord Tobius Faros before his long illness and eventual death."

"I don't see what this has got..." began Llyat before Heliana cut him off.

"Llyat, just shut up and let me finish. Ailith was my secret. We met during the early years of my service with old Marus. I was so young and at the beginning of my teens. Her Lord, Faros, had summoned our master to his rooms as he had developed a great pain in his lower teeth; the few that he had left. It was during their extraction that I first met Ailith. I mean, I had passed her many times before in the Underkeep but this time I saw how pretty she really was. From then on I found myself attracted to her scent. Many times we met in secret to share our passion for each other's lips and flesh but it was a secret tryst that was destined not to last. One day Ailith was summoned to Lord Blackfayer on a matter of utmost importance and she then disappeared forever. I was left distraught at the loss of my first love and over time I began to make enquiries around the Citadel, always in secret mind you. Golda Flintwind, the handmaiden to Lady Fullbane and the trollop that was murdered, told me that Ailith had been a member of the Thieves' Guild. It seems she had infiltrated the Court with the intention of stealing from the highborn and selling her ill-gotten gains back in the slums. She had been using me to get to our master and in the sight of all the gods I had fallen for her trickery. I felt so foolish and betrayed that I vowed that I would never trust another with my heart. That is why I have been so cautious with you Llyat. Yes we have fucked but I didn't want to get too close to you in case you also betrayed me. Seeing your sudden recovery from the ocean sickness and how much you were enjoying fighting those two from the Watch brought back memories of treachery and a great anger grew inside my head."

"What happened to her?" asked Llyat.

The youth was perplexed to find that the girl he so desired had enjoyed the most of intimate exchanges with another girl. He felt jealous and yet aroused at the same time and the contents of his breeches stiffened.

"Did you ever find out where Ailith went?"

"According to Golda, she was executed in secret by Sir Richemanus of the Nightfall, the Royal Executioner. Her corpse was chopped and sent to feed the Royal Hounds. Ever since then I have had a problem trusting people who come into my life. Llyat you are the first boy that I have ever fancied. I had hoped that things would have been different."

"But you can trust me," pleaded Llyat as once again he placed his arm around her and sought to give comfort. "I should have told you I was feeling better, I know that now. I didn't realise that I was actually going to hurt you this much. I was just thinking of myself and I'm truly sorry for the distress I have caused."

"Apology accepted," said Heliana who then smiled and reached up to grasp the hand that lay on her left shoulder. Their eyes met and she laughed.

"What!" asked Llyat, confused at the sudden change in Heliana's emotions?

"Your face. It looks like those two warriors have blackened your eye.

"Oh yeah," exclaimed Llyat. "Awesome indeed!"

Following all that had happened and his struggle to understand Heliana's behaviour, Llyat had lost awareness of the many the aches and pains inflicted by Tonousa's skilled sword arm. He started to feel each one of them creep into his head but soon his attention was drawn towards an enormous structure that stretched out from the cliffs and over to a rocky island deep within the ocean.

"Wow, look at that! I wonder what that place is," said Llyat as he pointed towards the fortress on the rocks.

"That is the Bards Guild young lad," rasped a voice from behind.

Both Llyat and Heliana jumped at Highroar's sudden appearance. He too focused his eyes on the structure that connected the two land masses on the distant horizon.

"We are going at a fine pace. It should take us just another hour or so to reach Valameer if Theoplous manages to maintain our current speed."

Llyat stared out towards the Bridge of Athuna and the distant buildings at the foot of its adjacent cliffs. A wave of sadness pass through him. He so wished that his friends were still alive and that one day he could tell them of his travels. While he stood in silent reflection the waves sprayed salty water upon figurehead's breasts where it then deflected onto Llyat's face. Heliana gripped his hand and Llyat understood how much the young woman loved him.

17

Amid a dingy dusk the Banshees Wail docked alongside a swarm of small fishing boats at the end of Valameer's long pier; one that stretched out to sea beneath the black shadow of the Bridge of Athuna. The wooden wharf pointed like a benevolent giant's finger that touched and tickled the vessels that caressed its sides. The hand that held the finger, the immense wall of formidable cliffs, stood guard, ready to crush the puny boats should the whim take it. Once the vessel had been secured a further half hour passed before its passengers began to disembark and touch their feet upon solid ground. Solaris disappeared beyond the western horizon and left a cloudless sky, illuminated by Mona who took the fire god's place for yet another of her night's watch.

Stepping off the gang plank Tonousa began comparing the buildings and structures around the base of the mighty cliffs to those she knew so well in the Capital. Unlike in Parandor those of Valameer were faced with gleaming white marble which created a distinct contrast to the black surrounding volcanic rock walls. The houses were all of the same cube-like design. Their small square windows were lit up by candles from within and the overall appearance appeared surreal and somewhat magical. There was one building that stood out amongst the pack, one that was far taller than the rest and had tall towers at both of its seaward facing extremities. Tonousa assumed that the building belonged to the Lady Flurdiana, the highborn official who governed the town and was the betrothed of the Sovereign's brother.

Being her first time in Valameer, Tonousa was struck by the cleanliness of the streets and wondered how the citizens managed to maintain it in such good order. Her eye then caught the beginning of the treacherous path that snaked its way up through the rocks to the point where the Bridge of Athuna joined the main mass of the land. Only then did she realise how difficult the climb out of the sheltered bay would be. Her military training concluded that any attack from above would leave the town cut off and vulnerable for once the steep path was closed there was no other way out except via the ocean itself.

Irabo set off to procure horses and a sturdy cart in order to take the travellers up this steep trail. Tonousa offered to go with him but Irabo pointed out he had once worked in Valameer when he had journeyed south from Falahorn. He knew the ways of the townsfolk and one individual in particular who would trust him with the loan of valuable property. Besides, somebody needed to stay and watch over the old physician. Llyat was insistent that he be allowed to accompany Irabo because as night had fallen it would unsafe for a person to walk out alone. After giving Heliana a peck on the cheek Llyat ran to catch up with Irabo as the warrior disappeared among the twinkling lights and dark shadows of the town. It was with more than a little apprehension that Tonousa, Heliana, and the Grand Physician watched the youth's departure for Llyat was still far too wet behind the ears to even look after himself. He would be more of a hindrance to Irabo than a help.

The three who remained did not worry for long as in no time at all Irabo and Llyat returned as promised with a cart and two horses. The chestnut coloured steed was saddled and harnessed to the cart that it pulled. On its broad and sturdy back sat Irabo. A black mare with a white blaze upon its forehead followed at the rear of the wooden cart; led by Llyat as he demonstrated his skill in handling animals. Tonousa was both relieved and surprised that Llyat could actually be of some use. Then she remembered that he had been a farm boy and thus was used to being around creatures of the land. The two young men approached the end of the dock and as they did so Irabo shouted out to the ever patient Grand Physician.

"As promised, I have provided our means of transportation."

"Good work Irabo," replied Tonousa as she moved forward, placed her hand upon the horse's nose and caused it to stop. "I think that I shall ride to the Guild fortress with you for it seems young Llyat is skilled with the handling of horses and can look after the black one."

"That I am Tonousa," replied Llyat with pride.

"Well done Irabo," shouted the Grand Physician who sat some distance away upon the chest that contained his precious belongings. "I was worried for a moment that we would have to walk there. I don't think that Llyat and Heliana would have enjoyed carrying my possessions up that incline. The cart will serve our purpose well."

A few minutes later the horses stopped before of the old man.

"Now Llyat, would you be as so kind as to help this bag of bones up on to the cart,"

"Of course sir," answered the youth.

While Llyat moved forward to help his master Tonousa was pulled onto the back of the chestnut horse by Irabo's muscular arms. There she made herself comfortable, wrapped her arms around his muscular waist, and felt his taught muscles as they brushed against her fingertips. The two members of the Watch waited for Llyat to finish the task of loading his master's belongings. Llyat's last task was to help Heliana climb on board. Looking back towards the vessel that had brought them to the town, Tonousa noted the Captain of the Banshees Wail and his First Mate descend their gangplank and move at pace along the creaking pier.

"I see you have already found transportation," commented Highroar as he approached. "That was quick work; I am most impressed."

"Yes it was," replied Tonousa. "It shouldn't take us too long now to get to the Guild. I reckon less than an hour. By then I think we will all be in need of much rest."

"My crew and I, as much as we would like to join you, will be searching out somewhere more suitable for sea dogs to spend the night. Although we have no intention of resting," he added as his right hand rubbed between his legs and a lecherous grin formed on his face.

"Nice!" muttered Tonousa under her breath, disgusted at the Captain's contempt for women.

"I must insist that my First Mate accompanies you on your journey," added Highroar.

Tonousa looked to Theoplous who stood next to his superior.

"I couldn't vouch for his safety," Tonousa replied. "He would have to fend for himself should anything happen.

"Do not fear woman, I can take care of myself," said Theoplous while pointing to the curved blade that hung from his belt. "It would be more likely that I would watch over you!"

"And what is that supposed…" barked Tonousa.

Before she could say anything further Irabo interrupted.

"Of course you can join us, although you will have to ride in the cart with the others."

"I will lead the black horse myself and give the young one a rest," offered Theoplous. "The lad has had a rough few days at sea and it cannot be easy living a life of servitude. I value my freedom more than anything else and as an honest sailor I will not let others do my bidding. I therefore offer my service to your party but only for this evening."

"If that pleases Llyat we will accept your offer and company," replied Irabo after which he looked over his shoulder. "What do you say to that Llyat? Theoplous wants you to rest your bony arse and guide the cart for you."

"Sure, whatever!" replied Llyat, unable to disguise the relief in his voice.

"Then that settles it," said Highroar smiling. "When you return, seek me out. I will be with my crew in the Winking Ogre."

Llyat jumped up onto the cart and took his place on the hay bales next to Heliana. Tonousa and Irabo began to move forwards through the dark foreboding streets and on toward the start of the cliff side path. Theoplous followed at the rear and led his horse with demonstrable competence along the cobbled streets. Tonousa scanned the shadows for signs of danger. Unlike the Capital that she knew so well there appeared to be no signs of violence, no bodies dying in the streets, and not one single beggar with a palm outstretched. The peacefulness of the town made Tonousa feel uneasy for there was something about Valameer that just didn't seem right. She pondered as to why the town was so quiet and why it was kept in such an immaculate state. At last she concluded it had something to do with the pending nuptials of the Lady Flurdiana and Lord Raorick Gylewu. It appeared that the town was seeking to make a great impression on the two highborn who would govern it together.

While Irabo led the horse from off the cobbled streets and onto the dirt track Tonousa began to survey the path ahead and its surface triggered distant memories. The narrow trail reminded her of one of Brynn Townsforth's military exercises when he had sent her among the Howling Hills during the time of her own training. Those hills were a range of natural swellings that lay to the south of the Capital. Their distinctive crooked summits could be seen from miles around and at night when silhouetted against Mona's light gave an eerie and unsettling appearance. That however was not the reason behind their name. The hills were unique for whenever a fierce east or west wind blew through the channels created by the steep rising lands, the sounds generated by the gusts of air reminded travellers of the distinctive howls of the kulkulkath; bizarre creatures similar in shape to scorpions although as big as oxen and covered in thick hair. The slightest drop of poison from the sting at the tip of the creature's tails would result in a most agonising death.

Tonousa's thoughts continued to drift amid the distant past. It had been a regular training exercise, one that had been carried out year after year by all trainees of the City Watch. Two members were always sent out for nine days, to survive on their instincts and hunting skills, deep within the shadows of the Howling Hills. The exercise was designed to develop trust and was the last to be undertaken before a student could qualify. Its purpose was to ensure that the trainees survived through mutual help and understanding. It was as a rule an easy enough task as the Howling Hills were abundant with wildlife that could, with a limited application of common sense, be caught and used for sustenance. Fortunately there were few of the dangerous kulkulkath in that region despite the noises that could be heard upon the wind. However, things had not turned out as planned for Tonousa. A group of renegade Lizardmen, numbering no more than five, had come down from the marshland. This was most unusual as the hills were a dry and desolate place and lacked the conditions that the scale covered creatures needed to survive. The Lizardmen had attempted to kill Tonousa and her companion, Serf Jakke. They had set an ambush and then attempted to drag the trainees along a dry stream bed and into their encampment; no doubt for their cooking pot. It was just by pure chance that Tonousa and Serf had managed to escape and kill their captors.

Sometime later Tonousa's mental meanderings were interrupted as Irabo shouted out an order for all to stop moving. Her day dream had gone on for far longer than she had intended and she soon realised that the group had arrived at the summit of the cliff path. There ahead, and illuminated by Mona's glow, was the start of the awesome Bridge of Athuna. As the horse came to a standstill Tonousa peered around Irabo and whispered into her companion's ear.

"Why have we stopped? Let's just keep going. I want to experience the bridge."

"Look over there," ordered Irabo while pointing towards a gap in the distant mountain range.

"What am I looking for?" she replied.

"There above the Ivory pass. In the sky against Mona's glow. Can't you see it? It's magnificent."

Tonousa stared towards the far off mountains and saw silhouetted against Mona the shape of a great reptile in full flight.

"Is that a dragon?" shouted Llyat with great excitement.

Tonousa glanced behind to see both Llyat and Heliana standing up on the cart and staring towards the night sky. Even the Grand Physician strained his failing vision and squinted as he tried to make out the nature of the distant shadow. Theoplous stood still besides the black mare, unmoved by the creature that swept across Mona's face.

"Do you think it can see us?" asked Tonousa.

"Not at all," said Irabo laughing. "Given the size of the beast and how small it looks to us, it must be a long way off. I wager that it is beyond the Ivory Pass and well into the Dragonas."

"It is magnificent," exclaimed Tonousa as she watched the behemoth before it at last disappeared behind the mountains and into the black horizon. "In all my life I never thought I would ever get to see one."

"It's so sad that they are almost extinct," replied Irabo as he held his mount at rest. "After the fall of Xenvagen at the hands of Sir Belquin, the villages of Falahorn and Griginor vowed to protect the magnificent creatures from the swords of the knights that hunt them for the alchemists. It is said that parts of the creatures are blessed with magical properties."

"I'm sorry to interrupt Irabo," shouted the Grand Physician, irritated by the delay to their progress. "If you haven't seen the impending storm already then look to the west. There are dark clouds heading this way. I don't know about you, but I would like to be inside the Guild before Aquaris decides to take a piss."

Tonousa looked to where Marus pointed and saw the great storm gathering in the west. The sea wind was blowing the tempest in their direction but before she could agree with the old man Irabo took the reins of the horse and urged it onto the stone floor of the bridge. Behind she heard the second horse begin to move and then the cart wheels as they clattered over the hard cobbled surface.

It took a full twenty minutes to cross the vast Bridge of Athuna despite moving at a steady pace. The travellers passed over the immaculate town of Valameer way below, and then the spewing foam of the ocean. The storm continued to gather, born out of the vastness of ocean and always getting closer. On reaching the tower with its portcullis that bared the way, Irabo dismounted from the horse and allowed Tonousa to move forward on the beast's back and take hold of the reins.

"State your business," shouted a voice through one of the murder holes.

"We are members of the City Watch and Guardians of the Citadel of Parandor. We seek the wisdom of the Bards of Valameer on an important matter that threatens the welfare of the Realm," replied Irabo in a voice just as loud.

"How many are you?"

"There are six of us. We seek assistance and an audience with the Grand Musician. We bring grave tidings from the Capital."

"And that takes six of you to do that does it?"

Without warning the booming voice of the Grand Physician bellowed forth. The old man was impatient, frustrated, and fearful of the deluge that would soon fall upon his head.

"Look here friend. I am Abrahamus Marus, Grand Physician to the Sovereign Ruler, Phauless Gylewu IV. In his name, we demand an immediate audience with your master, Owasorin Fusepelt. Now, open this fucking gate!"

A moment of silence followed as the party from Parandor stood and looked at the solid portcullis before them. From her position on the horse, which she had called Glorius for want of a better name, Tonousa wondered if the next noise she heard would be the pulling of bow strings and the whistling of arrows.

"I don't like this," muttered Theoplous as his eyes flicked with suspicion.

Several minutes passed while the travellers waited in the cold night air. The weather was turning foul and the first mist from the approaching clouds began to envelop the group as if a portent of the deluge to follow. The portcullis began to ascend, inch by slow inch, and the tension within the travellers mounted. Irabo gripped the reins of Glorius and started to lead the mount towards the gate of iron. Tonousa could not imagine what they were going to find once inside the walls. Thus far, the famed hospitality of the Guild had been far less than she had expected yet being a member of the City Watch she understood the reasons behind the harsh greeting of those responsible for protection of the fortress of learning. The gatekeepers were after all just doing their job. Glorius nudged forwards and carried Tonousa under the portcullis. She noted the sound of the horse and the cart behind and the deep breaths of its apprehensive occupants. Tonousa then glanced down to her right to the man who led the black mare and she thought about Ligart Highroar and his insistence that Theoplous accompany them into the Guild. It clearly wasn't just to allow young Llyat to rest. No, there was something not right about the dark skinned First Mate of the Banshees Wail. She vowed to watch him like an owl for her instinct eroded all trust and her senses cried out for extreme caution.

Within moments of their arrival inside the stone courtyard, the vast iron doors of the main building swung open. Down the few steps that led from the entrance strode a young man wearing a red doublet lined with golden embroidery and flanked on either side by two bronze armoured Knights bearing the recognisable sigil of the Bards Guild upon their left pauldrons. The young man made his way forward to greet the travellers who had by then come to a stop in the centre of the courtyard. When he reached Irabo the man in red and gold offered his hand out in a gesture of welcome and then spoke.

"Good evening dear cold and weary travellers. My name is Dayis. I am the master who supervises entry into the Guild. I am a simple meet, greet, and treat sort of chap. What brings you all the way from the Citadel of Parandor in such a hurry and at this late hour?"

Before either Irabo or Tonousa could respond the booming voice of the Grand Physician rose over the sound of the howling wind.

"I seek an audience with the Grand Musician. I bring grave tidings from the Capital."

"And what tidings would those be?" replied Dayis as Tonousa watched him lean to one side in order to direct his comment towards the back of the cart. "The Bards Guild is a fortress and its position above Valameer offers us the highest protection. What makes you think that any of the issues that bother the Capital should be of significant concern to us here?"

"I bring grave news that the Grand Musician must hear," shouted the irritated old man. "Unfolding events that will affect everyone across the Realm. Whispers that utter a fearful name wherever they are heard. I have news of Death Tubaria."

Tonousa watched as the young master of the Guild gasped. The colour drained from his face and left it spectral grey.

"I see from your sudden pallor that you have heard such words before young man,"

The Grand Physician rose to his feet and climbed down from the cart. His old bones carried him past Tonousa and Irabo and over to the young man at the foot of the steps.

"Of course I have heard that name," stammered Dayis in an attempt to recover his composure. "Who hasn't heard of the terrors that once gripped Parandor?"

"Then you will understand the urgency of my visit. As I told your guard on the gate, I am Abrahamus Marus, Grand Physician to the Royal Citadel and I stress that I must speak with your master at once."

"But...but...but..." stammered Dayis.

"Look my lad, the next fucking butt will be the one that connects with my boot, so quit stalling and let me inside."

From her seat atop of Glorius, Tonousa winced at the crudity of the Grand Physician's words and vowed that she at least would remain professional and uphold the reputation of Parandor.

"It's not that my Lord," continued Dayis. "We have been in a state of high alert ever since another arrived several days ago. He too had talked of the impending horrors of Death Tubaria and the stirrings to the east."

"Then I must speak with this man also," snapped back the physician.

"I think you had all better..."

"If you're going to tell me to fuck off then they will be the last words that ever leave your mouth lad!" snarled the old man. "You bards are not the only ones who wield magic."

Tonousa could not control herself and she giggled. The sight of the Grand Physician arguing in the rain that now poured down in torrents was just too much to bare and it fired her sense of humour. Soaked to the skin, Irabo turned around and glared. In that moment Tonousa realised she needed to control her behaviour.

"I was going to say..." sneered Dayis, "...before you rudely interrupted me old man, that I think you had all better come inside. If your business concerns Death Tubaria then I agree that you must speak with the Grand Musician at once."

Tonousa dismounted and Irabo handed the reigns to a stable boy who had appeared from out of the shadows. Dayis and the armoured knights then proceeded to escort the cold and water sodden visitors through the large iron doors and into the imposing building. As they moved forward Tonousa tuned into Irabo's question.

"Dayis, what about our horses?" he began. "I hope your Stable Masters will look after them well for we have them on loan."

"They shall be cared for as if our own, please do not worry."

"And our belongings?" added the Grand Physician.

"I will send someone to bring them up to you."

The group walked into the hall that led to a staircase at its opposite end. Apart from the hallowed music that echoed through the air, the space through which they moved was otherwise silent. The muted students of the Guild passed like shadows and glanced for but a brief second at the strangers before dropping their heads to continue on as in a trance. The way that they conducted themselves reminded Tonousa of those who served in Parandor's Temple of Fatumai. She began to reflect on the differences between the student bards and the novice priests and concluded that there were none. Both carried themselves with an air of humility and peace and no doubt both had equal, although different, beliefs and magical practices. It was well known that both used the power of their words and music to control the minds of their gullible audiences.

Dayis continued to lead the six visitors through the torch lit hall, on up the stairs at its far end, and onto the second floor. The two Knights who had escorted them remained at the top of the stairs. Water droplets dripped off their armour and formed small puddles where they resumed their guard. After traversing the corridors of the second floor for some minutes Dayis stopped in front of a large wooden door that was set back into the left hand wall of one particular corridor. It was surrounded by an ornate arch in whose stony apex was the carved sigil of the Bards Guild. Dayis struggled for several seconds under his red and gold robe but after a short while pulled out a set of keys. He then proceeded to try several inside the door lock until he found the correct one. Tonousa meanwhile was distracted by Theoplous who seemed to watch every move that Llyat made. She became ever more convinced that the sailor was a significant threat yet she still could not put her finger on what it was about him that fuelled her anxiety. A click indicated Dayis had managed to find the right key.

"Please wait inside this room while I fetch the Grand Musician," he ordered.

"Of course," replied old Marus. "I hope he won't keep us waiting long."

"I believe he will not."

With that Dayis strode off down the corridor, turned a corner, and vanished from sight.

"What a peculiar little man," mumbled the physician.

"You also would be on your guard if six strangers turned up at your gates demanding an audience," said Irabo as he stepped into the room.

The others followed and Tonousa was the last to enter. She had waited for Theoplous to go ahead before making her move. Her intention was now to watch his every move. Suspicion gnawed away at her and she felt far from at ease. The sailor had imposed his presence on her and he would have to work hard to gain her trust. Once she had closed the wooden door Tonousa noted the strangeness of the room in which they now all stood. It was a large circular space that stretched up towards the heavens and she realised she must be in the base of one of the towers of the Guild. Apart from the wooden door they had entered through there were no other means of exit. Small stained glass windows were spaced at regular intervals around the walls which themselves were covered in bookshelves, full of curious and forgotten lore, and accessed by a series of ladders and gantries that reached ever upwards and into the distant darkness of the rafters. Light was generated by five burning torches on metal stands that were placed around the desk and chair that occupied the centre of the circular space. The hammering of the rain against the window panes continued, brought on by the storm that grew wilder as each minute passed. The room with its musty smell brought back memories of her own father's library back in Parandor.

"Now isn't this something," gasped Heliana as the sheer awe of the library stirred her emotions. Even Irabo stood speechless as he looked up at the never ending rows of dusty books.

"What did you expect?" asked the Grand Physician, seemingly the only one of the party not overwhelmed. "Did you think we would be led into the dungeons?"   "I didn't know what to expect," replied Tonousa.

She had spoken the first words that had come to mind and they were the same as those that bounced within the heads of her companions. Even the First Mate of the Banshees Wail stood astonished as his gaze moved from Llyat to scan the room. It was as if Theoplous had ever seen a library before. Perhaps that was to be expected given that he had spent most of his time at sea where there was no need for such things as books.

"A curious place," Tonousa whispered to herself before moving to the centre of the room.

"My friends, this is the safest place in the Guild," squawked Marus. "I believe that young Dayis brought us here because he knew we wouldn't draw attention to ourselves in this library. I sense Tonousa that even you picked up on how edgy that young master was when he first greeted us."

"Yes, I did notice that. Strange, wasn't it," she replied.

"They took an age to let us through," added Llyat as he leaned against a bookcase.

"Yes indeed," replied the Marus. "The Guild is on high alert and that messenger that Dayis spoke of seems to have got the musicians spooked."

"I don't like it," chipped in Theoplous. "There is something about the air in here that is foul."

"What is there to like?" snapped the old man as he turned to face the dark skinned sailor. "Remember that there have been several murders, all connected to the cult of the Death Tubaria. Each involved the deepest magic, so powerful that even the smallest amount of Masslewort can detect it. We have sailed many days to seek the assistance of these bards and are fortunate to have been granted entry by their guards and steward. Forgive me master of the sea but there is nothing at all that I like about this situation. You should be grateful to have been be given the honour of waiting with us in this most splendid library, the best that any of us will ever see."

Tonousa looked on as the Grand Physician spat out his words. Theoplous backed against the bookcase as the sentences seemed to push against him. Tonousa duly noted this strange manifestation of power and it was several seconds before the sea dog responded.

"Forgive me Sir, but I intended no offence. Why I wonder is this remote place on such a high state of alert? I do not understand it. On the journey here you often spoke to Captain Highroar about your purpose in travelling to Valameer. You told him of the murders in the Capital on numerous occasions. The drunken whoremonger was unable to keep your secrets from his crew; his lips are as loose as those of the sluts he likes to fuck. I know of your purpose here in Valameer but you do not know mine."

The room hushed as the physician and Theoplous squared up to each other. The rest of the party watched and feared where the confrontation would lead. Tonousa made eye contact with Irabo after which he mirrored her actions and placed his right hand on the hilt of his blade.

"Well, that is most revealing," sneered the physician. "So, your master cannot be trusted with secrets. No matter Theoplous, we both understand each other now."

"I respond better to Theo," replied the First Mate.

"Well then Theo the truth seeker," continued Marus. "Speak now, why did you join us on the pretext of helping young Llyat? Be open and honest, and I may yet forget your rudeness."

"A sailor hears many things, whispers from the far north, and natter from the depths of the south. From the Lotus Isles far away to the Bay of New Hope. There has been talk of sinister stirrings and the resurrection of a cursed city. Covert messages on the wind, all the way from Avol..."

Before Theoplous could finish the name, the door to the library tower opened and Dayis strode into the room. As attention switched to the young bard, Tonousa removed her hand from the hilt of her sword and once again Irabo mirrored her actions. The tension settled while Dayis stood by the door, drew a deep breath, and made ready his announcement.

"My prestigious guests," he began. "I present to you the Grand Musician of the Bards Guild of Valameer, The Most Venerable Owasorin Fusepelt!"

A second later the hunched figure of the ancient musician, wispy bearded and dressed in his finest purple robes, progressed as would a snail into the centre of the room. Tonousa calculated that the old bard must have already been close to the library as it had taken Dayis such a short time to reappear. The master musician walked with a gnarled wooden stick that supported his faltering gait. Two other men followed and took their place behind their leader. One was dressed in damson coloured robes and had a distinctive black beard clung for life on the tip of a bony chin. It complemented his long coal black hair. Wasting no time he helped the ancient one forward towards the desk and chair. This plumb coloured bard reminded Tonousa of the snake like Xix Blackfayer. She closed her eyes for one second and prayed that that he was not as venomous as his counterpart back in Parandor.

The second of the two then captured Tonousa's attention. He was a great deal younger and was dressed in fine clothes, not to dissimilar to those worn in the Sovereign's Court. She guessed that the man was not much older than Irabo but there was something about his demeanour that made him appear older than his years.

"Forgive me," croaked the Grand Musician as he shuffled forward. "My legs are giving up on me. In recent days I have had to take to using this infernal staff to support myself."

"And you've been the better for it sir," replied the dark haired man.

"Nonsense Alfraba, It's slowing me down."

"As you say!" said the dark haired man.

"Allow me," interjected Irabo who moved behind the desk, pulled out the wooden chair, and placed it in front of the old man.

The dark haired one then helped the frail old man into the chair but Tonousa's gaze was elsewhere. He eyes focused onto the second man. It was clear that he was not a student of the Guild despite the lyre that was strung around his neck. With deep suspicion she sought to assess any threat and once again her hand fell upon the hilt of her sword. Then she was distracted for a brief moment as the old man struggled to sit. Even Llyat who had become bored raised his awareness as the feeble one tried to catch his breath. A moment later his cracked lips moved.

"Which one of you is called Marus?"

"That would be me, Your Honour," replied the Grand Physician while stepping before the old Bard. "I am Abrahamus Marus, Grand Physician to our Sovereign Ruler, Phauless Gylewu IV."

"And the others, who are they and why may I ask are three of them armed?"

"The two dressed in the leathers of the City Watch of Parandor are Tonousa Amberstone and Irabo Basequin," responded the Grand Physician as he pointing towards each in turn. "The dark skinned man is Theoplous Danmar, First Mate of the Banshees Wail, the vessel which brought us here and which remains docked Valameer's harbour."

"I respond best to Theo," said the First Mate and as he placed two fingers to his forehead in the fashion of a sailors salute.

"And the child servants?" barked out the black haired man "Do they have names?"

Llyat and Helena stepped away from the library walls to join the rest of the group in the centre of the room.

"Forgive Master Peaceore," laughed the Grand Musician. "He has always had a suspicious mind but it seems that in these last few days it has increased tenfold."

"I'm sure Peaceore has his reasons," replied Marus. "But in answer to his question, may I present Heliana Pulchra and Llyat Emgar, my servants from Parandor."

"Pleased to meet you," squeaked out Heliana while she curtsied in the fashion of the Capital.

"Likewise!" added Llyat with an exaggerated bow.

"Now that we are all acquainted...What is it Dayis?"

Tonousa turned her attention to the young steward by the open door who waved his arms aloft in a state of agitation while seeking to gain the Grand Musician's attention.

"If you will forgive me masters," began the young Steward "I will leave you and see to our visitor's belongings. I will assign them chambers where later they may rest after their long journey."

"Thank you Dayis," replied the Grand Musician squinting. "You have been most helpful."

"The honour was all mine."

The man in red bowed low, turned, and then walked through the open door. The heavy piece of wood then slammed shut and a deep heavy silence fell. A moment later the ancient bard looked away from the door and back to the Grand Physician. His frail yet loud voice echoed throughout the tower and drowned out the sound of the rain that continued to pour against the library windows.

"Forgive the directness of my next question," he began. "What brings you, the Grand Physician of Parandor, to our hallowed halls along with your servants and an armed escort? Young Dayis told me that you bring tidings of Death Tubaria; is that correct?"

While the old man spoke Tonousa watched the sullen stranger with the lyre. Here was yet another for her to hold in high suspicion.

The Grand Physician was soon in full flow as he described his investigation and the reason for his visit to the Guild. He told in some detail of the murders that had occurred in the Capital, including the last, the stable boy on whose body the mysterious runes had been carved. He went on to explain how those marks pointed towards a potential resurgence of the ancient city of Avolire.

It was then Tonousa's turn to speak out. She was instructed to relay the detail of how she had been summoned to the court of Phauless Gylewu and ordered to investigate the murders; an order that had been issued against the advice of Xix Blackfayer. During her report Tonousa made sure that she covered every detail and when it looked like she could forget something important, her memory was prompted by the ever attentive Irabo. It was when Tonousa reached the part where she mentioned that a secret investigator was working for the Sovereign Lord that the sullen man with the lyre moved forward to engage with the group.

"I think it's time that I introduced myself," said the man as he moved alongside Tonousa and offered her his hand of greeting. "Allow me to make myself known to you all. I am Thias Calavan, appointed bard of the Realm, although I spend very little of my time in the Citadel. It is I who have the honour of being Phauless Gylewu's secret investigator, as you so put it. "

"You?" gasped Tonousa with surprise as she shook the hand of the sullen man. "Are you the one that our Sovereign Lord sent to the Grey Keep to question the dwarf that killed Lord Tullage?"

"Yes indeed. I am that same person," replied Thias.

As she let go of his hand Tonousa swore that she saw a glimmer of recognition form on young Llyat's face and also on that of the Physician.

"Well then," Tonousa began without hesitation. "Why are you here in distant Valameer when you should be either at the Grey Keep or back in the Capital reporting to our Sovereign Lord and his Council? What have you discovered on your travels? Did you locate the dwarf and what knowledge did you obtain from him? Did he know the name of the person who has stolen the Lore of the Dead?"

"Has the Lore of the Dead been taken?" gasped the Grand Musician while he wavered on his chair and required the assistance of Master Peaceore to prevent him from falling.

"This is also the first time that I have heard of these matters," added Marus with equal surprise. "Tonousa, why wasn't I told about this before? I thought the Lore was locked safe inside your father's library?"

"It was," flushed Tonousa, realising she had let slip a vital piece of information. "I am ashamed to report that the book was stolen from the Royal Archives some years ago."

"I think you had better start at the beginning Tonousa… and leave nothing out," commanded the Physician.

Tonousa sighed. She then recounted the story of how on the day of the discovery of the young stable boys murder, her father had informed her of the theft of Lore of the Dead, an event which itself had been kept most secret. Feeling foolish at having implicated herself and her father in the suppression of this knowledge she realised that having now spoken of it there could be no turning back. It was as if her mind road a tidal wave and leaped forward without hope of knowing where it was going. The moments that followed felt like the longest of her life.

"...So the Lore of the Dead has been taken, that is indeed unfortunate," repeated the Grand Musician with a degree of calmness embedded in his voice. "Goodness me Alfraba, and you said I was paranoid."

"I don't understand what all this means?" added Tonousa. "The pages that contained the ritual of Kha had been destroyed before the book was stolen. That act was committed by my father on the orders of Xix Blackfayer. He told me that it was done to prevent any future re-enactment of the ritual. Unless Grovrouk the Despoiler was taught the words of the ritual by Lord Tullage in the cells of the Grey Keep then there is no possible way for the cult to try and resurrect Kha."

"Thias, I think it is time to tell our guests the results of your investigation and of what you recovered from the village of Maplehill," ordered the Grand Musician.

"Maplehill!" spluttered Llyat, unable to contain his excitement. "I thought you looked familiar. Now I know who you are."

"And the same I might say of you young Llyat..."

"I'm sorry to break up this very touching reunion," interjected the irritated Grand Physician, "What did you find in Maplehill? Was it what the Knights of Avolire were looking for?"

"Let me show you," replied the Thias and he turned to address the still bemused youth.

"Llyat, behind you and hidden in plain sight there is a secret compartment where the Grand Musician keeps objects of great value and power."

"Yes, that is true. I do save some very interesting items," croaked the ancient one. "Such a cursed object needs to be locked away and this place is secured with magic. It cannot be opened in my absence, just in case any of you get any ideas of lining your pockets!"

"Llyat," continued Thias. "If you would as be so kind to bring me a book off the shelf behind you. The one labelled 'The Secrets of the Stars by Anyle Belanore'."

Tonousa watched with great interest as Llyat, despite his limited reading ability, made his way over to the bookshelf and began his search for the book that the young bard had requested. During his poke through the leather bound tomes that piled high upon the dusty shelves, Tonousa's mind went wandering. An idea came to her. Perhaps the Lore of the Dead with its passages to summon the Lord of the Underworld might contain something else in addition to the rituals that were the prime cause of her investigation. The manner in which the Grand Musician had reacted to the news that the book had been stolen perplexed her. She tried to second guess how that dreadful book could be linked to whatever Thias Calavan had found in Maplehill and she grew excited as she realised the mystery would soon be revealed. With this additional knowledge she hoped to gain a greater insight into her investigation and the identity of the serial killer that she sought to unmask.

The loud ticking and rumbling of clockwork gears brought Tonousa out from her thoughts. She looked over to where Llyat stood and clutched a thick leather bound volume. As she sought to determine the origin of the noise the image of a section of bookshelf melted away and left behind a stout wooden door which then moved forward from out of the contours of the wall in time to the clunking of gears. When it came to an abrupt halt it revealed a hidden alcove.

"Most impressive!" muttered Irabo taking his hand from off the hilt of his sword.

"You have no conception of our skills if you are impressed by that young man," said Thias "This is just a parlour trick."

"Thias!" snapped Peaceore, irritated by the delay. "Our Grand Musician will be long dead before the end of your story if you carry on at the rate of a sea cucumber. Hurry up lad."

"Easy now Alfraba," croaked the Grand Musician as he raised his hand to signal an end to the verbal sniping. "Let Thias have his moment. Remember that he delayed his departure so we must indulge him and allow him this moment to let his voice sing out."

"I thank you Grand Musician," smirked Thias; a look that did not go unnoticed by Tonousa.

"What is it that I'm looking for?" shouted Llyat.

With his back to the group Llyat fumbled his way through various objects that lined the hidden shelves. Tonousa watched on with some amusement as Thias jumped forward to intercept Llyat's right arm before it could pick up a scab infested four fingered mummified hand.

"No, Llyat!" shouted the young bard. "Do not touch it. The hand will petrify you for at least a week as you do not have the appropriate enchantments to protect you."

Tonousa giggled when Thias then slipped as he gripped Llyat's wrist. The bard fell backwards and pulled Llyat over on top of him. The fall was part arrested by the wooden shelves and for a brief moment they shook with some violence. Then as Tonousa continued to follow the comical events a small jar of dried herbs on the top of the highest shelf began to wobble. It rocked, rolled, plummeted, and then emptied its contents over the youth from Maplehill. The jar then bounced off Llyat's torso and onto the hard stone floor of the library tower. In the next instant a brilliant flash of light filled the room and Tonousa shielded her eyes to prevent being blinded.

Once the intense flare had dissipated Tonousa removed her hands from her eyes and allowed her vision to adjust to the dimming light within the tower. She looked for danger and with her fist gripped upon her sword saw that all present had been startled to the same degree.

"Llyat." shouted Marus. "You stupid moronic mathulath; what did you think you..."

The old man's rant came to abrupt halt as he glared at his young servant slumped on the floor, still with his back against the shelves. Thias sprawled in a heap, stared at Llyat with a look of complete disbelief. Tonousa gawped at the youth, half expecting him to have been turned to stone but before she had a chance to speak, Heliana screamed.

"Llyat. You're glowing!"

.

18

"Llyat!" screamed Heliana. "You're glowing; you're fucking glowing!"

Once the violent flash of light had dispersed, Thias's first thought was to cover his head lest anything further should fall from the shelves above. When that didn't happen, he like everyone else looked to the young boy from Maplehill and his jaw dropped in astonishment at what he then saw. Llyat was indeed glowing. It was an eerie ethereal light that leaked from out of his core and showed no sign that it would soon stop.

"What's happening to me?" pleaded Llyat with a whimper as he jumped to his feet and stared down at hands that poked through the ends of the sleeves of his red tunic.

"What did you touch Llyat?" demanded the Grand Physician as he tried to raise his voice over Heliana's hysterical screams. "What in the name of the gods did you put your grubby paws on?"

"I didn't touch anything! I was just knocked to the ground. I was about to take hold of that withered hand like thing when this man here threw me to the floor. That was when the powder landed on me."

"Powder!" shouted Peaceore. "Are you sure boy?"

"He is telling the truth," added Tonousa. "I swear that I saw it fall on him. It dropped from above in a glass container. There, look, you can still see where the jar smashed against the floor. That's what triggered the brilliant flash of light."

Thias looked over towards the broken shards of glass, ignored the glowing youth next to him and crawled several paces forward on his hands and knees. He reached out with his right hand and touched the remains of the herb mixture that lay amongst the glass. As he was so occupied Irabo sought to calm the hysterical girl while the two old men muttered together in anxious and hurried conversation. Thias rolled the herbs between his thumb and index finger and then switched his attention from his finger tips to the glowing youth beside him.

"What is wrong with him," shrieked the Heliana. "Is he infected? Is he enchanted? Isn't there anything we can do for him?"

"All is well Heliana," replied Thias in his reassuring manner. "Everything is going to be alright."

"But he's glowing. He's still fucking glowing."

"Am I going to die?" sobbed Llyat, breaking from his shock.

"I wouldn't think so," added the Grand Physician who then moved forward and put his arm around the glowing youth. "Death or indeed any other serious effects would have happened by now..."

"Serious effects!" sneered the dark skinned sailor. "The boy is lit up like Solaris."

"He's still glowing," wailed Heliana. "He's still fucking glowing! Please make it stop."

"Heliana please calm down," shouted the Grand Physician. "At least while we figure out what's going on and what we can do about it."

"What is happening to me?" pleaded Llyat.

Thias looked towards the occupants of the tower for in that moment he was sure that he recognised the distinctive texture of the power between his fingers.

"You must have an antidote or some counter concoction Owasorin," insisted the Grand Physician. "By the shadows of Mona's breasts, what is that stuff?"

Before the Grand Musician could croak out a reply Thias stood up, wiped the residues of dust off his tunic and trousers, and then spat out the answer.

"Masslewort. The powder that covered Llyat was ground Masslewort."

"You mean..." gasped Peaceore.

"Yes indeed Master P," continued Thias. "There is no mistake. It is Masslewort and that would mean that the glow is the Kundalish Aura. I have never seen so extreme a display."

"Will someone please talk to me!" shouted Llyat who through his self-generated light looked as pale as a spectre. "What shit is happening to me?"

Llyat began to retch. Thias looked across to Master Peaceore and the Grand Musician and knew they both had realised the significance of what had just happened; 'The Time' was now upon them. The bards then scanned the other occupants of the room, each one confused and some more worried than others. Having helped the hysterical serving girl to sit on the floor Thias decided to tell the visitors of his conclusions and all that he knew. He would have told them anyway but fate had forced his hand so sooner than he had anticipated. If as it appeared, the boy Llyat was 'the One' that they had been waiting for, then it was time to reveal that important fact to the others. Llyat also had to understand the implications of his destiny and what the Fates had conspired for him.

"Is anyone going to explain why Llyat is showing this intense degree of Kundalish Aura or are we just going to have to work it out for ourselves?" demanded Tonousa.

"Yes, I too would like to understand what is going on," grumbled the Grand Physician. "Llyat, when were you touched by magic? What other secrets do you hold?"

"I've never, ever, been in contact with magic before. Not at any moment of my life. I mean, I've seen you perform it Master on several occasions during your work and then there was the knight in the skull helmet that murdered my parents. He used it. But apart from that I've never known or seen of it."

"Then why are you displaying the Kundalish Aura lad?" asked the Grand Physician, irritated by the negative response. "You had better not be hiding anything from me. If I find out you've been lying to me young Llyat then I'll have Irabo throw you back in the river where he found you, debt or no debt."

"In all honesty sir, I'm telling the truth," continued Llyat.

Thias noted the tears that welled in the glowing boy's eyes.

"Alright lad, I believe you," replied the Grand Physician. "Others wouldn't but your emotions do not speak of deceit. I can see that you are telling the truth."

"But why Llyat?" shrieked Heliana. "Can someone please explain what is going on? This is too much to bear. He has fucked me so does that mean that I am also possessed by some strange and evil spirit? Please, somebody do something?"

"Grand Musician, is there something we could do to help the poor boy?" added Master Peaceore with a raised eyebrow.

"Perhaps," replied the Grand Musician as he stroked the hair on his face and deliberated.

"What do you suggest?" added Thias.

"Alfraba, if you would be so kind as to go and locate Master Ulthirn….Oh, and find Dayis too. We may need his help this evening after all," croaked the Grand Musician and he turned his head towards Thias. "This explosive display of Kundalish Aura is something that needs to be suppressed and Master Ulthirn knows many incantations for soothing magic. We cannot have young Llyat walking around the Guild looking like a lighthouse."

"As you wish Grand Musician," replied Peaceore after which he bowed in deference to his superior, left the room in haste, and secured the door behind him.

The tower fell silent save for the crackling sound of the torches that lit the room and the rumbling of the thunderous storm outside its walls. At last Heliana's sobbing ceased.

Each of the remaining occupants looked at each other and they waited in silence not knowing what to say next. Lightening illuminated the interior of the library and deep tremors followed a second later as the great storm broke upon the fortress of the Guild. Pellets of hail rattled hard against the window panes. The Grand Physician raised his voice to speak once again.

"While we wait for some cure for young Llyat's ailment will you please continue with your story Thias? What was it that led your investigation to the town of Valameer and what exactly did you find in Maplehill? Hurry and tell me what you discovered at the Grey Keep and what if anything came from the mouth of the dwarf. I hope to at last conclude my investigation and have the City Watch detain whoever is behind this most evil of plots?"

"Where to begin?" replied Thias.

The young bard was certain he would have to declare the knowledge he had gained over the past week, the link between the village of Maplehill and the 'One' now revealed as Llyat Emgar.

"Yes, start at the beginning," added the most ancient of the musicians. "Tell them everything."

"Everything indeed!" demanded the Grand Physician. "But first, tell me why you were so shocked when Tonousa mentioned that the Lore of the Dead had been stolen?"

Thias paused and pondered as the assembled group waited with growing impatience.

"That is as good a place to start as anywhere," began Thias. "But what I am about to tell you will throw a whole new light upon what we have just witnessed; Llyat's response to Masslewort."

"Oh for fucks sake, quit stalling and get on with it," barked the frustrated Physician.

"Starting with the Lore," continued Thias. "You need to understand the true purpose of Lore of the Dead. For those who are not familiar with it, the text is full of instructive passages, rituals, and incantations of the worst kind. If you could imagine the power that the Bards Guild possess, then multiply it one hundred fold, you would have some idea of the immense forces contained within that evil book. The Lore appears to be a central to this investigation and that is why my music masters and I appeared so shocked when you revealed that the book had been stolen some eight years ago. Even without the burnt pages that allow for the resurrection of Kha, if the book falls into the wrong hands it has the potential to bring about our doom."

"Yes.... but...." added the Grand Physician. "The Ritual of Kha has been destroyed. If the incantation has been committed to memory then it would have had to have been stolen during the time of Lord Tullage's madness. He must have committed the incantation to memory and then passed it on."

"Don't you see?" added Thias, angered by the Grand Physician's continued interruptions and speculation. "There is more to the Lore of the Dead than the ritual of Kha? Whoever is responsible for events in the Capital, and indeed the others that I am about to describe, has a most detailed and sophisticated plan. This is not just the actions of a misguided cult playing at resurrecting an ancient evil from Underworld. Something far greater is trying to force our hand?"

"What do you mean?" asked Tonousa.

"The cult itself, if it still exists, is being pulled by strings by a master as yet unknown. You are preoccupied in finding the Lore of the Dead such that you can prevent further murders in the Capital. The real power and meaning of that book is its ability, through certain other specific passages, to facilitate the opening up a portal into the Underworld itself. That would unleash an untold malevolent power upon those who managed to unseal the way between the worlds. If indeed the murders you investigate were carried out by the orders of the cult of Death Tubaria then they themselves are being manipulated for they are unaware of the true messages hidden within the pages of the Lore. The Capital and its inhabitants are being controlled by persons unknown and as yet they are hidden in the shadows."

"But what about the burning that my father spoke of?" asked Tonousa as she tried hard to follow the twists in the plot? "Why did my father and Xix Blackfayer destroy those pages after Lord Tullage's arrest and incarceration?"

"The pages contained an evil ritual that was part of the cult's first attempt at taking power," continued Thias. "But like I said, whoever is responsible for a much deeper and more devious plot is trying to distract you with a search for the Lore of the Dead. They may already possess the full contents of that evil writing. After learning of one particular passage in that cursed tome last week, and following discussions with the Guild Masters, I have to tell you that the situation we find ourselves in is far worse than any of you could ever have anticipated."

"Stop talking in riddles man," snapped the Grand Physician. "This is just speculation. Did you find out anything at the Grey Keep? Did Lord Tullage pass on any information to his cell mate or indeed anyone else there? What of Lord Raorick, brother to our Sovereign Lord? What did he have to say about Lord Tullage's death?"

"Raorick is dead," added Thias as a sense of disbelief rolled through the room.

"Dead!" gasped the Grand Physician. "How can you be sure?"

"I saw the body myself" replied Thias without hesitation. "He was slain and his corpse left to rot with the rest of his men."

The statement captured the attention of those from the Capital. Heliana gawped as she heard of events at the Grey Keep. Llyat sat beside the secret cupboard and continued to glow. The sailor scowled and furrowed his brow. Then Thias described his journey along the banks of the Tiaryer, his time in Maplehill, and his journey east through the wastelands after his encounter with the Knights of Avolire.

"You saw them on the road?" said Llyat. "You saw them before they attacked my village."

"Yes I did," said Thias, turning his head to face the young boy. "They murdered an innocent man, a farmer I think. Took his head clean off his shoulders with a blade like no other I have seen. Even their armour seemed different. Lighter, more stylish, and easier to move in. It was made of a metal that…"

"Yes, yes, yes," interrupted the Grand Physician as he sought to regain control over Thias's ramble. "So you are telling us that the Knights of Avolire took out Lord Raorick and the rest of the Grey Keep."

"Please sir, let me finish. It wasn't the Knights of Avolire that murdered our Sovereign Lord's brother…"

Thias then told of his encounter with Sir Cristofre Randle, his subsequent duel with that knight, and the discovery that the dwarf called Grovrouk the Despoiler was missing form his cell.

"So who let the dwarf go?" asked Tonousa. "Or perhaps abducted him?"

"Amongst the dead, littered over the flagstones of the courtyard inside the Grey Keep and scattered amongst our own dead, there were others. Their blood defiled the ground where our people lay rotting."

"Who dammit?" exclaimed the Grand Physician.

"Lizardmen!" replied Thias without emotion. "Lizardmen of the Eastern Marsh."

Thias watched out of the corner of his eye as the dark skinned sailor dropped his hand to the hilt of his blade. He then scanned the eyes of all who had listened to his words. There he saw doubt, fear, and intrigue etched upon their faces. Tonousa was the first to respond.

"What in the name of the gods the do the Lizardmen want with Grovrouk the Despoiler? I don't see the connection."

"Before I could question Sir Cristofre on what had happened, he transformed before my eyes," continued Thias. "I mean, the man I thought was Sir Cristofre. He was a changeling, one of the Lizardmen shamans who had lain in wait should anyone venture upon the Grey Keep. We fought long and hard and in the last moments of that foul creature's life it hinted that the dwarf was in possession of the arcane knowledge needed to bring about the resurrection of Kha. It denied being associated with Death Tubaria and told me that I was far from understanding the twists and turns of events that we here tonight seek to understand."

"Did you ever find the dwarf?" asked Tonousa. "Was he still alive?"

"Alas I couldn't find any trace of the little man and I wasn't going to follow the Lizardmen into the marshlands alone and without help. I had a choice to make, either to return to the Capital with this news, or travel over to Valameer to seek the assistance of the bards. I chose Valameer."

"So now we have the Eastern Marsh as well as Avolire to contend with."

"I beg pardon for interrupting," stuttered Heliana and as she steadied herself. "But there is one obvious fact that you seem to have missed out of your story. Why is Llyat glowing like this? Is it something to do with what you found in Maplehill or the Lore of The Dead that you've mentioned?"

"Ah, that is where things get more interesting," answered Thias as he make his way back to the secret shelves of the Bards. "I went to Maplehill with the intent of seeing if an old friend. I wanted to know if he still possessed an object that had been linked to the previous activities of Death Tubaria. To my good fortune he still had it and so the cursed object became mine. I realised then that the goddess Fatumai had blessed me; given me a push towards the dark days that are to come."

"By the gods you're enjoying stringing this tale out," barked the Grand Physician.

Old Marus grew ever more frustrated as each second passed. His face turned blood clot red and for a brief moment Thias thought that perhaps the old man's head was about to pop.

"If you knew what I had discovered then you would also be afraid to reveal it."

"What did you come to own?"

"This!"

Thias then reached forward and from amongst the clutter of the dusty shelves he pulled out an emerald encrusted golden dagger and held it forward for all to see.

"Is that what I think it is?" gasped Tonousa. "Is that the Dagger of Kha?"

"Yes Tonousa, you are correct," replied Thias.

"I'd know that cursed object anywhere," she added. "Ten years ago, during the chaos that Lord Tullage brought down on us, the dagger was found by a young lad who the cult then tried to kill. Because this foul object has resurfaced it confirms that those who follow Death Tubaria are responsible for the recent murders."

"That's what I thought too until I arrived here and showed it to our Grand Musician. Then I learned of something far worse."

"Bears bollocks!" snapped back the old Physician.

"He speaks the truth," croaked the Grand Musician before old Marus could spew out further expletives. "In the week that young Thias has been back at the Guild he has carried out extensive research into this dagger on my request. We have discovered a connection between the cult of Death Tubaria, the Dagger of Kha, and the Lore of the Dead. All link together around the impending conjunction of Enderdetag. It leads us to one possible conclusion. We believe that the Lore contains more hidden and dangerous writings than the ones supposed to have been destroyed. In fact Tonousa, some of us do not believe your father destroyed it."

"So what else does the bloody book contain then?" barked out Marus.

"Please Abrahamus. Enough of the interruptions," croaked the Grand Musician who then rose to his feet and gestured towards Thias. "If you don't calm down I will instruct young Thias to play his lyre and put you to sleep for an hour or so. Believe me, I am serious."

Thias looked towards the Grand Physician who stood with his mouth wide open. The bard then nodded in the old man's direction and tapped upon his lyre. Despite his inner anger the Physician lowered his head with as much humility he could muster.

"Forgive me Owasorin, I meant no disrespect."

"You're apology is accepted my old friend," replied the musician as with considerable effort he lowered himself back into his chair. "Now if we may continue."

"Yes, please do," grumbled Marus.

"It appears that from young Thias's research, information that complements my own knowledge of history, prophecy, and religion, we can conclude that amongst the incantations and spells that the damned book contains is the disguised description and location of the lost Gems of Thamous," continued Fusepelt.

"The Gems of Thamous!" squealed Marus in disbelief. Tension flowed from his muscles to the point that he almost dropped with shock.

"Sir, are you well?" shouted Heliana as she rushed past Irabo to her master's side. "Are you in pain? Tell me what I can do? Should I can go and find the relevant remedy? Tell me which one will help."

"I'm fine, do not fuss so Heliana," replied old Marus as he supported himself on the young girl. "It's just that I thought that he spoke of the Gems of Thamous."

"I did," snapped back the Grand Musician.

"I don't understand," said Heliana. "What are the Gems of Thamous?"

"Come on hog head," shouted Llyat from his place near the wall. "Even I know what that they are, despite living all my life in a shit hole.....What's happening to me now? Why is everyone staring at me again? Am I changing into something inhuman?"

"No young Llyat," added Thias with a smile. "It appears that you are now back to your normal self. You have lost your radiant glow."

"Really?" responded Llyat. "Thank fuck for that!"

Before Thias could comment further Heliana raced from her master's side, flung her arms around her lover and embraced him. Then she planted her mouth upon Llyat's, forced her tongue into its wet opening and kissed him with great passion. A few seconds later she pulled away and began to slap Llyat across the shoulder. With each blow Llyat recoiled further back into the wall.

"What the hell is this about?" he shouted between slaps.

"For being so bloody stupid," raged Heliana. "You could have killed yourself with that stuff. For fuck sake it's like on the Banshees Wail all over again. I won't let you end up like Ailith, I just won't."

"Let's return to our investigation, or we may never get to bed this night," ordered Tonousa.

"I agree," added the Grand Physician. "With the great storm raging outside I want to conclude our investigation before we turn in for the night and prepare to leave tomorrow. If, as suggested, the Gems of Thamous have something to do with the murders in the Capital then I would sleep easier once that theory has been dismissed as idle speculation."

"But what are the Gems of Thamous?" asked Heliana as she faced the centre of the library.

"I think we should let young Llyat tell us," added Thias. "Being so fond of old stories he should be able to describe what they are and how they link to the Death Tubaria."

All turned to look at the young man who stood against the wall. Thias contemplated whether this poor simple soul could ever understand the ramifications of his destiny; his link to the shadows and whispers of evil that now threatened to engulf the Realm. Then the bard's thoughts turned to the Dagger that he still clutched in his hand and he began to wonder how different things would have been if his friend Vostag Heyn had not taken possession of it after the attempted murder of his young son Methladon. However, before Thias could get deeper into his thoughts Llyat began to speak. Words flowed with a softness at first but then got louder as his confidence grew.

"From what Denius Castor once told me, the Gems of Thamous are five distinctive jewels. They are dragon gems that when brought together can either open the door to the Underworld or seal it forever. Castor told that it was a farm boy who had brought down the mighty Urthanock and sealed his body deep within the Underworld, but I was deceived. Heliana showed me the window in the Citadel and confirmed that Urthanock had been defeated by Sir Raulyn the Grand using an axe called Fortune's Edge. You remember don't you Heliana, my first day in the capital?"

"Llyat, please stick to the point, there's a good lad," ordered the Grand Physician.

"I'm sorry Sir, I got caught in the moment by my memories. The gems, or dragon stones, according to the songs and tales that I heard back home, were cracked open under intense fire and the darkest of magic was then poured into their centres. I never understood how that could happen but what I do know of such things? Denius Castor told me that the person who did this knew that a day would come when a great evil would seek to reunite them and force open the door to the Underworld. I thought it was just an old legend and never once believed it could happen for real."

"Very good Llyat," added Thias after the youth had finished his tale. "You seem to have covered all that is important about the origin of Thamous's Gems."

"I'm sorry," shouted Tonousa, her voice trying to compete with a deafening clap of thunder from high above the tower. "Thias, I must have missed something. You have just said that Llyat had covered the origin of these gems. Where did they come from, or wasn't I paying attention? Please confirm their origin."

"I agree with Tonousa," added the Grand Physician. "Llyat's story was short on facts. Please explain in more detail."

"Very well then, and to put it in the simplest of ways," continued the young bard. "The Gems of Thamous were created amid dragon fire, spewed out from the belly of one of the greatest of beasts ever to roam the Dragonas. They were forged by the mightiest of dragons, the Great Thamous himself."

"Wyvern!" added Irabo before could Thias continue.

"I'm sorry," said Thias as he span around. "What did you say?"

"I said wyvern."

Thias was not the only one present who was taken aback by Irabo's remark. Even Theoplous who had been skulking in the shadows looked at Irabo with suspicion.

"I think you are mistaken my friend," responded Thias. "According to my research this past week, the legends all point to Thamous being a dragon. The beast is the one creature still alive that knows the location of the gems, except perhaps whoever has possession of the Lore of the Dead."

"Well I tell you now that your research is flawed," replied Irabo.

"I knew it!" sneered the Grand Physician. "We have a fucking expert in our midst."

"You misunderstand my motive behind the correction," continued Irabo. "I cannot confirm that the gems are involved in this chain of events but I can confirm that Thamous is a wyvern and not, I repeat, a dragon."

"And how do you know this for certain?" asked Thias as his face grew ever more sullen. "Whatever this young man from the City Watch of Parandor knows, now is the time to tell it. There must be no secrets and no holding back."

"I was born in Falahorn," continued Irabo. "As some of you will know it is the town just to the north of the Ivory Pass?"

"Of course I know of Falahorn," replied Thias, frustrated at yet another distraction.

"My family, before they died, were friends with those who were sworn to protect the creatures that live in the Dragonas. It was from them I learned of the wyvern Thamous that lives within those desolate and barren lands."

"And why are you choosing to tell us this now? How is it important?" replied Thias.

"With all that has happened this evening I felt it important that we were as accurate as possible with the facts," added the warrior. "After seeing Llyat glow like candles in the Temple of Fatumai, and on hearing the unexpected revelation of the events at the Grey Keep, I felt it best to clarify the nature of the beast."

"You did right Irabo," added the Grand Physician. "But now is not the time or place to argue on the differences between a wyvern and a dragon. Anyway, I am sure that everyone present knows what they are."

"I don't!" said Heliana.

"Well, it is all to do with..." continued Irabo, before the old man interrupted him.

"Like I said Irabo, there are more important things to discuss right now. Please Thias, do continue. Can you explain why you think the Gems of Thamous are connected to the murders in the Capital and what do they have to do with the Dagger of Kha?"

"Oh isn't that obvious?" replied Thias as he turned and held aloft the emerald encrusted relic for all to see. "This blade is more than just a dagger. It appears that the cult did not realise what they had in their possession..."

"Stop talking in sodding riddles," demanded the Grand Physician.

"I'm sorry, it's becoming something of a habit of late. What I mean to say is that the dagger itself has no significance at all. It is the largest of several emeralds embedded in the hilt that is important, for it is one of the five. One of the lost Gems of Thamous."

"Bullshit!" roared the old physician.

"I'll forgive that interruption Abrahamus, as long as it your last," croaked the Grand Musician. "One more and I will ensure that young Thias carries out my threat to silence you with his strings. Now young Calavan, please continue. Tell them what else you have found out."

"Of course sir; at once. I have studied the documents that cover the Prophecy and the Gems. With the help of Master Ulthirn I managed to identify the potential locations of three of the five. The first is now in our hands. It is the emerald set into the Dagger of Kha. Another is reputed to be hidden somewhere back in Parandor. It is a ruby cut into a heart shape and last reported to have been made into a pendent. The third was set into the head of a golden staff, a sort of sceptre. Furthermore, we believe it last surfaced as a gift from Sir Raulyn the Grand to someone who hailed from Avolire. That was a very long time ago.

"It is called the Sceptre of Urthanock," added Theoplous and in that moment Thias realised that he had ignored the sailor's presence.

"Where have you heard of it?" asked Thias, turning to the First Mate of the Banshees Wail.

"As I was telling my companions before the Grand Musician arrived," began Theoplous, "I have heard many a rumour rising up from across the distant shores of the Realm. They talk of the ruined city of Avolire and the army that is massing in the north. The Knights of Avolire, it is said, have joined forces with the Lizardmen of the Eastern Marsh under one single banner. I am a son of the Lotus Isle and my people do not often bother ourselves with the problems of the Realm of Phauless Gylewu. From the stories that I have heard in the taverns along the coast I have accumulated knowledge that may aid your investigation. I have also heard rumours of a great recruitment of men, sucking them in secret behind Avolire's cause, whatever that may be. It is also said that in the mines deep below Avolire's ruins, slaves are being forced to search for a magnificent diamond. It is the Seer's Stone that those who now control Avolire seek to use for their own ends."

"Thank you for that information," said Thias in response. "What was your name again?"

"Theoplous, but I answer to the name of Theo."

"Well Theo the sailor, you have confirmed something that we had ourselves deduced from the tomes. The Seer's Stone is in all probability buried somewhere beneath the ruins of Avolire but it concerns us that those who dwell in that city are seeking the Gems of Thamous. If you have any idea who commands their ranks, then please do enlighten us for it will help bring an end to our mystery."

"In all the stories that I have bought with the promise of beer or strong spirit there was always the same name mentioned. It was the one constant in all tales and it was the name of a woman. She goes by the title of the Lady of the Silverwynn."

"The Silverwynn!" gasped the Grand Physician. "Now there is a name I haven't heard for many a year."

"I am sorry sirs," asked Llyat. "Please forgive my ignorance. I have tried to learn all the names of those that live in the Royal Citadel but that is one name I have not heard before."

"Likewise," added Tonousa. "That person is unknown to the City Watch. Abrahamus, please tell us who this Lady is, and what the Silverwynn are."

"At least this is something I can answer," smirked the Grand physician, a gesture which didn't go unnoticed by Thias. "The Silverwynn is not a creature, nor is it a location or object. Silverwynn is a surname. It is the ancient name of a family that was once prominent in the lands to the north east, beyond the far edge of the Dragonas. If our mysterious seafaring friend is referring to the Lady of the Silverwynn, then he must mean Sanura of Calistorn. Have any of you heard of that place?"

Tonousa was the first to answer.

"Yes, I know of it. That was the city that tried to break away from the Realm and establish its own independent rule. I remember a story Danisun Dain once told me when I first joined the Watch. Way back in time when that town was in open rebellion against the rule of the Gylewu family, our current Sovereign's great, great, great, whatever, grandfather Malistaire sent a regiment of knights to Calistorn and destroyed the city."

"That is true Tonousa," replied the Grand Physician. "It is said the slaughter was great, that the family of Gylewu was cursed and will be punished for their deeds throughout all time."

An intense lightening flash lit up the tower. It was followed without pause by a crack of thunder that rattled the windows in their frames. As the rain poured down Thias looked to each of the seven occupants of the room, all attempting to assimilate the information that had been brought before them. Thias's thoughts turned to the Prophecy of Enderdetag and the question of whether it was playing out in front of his eyes. Then the Grand Musician spoke from his chair.

"So, The Lady of the Silverwynn is commanding the Knights of Avolire and those who side with them. This is grave news indeed."

"She must have found solace within Avolire," continued the Grand Physician. "The traitorous scum were always looking for someone to champion their cause. She must still hold great hatred towards the Gylewu family for their role in the termination of the Silverwynn line. At least we now know who is responsible for the murders in the Citadel."

"Do we?" asked Tonousa with a look of great surprise. "We now understand that the Lady of Silverwynn is involved in some way looking for Gems of Thamous, but as far as I can work out we are still no nearer knowing who is killing the good people of Parandor. As I explained in my report, Lady Thinata Fullbane and Cassius Underscroft of the Thieves Guild believed that someone inside the Court was peddling illicit substances. That I now see is a likely ruse to hide our murderer's true motives."

"It's not just the Lizardmen and Knights of Avolire that cause me concern," added Theoplous. "There have been sightings of other creatures moving across the Realm. Skyfawn are increasing in numbers along the eastern coast. Kulkulkath have been seen north of the Howling Hills and in the mountains surrounding the Ivory Pass. There have also been hints of ogres moving close to the Dirmark."

"That, I also have heard," replied Tonousa. "It was something that has troubled me ever since Hotch of The Murdered Wolf made mention of them being seen in the ruins of Barad Elestor. I had put it down to beer fuelled fantasy but it does seem that we must now accept that evil forces are being massed against us. We need a plan and we need to act with haste."

"What concerns me right now is how fate has caused us to all converge on the Bards Guild on this thunderous night," continued Thias. "It is as if we have all been brought together for a purpose. I can understand why I am here, and you and your escort Abrahamus, but with you Theoplous I struggle to work out the reason for your presence. You said that you had important information but you have yet to reveal your true intentions."

"Those are my thoughts as well," added Tonousa. "At first it seemed you were concerned over the welfare of the two young servants but I have noticed that you have been watching Llyat like an owl over the field ever since we arrived in Valameer. Speak the truth behind your plans."

Thias watched as Tonousa placed her hand back on the hilt of her sword. Irabo mirrored her action and it seemed that a fight was inevitable.

"Yes, I have been watching the lad," glared the sailor as he too rested his right hand his sword. "It is he alone that I am interested in for he is the 'One' I have been sent to find. My people, the men and woman of the Lotus Isle, believe in the Prophecy of Enderdetag; the 'End of Day's alignment'. Our astrologers have studied the stars and followed the teachings of Anyle Belanore. They predict an imminent conjunction in the heavens. I was supposed to consult with the Grand Musician on this matter and confirm my findings within the Orrery of the Guild. Never had I expected to overhear my Captain talk of a boy that came from Maplehill on the very boat that was taking me to Valameer for my hoped for meeting with you bards. The more I watched the lad, the more I became convinced that young Emgar is the One."

Thias turned towards Llyat who once again stood transfixed in a state of bewilderment, his pallor highlighted by another flash of lightening. It was obvious to all that the simple sailor who had attached himself to the Grand Physician's retinue knew much more than he was willing to divulge. Thias focused his attention on Llyat, as in fact did everyone else. The events of the last hour had been too much for the youth and his eyes rolled into the back of his head. Llyat fainted and fell to the floor with a thud.

19

Four slaves were forced into the wooden elevator on route to the surface. Only then could they begin to understand the mechanics of the contraption that had raised them from the mines. The cage had four strands of thick rope, one attached to each of its corners. Those four where then brought together and wound to create one thick rope that ran up through a series of pulleys before being attached to a very large wheel. The wheel itself was joined to the wall of the ruined building. Trapped within its circle was the most hideous creature that Methladon had ever seen. It was a grotesque beyond description and a most inhuman beast. Its bearded and wild haired head appeared disproportionately large for its body and its mottled grey skin gave it a stone like appearance. The linen cloth around the creature's waist offered limited protection as its cock rubbed against the central hub of the wheel.

"In the name of Solaris; what is that thing?" said Methladon as he was pushed forward by Ssnakash.

"What's the matter boy? Haven't you ever seen an ogre before?" replied Tycus.

"Never!" replied Methladon as the conversation continued. "I've heard stories of them but I never believed them to be real. I didn't think I would ever see one. They are repulsive."

"And they may find your form revolting, just as I do," hissed Ssnakash. "Believe me boy, before the end of today you are going to see a whole menagerie of creatures, some of which you would not believe possible, even in your nightmares. The fools that dwell south of the Grey Mountains have no idea what is coming for them."

"What do you mean?" asked Methadone.

"Shut up and keep moving. The Lady of the Silverwynn waits for you."

It was the first time that Methladon had seen the light of day since his arrival in Avolire and it took a while for his eyes to adjust to the brightness cast by Solaris. Forced to march through the crumbling streets of the once proud city Methladon soon recognised the very same spot where he had first seen the Lady of the Silverwynn when she had welcomed back Commander Rhaizen and his troops from their mission south of the Grey Mountains. It was to that very place that he and his fellow captives were taken. On route to the old church Methladon saw much that stimulated his curiosity. There were armoured Lizardmen patrolling the streets alongside knights in black armour. Skyfawn clustered around the spire of yet another crumbling church. Then in the shadows he saw several large scorpion like creatures, caged and tormented by a second hideous ogre. It was clear that something most evil was taking root in Avolire. Hideous beasts were indeed gathering.

The imposing hall of the ruined church, unlike the mines of Avolire, was almost devoid of activity. While the underground was a mass of confined sweat soaked humanity, a colony of ant like slaves imprisoned and watched over by a swarm of Lizardmen, the great space of the ruined church seemed empty in bleak contrast. Through its ancient stones Methladon was forced to walk by his tormentor Ssnakash until he reached the main chamber of the ruined building. He squelched through deep puddles of water that covered the uneven stone flagged floor; pools that had collected in long worn away footholds following one of Aquaris's discharges from on high. The liquid of life had found its way through the part collapsed rib-vaulted ceiling of the once great edifice and having no natural run off it had accumulated on the worn stone. Methladon sought to assimilate his immediate surroundings although each time he stopped he was forced on by Ssnakash. The youth could not help but wonder at the amazing architecture. In his mind he imagined the hall in its original state, with its pews filled with the devotees to some ancient god or other, praying for a better life, free from torture and the plagues that returned like clockwork. No doubt they too would have wished for abundant resources, benevolent leaders, and other such fantasies. He looked upon the smashed and defaced statues set at regular intervals into recesses and which depicted the important ancestors of those who had once ruled this part of the middle world. The wanton destruction made Methladon both sad and angry at the same time. He could not understand why anyone would allow such a once great city to fall derelict.

"Keep walking scum," hissed Ssnakash as Methladon felt another blow upon his back.

"I'm fucking moving!" winced the blacksmith's son through gritted teeth while he sought to catch up to the three other wretches in his group.

"I thought I told you keep your head down!" exclaimed Lancet as Methladon drew alongside and stepped over yet another grey gecko that scuttled before his feet. "I hate theses little fuckers. They swarm around here like rats... Meth, you've got to stop being such a pillock; you're going to get us all killed if you carry on like this. You attract far too much attention and have been singled out by the masters. I will not suffer any further punishment on your behalf."

"Says one who sells his sword for a few groats," added Tycus. "You mercenaries are all the same. You'll do anything if there is a sniff of money to be made but as soon as the going gets difficult or the money flow dries up, then your true nature reveals itself."

"Silence scum!" bellowed Ssnakash as he cracked his whip. "You're purpose here will be revealed soon enough. Until then, keep your worthless mouths shut."

Methladon and his fellow slaves had no idea why they been brought to the surface from the depths of the mines for the Lizardman had offered no explanation. Neither had the black knight who had brought the order. It had been a week since the slaves had discovered the Sceptre of Urthanock and every day since that moment groups of prisoners had been taken to the surface. Once taken above, none ever returned and the number of slaves was starting to noticeably dwindle. Methladon had tried to engage with Ssnakash on this observation but each time he had opened his mouth he had felt the sting of the lash. It always took the form of at least three strikes across his naked back while two of his fellow prisoners were forced to hold him down. Methladon's defiance did not make sense to most of his fellow prisoners. Lancet and Tycus had tried to talk sense into him on numerous occasions but that just made Methladon more determined to find out what had happened to the ones who had disappeared.

The companions in misery had already lost two others from their team during the week that had followed the sceptre's discovery; crushed in the process of shifting a heavy rock fall. Despite Urthanock's rod having been found, the remaining slaves had been forced to continue to work the mines and recover whatever minerals could be used to fund Avolire's cause. There was one other who had just been allocated to Sslondart's team and he was a most pitiful wretch. On several occasions Methladon had tried to befriend the fair haired man but had was always been met by a wall of silence. This walking skeleton carried on as best it could despite its prolonged state of starvation. Many times Tycus and Lancet had commented on the sad loner's lack of life time and that Methladon should not concern himself with one so near to death. Lancet wished for the man's release, if only to end his suffering, but Methladon disagreed and that opened a rift between the two of them. The blacksmith's son felt that all life was precious and that no matter how weak a person became it was their duty to resist the call to death and their oppression by others. *'No man should ever be forced to live as a slave'* became the driving force behind Methladon's drive to survive. They needed, he had said in his own words, *'to stand firm and resist moving into the black'*. Lancet had continued to argue and remind Methladon that his continuing attempts to escape would get them all killed. Such disagreements always ended with Tycus breaking up the fight between the two frustrated protagonists. Now within the confines of the old church the Lizardman's voice rang out.

"Here are the four prisoners you requested my Lady," hissed Ssnakash.

"Thank you my loyal servant," replied the Lady. "You are now dismissed."

"Service is all," replied Ssnakash who then stood to attention, raised his arm in salute, and proceeded to leave the church. As the creature walked away Methladon looked to his surroundings and began to formulate a plan to kill the woman that stood before him. He saw several objects that would be heavy enough to smash her skull and splatter its contents across the floor of the sanctuary. A great desire for revenge burned inside but as he looked towards his companions he made eye contact with the emaciated prisoner. The words of Lancet and Tycus echoed through his thoughts; *'think of us before doing anything stupid.'* Methladon was sure that he could take out one or two of the Knights, even Nictis perhaps. He was certain that Tycus and Lancet could do the same before they too were felled but he could not depend on the weak one. The odds were stacked against him and a quick death would no doubt follow any act of aggression.

"Maggots! Show your gratitude for the honour of an audience with the Lady of the Silverwynn," barked Captain Nictis once Ssnakash had left the sanctum.

None of the four prisoners moved. Methladon understood what the Captain demanded but he, like the others, had no intention of satisfying either Nictis or the Lady without some degree of dissent being shown.

"I said show your gratitude!" barked Nictis.

Still the four men ignored him. Then as the Captain stepped two places forward, the emaciated fair-haired man fell to his knees where his joints met the pool of piss he had just voided.

"At least one of you has the sense to show respect to our Lady, your Queen," yelled Nictis as he moved ever closer.

"Go to hell!" snapped back Tycus, spraying saliva from his mouth.

"You will show gratitude," ordered Nictis. "Kneel now, you fucking bastard."

Methladon winced as Nictis swung his gauntlet into the face of his fellow slave. Tycus dropped to the floor, teetered on his hands and knees and he spat again. This time his spittle was mixed with blood and bits of broken tooth. As soon as the pink froth hit the stone floor Nictis slammed his right boot into Tycus's back and drove him flat against the hard surface. Then he turned towards Methladon and Lancet.

"Now do either of you want to continue to resist?" he screamed while kicking Tycus in the ribs.

"No sir," muttered Methladon and Lancet in unison.

"Then fucking kneel!"

"Nictis; enough," ordered an authoritative voice from high on the alter platform and Methladon looked up to the menacing figure of the Lady of the Silverwynn.

"I need the 'One' alive and without lasting defect. He must be intact if he is to serve my cause. Do you have a name boy?"

Methladon was shocked that the Lady had singled him out with her pointed finger.

"Methladon, Methladon Heyn," he stuttered.

"Then Methladon Heyn, you must tend to your friend. I must however request that you honour me and kneel in my presence or else I will have no alternative but to order Captain Nictis to continue your education."

"Of course Lady, as you desire," replied Methladon.

He and Lancet immediately fell to their knees and bowed their heads in submission.

"Very good," said the Lady with a smirk. "See Nictis, if you ask in a nice manner then you are much more likely to achieve compliance. Now Heyn, see to your friend."

Methladon rose from his knees and moved across to Tycus who lay motionless upon the floor. After checking for a heart throb at his neck he was relieved to find that the man was unconscious and not dead as he had first thought. He turned his fellow slave onto his back, pulled him up by his arms, and rested his back against the wall. As he did so Tycus regained consciousness and muttered under his breath although Methladon struggled to make meaning of the words.

"Tycus, its Meth. Everything is going to be fine," he whispered.

"Wat... Need Wat..." groaned Tycus through blood stained lips.

"Nictis, get the slave some water," ordered the Lady of the Silverwynn.

"As you command Lady."

Methladon's anger simmered and his three circled mark on the back of his head began to fizz.

"Having found the sceptre that you had been searching for," shouted Methladon. "Why can you not just leave us be."

"I sense much fire inside you and quite a bit of venom too!" answered the Lady. "People with your spirit are few these days. Tell me Methladon Heyn, can you swing a blade?"

"I was the best swordsman my village ever had. That was before your knights burned it down."

"And yet my men managed to overpower you with ease," added the Commander as he slipped his right hand to the hilt of the weapon that hung from his belt.

"What the fuck do you want with us?" demanded the youth.

"Meth, shut up and kneel back down," shouted Lancet.

"Listen to your friend Methladon Heyn," laughed the Lady. "He at least talks sense."

"Do as she says," mumbled Tycus from against the wall. "Do not risk all of our lives by teasing these bastards."

Methladon switched his gaze from the Lady to Tycus. He realised that his fellow slave was right in his assessment. He needed a new strategy if he was to avoid having their deaths on his hands.

"Your friend from the Lotus Isle speaks much sense young Methladon," continued the Lady. "I cannot hold my men back for much longer, isn't that right Commander?"

"Believe me boy, you will pray to die if you continue to resist," added Rhaizen. "Drop to your knees lad and speak only when requested."

Methladon followed the order for he was at a loss as to what else he could do. Part of him wanted to make a break for freedom but that would result in the butchering of his friends. So he did nothing.

"Good," continued the Lady as she returned to her throne. "At last we make progress."

"Which one do you want to start with," added Rhaizen, his eyes focused on the four prisoners?

"I doubt that the thin and pasty one will survive what I have planned," answered the Lady "The one from the Lotus Isle has yet to recover and as I said before, I need an intact specimen."

"What about him" added Commander Rhaizen, finger pointing at Methladon?

"No, not just yet. I need to warm up the sceptre before I play with young Heyn. So out of the four, it seems the most suitable candidate is you, you lucky man."

It was the Lady's turn to raise her hand and she pointed her digit at Lancet.

"Do your worst," snapped back the mercenary.

Rhaizen moved from behind his Queen and stepped off the platform. He then took hold of Lancet by the neck and thrust him forward towards the Lady. Lancet did not try to struggle and Methladon thought this rather strange for the mercenary had never before shown signs of surrender. Now he appeared ready to accept whatever fate had planned for him. The Lady of the Silverwynn looked down on her slave while holding the sceptre before Lancet's eyes.

"I want you to keep your eyes open and tell me all that you see," ordered the Lady. "Describe it to me in every detail. I want to know if you experience your deepest desires or your worst nightmares."

"And then what?" asked Lancet as he submitted to the Lady's will.

"Just wait and see!"

Rhaizen then took hold of Lancet's hair and forced his face toward the diamond at the top of the sceptre. A pale blue glow seeped out of the Seers' jewel and forced the prisoner into a trance.

"Tell me what you see?" asked the Lady as she bent over Lancet's ear. "Relate your visions."

Lancet began his reply in a voice that was devoid of emotion.

"I am alone and there is nothing but the black. I see myself falling for eternity. All is empty and without hope. Emotions do not exist in this place. Now I see my mother appearing alongside of me. She is older than I remember and the further we fall the more ancient she becomes. She is withering and her flesh crumbling. The dust is blowing away and I am left falling on my own again. I am joined by a girl..."

"And who is the girl?" asked the Lady.

"My sister. It is my little sister. I see her looking at me with accusing eyes. It was my fault she tells me. It was my fault that she died. No...Stay back!"

"What do you see now?" demanded the Lady as Methladon watched with a stunned curiosity.

"She's clawing her way up through the dirt," whimpered Lancet as fear gripped his voice. "Her skin is rotting and her eyes empty of life. She is groaning yet gasping for air at the same time. No, she's alive. We buried her alive. It was a mistake. Everyone is judging me."

"Who dares to judge you?"

"The town! My family!" shouted Lancet. "Take your fucking accusing eyes from my soul. It was just meant as a bit of fun. She should never have drunk the liquid... Keep away... Keep away from me."

Without warning Lancet picked up a piece of fallen masonry and threw it backwards back over his shoulder where it connected with the side of Commander Rhaizen's skull helmet. In an instant Lancet was up on his feet and he ran off down the aisle of the church. Rhaizen, whose blood covered face radiated bull like anger, reached down and drew his curved blade from its scabbard. In one single skilled movement he launched the sword like a javelin towards his target. Lancet did not have time to swerve or duck before the sword pierced him through the centre of his back and dropped him to the ground.

"Oh fuck Lancet! What have you done?" cried out Tycus from against the wall.

Nictis had chosen that very same moment to re-enter the church with the pot of water he had been ordered to fetch. On seeing the events unfold, he threw down the earthenware jug which smashed against the floor. He too drew his blade and rushed over to where Lancet lay wounded. As he leaned over the slave Nictis laughed. It was the same crazed cackle that Methladon had heard when Mal Castor had been sacrificed before the Lizardman priest.

"I want my voice to be the last you ever hear," barked out Nictis.

With a swing of his sword, the Captain decapitated Lancet. The head flew several paces down the aisle while crimson pumped out of the severed neck and mixed with puddles of water. Methladon wanted to scream but he had been emptied of spirit. The mark on the back of his head burned with great intensity and his anger continued to grow. A minute later he didn't care what else happened to him for he just wanted to kill Nictis and if need be he would die in the attempt.

"Captain! My sword," ordered Rhaizen as he wiped a trickle of blood from his face.

"As you so wish," replied Nictis.

The Captain pulled the blade from out of Lancet's body to the sound of a slippery suck.

"Which one do you want to try next my Lady," asked the Commander?

"It will have to be the starving bard," she answered.

Methladon looked to the wretch that knelt beside him, the man whose name he still did not know. In a low whisper he spoke to himself. 'So you are one of the Bard's of Valameer; just like the one that visited our village during happier times. Perhaps a bard's magic can resist the will of these tormentors."

"No, please, please," screamed the wretch as Rhaizen approached. "I'm too weak. My mind will not survive the stone."

Rhaizen snatched at the hair on top of the bag of bones and pulled the bard onto his feet. Methladon knew he would have to do something at once if he was to save his fellow slave. An idea then appeared as if from nowhere. He swung out his right leg and took the feet from under Nictis. The Captain dropped like a stone and his armour clattered against the hard floor. Methladon reached for Rhaizen's sword and made to attack. In the commotion that followed, he saw the bard free himself from the Commander's grip and run to a distant corner of the church. Then as he tried to attack, Methladon's bones were filled with an unimaginable pain. It was as if each were being split apart from within. No longer able to feel the floor beneath his feet and despite the agony that seared through his body, Methladon realised that he was floating in the air. The sensation of being pulled apart grew even more intense and when he looked to Rhaizen he understood what was happening. The Commander held out an arm and pointed at him while uttering strange and unknown words. When the chant ceased the Commander's words again made sense.

"Put down the sword lad."

Try as he might Methladon was unable to move any of his limbs or turn his head. Despite feeling the need to scream out he gritted his teeth for he was determined not to give his tormentor satisfaction.

"Fuck you!" mumbled Methladon.

"Drop your weapon," ordered Rhaizen and the Commander twisted his wrist and induced another bolt of agonising pain.

"Do as he says Meth," whimpered Tycus. "This is not worth dying for."

"Captain Nictis," shouted Rhaizen.

"Sir!" replied the Knight as his armour clattered to attention.

"Kill the other two, take your time, and make them suffer."

"At once Sir."

Methladon sensed Nictis draw his sword as he moved towards the throne at the front of the church and he realised that unless he obeyed the hated Commander he would be responsible for the deaths of his friends. With considerable effort Methladon released his grip on the sword and allowed it to fall to the floor.

"Good!" sneered the Lady of the Silverwynn. "I find gentle persuasion always works best. Your compassion for your friends has defeated you Methladon Heyn. Commander, now make him kneel before me."

"My pleasure!" snarled Rhaizen as he moved his hand forward.

Methladon felt the agony surge throughout his body and he began to float towards the evil woman. Limbs that he no longer controlled were now manipulated by others. His legs twisted into a kneeling position and he gave up on them. The spasms of pain then lessened and he looked to Rhaizen again. The fearsome knight had grown pale, appeared drained of energy, and seemed to struggle to keep Methladon subdued.

"Methladon Heyn, I hope we understand each other," continued the Lady. "I do not want my Commander to use all his magic on you for you would not survive the ordeal. Are you going to cause me any more trouble?"

"No."

"Good," replied the Lady. "Release him."

Rhaizen lowered his hand and as he did so his limbs faltered and he was forced to steady himself against the stone throne on which the Lady of the Silverwynn sat.

"Look into the Seer's Stone just like your friend and tell me what you see."

"I will only do so if you promise to free my two companions," replied Methladon.

"Of course dear boy," she smirked. "You have my word as the rightful Ruler of Parandor. I will not harm your friends if you comply with my demands. But should the jewel send you mad or you beg for a merciful death, then who do you suppose will be around to ensure the promise is kept? Now, look into the stone and tell me what you see."

Methladon contemplated defying the Lady but once again his thoughts returned to the plight of his fellow prisoners. He would have to trust in her word that his friends would be freed. Perhaps he could survive the connection with the Seer's Stone. Realising he had no choice in the matter he took a deep intake of breath and stared into the diamond that had been thrust within a few inches of his face.

"What do you see Methladon Heyn?" demanded the Lady.

At first it was just the reflected sparkle from off the surface of the stone as it glinted in the little light that shone through the holes of the derelict roof. Then as he looked deeper into the stone he began to see a different light. He focused his attention on it and soon became obsessed with its presence. The bright glow drew his mind inward and forced him to look even deeper into the stone's crystal structure. A second later Methladon felt his mind ripped from out of his head and pulled into a curdled milk-like limbo. He heard the faint voice of the Lady of the Silverwynn ordering him to tell her everything but even though he tried to move his mouth to speak he could not do so. Surrounded by mist and light he found it impossible to control his mouth. Then as his trance deepened he wondered if Khaizen had once again taken control of his body.

When the mist began to clear Methladon found himself floating face down. He was high up in the sky and looking at a vast city that sat on the edge of a bay close to a vast and limitless ocean. The city was on fire and it soon became consumed by a mass of orange flame and dense black smoke. Methladon sensed he was going to fall into the burning ruins but he did not. He remained suspended in the air and hovered as if on a spit. There he was held in the hot air that rose from the conflagration. It was a fierce heat and the high temperature began to make his flesh melt. Skin pealed and fat globules dripped from his face where they fell like oil filled rain drops only to sizzle out of existence within the fire below. He wanted to scream out but no sound left his mouth. He attempted to close his eyes but he had also lost control of his lids. The skin of his face continued to cook and expose the blood streaked bones of his skull. He prayed for release from his torture but none came. Locked inside a wave of agony he knew there could be no turning back.

Then the image before him changed and flesh returned to cover his face. He open his eyes but instead of the burning city, he now found himself in the centre of a great battle with knights and warriors of all creeds and colours locked in fierce conflict upon the barren ground outside the walls of the city. The armour of some of the knights he recognised, being identical to that worn by those who had destroyed his village and taken him prisoner. Fighting against the black swine were warriors in padded leather armour and others in steel who displayed a unique sigil on their left pauldron. It depicted a golden cross on a background in four colours, copper red, bronze, silver, and grey. The knights with the golden cross were being slaughtered in a systematic and vicious manner by those who donned the black. While he surveyed the carnage of this mighty battle, Methladon began to focus on two warriors engaged in a fight to the death upon a pile of mutilated corpses. One was disfigured, burned across the face, and he wore the same black armour of those who were in ascendance. The second had what at first appeared to be armour made entirely of gold, but it was lighter than any metal that Methladon had ever seen for it did not affect the warrior's movements. He tried to look for detail in the second man's face but just as he felt he was about to see more, the image before him faded and began to change again.

Methladon next found himself in a grand marble hall filled with fine Lords and Ladies. Above them golden banners hung from the rafters and the sound of a trumpet fanfare echoed through the air. He looked towards the centre of the crowd where the mass of people then parted and gave way to expose two marble thrones, one white and one black. Upon the black chair he recognised the Lady of the Silverwynn. She was older and yet somehow more beautiful. He then noticed that the entire crowd had begun to stare at him and without warning another fanfare trumpeted out. It was followed at once by words from one of the Lords who stood adjacent to the Lady's throne.

"All hail the King, the Sovereign ruler of Parandor and Keeper of the Peace, Savoir of Avolire, and Guardian of the Underworld."

It was then that Methladon realised that he no longer wore the ruined and dirt soaked clothes of a prisoner and slave but garments fit for a king, multi-coloured and topped with a golden crown.

"All hail the King!"

Methladon lurched backwards, dazed, and confused. He stared back at the Seer's stone that was but inches from his face while torrents of sweat oozed out from his pores. The mark on the back of his head burned with a ferocity he had never experienced before nor wished to again.

"I too have seen a glimpse of what the Fates may have planned for us Methladon Heyn," said the Lady of the Silverwynn. "I do not understand all of what may come to pass but most is much clearer to me now."

As Methladon knelt before the imposing highborn lady he began to wonder how she knew the detail of his visions for he could not remember having spoken.

"I saw myself as Ruler," began the bewildered youth. "How can that be so? Such things can never come to pass."

"Stranger things have happened in this Realm, long before you were born," she continued. "I remember a time when every person went out of their way to help others. Those were the days of glory, long before the family of Gylewu usurped the throne and stripped this once fine city of its riches. I have seen many strange things Methladon Heyn; happenings that would make your blood curdle and spew out the contents of your stomach."

"I take it you have looked into the stone yourself?" answered Methladon.

"Me!" laughed the Lady. "Look into the Seer's stone... No I have not. I harness a power far greater than that contained in the diamond and the rest of the Gems of Thamous. I have looked into a fracture and seen inside the Rift. I have felt its energy and power and have become acquainted with that which lies inside. It revealed to me a future where I rule the Realm. There was a young man by my side, but not until now did I think he would be one as young as you."

"Forgive me my Lady but haven't you told him too much" growled Rhaizen?

"Your concern is noted Commander.

The Lady lowered the sceptre and took hold of Methladon's face with her other hand and forced his eyes to look into her own.

"There is nothing that can be said that cannot be retracted; yet this boy who kneels before me now shows great potential. He may or may not be the 'One'."

"As you so instruct Lady," replied the Commander.

"For now Methladon Heyn, you have caught my attention, but we shall think on what we have witnessed here today," she added before turning her attention to Nictis. "Take them back to the mines and keep a very close eye on them, this one in particular. Post at least two of your scale scum to guard over his cell."

"As you command Lady," replied Nictis as he then addressed his captives. "You heard the Lady's words so now let's get back to work. Heyn, take care of your dark friend."

Methladon rose to his feet and made his way over to the wall that had kept Tycus from falling.

"Leave me Meth, I'm done for," Tycus moaned as Methladon approached.

"Come on friend, I will not give up on you yet. I will find you water when we are back in the mines. Even these bastards won't deny you water."

"Here, let me help you," whispered another voice.

Methladon had forgotten about the starving wretch whose life he had earlier saved and with his help he began to lift Tycus from the floor.

"Thank you bard," said Methladon.

"No, thank you my friend," replied the living skeleton. "I owe you one for saving my life."

"Come on you fucking maggots!" screamed Nictis. "That hole in the ground isn't going to dig itself. Move your sorry arses or Ssnakash will give you all twenty lashes on the hour."

"We heard you!" snapped back Methladon.

The two men threw Tycus's arms over their shoulders and helped drag his limp frame through the scuttling geckos that sought to avoid their feet.

"I'm Methladon, Methladon Heyn."

"Yes, I know," replied the bard. "That cunt of a woman said your name often enough. She was trying to connect with you."

"What do you mean?"

"It is something that the Masters of Bards Guild believe in," continued the emaciated man. "There is much power in a name and it can be used to bend its owner's will."

"What about you? What beliefs do you follow?"

"I used to have faith in the Fates, the gods said to bestow order upon the Realm; but my belief died soon after I was brought to this furuncle of a city; one where we will both end our days."

"So you don't believe like your fellow Guild masters that there..."

"I'm not a Guild Master, nor indeed am I a bard," said skeleton man.

"But the Lady called you one, and you confirmed you were from Valameer."

"I do come from Valameer and I have lived many years behind the walls of the Guild. But I am neither a bard nor a master. I served those within the Guild in my role as steward."

"And do you have a name, steward?"

"Yes I do. It is Dayis."

20

Llyat woke from a most idyllic slumber. The mattress on which he lay felt wonderful and soft to the touch. It was unlike anything that he had ever before felt against his skin. His mind fought against the urge to wake as he sensed the womb like warmth around him. He savoured the delightful caress of the fresh linen sheets and soft woollen blankets. Wherever he was he felt safe and secure. Someone had taken great care when they had put him to bed. The youth tried to remember what had happened back in the library before his memory had clouded and then left him. With difficulty he tried to piece together his fractured thoughts into some cohesive story and to work out what had happened. After some minutes passed he remembered the glow that had scared him. It had disappeared during a heated conversation about events within the Realm and something significant that had occurred elsewhere. He could half remember a garbled story about the Gems of Thamous and the adventures of the bard who had visited Maplehill before its destruction. Then as the mist of forgetfulness lifted he recalled that the First Mate of the Banshees Wail had been looking for him. That was as much as he could remember and Llyat realised that his mind must have then shut off. Now it had switched back on and had forced him to surface within unfamiliar surroundings.

While he lay within the bed's cocoon Llyat merged into the present. He heard four different voices which continued on with no apparent regard for his presence. First of these he recognised as the stern voice of his master, the Grand Physician. The second, the person that the old man conversed with most, was the young bard Thias Calavan. Of the other two he then noted the voice of the steward called Dayis who had taken them to the library earlier that evening. The last of the four he could not recognise although for some reason he felt that he should have known who it was. Llyat continued to listen but he kept his eyes closed and gave no indication that he was awake. His master was arguing and it was obvious that the old man refused to believe the words that penetrated his ears.

"Bullshit! It cannot be this boy."

"You saw what happened with the masslewort," replied Thias. "The sign was clearer than could have ever been anticipated. I am certain that this boy is the one that the prophecy speaks of."

"It cannot be Llyat, it just cannot be," continued the old man.

"I'm afraid that after all the Grand Musician told us in his library and then embellished by that pox-faced sailor, there can be no doubt about it; he is the 'Marked'," added the fourth. "You said yourself Abrahamus that the lad hails from Maplehill."

"But he can't be…"

"The odds do favour it being the case," added Dayis. "I maybe just a steward but I do know the words of the prophecy. It does seem that the Marked of Maplehill has finally revealed himself to the bards."

"The Prophecy of Enderdetag is upon us," added the fourth voice.

"We had better take care in all that we say or do from this point forward," added Thias.

"There is no way that the enemy could overhear us within these thick walls," added the physician. "As the Grand Musician himself said but an hour ago, this is the most secure place in Valameer, if not the whole Realm."

"It's not the enemy that worries me," added Thias.

"Then what is it man?" demanded old Marus.

"The boy is awake and has been so for several minutes. He is just pretending to be asleep."

On hearing those words Llyat opened his eyes and sat up against the wood panelled wall at the back of the bed. That was when he noted with some surprise that he was still fully clothed.

"How long was I out for?" he asked as he tried to focus his on his surroundings.

"Just half of an hour or so," answered his master. "I'm glad you are well again boy. I've taken a liking to you and I could not forgive myself if something untoward happened to you. Even this mix up about the legend and a mark…"

"He is the Marked, Abrahamus," interrupted Thias. "You have to believe it. He is without doubt the One."

Llyat saw from the expression on his master's face that the old man was close to losing his temper and he wondered how long it would be before he exploded with rage. He then scanned the room to see where he lay and found himself upon a solid four poster bed in a room lined with wooden panels. There was a single window upon which the rain from the storm continued to drive. Against one wall stood a dresser, complete with a mirror and surrounded by an intricate and detailed carved boarder. By its side Llyat recognised his master's trunk, the one he had packed with Heliana's help and that they had brought all the way from Parandor. It was then that he realised that he was in the room that the Guild had allocated to his master. The argument between the Physician and Thias continued and Llyat tried to follow all that was said although like the conversation in the tower library he struggled to understand much of it. He saw the concern etched on the faces of Dayis and the fourth man as his master and the bard continued to argue. Llyat listen hard as the men repeated the same two phrases over and over again, the very ones that Llyat had heard mentioned in the library, the Prophecy of Enderdetag and the Marked of Maplehill. A shudder passed through his essence as he recalled that the Marked was the one sought by those who had murdered his father.

"Excuse me!" interrupted Llyat. "I know you are talking about me. What is going on? I promise that I will try to think of any information that could be of use to you; not that I am likely to know stuff."

Llyat knew those words to be a lie. Of course he had heard of the Marked. It was a name that continued to haunt his thoughts. Part of him wished that he had the courage to tell his master that the reason for the attack on Maplehill was because the strange knights were looking for him. If only he had spoken of it back in the Capital he would perhaps now be protected from the strange events that had ensnared him.

"Please tell me," pleaded Llyat once again. "What is this Prophecy of Enderdetag that you keep mentioning and why do you seem convinced that I am connected to it?"

"I think we should let our expert in this matter explain," replied Thias who then pointed to fourth man. "Allow me to introduce you to Master Ulthirn. He is one of our teachers here in the Guild and he specialises in the movement of the Heavens. He is also the foremost expert on the Prophecy in all of the Realm."

From his position in the bed Llyat looked out towards the one called Ulthirn. The man, if you could call him one, was so slender in appearance that he looked like a stick that had fallen from a tree. He was dressed in similar robes to those that Master Peaceore had worn earlier. What confused Llyat was that even though Master Ulthirn appeared to be a man, there was something uncomfortably woman-like about him. Then as they made eye contact, Ulthirn moved to the bed and began to recite verse. It did not take long for Llyat to realise that it related to the Prophecy.

When the Marked is found amongst the Maples,
And the armies of the East shall walk again,
With the Enderdetag alignment in the Heavens,
Then shall be the end of good men.

When the Oracles crypt shall be opened,
When the choices we make must thrive,
The Powers of Evil shall be woken,
And none then alive will survive.

From the innocent the savoir shall awaken,
To the Bards he shall appear,
To reunite the Gems of Thamous,
And destroy the Lord of Fear.

"That Llyat is the Prophecy of Enderdetag," added Master Ulthirn. "Written down by the great Anyle Belanore after a life time studying the stars and orbs that move above us."

"So what has this prophecy got to do with me?" replied Llyat while feigning ignorance.

"The Marked found amongst the Maples, that's what!" added Thias. "The Maples we believe is a reference to Maplehill. From Master Ulthirn's studies, the Marked should be able to generate Kundalish Aura in a natural way without prior contact with magic. My suspicions were raised when you covered yourself in masslewort back in the library, but it was only after you passed out and you had been brought here by Dayis and Master Ulthirn that we became certain. You are the Marked of Maplehill, unless of course you know of anyone else who would better fit the description."

Even though Llyat knew the truth, he couldn't help but wonder if it was all a dream or some great mistake. Sat upon the bed he thought of two others from his village who would better fit the role of the Marked. The first was Elita Darcha who had been marked and mauled by a skyfawn but she was dead. The second was his friend Methladon who bore a three circle birthmark on the back of his head. It was similar to the one found on the body of the stable boy back in the Citadel but it couldn't be him for he was also dead. Llyat remembered only too well the moment that his friend had been slain amid the carnage that had descended on Maplehill. With no other names to choose from Llyat realised that there was just one possibility left. He was the last from his village still alive and had to be the one that the prophecy spoke of. Llyat Emgar had to be the Marked.

"They were looking for me," said Llyat after a brief pause. "You are right. I am this marked one. There is no other it could be. "

"Now don't just agree with these bards for the sake of ease," barked out the Grand Physician before Thias raised his hand and demanded quiet.

"Please Abrahamus, let the boy continue. Llyat, you must finish what you were going to say. Who was looking for you?"

"The man in the skull helmet," replied Llyat. "The leader of the knights that destroyed my village and murdered my family. He had said he was looking for the Marked."

In the silence that followed this revelation Llyat sensed the degree of his master's shock.

"Are you saying that you were aware they had been looking for you?" demanded old Marus. "All this time you knew that you were part of this complicated chain of events and yet you chose to hide this information from me. Llyat, I must say that I am disappointed in you."

"I felt it best at the time, given all that had happened to me and what with this murder investigation underway. I felt lucky to be alive and did not want to implicate myself in any way. I really wanted to tell you, in all honesty sir, but I never had enough courage or confidence to speak out. I'm so sorry."

"I will accept your apology Llyat," replied the Grand Physician, dismissing the youth while turning his attention to the others in the room. "Now that Llyat's true identity is out, could one of you three please explain the rest of the prophecy to me or do I have to do the research myself? Well……I am waiting?"

Before any could answer, loud knocks rapped upon the door and Thias opened it without waiting for permission. There stood a young woman about the same age as Llyat and dressed in similar robes to Dayis. She looked to all in the room and then entered.

"Ah Dayis, I'm so pleased to have found you. Masters Peaceore and Fusepelt said that I would find you here. You are needed at once in the wine cellar."

"Can't this wait Hara," replied the steward. "Can't you see that we are busy?"

"The Grand Musician said it couldn't. You are in charge of the wine cellars and you need to sign off the delivery of a consignment from Valameer that has forced its way here through the storm."

"I don't care what…" grumbled Dayis.

"Thank you Dayis," interrupted Master Ulthirn. "Your services are no longer required here. Please see to your delivery and then have some food sent up for Llyat. He is going to need all his strength over the course of the next few days."

"But…but…" moaned the steward.

"Dayis," continued Ulthirn. "You are dismissed."

The steward and the young girl closed the door behind them and Llyat realised that some of his fellow travellers to Valameer were absent.

"Sirs, I beg your pardon. Where are the others? Where is Heliana?"

"Fret not, they are all well," replied the Grand Physician "I do understand the strength of bond between you and young Heliana and why you would worry about her. I too fear for the girl. She is like the daughter that I always wished for and yet never had, but that is a story for another time. In answer to your question young Emgar, she is quite safe. Those of the City Watch and that pox faced sailor have accompanied her to the Guild's dining hall. Master Peaceore had promised to feed them well."

"Are sure Heliana is safe?" asked Llyat in a way that betrayed his emotions.

"She was a little shocked when you glowed in so strange a manner and then passed out. But it is nothing that a little food and a mug of warm mead will not remedy."

"Mead!" gasped Llyat. "Do they have mead here?"

The youth was reminded of the last time that he had drank the amber liquid back on old Chirth Hadra's farm. It seemed odd to miss a place of so much torment.

"Of course some of us have access to mead," said Master Ulthirn as he laughed. "But let us not think of that now for we still need to clear up the matter of the Prophecy."

"Master Ulthirn is correct," added Thias. "We must work out what we should do next."

"I must remind you that before we decide on anything we need to interpret the Prophecy properly," muttered the Grand Physician.

"Let me tell you what we have deduced so far," continued Ulthirn. "The first verse speaks of the Marked being found in Maplehill and the 'armies of the East' walking again. From what we have heard today I believe this relates to the Lizardmen of the Eastern Marsh preparing to take up arms and move south. The second verse speaks of an Oracle. We believe this could be the burial place of the famous Oracle of Frasteria which legend indicates is sited somewhere near the ancient Barrow of Harico. If we can locate the site of the Oracle's tomb it may lead us to the location of the door to the Underworld."

"I thought that knowledge was supposed to be contained within the Lore of the Dead," said the Grand Physician while his hand stroked the hairs of his beard.

"So did we, but it appears that may not be the case," continued Master Ulthirn. "The next point of issue is that only the Marked is able to enter the Oracle's tomb, overcome its defences, and gain knowledge of the location of the door that we must seal forever. The prophecy hints at a significant decision to be made, a choice of some kind that will determine whether or not the evil within is released upon this Realm."

"But the doors to the underworld are at this moment shut," added the Grand Physician. "They require the Gems of Thamous to open them and to also seal them again. Therefore, without the Gems the evil cannot be released."

"That is the one part of the prophecy that we have yet to understand," continued Master Ulthirn. "I must tell you now that we believe that a great evil is about to be unleashed upon us and that it will bring about the return of Urthanock, the Lord of Fear."

A violent rumble of thunder shook the foundations of the building but for once it had not been preceded by a flash of lightening.

"Now you are just teasing us," moaned the Grand Physician.

"I wish I was Abrahamus," replied Ulthirn. "It appears the Lizardmen have already started their push south. They have eliminated the garrison at the Grey Keep and all the signs point to the Prophecy being enacted. The Fates have chosen young Llyat to be our most unlikely saviour."

"But Urthanock!" gasped the Grand Physician. "It just cannot be. He was destroyed by Sir Raulyn the Grand, his body burned, and his essence sealed forever in the Underworld."

"And yet his servants are massing in Avolire," added Thias. "There is one more piece to this puzzle that worries me; something that has plagued my thoughts ever since your party arrived here."

"And what is that?" asked the Grand Physician.

"The shape shifting Lizardman that I slew at the Grey Keep implied the enemy had already infiltrated the Capital..."

"Tell us something that we haven't already guessed!" sneered the Grand Physician. "I suspected this sometime ago, as did our Sovereign Lord, even though we didn't then know it was the scale skin buggers that were behind it."

"The Lizardman also suggested the culprit to be one of our Sovereign Lords trusted advisors, an individual with access to the Council."

"If you think for one moment I am a Lizardman young man then you are very much mistaken," snapped back the Grand Physician.

"Forgive my rudeness Abrahamus, I meant you no disrespect," replied Thias while dipping his head in reverence, "You don't have the right temperament to be one of the enemy and would have given yourself away at once. I have my own ideas as to who lies in wait by the side of our Sovereign."

"As do I," continued Marus. "Lord Amberstone, according to his daughter, appears to know more than he has so far declared. I also believe that Blackfayer is hiding something."

"If I was a betting man I would put my money on Lord Blackfayer."

"As would I Thias, as would I?" said the old man.

"So what do we do now?" asked Llyat, aware of the sounds of a disturbance outside the room.

"We need to find the missing Gems of Thamous before those bastards from Avolire get their pustulent hands on them," continued Thias. "If the sailor is to be believed then Avolire may soon have possession of the Seer's Stone. At least we have control over the emerald."

"What of the others," asked Llyat? "How do we even go about finding them if we have no clues as to their location. You said yourselves that the Lore of the Dead was the one record known to contain knowledge of their hiding places."

"There is in truth one other source of that information," replied Thias. "The creature Thamous that first helped generate the power held within the gems. We must keep the dagger locked inside this Guild until we can gain ownership the others."

"Where is the dagger now?" asked Ulthirn.

"I gave it to Dayis to put back into the hidden compartment," replied Thias. "It will be safe there. However, we need to act with haste and before Avolire becomes aware of what we know and what we are planning…"

The commotion outside grew ever louder until the sounds inhibited the flow of the conversation inside the room. Thias felt unnerved as did Master Ulthirn who moved towards the door.

"I'll go see what all the noise is about. At this hour the students should be asleep," he shouted as he exited through the door and closed it behind him.

Thias turned to the Grand Physician. "If the warrior from the City Watch is correct, his friends in Falahorn maybe be able to help us locate Thamous's lair within the Dragonas. We should set out at once on that mission but I think it would be best if Llyat remains here under the care of the Guild, at least for the time being."

"Why? I want to come along," protested Llyat, ready to jump from the bed.

"The Marked must be protected," added Thias. "We cannot allow you to be discovered by the enemy and used for their own ends. The Dragonas is also the most dangerous of places."

"I can take care of myself," protested Llyat as he hopped off the bed. "Tonousa and Irabo have been giving me lessons."

"So we can see," smirked the Grand Physician. "That must explain your black eye. For a while I thought perhaps you had crossed Heliana again."

Before Llyat could respond another loud knock rattled the door.

"Who in the name of the gods could make such a racket at this time of the night?" muttered the Grand Physician as he moved towards the door.

"Perhaps a student looking for Ulthirn," responded Thias.

A second louder knock was followed by a third.

"Alright… Alright. I'm coming!"

The Grand Physician snatched at the door's handle and opened it in haste.

"Oh it's you! What do you want now?"

The old man stopped moving and let out a forceful expulsion of air. It was as if he had been punched and he then fell to the floor. Having moved several paces forward himself, Llyat saw the puncture wound above the physician's heart from which life blood pumped out onto the floor of the chamber.

"No!" screamed Llyat as he dropped down to offer aid to his fallen master.

He placed both of his hands over the hole and attempted to stem the flow of the crimson liquid that rose from out of the old man's body. The pressure forced the blood to squirt between his fingers and it soon covered his arms, his chest, and even his face.

"Watch out!" screamed Thias.

Llyat looked up to see a metal blade descending towards his head. He closed his eyes and waited for the end to come but after a loud clash of metal upon metal he forced them open once again. The blade that had intended to destroy him had been parried by Thias using a metal candle holder grabbed from off the windowsill of the room. Llyat looked up to the face of his attacker and recognised the man at once. The eyes of the steward Dayis met with his own as the metamorphosis under the steward's clothes began.

Dayis changed into the form of a hideous Lizardman. The creature then pounced forward. It leapt over Llyat and the fallen body of his master and rushed on to engage Thias in a fierce fight. With a swift flick of its reptilian tail it knocked the bard from off his feet and onto the hard floor. Then the creature turned towards Llyat, snarled, and hissed through its snake like face.

"The traitor's son must come with me now," hissed the creature.

"Llyat, for fucks sake run!" yelled Thias.

Before the creature could react, the bard launched himself from the ground and threw his arms around the reptile's neck. The beast squirmed and thrashed as it tried to release itself from Thias's grip. It swung its tail like a whip and its fetid jaws attempted to bite down on the bard's hand. Llyat felt helpless and had no idea as to what to do next. Once more his life was in great danger but he could neither run nor find the courage to go to the aid of the young bard. He was transfixed as if nailed through the feet to the floor.

"Llyat, get the fuck out of here. Find your friends," shouted Thias.

The bard hung onto the thrashing creature. The struggle continued and the pair crashed into the dresser. They then smashed against the mirror which caused the creature to drop its jagged blade.

"I can't just leave you!" screamed Llyat.

"You must," came the muffled response

The Lizardman flung itself backwards in another attempt to dislodge the bard from its back. It was a fight to the death and Llyat knew that if he didn't act soon then the creature would win the battle. Then fate pushed an idea into his mind. The reptile managed to throw Thias off its back and the bard careered across the room and ended up against the wall. Llyat meanwhile raced across the open space to his master's trunk and flung its lid open. Then as the creature turned its attention towards him, Llyat found amongst the folded linen the object he was looking for. In the flickering of an eye he gripped the hilt of Destiny's Song, swung the blade forward, and readied himself to face the wrath of the oncoming beast.

"Leave my friend alone frog fucker!" shouted Llyat with a surge of anger.

"Do you think that a mere child can stop me," hissed the Lizardman "The Dagger of Kha has already passed through the Mighty Rift to my master and soon this Guild will be raised to the ground. The traitor's son must be taken to Avolire. Not even the Marked can stop us now."

"You'll have to take my carcass because you'll never take me alive," shouted Llyat.

"So be it, I did not expect more," snarled back the Lizardman.

"You're forgetting one important thing," yelled Llyat as his blade swung forward.

"And what is that? What does the traitor's boy want me to remember?"

"That there were two of us in this room."

The creature did not have time to respond before a blade pierced its neck, ripped forward and sprayed its putrid purple ink out from between its scales. Arteries and veins were severed in unison. The creature gurgled, spluttered, and fell to the floor as even more of its life liquor squirted out. Llyat was transfixed as he watched the final moments of the reptile's life. Then he looked at the devastation inside the room, the smashed furniture, the broken mirror, and the bloodied and bruised bard who stood over the scale covered corpse. Thias breathed down to his boots and wiped his weapon with the edge of his cloak.

Llyat ran over to the doorway, dropped Density's Song to the floor, and knelt by his master's side. The blood which had at first gushed out from the puncture wound in his master's chest had slowed to a faint trickle and the old man's skin had turned a whiter shade of snow. He grabbed hold of his master's hand and held it close to his own chest. Salty tears welled in his eyes. They soon trickled out and rolled down his cheeks.

"Sir, stay with me," the young man sobbed

"He's gone Llyat," added Thias.

Llyat felt the pressure of a hand upon his shoulder. He reached to grasp it as he pulled him up from the ground. Another flash of lightening lit up the room followed by two loud rumbles of thunder.

"We can't just leave him here," he sobbed.

"We must," replied Thias. "Those last two thunderclaps were sent by the gods to warn us. We are in great peril. I fear the Guild is about to fall."

21

There were few occupants in the dining hall of the Bards Guild that late into the night. The visitors were shown to one of four long tables that stretched the full the length of the grey stone room. Tonousa noted that the others present comprised a mixture of masters, students and the occasional steward who attended to their suppers. Some, having finished the act of eating, still sat upon the wooden benches while engrossed in their studies, their avid eyes buried deep within the books that they read with obvious relish. She smiled when one of the students managed to make a small metal orb glow green and rise from the surface of the table.

Master Peaceore allocated the hungry visitors seats as Tonousa scanned the room one last time. While the wind and the rain continued to hammer on the arched glass windows she experienced a sense of significant foreboding but dismissed it as paranoia brought on by being in such a strange place. Her legs then folded and she rested her backside next to Irabo, now deep in his own thoughts. Sat opposite Theoplous she looked at the sailor with suspicion before her attention switched to the girl who sat beside him.

"Do you think Llyat is going to recover?" whispered Heliana.

"I'm sure he is going to be fine," replied Irabo without conviction. "He has your master looking after him and of course the bards. The Fates seem to be working for your friend's good fortune."

"Cut the shit," groaned Tonousa. "Not all that nonsense again. There are no such Fates."

"I am sure that the goddess Fatumai disagrees," added Theoplous as he smiled.

Tonousa ignored the sailor's words and manoeuvred herself along the bench until she faced her colleague.

"Do you honestly expect me to believe that it was fate that brought the boy to the Guild? Or that fate caused him to pass out just as Theo was about to tell his story."

"I do," replied Irabo, "and one of these days we will be able to settle our differences."

"When and if that time comes young Irabo I shall apologise with great humility, but until such a day I will remain a complete sceptic."

"And your unwillingness to embrace the joy of faith leaves you as limp as a witch greeting."

"Not that you'll ever know!" spat back Tonousa.

The conversation at the table was interrupted by a serving girl who appeared out of the shadows from behind Heliana.

"Master Peaceore asked me to see to your needs," she began. "I'm guessing you are all very hungry given your long journey from the Capital."

"You could say that!" agreed Irabo. "In fact I could eat a whole pig."

The four companions laughed together but the serving girl did not share the joke.

"I'm afraid pig is off the menu at the moment," she continued. "Most of our supplies from the south to Valameer are being rationed now. Just a small amount of pig is ever allocated to the masters and students of the Guild. The rest is being held in reserve for the upcoming nuptials of Lord Raorick Gylewu and the Lady Flurdiana."

"Oh, so you haven't been told then," began Irabo but a blow to his shin from Tonousa's foot ordered him to be silent.

"Told?" muttered the wench. "Told, what?"

"Oh nothing," added Irabo as he lied to avoid further contact with his colleague's boot. "It just that I heard that Lord Raorick was getting cold feet."

"Well that would be a waste of all that fills our stores," continued the girl." Perhaps I might be able to bring you some of the fine wine that our steward Dayis had sent from the Capital. He said the Lord of the Grey Keep would be most happy to have wine from his brother's city here in Valameer on the day that he weds and beds."

"Are you asking us to believe that most of the time you don't have sufficient provisions of food and drink at the Guild?" questioned Irabo.

"We have what we grow ourselves sir and that which we can buy in the markets of Valameer. You should understand that we have to grow most of what we need at the Guild ourselves... I think there is some parsnip soup left over from earlier this evening and maybe some scraps of boiled chicken rumps and bread. I will see what I can find for you all."

With that the wench disappeared from the table and made her way out through one of the doors of the hall. Once she was out of ear shot Tonousa turned to Irabo.

"I am not sorry for kicking you," she began. "You are such a dimshit. You almost gave the game away. We cannot be sure who we can trust so for now let's just keep what we know between the four of us and the senior members of this Guild."

Tonousa nodded to her right and as Irabo followed her lead his gaze fell upon the Grand Musician and Master Peaceore at another of the tables; both engaged in a deep and intense discussion.

"I just didn't think," added Irabo as his cheeks flushed. "I got caught up in the moment and forgot myself."

"You must be more careful," continued Tonousa. "But, like I said, we don't know who we can trust. Given the events at the Grey Keep and the slaughter of the garrison there, we need to be on our guard the whole time that we are here. From what I heard in the library earlier, the servants of Avolire could already be amongst us and waiting to strike. At this moment in time, I can trust no one but the four of us sitting here."

"What about my master," responded Heliana as she tried to keep her voice to a whisper? "And what about Llyat? You can trust them."

"In normal circumstances I would agree Heliana, but after watching young Llyat glow like the beacon at the mouth of the Tiaryer I'm now not so sure. It seems far too much of a coincidence for the lad to be linked to events in the Capital, the Grey Keep, and tonight's revelations in this Guild. The manner of his sudden appearance in Parandor does make me question if he is all that we are led to believe. As for your master the Grand Physician, he seems too wrapped up in his investigation. His regular outbursts are leading us nowhere fast."

"So I take it from what you are saying lady, that you now accept me as a friend and someone that you can trust," added Theoplous.

"I have no reason not to," replied Tonousa. "Given your behaviour ever since we arrived in Valameer and all that you have spoken of, my instinct tells me I should call you friend. I do hope I am right in my assessment and I apologise for my earlier accusations."

"Apology accepted."

Another great discharge of thunder shook the hall to its foundations. It had not however been preceded by any flash of lightening and as Tonousa glanced around she noted that most of the others present had an equal degree of concern fixed upon their faces.

"Sounds like Bycphy and Hamthor are at odds with each other again" laughed Theoplous. "That is one bugger of a storm raging outside. I'm so glad not to be at sea."

Tonousa scanned the room and saw that the Grand Musician and Peaceore had ceased their conversation. They too were also listening and watching for signs of danger.

"I don't think that was the storm outside," uttered Tonousa.

"What do you mean?" asked Heliana.

"There was no flash, no lightening," she continued. "And the room shook with a different sort of violence. Whatever caused that noise came from below and not from the sky outside. Wait here."

Tonousa made her way over to the Grand Musician and Master Peaceore for she sensed that they too had concerns about the strange noise they had just heard.

"That wasn't thunder was it?" said Tonousa with quick authority. "Please tell me that it was one of your students making mischief below."

"I'm not sure what it was myself," replied the Grand Musician. "I was just about to send Master Peaceore to investigate. It appeared to emanate from the cellars of this hall."

"What do you keep down there?" asked Tonousa.

"Just food, wine, and a few other supplies," replied Peaceore. "It is where we are storing all that we have set aside to celebrate Lord Gylewu and the Lady Flurdiana's wedding."

"Would you mind taking me down there Master Peaceore?" continued Tonousa. "I have a bad feeling about this. In fact I don't like it one bit."

"Of course, anything to assist."

Peaceore led Tonousa to the stone steps that spiralled down into the cellars below the Guild. As they progressed forward Tonousa began to feel a sensation of heat that that rose up from the very bowels of the building. For an instant she wondered if the stone stairs that had been cut through the rock on which the old building stood led straight into the Underworld. Her nose began to pick up the scent of burning meat and a sting of smoke then filled her nostrils. As it strengthened she pointed to her nose and looked questioningly at Master Peaceore.

"It always smells a bit down here and I think we are picking up aromas drifting down from the kitchens," he stated without apparent concern.

Once the pair had reached the wooden door at the foot of the stairs Peaceore produced a large ring containing numerous iron keys. They came in all shapes and sizes and as he struggled to locate the one that would unlock the door Tonousa noticed an orange glow that seeped through the gap between the wood and the stone floor. Once the correct key had been located, Peaceore thrust it into the door lock and turned his hand. As soon as the door opened an intense wall of heat shot out as if from a dragon's belch. Acting through instinct, both shielded their eyes against the fire that raged within the cellars. Tonousa's eyes adjusted first to the bright glow and she sought to assess the nature of the danger. A store of hanging carcasses, crates, and the wooden structures that supported the roof of the vast underground storeroom now burned with a great ferocity. Fat dripped off the roasting meat and fell onto the stone floor where it flamed and spit out hot globules like bacon in a pan. It was more than a fire, it was an inferno, and Tonousa struggled to understand how it could have started and taken hold with such speed.

"The Lady Flurdiana's feast!" gasped Peaceore as he rushed forward, took hold of a discarded piece of sack cloth and attempted to smother a patch of burning fat upon the floor. "Whosoever is responsible for this disaster is going to pay with their lives!"

"We need to warn everyone upstairs," shouted Tonousa above the roar of the flames. "We need to get everyone out."

"No need," replied Peaceore. "I will soon have this under control."

The bard master thrust his right hand forward and held it towards the fire. He muttered something under his breath, a strange incantation that Tonousa could not understand. She stood and fumed as Peaceore become more frustrated as each time he muttered his words nothing happened. The intensity of the fire increased by the second and thick acrid smoke began to impede Tonousa's vision.

"We have to get out of here," she shouted from the doorway. "We have to leave right now."

"I've told you already," snapped Master Peaceore. "I will soon have this all under control..."

A sudden explosion threw Tonousa from off her feet and forced her backwards onto the stone steps behind her back. Despite her stunned state she tried to work out what could have caused the fiery explosions. There was a distinctive smell to the smoke that surrounded her and it reminded her of something from her past. Memories flooded back and soon she recalled seeing strange weapons once brought to Parandor by a visiting ship from the East. She remembered the alchemist's black powder that had been used to created similar explosions. Perhaps someone by mistake had brought a barrel of that same powder down into the cellar believing it to be wine. From her position against the stone stairs she looked back towards the opening of the door and into the room beyond. To her horror she witnessed the roof of collapse in on itself with a deafening roar.

Vast amounts of rock and wood fell and a ball of smoke and fire filled the space it had left behind.

"Oh Fuck!" shouted Tonousa as she stared at the heap of smouldering rubble where just a few seconds before the fire had raged.

The warrior was at least pleased to see that the roof collapse had extinguished most of the fire but then her eyes fell on the crushed remains of Peaceore. It was at once obvious from the few mangled parts that she could see, that there was nothing that anyone could do for him, not even those who knew magic. Then the walls rippled as if an earthquake were underway and she realised the significance of what was happening. The displacement of the rock and timber supports meant that the structural foundations of the Guild had been compromised and the building was in danger of imminent collapse. All those above her were in extreme peril and she knew that she had to do something to warn them.

Tonousa acted at great speed. She was at the top of the winding spiral stairs that traversed the shaking rock in less than a minute although each second seemed endless in its passing. She had but one thought on her mind, to warn the rest of those in the Guild, that the bottom was about to fall out of their world. Once at the top of the stairs Tonousa raced through the corridors that took her back into the main hall. She knew that the dining room of the Guild, being directly above the cellars, would have sustained most of the impact from the blast. She ran through its stone arched entrance and collided with the young girl who had earlier severed her at the table. Both crashed to the floor amongst a clatter of pewter plates and a shower of spilt ale. The next thing that Tonousa felt was the hand of Irabo as it reached down and took her own and then began to pull her up from the floor.

"Less speed more supper," he laughed. "What's the matter, you look as pale as pigeon shit?"

"We need to get everyone out of here right now," replied Tonousa as she scanned the hall and pointed to the few students and masters who still sat eating.

"Tonousa, tell me what is going on."

Before she could answer the vast dining hall echoed to a deep groan which was then followed by an intense creaking and warping of the walls. All present stopped what they were doing and listened to the cries of woe from the once solid walls of the ancient structure. Even the young serving girl, having climbed back onto her feet, moved away in complete silence, so frightening was the sensation. Tonousa alone knew what was about to happen and she set about trying to save lives.

"Everyone, listen to me!" she shouted. "We need to clear this hall at once. The cellar supports have been compromised. The whole floor will collapse at any moment."

"Stay and drink with me and I will make the ground move for you," slurred an inebriated student from an adjacent table.

"I'm serious." shouted Tonousa. "The Guild is under attack."

Tonousa then caught the eye of the Grand Musician and in a moment of clarity realised that he understood the seriousness of her message. He may have been old and his senses impaired but he was quick to comprehend the truth behind her words.

"You heard the officer of the Watch," croaked the Grand Musician as he stood from his bench and shouted as best he could. "Everyone out of this instant."

With some reluctance those present began to rise from their arses. They huffed, puffed and grumbled and then began to congregate into small groups. Once more a heavy groan reverberated through the walls which then trembled a second time. She watched the dawdlers and her frustrations grew.

"What is happening?" cried Heliana over the commotion. "What did you discover below?"

Tonousa was about to reply when an enormous crack opened up and the floor before them gave way. In an instant she grabbed hold of Heliana and dragged her to safety against the wall. With fate pushing his back Theoplous jumped towards the wall a second before the vast majority of the floor collapsed inwards. Shards of wood, clumps of stone and flying furniture took to the air before they too fell down into the vast rocky cavern that appeared where solid ground once lay. Dirt, dust, and smoke then filled the space of the once great dining hall like a sea fog rolling in off the ocean.

Tonousa, relieved to find her companions alive beside her, felt a sudden sadness for the fate of the students and masters who had been too slow to evacuate the hall. There was no sign of the Grand Musician nor indeed the young servant girl as Tonousa strained her eyes to see through the billowing smoke and debris. Whoever was behind this attack knew what they were doing and it was clear from the still trembling walls that the whole of the Guild could collapse at any moment.

"What the fuck is going on?" screamed Heliana, expressing her fears as she pressed herself against the wall and away from the deep pit that lay only inches from her feet.

"I'm not sure," replied Tonousa while surveying the chaos and screams of panic from the few others who still clung to the walls. "There was black powder in the cellar. I believe that it was put there on purpose."

"This is not time for an investigation," grunted Theoplous. "We can speculate once we are out of this death trap. I fear the rest of this building is going to fall."

"The sailor is right Tonousa," added Irabo. "We must leave right now."

Tonousa nodded her agreement and the group of four began to move off the already weakened floor residues onto which they clung to life. Tonousa turned, pushed Irabo forward, and looked on as he edged his way along what little was left. His progress was slow but after several minutes he made it through the arch and out of the hall. Heliana was next to traverse the ledge, followed by Theoplous. Tonousa watched with growing impatience as the others completed their short journey before her time came to follow in their footsteps. She edged her way forward, always with her back to the wall, and as she did so she felt the unmistakable tremors pass through the stone. The cracking and creaking of timbers shattered any hope of silence as the structure of the Guild strained to remain upright. Time was short and they had to leave without further delay.

On reaching the corridor beyond the arch, Tonousa came upon a scene of pure panic. Guild members raced in every direction as if decapitated; their bodies rushing as if with a will of their own. On reaching her companions she wasted no time in collecting her thoughts for the nightmare was far from over. Then without warning she was attacked and knocked to the floor. In her confusion she first thought was that the floor must have moved beneath her but then realised she had been assaulted. Someone had hit her with an object across her back and thrown her to the ground. Tonousa screamed out in agony from her prostrated position on the cold stone floor. Then she heard the sounds of steel on steel, followed a moment later by a death screech, a hiss, and a thump on the floor beside her. As Heliana added to the noise with screams of her own, Tonousa rolled over and despite the pain in her back somehow managed to jump to her feet. She drew her blade from its sheath, readied herself for action, and then saw what it was that had attacked her.

There, motionless on the floor with Irabo's blade through its heart, was one of the students of the Guild whose hand still gripped a jagged blade. Tonousa watched in astonishment as the blond and blue eyed features of the student changed into a scale covered Lizardman. Heliana screamed.

"What the fuck is that?" gasped Tonousa.

"It's a Lizardman of the Eastern Marsh," shouted Theoplous, his blade drawn from its scabbard and readied for whatever came next. "It's one of their shape changers. They do not have many of them but they are dangerous fuckers."

"The Guild is finished," bellowed Tonousa above the chaos. "We must go. There may be many more of them."

"What about Llyat," shouted Heliana? "What about old Marus? We can't just leave them."

"Irabo, do you remember where they took the lad?"

"Sure," replied the young warrior as he pulled his blade from out of the Lizardman's chest. "In a room down the corridor, just off from that library tower."

"Llyat and the old man are your responsibility now. Get them out of here at the cost of your life if need be. The rest of us will make for the bridge."

Irabo nodded his head and indicated that he understood the instruction. Then with his blade in his hand he turned and raced off along the corridor towards the library tower. Tonousa looked to Heliana and placed both her hands upon the young girl's shoulders.

"Irabo will get Llyat and the old man out, I promise you. My priority is to get you and the sailor to safety. He knows much that I need to hear and understand."

"Do not worry about me. Believe me, I can take care of myself," added Theoplous as he waved his blade. "Be careful, there are bound to be more of the creatures lurking in the shadows."

"I think that is most probable," continued Tonousa. "Now, let's move!"

Tonousa strode off down the same corridor that Irabo had taken just a few seconds earlier. Heliana and Theoplous followed close behind. Amid her heightened state of awareness Tonousa was determined not to be surprised a second time. She would not drop her guard or make the same mistake as she had done with Nedes Karoly all those years ago. On reaching the main entrance they found a scene of chaos. Amid the aimless panic of crazed students Tonousa surveyed the hall. Spotting Irabo in the distance she saw he was already halfway up the great stone steps as he raced towards the second floor where the Grand

Physician and Llyat had last been seen. At base of the stairway and to her great dismay Tonousa spotted something that took her breath away. In the very same place where the two armoured knights had once stood guard there rested two enormous wooden barrels.

"By the gods! They are planning to bring the whole place down," she exclaimed pointing the objects out to Theoplous and Heliana. "Look, over there. There are more of those fucking barrels."

"What barrels?" demanded Heliana, oblivious to the words significance.

"There under the stairs. At first I thought they were just casks of wine, but now..."

Before Tonousa could finish her sentence several explosions of blue light burst into the confines of entrance hall. Strange popping sounds followed as the points of light energy dispersed only to be replaced by the presence of those that that she feared most.

"Run," shouted Tonousa, "The Guild has fallen."

The few students and masters that were still present raced for their lives but as they did so they were hacked down as a mass of Lizardmen who arrived out of nowhere and who wielded their weapons with devastating effect. Blood flowed in torrents and severed limbs slithered across the sticky floor. One of the creatures materialised right in front of Irabo who without hesitation severed its legs and sent it toppling over the balustrade and to the ground below. Tonousa watched with admiration at the way Irabo swung his blade but then she noted another of the creatures besides the stairs. This new one clutched a burning torch and she knew at once what was about to follow.

"Irabo!" she screamed. "Get off the stairs. They are about to be destroyed."

Tonousa then ducked as a Lizardmen charged towards her with its blade aimed at her neck. In one swift motion she span around and kicked out with her right foot. The foul creature dropped to the floor whereupon she slashed through its throat without further ado. The severed neck spewed warm fluid all over her boots and she felt its heat on her feet. Looking once again to the stairs she noted the trail of burning power, well on its way to the barrels that had been left where they could do most damage. The explosion was seconds away. Just as Irabo reached the top stairs Tonousa flung herself over Heliana and pinned her to the floor in an attempt to shield her from the imminent blast. In a blinding flash and with a deafening roar the room shook beyond its foundations. When at last Tonousa opened her eyes the once impressive staircase was no more. All that was left was a pile of stones and dust. Great cracks had appeared in the adjacent walls.

Glancing up through the smoke to the first level balcony where she had last seen Irabo, she looked for signs that he had survived the blast. Then as the haze began to clear she saw him, his attention taken by a fight that had broken out between a student, a Guild master, and a Lizardman amongst the rubble below.

"Irabo!" bellowed Tonousa. "Find Llyat. Get him out of here."

Then she remembered Heliana who still lay pinned beneath her body.

"Are you okay?" she asked.

"Not at all," said Heliana with a whimper. "What is happening? What are those things...?"

Tonousa jumped to her feet and with Theoplous's help dragged Heliana off the floor.

"No time to explain," she added. "We have to get away from here now."

"But what about Llyat," screamed Heliana?

"As I told you before, he's in Irabo's hands now."

"I'm not going to leave him here. I'm not going to let him die alone. He's..."

Theoplous hit Heliana on the head and knocked her senseless, an act which caught Tonousa off guard. The young girl fell forward and the sailor caught her, scooped her up in his arms and then flung her over his shoulder. With a deft movement of his hips he then span round and drove his sword into the stomach of yet another Lizardman who attacked from out of the smoke. As soon as the blade had completed its mission Theoplous withdrew it and the creature fell to the floor.

"This bitch whined too much," sneered the sailor. "Now, let's go."

The two warriors raced on through the smoke and rubble that now littered the entrance hall. More of the hideous creatures appeared and each brandished a weapon and looked for a kill. With each attack Tonousa and Theoplous cut down their foe with a mixture of skill and brutal slashing.

Rain fell in torrents as the two warriors with their servant baggage raced out through the iron doors of the Guild and down into the courtyard. The continuing rumbles of thunder and the lightning bolts that lit up the night sky added to the scene of utter pandemonium. The stables were ablaze and those horses that had been released raced around the courtyard in panic. Those still trapped screeched out in terror as their flesh cooked in the ever spreading flames. Many Lizardmen were locked in combat with stewards, students, and masters. The men who spent their lives in song and verse sought to defend themselves with any weapon they could lay hands to or with what little magic they had the energy left to create. It was a one sided battle for the Lizardmen had been prepared and had used their tactic of surprise with great effect. Tonousa and Theoplous continued to take down more of the reptiles. With a frenetic entrance, Glorius the chestnut horse from Valameer, broke out from the burning stables and entered the courtyard. The mare had been saddled and readied by persons unknown. Swinging her blade from side to side Tonousa made her way over to the frightened horse. She reached out, grabbed the reigns, and calmed it as best she could. After what seemed like forever she managed somehow to settle the horse amid the raging battle.

"Theoplous, take Heliana away from here!" shouted Tonousa. "Get her to safety. Warn the people in Valameer."

"What about you" replied the sailor as he slung Heliana from his shoulder onto the body of the horse?

"I will take care of myself in other ways."

"As you so wish," he replied without emotion.

Theoplous clambered into the saddle behind the still unconscious girl, gripped hold of the reigns and kicked the horse with both feet. Glorius reared and then set off at a gallop. Tonousa watched as the horse carried her two companions away, out through the gatehouse, and onto the Bridge of Athuna. A lightning bolt struck the walls of the Guild and caused a further section to drop. The stones fell with a mighty crash but the light had been sufficient to illuminate Tonousa's options.

"Today is not my day to die!" she screamed as yet more Lizardmen leapt in her direction.

The first of her attackers fell, followed by the second, and then a third. Each time another took its place as the fearless woman of the City Watch stood her ground. It was as if they toyed with her but she vowed that she would not be beaten or taken. As her foes fell one by one Tonousa looked for a means to escape. Soon an opening in the swarm of scale appeared and offered a brief opportunity to break out from the courtyard. She raced forward through the gap and felled yet another reptile as she ran. Her lungs felt they would burst from the effort, such was the speed that she ran. On she raced, pushing her body to its limit for she knew she would not get a second chance.

Finding herself on the grey hard stone paving of the Bridge of Athuna, with ears deadened by the crashing of waves, she tried not to slip on the rain soaked stone. There was no other option other than to run the full length of the bridge if she was to make her escape. Even though she was fit, the effort required would be immense. With numerous Lizardmen in pursuit she never once slowed down. From is origin high in the sky, the most intense of lightning strikes hit bridge before her. It smashed into the stone and punched a large hole in its centre. A section of the bridge collapsed and it fell with a deafening crash into the boiling water below. Tonousa skidded to a halt, tottered, and almost fell over the edge of the gap that had formed.

"Fuck you Hamthor!" she shouted to the heavens. "I will not give up my life to you or any of your kind. Leave me alone to sort out my own destiny."

The sound of her pursuer's footfall had also ceased and so it was that Tonousa turned to face the direction of the burning Guild. The way back was barred by five armed Lizardmen, each with different shaped blades. They crept ever closer, hissed, and snarled as they sought to coordinate their attack.

"For Parandor!" screamed Tonousa as she leapt forward to meet the first. Steel met steel and Tonousa's sword was taken from her hand. The Lizardman that had disarmed her then approached for the kill. Sucking in all her reserves of strength Tonousa closed her eyes. With every ounce of energy she could muster she launched herself into her assailant and took them both over the side of the bridge and down into the raging water. The Guild continued to burn and its glow lit up the night sky. There would be few, if indeed any, who would survive this dreadful night of destruction.

22

Llyat wept as he held his fallen master against his chest. He did not want to leave the old man on the cold floor of the bedroom and despite Thias rubbing his shoulders he saw no hope of an end to his grief. In just a matter of a few weeks he had lost his mother, his father, all his friends from Maplehill, and now the man who had taken him into his care. His new guardian lay lifeless on the floor and Llyat was convinced he was now destined to lose everything that was once precious in his life.

"I can't just leave him here," he sobbed.

"Look Llyat, we have to go. The Guild is about to fall and we need to leave right now," ordered the bard.

Llyat's sobbing turned to a wail. "What about his body? We need to take it with us. We need to give him a decent and proper funeral. We can't just leave him to rot."

"Pull yourself together Llyat," snapped back Thias. "Don't make me drag you away. Given all that has happened and your importance to what has yet to come, I must somehow save your worthless hide. If I have to carry you away unconscious, then I will."

"But...but... " muttered Llyat.

"There is no time for argument," replied Thias as he gripped Llyat's shoulder to the point of pain. "Now move your useless mound of bones and get to your feet."

Llyat looked down at the body of the once Grand Physician of Parandor and placed his hand for the last time on the old man's chest. Then he wiped his eyes with the cuff of his tunic, rose to his feet, and picked up Density's Song. Turning towards Thias he attempted to restrain his emotions.

"That scale scum called me the 'Traitor's Son'," he said as he pointed to the fallen husk of the Lizardscale. "What did he mean by that? Why would he want me to go to Avolire? Why do I have to be the fucking Marked? I never asked for this. I just want to..."

"Be quiet lad. Those are questions that will have to wait for now. I need to get you out of this building and to some place of safety where we can rethink our strategy. First we must cross the Bridge of Athuna and seek refuge in Valameer."

"What about the others?"

"With any luck we will find them on our way but we must go without them if we have to; do you think you can handle that blade?" answered Thias.

Llyat looked at Destiny's Song as it sat in his hand.

"I think so," he replied.

"Good but just remember that you can do more with it than just sticking the sharp end in."

Thias then led the way out of the room and on into the corridor beyond. Llyat followed, his mind stretched into overload. There were so many questions that ran through his head. He hoped that the list would end but as each moment passed new and more haunting ones appeared. He had lost control of his life and Irabo's ideas on Fate returned to confuse him further. The pair moved at pace along the passageways of the Guild and Llyat began to notice the chaos that surrounded him.

He looked with astonishment as the students and masters ran and shouted out their terror. Some screamed and called out warnings; something to do with the deep rumbles they had earlier heard emanate from under the dining room. Someone then shouted that the hall had collapsed and if that was true, Llyat prayed that Heliana and the others had left before the bottom had fallen out of the Guild. He refused to engage with the thought of losing the woman that he loved. Then the commotion grew ever louder as more voices echoed through the building. A young student girl ran towards them and Thias reached out. He grabbed the distraught woman by the sleeve of her robes.

"What's happening?" he demanded. "What's going on down there?"

"The Guild is under attack," hollered the girl. "It's the Lizardmen. At least twenty of them I would guess. They appeared out of nowhere moments after the dining hall floor collapsed. The bastards popped out of tunnels of blue light as if by magic."

With the force of fear in her legs the girl managed to break free of Thias's grip and continued to race off down the corridor.

Thias turned to Llyat. "You are going to have to use that sword sooner than I expected."

"What about you?" replied Llyat as he realised that Thias was unarmed. "Should we go back for that creature's weapon?"

"We don't have time," continued Thias. "From what the student said, I assume that the Lizardmen have invoked the Rift and that more of them will continue to arrive. I may not have a blade but I can look after myself without one."

Thias muttered something under his breath, strange words that Llyat had never heard before and as he watched the bard's hands burst into flames. The fires crackled and the flesh began to smoke and yet Thias seemed to experience no pain.

"Fuck me!" gasped Llyat.

It was hard for the youth to believe what his eyes could see and yet given everything else that he had witnessed in the past few hours, flaming hands now seemed somehow easy enough to accept.

"Like I said," continued Thias. "I can defend myself. Now come on."

Thias led and Llyat followed. They continued for a short distance until on turning one corner they saw walking towards them, dressed in distinctive leather armour, three Lizardmen with weapons drawn and ready to strike down anyone or anything they came across.

"Prepare yourself Llyat," shouted Thias. "Fate has called out our names."

"For Maplehill!" screamed Llyat as he gripped Destiny's Song with both hands.

"For the Guild, and Parandor," shouted Thias, his fists raised and ablaze.

The first two Lizardmen charged forward. One that carried an iron mace engaged Thais, whereas the smallest of the three who held a jagged blade jumped towards Llyat. The weapon descended in an arc but Llyat managed to deflect the blow by thrusting Destiny's Song up and out. Before the creature could regain its balance, Llyat rotated his sword and thrust forwards with all his strength. The blade sliced through the leather armour, past a barrier of reptilian scale, and into the soft flesh of the creature. The beast did not even wince. It grabbed hold of the blade and snarled into Llyat's face. Then it pulled the sword deeper into its own chest.

"Is that all you have got little boy," it hissed.

"Not at all" shouted Llyat.

The youth he kicked up to where he assumed the creature's balls would be, if indeed it had any. He connected with something soft and squelchy and the creature howled out in pain. It dropped its own weapon and released its grip on the blade that had pierced its chest. Llyat pulled Destiny's Song from out of the creature, swung it around at arm's length and decapitated his foe. The body to fell to the floor before him while the head flew several paces away and bounced off the wall of the corridor. Llyat was taken aback by his first kill but soon regained his composure. He then turned his attention back to his friend. Thias punched the air and with each movement released a fire ball in the direction of the mace wielding creature. With each blast of fire the Lizardman countered with a swing of its weapon and deflected the balls of flame back towards the bard. Thias dodged every counterstrike. Then Llyat readied his blade again as the third Lizardman charged forward into the fray but the reptile did not get far for another blade slashed through its throat and dropped it to the floor. Llyat looked on with surprise as amid the smoke and fire that billowed up from the hall below he saw the silhouette of Irabo. The warrior from the Watch stepped forward and thrust his blade into the back of the creature that had picked its fight with Thias. It was a fatal blow and the Lizardman fell to the floor where it writhed for several seconds before its life force departed the Middle Realm.

"It's good to see you're both awake," shouted Irabo. "The Guild has fallen."

"No shit!" replied Thias, his voice oozing sarcasm. "We were trying to get the fuck out of here."

"Likewise," continued Irabo, "but Tonousa sent me to find the lad and the old man. I am pleased to find you are here Llyat, but where is the Grand Physician?"

Llyat did not have to speak for Irabo to understand the meaning of the silence that followed.

"As much as I hate to break up this happy reunion," added Thias while turning off the fire from his fists. "We must leave now. The flames below are getting ever closer and I don't know about you but I have no desire to die this night."

"That will be for Fatumai to decide," answered Irabo with his usual calm.

"Come on this way," ordered Thias as he pointed down the corridor in the direction that Irabo had just come from.

"No, that's a lost cause. The stairs are gone. I was lucky to have just made it to the top. We must find another way out," responded Irabo.

Llyat stood and watched the verbal exchange as the corridor around them burned. Then he saw himself back in Maplehill, trapped in the floor space beneath his house alongside his mother as the building above them burned. He felt a surge of guilt knowing that he had escaped at the cost of his mother's life. The pain and torment burst into his thoughts while he felt the tingle across his finger tips from the blistered scars that he had incurred on that fateful night. If he and his friends did not act soon the Guild would be their funeral pyre.

"Please," pleaded Llyat. "For the sake of the gods we love, let us escape from this nightmare…"

"Llyat, this is no time for prayer," snapped back Thias. "Follow me… I think I know how we can get out of here."

Thias raced over to the nearest door in the corridor and kicked it open. The force of the blow broke the lock that had sealed it and Thias raced in through the opening. Llyat and Irabo followed as the wooden roof of the corridor behind them ignited into a ball of flame. Timbers crashed to the floor while Irabo slammed the door shut to delay the ingress of the heat and flames. There was no way back and it seemed the three were trapped within the confines of the room that they had just entered. Llyat recognised the chamber for its walls were covered in a multitude of shelves on which rested thousands of books. Thias had brought them back into the library tower. No flames had yet taken hold in the magnificent room but Llyat knew that it would be but a matter of time before the fire in corridor breached the wood of the door. Very soon the history and lore of the Bards of Valameer would be lost forever, turned to ash, and erased from the memory of man.

"What now," asked Llyat in panic? "This is a trap. We are doomed"

"Have faith," replied Thias. "All is not as it appears. We are far from finished."

"If you think that we could climb out those small windows then think again," said Irabo as he surveyed the room and the small arched openings placed at random around the tower.

"No, not the windows," said Thias as he dismissed the suggestion. "Quick, the table. Help me to move it for the flames are beginning to lick through the door."

Even as he spoke the fire began to force its way in between the wood and the stone floor. A few seconds later smoke began to fill the room and the door began to burn with an intensity that showed it wold soon collapse. Llyat wasted no time and just beat Thias to the table. Irabo moved at a more considered pace with his sword readied while he scanned the room for danger.

"Quick, help me turn it onto its side," ordered Thias while he grabbed hold of one of the sides of the table.

Llyat took hold of the other end and between them they flipped the table onto its side, scattering its contents over the floor. He was surprised on how heavy the table felt considering the light wood that had been used to make it. He decided that some magical property must have been given to it like the hidden shelves that had contained the dagger; the secret shelves that still remained open and exposed. Once the desk was on its side it revealed a square stone slab in the floor. Thias tapped it three times with his right foot and the stone began to move. Within a few seconds it had retracted down and back under the adjacent floor. As the red glow of fire filled the room it illuminated the first steps of a winding stairway that descended into the rock below.

"Get into the passage now," ordered Thias.

Llyat made towards the opening but a sudden explosion of blue light flashed in his intended path. Then as the ethereal glow vanished with an explosive pop, it left in its place another of the Lizardmen. Llyat froze with fright. He began to shake with fear as he realised that the terror continued. The fire began to take hold over the book lined walls and the smoke that filled the room got ever denser. The Lizardman charged towards Llyat but before he could reach him Irabo jumped between them.

"Llyat, get out of here," he shouted as he deflected the strike of the reptile's blade.

"What about you" screamed Llyat?

"Thias, get the boy out of here."

Llyat half expected that Thias would drag him kicking and screaming towards the opening in the floor but he couldn't have been more wrong. Instead, Thias raced across the tower room towards the mysterious shelves and shouted out words that Llyat did not understand. The bard then grabbed hold of the withered scab infested hand. His whispered spell now protected Thias from its magic and he threw it towards the Lizardman. It struck the creature at the base of its scaly tail. The reptile ignored the transient blow, hissed, and continued one more step towards Irabo. Then in the next instant it froze on the spot. Llyat looked on as the creature turned the colour of stone and as it hardened like concrete it ceased to breathe.

"Awesome!" said Thias as a great smile spread across his face. "Instant petrification."

"Where do these steps lead?" demanded Llyat as he walked over to the hole in the floor and peered down into the darkness.

"This exit is a close kept secret," replied Thias as he started to lead the way down. "It was designed such that if the Guild was ever under attack we could get the Grand Musician out undetected."

"Blessed be the architect," said Irabo.

The trio moved with great care down into the darkness. The pressure on the stone steps activated some hidden mechanism and Llyat heard the slab above begin to move and close. Soon they were plunged into darkness and Llyat heard the bard mutter more strange words. This time he recognised one of them.

"Promethelumous," mumbled Thias and again his hands burst into flames and lit the way.

"What about the others" asked Llyat? "What about Heliana? What about Tonousa?"

"She is a skilled warrior," replied Irabo. "The best I have ever known. She will get Heliana to safety somehow, even if she perishes in the attempt. I have complete faith in Tonousa Amberstone."

Llyat did not know what to say. He could not help but think about the girl who had in recent days made his life complete. The thought of her burning alive in the Guild, or being hacked to pieces by the murderous beasts, was all too much to bare. Yet he knew he had to stay strong and live long enough to see her just one more time. When Thias reached the end of the stone staircase he stopped and took a deep breath. At the bottom their escape route ended in a deep pool of water with no path around it. It seemed they could go no further.

"Oh fuck, we're trapped," exclaimed Llyat as he stood before the murky depths. "There is no way out. What have you done Thias?"

"Keep your head young Llyat," replied the bard. "The tide is in and the exit is under the water. We just need to swim down a short way, then along a submerged tunnel about the length of ten tall men. It will then slope upwards into a small cave at the foot of the island. If my memory is accurate there should be a small boat hidden inside the cavern that we can use to reach the mainland. I pray we have the strength to fight the stormy seas and make the shore alive. By the will of the gods, I hope you both can swim."

"I can, just about," replied Llyat while he pondered how he was going to manage such a distance under water. "Although I am out of practice."

"I can," added Irabo. "Swimming is one of my stronger skills."

"Good," continued Thias. "I'm a strong swimmer too. We can both help Llyat."

"Are you sure about the distance?" asked the trembling youth.

"I'm positive... Irabo, you go first. Take a lungful of air and just use your arms to guide you. Llyat once you are under the underwater, hold onto his feet. Do you think you will be able to pull him along Irabo?"

"I can but try," answered the warrior.

"That's good. I won't be able to maintain the flame once we are underwater so it will be very dark. Come we must go before the passageway is compromised."

Llyat hesitated and watched as Irabo moved down the few steps and began to submerge into the deep water that covered their route to freedom. Once again the memories of the fateful night in Maplehill pervaded his thoughts; how he had escaped from the massacre and had then ended in cold water of the Tiaryer. This time however it was different for he had friends guide him through this new nightmare. He tucked Destiny's Song into his tunic belt and with much trepidation took his first steps into the black."

"Take a deep breath now," said Thias from behind.

Llyat looked forwards to where Irabo had disappeared and realised that it was now or never. In fact he took several deep breaths. Then on holding onto his third intake of air he lowered his head into the cold and salty water. Within a second Llyat felt waves of panic as he tried to locate Irabo's feet and take hold of them. Seconds passed like hours under the freezing water and he realised that if he didn't find them soon he would drown. Then, after several more seconds, a boot kicked him in the face and pointed out the location of his saviour. He reached out and grabbed the damp leather around his friend's foot and held on for his life. As he moved forward, dragged along by Irabo, he tried to close down his visions of drowning, of finding the tunnel collapsed, and ending his short life in a cold wet tomb.For what seemed like an eternity Llyat was dragged along inch by inch through the mind numbing passageway. He felt the pressure mounting inside his chest as he struggled to keep hold of his breath. He so much wanted to open his mouth and gulp in air. As his vision began to cloud he prayed that the young man of the City Watch would once again deliver him from a watery death. Just before Llyat was about to give up all hope and gasp in water he realised that he was moving up. He opened his eyes, stared through the salty sea ahead. There he saw the waterline and above it a flickering light. A second later his head broke the surface and he sucked in the cold air as his hunger for life returned with a vengeance. Lungs deprived of life sought to empty the cavern of its gases. Once he had regained a little of his composure he looked around and saw that as promised he was inside the interior of a small cavern. There ahead of him was an old wooden jetty. The fearful darkness of the cave was lit by flaming torches that he assumed were controlled by similar forces as those that illuminated Parandor's Underkeep. While his thoughts dwelled on the Capital Llyat felt a hand grab hold of his sodden clothes and it pulled him on towards the wood. Soon he was dragged out of the cold water and left like a floundering fish upon its splintered surface. Sitting up and thankful to still be alive, he scanned the surface of the water for Thias. There was however no sign of the bard within the treacle darkness of the subterranean pool. Llyat turned to Irabo and shouted:

"Where is he?"

"He should have been right behind us," replied the warrior.

Both men nervously watched the surface of the water for what seemed like an age. They focused on the rippling swell which at the far end of the cavern led out to the vast ocean beyond. There was still no sign of Thias. Llyat's gaze fell back upon the small wooden boat that was tied to the jetty but there was no evidence of the bard there either. In the silence that followed Llyat assumed that Thias must have drowned but then he noticed a small number of bubbles rising to the surface of the water. The bard then burst through the surface and gasped for air. Llyat sighed in relief.

"What kept you?" shouted Irabo as the bard swam towards the jetty.

"I was just trying to hold the dramatic tension," replied Thias as he laughed.

Seconds later the bard began to pull himself onto the wooden structure.

"I am so glad we are all still alive," panted Llyat. "I didn't think we would make it."

"It's not over yet," replied the bard while standing. "We still have to reach the mainland."

"Then let's get going," ordered Irabo. "No offence Thias, but I've had enough of your Guild."

"You know what," answered Thias. "So have I."

23

In a deep state of shock Methladon and Tycus were led back down into the mines of Avolire. They had been stunned to hear that the Bards Guild of Valameer had been infiltrated by the Lizardmen. It seemed impossible to believe that the all-powerful bards with their mastery of magic, sorcery skills that rivalled the wizards of Parandor, had been unable to prevent such a deception.

"Tell us Dayis," demanded Methladon as with the steward he helped the broken Tycus onto the stone slab that would have to pass as his bed. "How did these bastards capture you?"

"A group of us had ventured north into the Ivory Pass in search of kulkulkath carcases," replied the steward. "The beasts' venom has great healing properties if diluted and we were running short of it back in the Guild. Someday I must tell you of its remarkable effects. One drop diluted in a barrel of water can heal thousands yet the smallest drop placed on the tongue in its pure state can kill a man in an instant. Did you know that it isn't just the kulkulkath that use the Ivory Pass, the giant wormnoses also use it as a graveyard?"

"Fucking fascinating, but keep to the point," winced Tycus from upon the makeshift bed.

"I'm sorry!" said Dayis. "Where was I?"

"You were telling me how you were captured and brought here," prompted Methladon.

"Yes, quite so. We came across some strange tracks in the pass the likes of which I have never seen south of the Grey Mountains. My curiosity got the better of me and I allowed the rest of my party to return back to Valameer while I followed the footprints north, skirted around Falahorn and entered deep into the Dragonas. Within that land that I came across a caravan of Lizardmen. It was strange for them to be that far west and so distant from the Marsh given the intensity of the heat out there. Like the fool that I am I drew too close and the goddess Fatumai dealt me a most fateful blow. I was discovered and soon overpowered. I tried to fight back with what little magic I knew but they were too strong and large in number."

"How long ago was this?" asked Methladon.

"About two months I think. They took me east, right across the Dragonas along with others they had taken by force. Most of us were put to work down in this mine. The others, the lucky ones, were given a stark choice, either serve in Avolire's Army or die."

"I'm sorry for your troubles," groaned Tycus as at last he managed to sit up and swing his legs towards the floor. "I don't want to hear any more of this shit; what use is it to me? We will be stuck here until that Silverbitch decides to torture us again. Who knows what poison she will fill our minds with..."

"Take it easy," ordered Methladon. "Save your strength."

"Save my strength you say!" sneered Tycus. "Save it for what? I see now that nothing will ever come of your false hopes of escape."

"I'm still trying to figure out a way of getting us out," replied Methladon. "I didn't ask for any of this and I do not ask that you treat me as your leader."

"You stood up to the masters," added Tycus. "You stood up to Nictis. You stood up to her."

"And look where that got me!" bellowed back Methladon. "She showed me what she said was my future, a future that I do not even dare to contemplate. I will get us out of here, I promise you that, but I cannot do it alone. I need your support and encouragement Tycus. We need to understand our enemy better and discover what plans they have for the sceptre. This is my challenge and by the gods I will complete it no matter what the personal cost. They butchered my father, my mother. All gone because of that woman's lust for power. I will have my revenge for I refuse to die for nothing."

The three men looked to each other. Methladon felt the mark on the back of his head burn but he did not stop to think what it could mean.

"Look Tycus, I'm sorry," he continued. "I wish that I could have saved Lancet. I'm gutted that he had to die."

"Forget it," replied Tycus as he stood and swayed from the effects of his savage beating.

Methladon sighed. He didn't have the energy to argue. All three held deep fears for the future but one of them had to remain strong.

"Look," began the blacksmith's son. "I'm going to find us something to eat in order to keep our strength up."

"Oh really!" sneered Tycus. "A feast. I cannot wait."

Methladon felt his anger rise and was about to snap when Dayis intervened.

"I just want to say thank you once again for what you did for me," said the steward.

"Think nothing of it!" answered Methladon after which he turned and left the cell.

Several days later the young man from Maplehill wandered through the passageways of the stone prison, lost in his anger and thoughts. He struggled to understand the actions of his friend Tycus whose life he had saved on numerous occasions and for which he had received many beatings. The events in the ruined church weighed heavy upon his thinking. Had he not resisted in the way he had done then both Tycus and Dayis would have been murdered there and yet it was only Dayis who showed any gratitude. Although he had promised to get them out their nightmare he also knew that any plans could not be rushed. One wrong move against the knights or the Lizardmen would mean certain death for all. He moved clear of the prison block and roamed around inside the labyrinthine mine tunnels. For many long minutes he saw little evidence of activity throughout the torch lit rocky caverns. There were just a handful of his fellow slaves left and deep in his subconscious he knew the fate of those no longer at their labour. Without warning a Lizardman master called Sslondash approached.

"Boy," hissed the reptile. "Are you the one they call Methladon Heyn?"

"Yes, that's me, why?"

"The Lady of the Silverwynn demands your presence."

"And what if I refuse?"

Sslondash did not answer but instead pulled a knife from the sheath that hung from his belt and jabbed Methladon in the abdomen. The force was not sufficient to pierce the skin but enough to ensure that Methladon understood the creature's intentions.

"I understand," he answered with the limpness of a defeated soul.

Methladon was forced to walk ahead while the Lizardman followed and dictated the route that they took. They trudged through the caverns of the mine and after some time made their way up the wooden lift shaft to the surface. Once above ground Methladon was marched through the ruined city and the encampments of its flee ridden masses. They soon passed a large open square and then moved on to the stairs that led to the church where he had encountered the Seer's Stone and experienced his haunting visions of the future. Sslondash pushed him beyond it and towards a more complete structure that appeared of greater importance. It was almost palatial in construction and was situated at the rear of the ruined church.

"Where are you taking me?" demanded Methladon.

"I told you before, the Lady requires your presence," hissed Sslondash while he jabbed away with his dagger into Methladon's back.

Sslondash pushed the youth through the passageways that lead off into gecko infested rooms and soon the pair came before an ornate arch where a great dragon had been carved upon its key stone. In the space created by the arch stood a pair solid oak doors, fitted to fill its middle and kept upright with enormous bronze hinges. In front of the doors and with his right hand gripped around the hilt of his sword stood Commander Rhaizen. In his left he held the skull helmet.

"My Lady awaits within," he commanded as his eyes stared menacingly down. "Approach the door and knock but I warn you, do not to try anything stupid."

Methladon thought to reply but realised there was no point in antagonising the knight further. After feeling yet another sharp stab in his back he moved towards the wooden doors. There he stopped and knocked four times upon the solid oak. After a brief pause he recognised the female voice that answered from within.

"Enter" it shouted but before Methladon could push against the doors they swung open by themselves. Their rusty hinges screeched as the wood parted and allowed the youth entry.

Before him was the most magnificent of bed chambers. Despite the surrounding ruins it appeared to have survived the ravages of time untouched. An eerie light from the few candles present flickered against the dark stone of the room. Through the gloom Methladon focused on an enormous four poster bed. The linen upon it had seen better days as had the woollen quilt which was also frayed and torn. He assumed that the bedding had been subject to the same nocturnal insults as his own back in Maplehill for he recognised the pattern of rat's teeth where they had nibbled away in desperate attempts to satiate their hunger. The Lady, it seemed, was not immune from the vermin that scavenged through the ruins of the once mighty city.

"Are you going to keep me waiting much longer Methladon Heyn?" shouted a shrill voice from deep within the darkness of the room.

"Move your arse inside!" hissed the Lizardman as he jabbed again with his knife.

"Thank you Sslondash, that will be all," continued the Lady. "The boy is old enough to enter of his own volition."

Methladon turned his head and for a brief second and looked at the Lizardman behind him. The creatures face screwed in contempt, no doubt angered that a slave was to be left alone with the Lady. It hissed, moved one step towards Methladon, but then thought the better of it. The creature scuttled back the way it had come.

"Are you going to frustrate me Methladon Heyn? Do I need to call Sslondash back? I am sure it will be more than willing to have you beaten again and again. Let us put a stop to this nonsense right now. All you have to do is enter of your own free will."

A strange sensation took over Methladon's body. It was as if he was being controlled by an unseen force as he looked into darkness and felt unable to resist the urge to walk forward. Once several paces inside the youth sensed that he had regained control of his limbs. For a moment he suspected the Lady had used the power of the sceptre on him again but then he realised that the sensation had been different. The doors behind him slammed shut. He turned at once to face them and found himself staring into the blue piercing eyes and chalk toned skin of the Lady of the Silverwynn. Without the circlet of white stones around her forehead her ebony hair fell unrestrained to her shoulders and enhanced the natural beauty of her pallor.

"The first step over the threshold is always the hardest Methladon," said the Lady with a hint of tenderness to her voice and as she moved towards him through the gloom. "From this moment all will become easier, should you so wish it so."

The Lady then clicked the fingers of her right hand and the light from the burning candles grew much brighter. Once the room was fully lit Methladon stared at its grandeur. To his surprise the blanket and the linen that lay upon the bed now looked new and for a second he thought he must be dreaming. Perhaps the woman was once again playing tricks with his mind. He stared in wonderment at her bedroom, the likes of which he had never seen before even in his dreams. It seemed tragic that his brothers were no longer alive to hear him tell of it, nor indeed his friend Llyat, for he would have such a story to tell while downing ale in the Red Mare. The pain of all that he had lost was immense and yet somehow he sensed a new beginning. From somewhere unknowable he felt his fortune was about to change.

"What do you want of me?" demanded Methladon as he tried to ground himself in the reality of his predicament.

"So defensive and so angry!" laughed the Lady while she stroked Methladon's right shoulder with her delicate fingers as she walked past him towards the bed. "That is no way to speak to a highborn."

"After what you did to us in the church then what did you expect," he growled back.

"The Knights of Avolire recognise my authority over their prisoners," she continued as she sat on the edge of the bed. "There are certain expectations to uphold, if you know what I mean."

"Oh is that so!"

"Thief's, bandits, and outcasts all look to me as their saviour. They need someone to lead them out of the darkness having been forsaken by the gods. They look for someone to take back the riches stolen by the House of Gylewu and to restore the rightful power in this Realm."

"You mean you?" replied Methladon.

"Correct! Please be sure that you understand me. The House of Gylewu and Parandor will fall at my will and on my command."

"The city in the vision that you forced upon me? The city on fire?"

"Once again you are correct, but we are setting off on the wrong foot Methladon Heyn...."

"Please, my Lady, you don't have to keep saying my full name over and over again. Those who know me well just call me Meth."

"Well then... Meth, although I must say that sounds a rather cheap shortening of a fine name; please be seated. Take the weight off your weary legs and relax for I am not going to harm you."

The lady tapped the linen on the bed sheet beside her and waited for a response.

"With regard to my initial question. What do you want with me? Why bring me here if not to taunt me or make me suffer further?"

"To offer you an opportunity my young friend."

Methladon was taken aback, unsure if he could trust the woman. So much had happened to him since he had left Maplehill that trust in another would not come easy. He would never forget the murders of Maria Darcha, Mal Castor, and her unborn child. Nor would he forgo the memory of the punishment that he had endured in the mines, whipped each day by the Lizardmen masters. No, he would not drop his guard and would be mindful in all that he said or did.

"If you wish to offer me friendship then at least you could tell me your name."

"My name!" said the Lady as she laughed out loud. "I'm sure you have heard the slave masters shout it often enough as you toiled below ground. I am the Lady of the Silverwynn."

"Your real name," he added while his anger continued to ferment.

"You do make me laugh young Methladon Heyn... sorry Meth, but you are right, how can you learn to trust me if I cannot even speak out my true name."

"Then spit it out, who are you?"

"The name my birth parents gave me, is Sanura. I was the daughter of the now long departed Hailth and Frostaria Silverwynn, the once Rulers Elect of the City of Calistorn. You see I am the true Lady of the Silverwynn... Are you hungry by the way?"

"Starving, like all of your slaves! Calistorn? I have never heard of such a place. I thought I knew the geography of the Realm well and have listened to many songs from wandering bards but I have never heard that particular name mentioned. My father knew his maps and he never once made mention of such a city."

"It is not surprising that you have not heard of Calistorn in any of the songs of old. When my ancient city strived for independence from the rule of Gylewu it was wiped by law from all maps and documents. Its name was erased from the history and lore of the Realm; it was left to crumble and decay. But come now, where are my manners, let me get you something to eat."

The Lady snapped her fingers with her right hand and as Methladon stared in disbelief a golden table appeared from out of nowhere. Its surface was filled with the most magnificent variety of foods that he had ever seen. His stomach rumbled and he licked his lips, desperate to savour the succulent selection. Drooling like a dog to the bell as sweet aromas floated up his nostrils he longed to sink his teeth into the feast. Methladon lost control of his will and step by deliberate step, walked towards the temptations as if driven by some hidden force.

"I'm guessing that you know the ways of the magic," said Methladon as he gazed down at the spread. "I've already seen your Commander show off his tricks so there is no need to try more."

"Commander Rhaizen is a direct descendant of the old order of the Knights of Avolire," continued the Lady while she looked over the rim of the golden goblet at her lips. "He was born with a gift that enables him to control his magic centres. Like those he is descended from, Rhaizen can harness all manner of magical power, much more than the bards could ever dream of singing about, yet less than the wizards in the Capital and beyond. I however lack that same power."

"But the candles, the doors and the food? How do you explain all of this?"

"Nothing escapes you does it!" said the Lady before taking another sip of wine. "Within these four walls I am all powerful. A mysterious enchantment was placed over this room by those from the Eastern Marsh. It is a direct result of harnessing the power of the Mighty Rift. Those Lizardmen that serve me gave me this chamber as a gift. It was their way of ensuring my cooperation through the oncoming storm that is about to descend upon the Realm. Well now, what are you waiting for Meth, help yourself."

Methladon looked again to the food and his resistance melted away. He lifted a red apple from one of the several black metal fruit baskets but then pulled away and let it drop.

"Come now my young friend, if I wanted to kill you then you would have been long dead. I have had so many opportunities already. Poison may be the woman's way but you have nothing to fear from me. Please eat."

Methladon hesitated once again but then reached out to take an apple from the table. This time he selected a green one and he savoured the moment. He raised it to his mouth, sank his teeth through the fruit's tough skin and took a large bite. As the juice of apple engulfed his taste buds he knew it was the best fruit he had ever tasted.

"How do you find it?" asked the Lady.

"Delicious. A gift from the gods themselves. This apple is divine."

"Feel free to eat as much as you like my young friend," she continued. "But please, come sit next to me and share my goblet of wine. There is far too much for one person to drink and besides I do not like to drink alone. This brew will leave me with a bad head come the morning if you make me drink it all myself."

The Lady tapped the side of the bed for the third time and Methladon made his way over towards it. With some hesitancy he sat and made himself comfortable.

"What happened in Calistorn? Why did the city so want its independence?"

"So many questions from such a simple rustric," she said, pushing the goblet forward.

"I'm twenty three years old!" snapped back Methladon.

He snatched the vessel from her hands and took a substantial gulp of the ruby wine contained within its bowl.

"Stop pissing me off!"

"As you so wish Methladon. I will tell you the tale of Calistorn and how I ended up here in Avolire. It is a story that will put the House of Gylewu in a whole new perspective. It all began with the finding of a vast seam of black orichalcum outside of Calistorn and that triggered the greed of those that dwelt in Parandor."

"Orichalcum, what is that? I have never heard of it, let alone a black version."

"All will be revealed in due course," continued the Lady. "The story starts far from here, near our northern boarders and before you cross into the Dirmark; the lands of the dwarves. A simple farmer from one of the surrounding villages was out walking with his most trusted animal, a dog called Jedidiah, and he came across what at first he thought was pitch bubbling through the ground. However on closer inspection, it appeared to be a molten black metal, the likes of which no one in the Realm had ever seen before. Acquiring a stone jar from the nearest market he collected a sample of the strange metal and once cooled sent it to the alchemists of Calistorn for identification. There with great astonishment it was found to be the fabled orichalcum, a substance that when set becomes as hard as a dragon's hide and yet feels as light as a feather. As the seam lay on Calistorn lands it became the property of those who governed our city and that happened to be my parents. The riches that began to flow into Calistorn became the envy of Parandor and Avolire. Prosperity came when we sold some of the precious earth gift to lands across the Eastern Sea and we grew ever wealthier. It was then that the greed of Gylewu raised its foul head and demanded that the wealth that Calistorn had accumulated be given over to Parandor. My parents refused and incurred the wrath of the Sovereign Ruler, the great, great grand whatever of your current ruler Phauless. He demanded that the location of the source of orichalcum was disclosed. In response the people of Calistorn rebelled and formed an independent city state. They broke all contact and trade with the Capital and began to arm themselves. They forged a new stronger yet lighter amour made from the black orichalcum and never once revealed the location of its source."

"Is that the same strange plate that the knights who serve you wear?" asked Methladon as he reached out to the table and plucked a bunch of grapes from off one of the fruit bowls.

"Correct. My city sought to protect itself from the wrath of Parandor and yet they were not prepared. The Gylewus, supported by the other Houses of the Realm, marched upon Calistorn in an attempt to conquer my home and take its riches. What little armour and weapons that had been made by the time of their attack were secreted out of the city on the first night of fighting. The smugglers used the old sewers and then the ancient shepherd's paths to move the metal to Avolire. There they used it to bargain and to beg help from those who still dwelt in the ruins of that once great city. However the Knights of Avolire arrived too late to save Calistorn. The city had been put to fire and was ablaze long before they arrived. The knights found one lone and scorched survivor amongst the remains of that once proud city. A small innocent child lost in the world and without any family to call her own. It was a baby girl... me."

"Ah, so that is how you came to Avolire!"

The youth took yet another gulp of the endless supply of wine and being a most potent brew it soon began to cloud his senses.

"Indeed so and that is how I came to this god forsaken place. As I grew and as the years passed I was told stories about how I was found and how the city of Calistorn had been destroyed. I noticed similarities between my city and that of Avolire and realised that Calistorn still lived inside me. I would not let the House of Gylewu force Avolire to share the same fate as Calistorn even though it was already in ruin. It became my mission to bring down Parandor and rebuild Avolire. I vowed to restore it to its rightful place as Capital of the Realm."

"So you intend for Avolire to rule in place of Parandor?"

"Indeed I do. My mission is to unite the people and races of the Realm under one banner, that of the Knights of Avolire. I intend and take Parandor by force, both from without and from within."

"From within? How?"

"You now know of the great abilities of the Lizardmen of the Eastern Marsh. As well as being able to harness the power of the Rift to serve their ends, a small number of the reptiles have the ability to disguise themselves, just like the creature called the chameleon. You met the prisoner called Dayis earlier today. He has already been duplicated and substituted by the Lizardmen. Some time ago he was placed in a position of high importance in advance of the plan that we are unfolding at this very moment. However there is another of greater value that is whispered of within the shadows of the Capital. Some years ago my hidden one in Parandor replaced a key member of the Sovereign's Court and is wreaking havoc there as we speak. He has created a substantial distraction by invoking the old ritual of Kha and a string of murders."

Methladon shuddered as if some malevolent presence had passed through his essence. The mark on his neck burned as an image appeared in his mind, one where he was tied to four horses, stretched out and about to be dismembered. It was a memory he had suppressed and longed hoped forgotten.

"Death Tubaria?"

"The very one Methladon," continued the Lady. "My spy in the capital came across the old ritual in a book hidden within Parandor's library. He had discovered that the pages containing the exact words of the ritual had been removed but there was enough knowledge left within it to recreate a story of the resurgence of the cult and tip the Capital into a state of fear. Lord Tullage's previous attempt to resurrect the Kha was not kept secret. One of my spies at the Grey Keep knew that Tullage had passed on the incantation to his cell mate before he died; but that was a fortuitous bonus because what my spy in the Capital also found in the book was detail regarding the importance and probable location of the lost Gems of Thamous. This information we now know was also passed onto Lord Tullage's cell mate."

"So who is he? Who is your spy in the Citadel?"

"Who is he indeed?" said the Lady as she began to chuckle.

Then she began the laugh of the lunatics, to such an extent that Methladon thought she was in danger of falling off the bed. Seconds later she composed herself and took a deep breath.

"I shall not tell. That secret is between me and my spy. Apart from certain Lizardmen no one else knows of who I speak and I intend to leave it that way."

"Then answer me this. Why did the Knights of Avolire attack Maplehill? Why did they let me live yet kill those that I held dear to my heart?"

"Because of the Prophecy dear boy. Because of the Marked."

The Marked? Methladon had heard this phase uttered on many occasions by knights and the Lizardmen masters. There was only one mark that he was aware of, the three circle pattern on the back of his head. Before he could attempt to clarify what it was that the Lady hinted at, a loud knock sounded on the door of the bedchamber. Both turned to face the wood.

"Enter! It opens," she shouted.

The Silverwynn clicked her fingers and the wooden doors swung inward, moved as if by some hidden force. Three figures then marched into the room. All wore the same armour that he now knew to be made from black orichalcum. To his surprise they were not all of equal size. Two men of average height followed one step behind their leader, a small and diminutive figure that had to be either a child or a dwarf.

"Remove your helmets please!" commanded the Lady as the three stopped before the table of food. "For the deep magic of this place to work, the walls of the room need to see your faces."

"Forgive me my lady," began the short legged leader as he started to remove his helmet. "I apologise for my rudeness but I bring word from Valameer. The rumours were true. The bards had indeed found one of the Gems."

Methladon stared at the dwarf for he looked somewhat familiar. Then as his eyes examined the clean shaven head and wizened face of the small man he tried to picture him with a full beard and an unkempt head of hair that smelled of pig breath. The realisation was not slow in coming. It was the very same dwarf with whom he had shared the cage; he who had identified himself as Grovrouk and who had been unable to comprehend the manspeak.

"Your rudeness as always brings great amusement Grovrouk," began the Lady. "Prey tell which of the gems have they found? Which relic have they uncovered?"

"The Dagger of Kha," replied the dwarf who then nudged one of his companions with his elbow. A hand extended forward and in its grasp lay a golden dagger. "Here is the sacred relic of the Death Tubaria. Your spy in the Bards Guild was correct in his report."

"Excellent work Grovrouk," she continued. "You serve the Knights of Avolire well."

The young man looked towards Grovrouk and the dwarf stared back at his former cell mate. Methladon was confused. He struggled to comprehend how this little man who had been his fellow captive seemed so at home serving the Lady of the Silverwynn. How the dwarf had become one of them seemed a great mystery as was his sudden mastery of manspeak. Grovrouk then took charge of the dagger and passed it across the table into the waiting hands of the Lady. Methladon fixed his gaze on the blade's golden hilt. A memory stirred within, one from long in the past. It had to be the same blade that he had found by the river and that his father had once kept locked away in their home. His thoughts returned a fateful day during his tenth year. The chest that had contained the dagger had been left open by his father and Methladon with much curiosity had picked up the blade. His parents had chastised him for touching it, saying that he wasn't old enough to know of its origin or the full extent of its evil powers. He was told he should forget how it had been found and that his family's greatest secret should never be shown or mentioned again. Here in the Lady's chamber the youth found it hard to believe that this could be the same dagger.

Methladon felt the three circle mark burn with a ferocity that he had not felt since the day he had first examined the dagger as a child. It was as if a hot needle had been pushed through his skull and into the depths of his mind with the intention of destroying whatever memories were left inside.

"Fuck!" he shouted as he jumped up from the edge of the bed. "What did you just do to me?"

The Lady and the dwarf looked at Methladon, both surprised by this sudden turn of events. Grovrouk and the two knights dropped their hands to the hilts of their swords.

"I promise you Methladon, I did nothing," said the Lady. "Why did you cry out in such pain?"

"Something sharp pierced the skin at the back of my head. Is this more of your torture? It was like nothing I have ever felt before. What the fuck did you do?"

Methladon rubbed away at the back of his head while the agony spread through his body.

"Make the pain stop!" he screamed. "Make it go away."

Falling to his knees he clutched his hands across the back of his head. He cried out in distress for whatever was happening to him showed no sign of passing. As he writhed on the floor he saw the Lady place the dagger onto the table in front of her and then walk towards him. The dwarf and his escort remained motionless but continued to watch with suspicious eyes. The Lady then touched Methladon on his shoulder and spoke with a softness he had not expected.

"Tell me where the pain is and I will do everything in my power to ease your suffering."

"My head!" screamed Methladon. "The mark on the back of my head. It burns. Kill me please."

"A mark?" she whispered as she held him close and offered comfort.

"The back of my head... The back of my head."

"Move your hands, I cannot see," she ordered softly.

Methladon pulled his hands away and felt the Lady push his skull forward. She began to examine his skin below the hair.

Without warning she jumped to her feet and pushed Methladon to the floor where he continued to writhe in pain.

"Grovrouk!" she exclaimed. "Take the dagger and put it with the sceptre. I will come and find you and the Valameer raiding party later. Go now."

"Are you sure Lady?" questioned Grovrouk.

"No time for questions, just do as ordered or I'll throw you back into a cell."

"As my Lady wishes!"

With that Grovrouk snatched the dagger from the table and marched off with his escort.

Once the doors to the room closed Methladon felt well again. No longer did the pain shoot out from his head. Within minutes he was fully rejuvenated although a little shaken. He then looked up to the Lady as she stood before him and noted the strange smile on her lips as she offered him a helping hand.

"Thank you," he said as their fingers intertwined and she raised him to his feet. "Whatever you or this room did for me my Lady, I thank you for taking the pain away."

"I did nothing Methladon," she replied as she pulled him towards the bed. "The mark on the back of your head is a curious and most interesting one. You say it is a birthmark?"

"Yes, I was born with it, which is strange as I have no memory of it in my younger years. I assume that I must have always had it, well I would, wouldn't I?"

"Indeed you would Methladon although the Realm is now so full of strange happenings that I could believe almost anything. Even the great Sir Raulyn the Grand, slayer of the mighty Urthanock, never saw or knew of such bizarre events. There are secrets so hidden that only those deemed the most worthy can access them. Methladon, for now let us assume that what you have upon your head is nothing but a birthmark. Be seated again and let me check that everything else is in order with your body. I must make sure you are hiding nothing else of interest or importance."

Methladon cast a look of surprise. He had no idea what she had planned for him but as silence fell his mind created a new image of his captor, one that was more positive, even though he still was wary of her motives.

"After all I have said and done for you, why do you find it so hard to trust me?" whispered the Lady "What must I do to convince you of my sincerity?"

Methladon stared back and realised he had no choice other than to be compliant. He sat down on the bed and faced her.

"See!" she said laughing. "There is nothing to be scared of. I will not hurt you."

Without warning the Lady climbed behind him, moved her hands up to his neck and shoulders, and began to massage his upper body.

"Then what do you....ow!!"

Methladon felt a sharp pain surge through his back for the Lady had moved her hands onto one of the many open wounds beneath his tattered tunic. Her spindle like fingers sank into the deep cuts caused by Sslondart's whip.

"I'm sorry, I didn't mean too....was it your mark again?"

"No!" winced Methladon as she continued to move her hands over his back. "You touched a flesh wound, a gift from your loyal scum."

"Let me see your wounds," the Lady whispered while she blew air into his ear. "Now, take off your tunic so I may see what damage my servants have inflicted."

Methladon once again hesitated for two voices competed inside his head. One told him to trust the woman who for whatever reason was now trying to befriend him. The other continued to push for caution until he discovered her true motives. He struggled to decide which to follow but before he could make his choice the Lady began to remove his dirt encrusted tunic and in less than a heartbeat had exposed his muscular chest.

"My word, you are a fine specimen," she said having tossed his tunic aside. "I have not gazed upon such flesh for as long as I can remember. I will not forgive Sslondart for trying to make a pulp out of such a wonderful body. Please lie down so I may inspect your wounds further and in more detail.

Methladon paused for a moment before turning onto his back. His eyes fixed upon the ceiling. Amid his semi-naked vulnerability he watched with trepidation as the Lady cast her lecherous eyes over further whip marks on the front of his chest. Even with the vicious scars that dipped like canyons through his skin, there was no denying the attractiveness of the well-toned torso upon which the Lady's eyes roamed with growing excitement. Methladon lay motionless as the highborn woman started once again to rub and caress his body. The sensation stirred his emotions as if a ladle in a soup of sensuous teasing. He had felt such feelings just once before when Catriana Darcha's hands had addressed an urgent need inside one of the guest rooms of the Red Mare. He felt the movement in his trousers as his cock stiffened in anticipation of what was to come. The warmth of her hands upon his body caused him look down. The Lady's hands drifted across his belly and he saw the faintest traces of a blue light as her digits flicked across his bare flesh. He watched in disbelief as the hands swam across his lacerated skin and caused the wounds to heal before his eyes. Soon there was no sign that his lesions had ever been there.

"What the fuck!" gasped Methladon. "How did you do that?"

Without warning the Lady climbed on top and knelt astride his chest. He sniffed the pungent aroma of her quim, only inches from his nostrils and his cock filled with blood.

"Within these rooms I have great presence for I am harnessing the energy of the Mighty Rift. I can bend reality to my will and can wield greater powers than even the gods could wish for. In here I can do anything that I please."

"But what would happen if I was to leave this room?" asked Methladon while he tried to keep focused and resist the desire that grew within his trousers. "Would the wounds come back?"

"No, dear child," replied the Lady as she started to nibble his ear. "I maintain a small amount of magic when I leave these four walls and I can use it as I wish. However once the hours pass and that pocket of power fades, I need to recharge my energy centres within these four walls. Be reassured however, the changes that you take away with you cannot be undone."

Methladon's ears listened as she talked but his mind was elsewhere. The sensations induced by her lips were overwhelming. Ever since he had left Maplehill in the back of the cage he had felt nothing but pain and fear. Now pure pleasure took hold and it began to dictate all that he would do. Determined to enjoy himself at whatever cost he surrendered to the power of the Lady's seduction. With eyes shut tight he felt her lips pass down over his torso and on towards his belly. Her sensual lip flirts sent shockwaves down his spine and his toes curled within his boots. Then he felt her hand disappear under the waist band of his trousers and curl around his cock. Skilled fingers gripped and dragged it out into the coolness of the room. The Lady of the Silverwynn then took his manhood and buried it deep within her cavernous mouth. Methladon could not hold back and in a surge of rapture released his seed. The Lady smiled, turned her head to one side, and spat.

"Methladon Heyn, I am your friend. I don't want to hurt you. Do you see that now?"

"So it would appear," he panted as he gazed into her eyes.

"Methladon, I sense that you have great potential. I want you to consider joining my quest to reinstate Avolire to its rightful place."

The Lady climbed off and allowed Methladon to sit up at the edge of the bed. The idea of joining the Knights of Avolire seemed an attractive option but then his thoughts turned to his friends and fellow slaves trapped in the mines below.

"What about those who have shared my suffering and helped me through my darkest times?"

"They will continue to serve my purpose," the Lady snapped back. "The ores and gems that the mines produce help fund my cause. But you dear boy, out of all of those who I hold captive, show the greatest potential. Do not forget what you saw when you looked into the Seer's Stone. One day you could rule Avolire by my side. We should allow fate to run its course."

"There is no such thing and you are deluded," snapped back Methladon.

"If that is true we must end our conversation here!"

She snapped her fingers and the doors opened. Her words rebounded off the walls.

"Commander!"

Rhaizen appeared at the entrance to the door

"My Lady."

"Take Heyn back down to his friends. Ensure Sslondart gives him a good whipping and stress that it is my wish that the beating is of the most severe kind. I want him flogged within an inch of his life, but he must not die... You see child, there is no point trying to fight fate; it seems your fortune has again changed."

"Fuck you!" snapped Methladon.

"You had your opportunity but you couldn't last the course!" she sneered. "When we next meet, I will give you one last chance. Either join with me and serve my Knights of Avolire, or die at the hands Sslondart. Now Commander, remove this slug from my presence and have him taught a lesson he will never forget."

"As my Lady pleases," replied Rhaizen as he raised his right arm in salute.

"Oh another thing, ensure that his friends watch his beating, then burn them alive."

"As my Lady commands?"

"No, you can't!" gasped Methladon as Rhaizen grabbed him by the neck.

"Trust me Methladon Heyn, I can and I will."

Once again Methladon's birthmark fizzed. He broke free of Rhaizen's grip and raced across to the table. There he snatched up one of the black metal fruit baskets and spilled its contents across the floor. With all of his energy he launched himself at the Lady, intent on smashing the metal into her skull. He did not however reach his intended target for as he propelled himself forward the woman raised her hand. An unseen force shot from her palm and flung Methladon across the room where he fell against the wall beside the wooden doors.

"Stupid ignorant boy," she growled. "Did you not learn anything? Do you still not understand the power of this room?"

Slumped against the wall Methladon looked through closing eyes at the Lady of the Silverwynn. Instead of the young woman that had pleasured him and soothed his wounds he saw a haggard old crone with wispy white hair, a few decayed teeth, and many deep wrinkles. She didn't just look ancient, she looked beyond time itself. In the last moments before he lost consciousness Methladon heard her address Rhaizen one last time. Even her voice now seemed old and frail.

"Prepare the Lions of Avolire!"

24

The heat from Solaris had significant competition as the sun god raised his fiery form above the eastern horizon and chased away the remnants of Hamthor's storm. Upon the rocks amid thick black smoke and reddened flames stood the once mighty walls of the Bards Guild of Valameer. The noise from the fire was intense and the smell of destruction drifted over both land and sea as the conflagration continued to spread throughout the stone and timber structures that made up the fortifications of the once great edifice. A little to the north and a significant distance away from the craggy outcrop on which the building burned, a small rowing boat bobbed upon the waves. Two of its three occupants watched in awe as the flames soared upwards to meet the new dawn light.

Irabo stood at the rear of the wooden boat, mesmerised by the plumes of smoke and the rise of the embers that glowed like fireflies as they competed to see which could ascend the furthest into the heavens. Thias the bard sat in the centre of the boat with an oar in each hand and in a steady rhythm he moved them in and out of the water. His face was screwed to reflect his overwhelming grief as he looked upon the devastation of his once proud Guild. At his feet, curled up in a brown hessian blanket that had been found tucked under the central bench of the small craft, lay Llyat Emgar. The young peasant drifted in and out of sleep for he had been consumed by exhaustion and the challenge of his escape. Yet that same fatigue prevented him from deep slumber while tremors from both cold and fear coursed through his body. A recurring and persistent thought circulated through the chambers of Thias's mind; how lucky they three were to be alive.

Thias stared at the burning building for there seemed no other place to look. He gasped on the realisation of its isolation, now that the bridge separating the island from the mainland had failed. The once magnificent Bridge of Athuna, the greatest of all Realmgoth structures, had been destroyed. Thias rested the oars upon his lap, reached into his pocket and pulled out a bronze pendent with an inlaid amethyst at its centre. He held it within his hands as the dreadful images of the ravaged Guild brought yet another tear to his eye. That one drop held all the memories of his past, a tear full of the great times that had passed on the island. Powerful emotions poured through the young bard's head for he also felt a deep sadness for all those who had died while he had managed to escape. He vowed to remember this moment for it would be spoken of long into the future. Men would write and sing of this day for at least a thousand years.

Locked in that single tear was the memory of his maiden journey up the coast, the first time that his eyes had had gazed upon the Guild in the presence of many other raw recruits. How he had marvelled in its majesty on first seeing the awesome structure upon the rocks, the place that he would come to call home for so many years. Those who had taken him from the Capital had said that the Bards Guild of Valameer would be his spiritual home for all eternity. Its doors would never be closed to him. Now it had no doors and very few walls either. Before the time of the Guild, his life with his unsavoury father and then his subsequent foster parents, Vostag and Ruta Heyn, seemed pitiful in comparison to all that followed. Thias remembered how proud and excited he had felt to have been given the chance to start life anew amongst the bards; a golden opportunity to at last make something of himself. The masters and musicians of the Guild had welcomed him as one of their own from the very first moment that he had crossed the threshold their doors. Even though the training had been arduous, Thias had always strived to live his life to the full. Throughout every waking moment he had tried to be the best student that those who ran the Guild had ever taught.

The bard wiped away a second tear that had trickled out from his eye with the cuff of his damp tunic. The salt water on the material stung his eyes but Thias barely noticed. There was nothing he nor anyone else could do to take away the hurt that he felt inside. The slaughtered masters and students were not his blood relatives but they had been his family. They were the best he had ever known.

"How long do you think it will burn for?" asked Irabo?

"I don't know," replied Thias "There is no way of telling how long it will take. All the tapestries and books, all the instruments and furniture, they are aflame. It could take days to burn out."

"Do you think any of the others got away?" asked Irabo.

"I'm not sure. It's impossible to say," he replied.

Thias turned his head towards the coast line and the cove where the town of Valameer sat upon the ocean's edge. He focused on the buildings that sat in the shadow of its mighty cliffs, not yet touched by Solaris's light and devoid of Mona's silvery glow. Yet the town stood out with a myriad of light points which indicated that its people had long been awake.

"Tonousa is a first rate warrior," continued Irabo. "She would not have gone down easily."

"I hope your right and I pray she is still alive for all our sakes," replied Thias.

A sudden snort-snore rose from under the hessian blanket and Thias realised that Llyat had fallen into a deep sleep.

"So what happened to you two?" continued Irabo. "What became of the Grand Physician and why in the god's names didn't we see the attack coming?"

"We were taken by complete surprise. The Lizardmen of the Eastern Marsh had replaced one of the stewards with one of their own. Can you remember the man called Dayis? Well it was him. It looks like it was a well-planned attack and that they were just waiting for the right moment to strike. By the gods they are cunning shits. The changeling Dayis murdered the Grand Physician and then set about trying to kill young Llyat. We must be thankful that he failed. Do you think the lad understands all that is expected of him?"

"I can only hope so," replied Irabo. "Fate has deemed it appropriate to deliver the Marked to the bards as foretold in the Prophecy. It is up to us to ensure that he is protected at all costs. Have you any ideas about what we should do next?"

"I'm sure I'll have figured something out by the time we reach land and have had time to think on the matter. For now I think we should leave the poor sod to his sleep, given all that has happened to him this night. But in response to your question as to why we didn't we see the attack coming, that is easy to answer. We were blind to the fact that the Guild had been infiltrated. My worry now concerns where else these scale covered bastards have planted their changelings."

"If the Prophecy of Enderdetag is playing out around us then I'm guessing the purpose of the Lizardmens' attack was to further weaken the defences of the south of the Realm," added Irabo. "That would seem a logical follow up to what you told us about the destruction of the Grey Keep. Whatever their ultimate motive may be, they intend to destroy as many of us as they can."

"The Bards Guild of Valameer has always kept to its own business but you are quite correct in your assumption," responded Thias. "Any force that could pose a threat to the south by coming through the Ivory Pass would have been detected by the Guild and the news passed on to the Capital. I do not believe however that the destruction of the Guild was their prime mission. No, that was to retrieve the Dagger of Kha and deliver it to the Lady of the Silverwynn and the Knights of Avolire."

"So you think they now have two of the so called Gems of Thamous?"

"I do," continued Thias as once again he placed the oars into the water and began to row. "The one disguised as Dayis said that it had cast the dagger into the Mighty Rift. Do those words mean anything to you?"

"I have heard rumours of it back in Parandor. It was something that those who follow the faith of Fatumai often talked about. It is said to be a shaft of pure energy that exists between the worlds and is like the glue that holds the realities together. Even though I believe in the gods and in particular Fatumai, I never once thought such thing could exist in the real world. To me it was always a story, like so many that fill the ancient lore. If the Lizardmen have been able to locate and harness the Mighty Rift then I have answered my own question. That's how they took us by surprise. But if they can do that we are fucked for it means they can do anything they wish."

"My thoughts exactly!"

Thias did not know if such a thing were possible and whether or not it was the key to the attack. Yet now that that the Dagger of Kha had been taken and the Guild destroyed, it seemed a reasonable explanation with which to fill in with facts. Another thought then began to trouble the bard. It sneaked in at the back of his mind and fought its way to the forefront of his consciousness. The changeling Dayis had referred to Llyat as 'the traitor's son' and Thias struggled to understand its significance and how that squared with the fact that the boy appeared to be the Marked referred to in the Prophecy. Not being able to resolve the issue to his satisfaction he hoped the answer would come in time. As he continued to row his eyes became fixed on Irabo's grim face. Then he noticed Irabo looking at something ahead, an object that had captured his vision and forced his eyes open.

"There! Behind you!" shouted the warrior. "Look over there… In the water!"

Thias stopped rowing and swung his body round to face the front of the boat. Seeking to spot what Irabo referred to his eyes focused on some fallen wreckage. Atop of the wood lay a familiar figure.

"Do you think she is still alive?" asked Thias with great concern in his voice.

"We must hope so," replied Irabo. "As I told you earlier, she's a fighter. She won't give up her life with ease. Quick now, get nearer so that we can drag her on board."

Thias bent his back and rowed the boat towards the wooden wreckage with its limp cargo. Each muscle and sinew of his arms strained with the effort of the pull. As the boat came alongside Thias steadied it while Irabo reached over the sides and dragged the water sodden body of his friend into the belly of the boat. The small craft tipped and rocked in a most precarious manner as the extra weight was brought over its edge and the body dumped on its floor.

"What kept you Irabo?" moaned Tonousa as she lay on her back and coughed out salty gunk.

"We are so glad to see you made it out of there?" added Thias.

"You too," she replied. "Is it just the three of us?"

"Four!" replied Irabo after which he pulled back the hessian cloth to reveal the sleeping youth. "With great fortune the Marked has survived."

"Praise the gods, Heliana for one will be relieved."

"What happened to her? Where is she?" asked Irabo.

"The sailor Theoplous got her away to safety although he had to render her unconscious to do so. They made their escape just before Hamthor destroyed the bridge."

Tonousa pointed towards the remains of the once great Bridge of Athuna and to the large gap in the centre of its structure. Thias looked to the mass of fallen stone that stuck out above the crest of the waves. In that moment he realised how fortunate the Tonousa was to still be alive.

"It seems the gods have favoured me this night," she added. "Did you send fickle fated Fatumai to save me Irabo?"

"We need to get you to dry land and get you warm again," said Thias, ignoring the snipe.

"Aren't you supposed to have magic that you can use for moments such as this?" she replied.

"Perhaps in normal times. My energy was depleted getting us out of the Guild."

Thias then explained in great detail how the three had escaped using a secret flooded tunnel. She too then realised how lucky they were to be together.

"I'll borrow Llyat's blanket for I think I need it more than he does just now," said Tonousa as her teeth chattered. "He is asleep now so he's not going to need it. That boy can snore like the best!"

Thias watched as Tonousa took the blanket that covered Llyat and wrapped it around her shoulders. Thias returned the oars to the water and headed for the shore with what strength was left in his arms.

"Feeling better now?" he asked.

"Yes thank you," replied Tonousa "I think your Guild has seen better days. What happened in there? It was as if they knew the exact time and place to strike."

"We were just discussing that when Irabo spotted you floating on your raft. From what we can deduce it appears the Lizardmen had infiltrated the Guild some time ago, disguised as some of its members. We think that their goal was to watch for the appearance of the Marked and to take possession the Dagger of Kha once its presence had been revealed. I'm sure you recall that we were told it contains one of the Gems of Thamous, five of which together are able to unlock the door to the Underworld?"

"Don't start that shit again!" snapped back Tonousa from beneath the blanket that covered her face. She tapped her forehead with one hand and continued on with her rant "I've had it up to here with changelings, dragons, wyverns, gems and fucking prophecies. I need facts. I'm pissed off that someone has tried to end our lives this night. We cannot forget what our purpose was here in Valameer. We came to seek help from the Guild in order to find clues as to who is responsible for resurrecting the cult of Death Tubaria. What have we found out? Nothing, absolutely fucking nothing. When I next see Abrahamus, I am going to lash his ears with my tongue."

"You are going to have a problem there Tonousa" said Irabo.

"What do you mean?"

"Best ask Thias. He can tell you more."

"Well then?" demanded Tonousa.

Thias then retold the story of the night from his perspective. He began with the events in the library where Llyat had passed out from information overload. He then reminded her about how the Grand Musician and Master Peaceore had taken her and others down to the dining hall for drink and sustenance. Thias had then assisted the Grand Physician to carry Llyat back to his master's allocated room where they intended to look after him until he had recovered. He then described how they were joined by Master Ulthirn and one of the stewards called Dayis. Ulthirn was an expert on the Prophecy of Enderdetag and in his opinion he was sure Llyat was the one spoken of. This he said had been made clear by Llyat's projection of Kundalish Aura despite never having come into contact with magic before. Then he explained how Master Ulthirn then left the room to investigate a commotion which turned out to be the beginning of the attack. Thias finished off his tale by disclosing that Dayis the steward had been a changeling, how he had then murdered the Grand Physician and stated that he had sent the Dagger of Kha to the Lady of the Silverwynn in Avolire.

"Shit! That answers a lot of the questions I have been struggling with!" she replied.

"Quite so!" added Irabo.

"Put aside the lies of that Lizardman for one moment," continued Tonousa. "The attack on the Guild proves just one thing to me. Its purpose was to stop the Grand Physician and myself from completing our investigations into the Parandor murders. Whoever was responsible for those deaths must have sent word to the Lady of the Silverwynn. It was they who arranged for the attack so that they could silence us. Forget all the mumbo jumbo about opening the doors to the Underworld and harnessing some weird power. That's all just a diversion and a load of bear spittle. What we do know for sure is that there is a spy, an infiltrator, hiding somewhere back in the Capital. We have to find that person soon or else the old man will have died for nothing."

"It is unfortunate that I must disagree with you," said Irabo using his most forceful voice. "Fate has dealt her cards and pointed us in this direction. If Llyat is indeed the Marked that the Prophecy of Enderdetag speaks of, then it is up to us three to protect him at all costs. We need to help him locate and reunite the Gems of Thamous. He has to seal the gates to the Underworld and lock away its evil for all time."

"Oh for shit's sake Irabo," shouted Tonousa with so much angst that it took Thias aback. "Don't start blaming this all on fate. I will not buy into such rubbish. Please, if you would just look at the evidence before you, it is easy to work out. Avolire is massing its forces against the Capital and soon they will have enough men and resources to follow the Lady of the Silverwynn into battle. If her spy in Parandor and our murderer are one in the same then our Sovereign Ruler is in grave danger. If Phauless Gylewu was to fall then the realm would at once become unstable. That would give the Silverwynn the perfect opportunity to march south and wipe us all out."

"Open your eyes Tonousa," barked back Irabo. "Things aren't always so black and white. You don't have to understand the fine details to see that there is an even graver threat hanging over the Realm. Even that sailor from the Lotus Isle believes in the Prophecy. If what Thias says is correct, that the Lady of the Silverwynn has two of the five in her possession already, then it won't be long before she has the other three. We need to find them before she does. Thias, please support me on this one. Tell me that I am not losing my sense of judgement."

Thias stopped rowing and stared at both Tonousa and Irabo. A moment passed before he spoke again.

"You both make good points," he began. "Although I wonder where this conversation is going to lead us. Yes, I agree that the murders in the Capital need to be solved as soon as possible and the spy unmasked, but I also believe that Avolire is on the rise with a much greater purpose behind its plans. Ever since I encountered their knights upon the road and witnessed the murder a poor innocent farmer, I knew that the time for Avolire and Parandor to engage in battle was not long off coming. Tonousa, given your previous encounters with the Dagger of Kha and Lord Tullage's Death Tubaria, I am surprised that you don't also agree with Irabo. There must be a far fouler force at work. If the Prophecy of Enderdetag is unfolding before us now, the great Orrery of Anyle Belanore would show..."

Thias paused for a moment and looked once again to the burning Guild in the distance while realising he would never see the Orrery again. All the work and expertise that that had been put into creating the magnificent mechanism had been for nought. It was now just a tangled heap of twisted metal and ash amid the rocks upon which the Guild had sat. Another tear formed in his eye and he wiped it way with his sleeve.

"So what do you two suggest we do next?" asked Tonousa as Thias gathered his thoughts. "You can't expect to charge around the Realm trying to find three missing jewels without the slightest idea of where they are. That would be futile. It would also leave the infiltrator unchecked and able to strike whenever he wanted. Who knows who would be the next victim in his evil plan?"

"We know that one of the jewels we seek is already in the Capital. The heart shaped ruby!" said Irabo at once. "That means that we must find the location of the other two."

"But the two could be anywhere and it would take years to search the Capital. It would be like looking for a witch tit. As I said before, this is folly and madness."

"We wouldn't be searching like the blind at night," added Thias as an idea came to him. "I think Irabo holds key to finding the answers that we seek."

"Well then? Spit it out," she replied.

"Look Tonousa," began Irabo. "We are not far from the Dragonas. Three maybe four days hike through the mountains and beyond the Ivory Pass. We could make for Falahorn and then search out Thamous himself; ask him where the remaining gems are hidden. We just need to think of a reason to get him to tell us."

A further silence swept across the sea while the idea sank in. Irabo was sure that Tonousa would ridicule it and he was not disappointed by her eventual reaction.

"You can't expect me to agree to journey up north in search of a legendary dragon..."

"Wyvern!" added Irabo.

"And the difference is, prey tell" she demanded.

"Dragons have four legs. Wyverns have two. Do not believe anything you may have heard about them being inferior to dragons or that they cannot breathe fire. Those tales are lies and are not based on fact," snapped back Irabo.

"Whatever! So you want me to go with you in search of a mythical creature while there is a changeling killing those we are sworn to protect. I must insist that we head back to Parandor without further delay,"

"And leave the Lady of the Silverwynn to find the remaining three gems?" continued Irabo. "Please see sense Tonousa. If what Thias told us about the attack on the Grey Keep is true then she may already have the knowledge of their location from Grovrouk the Despoiler."

"Whatever we decide to do, it's obvious to me that Llyat is going to be a target for the Lady of the Silverwynn," said Thias, rubbing his chin. "After what has happened in the Guild tonight she may believe for a short while that the boy died in the fire. That buys us some time and gives us an element of surprise, as long as we are careful and do not give our presence away. Tonousa, I have a role for you, given who your father is."

"Say more?" she answered.

"Lord Amberstone is responsible for the Sovereign's library," continued Thias. "I am certain that amongst all of your father's books there will be some that contain information and clues as to where the Ruby is hidden. I want you to return to Parandor alone and spread the word that the rest of us were murdered during the attack on the Guild and that you are the sole survivor. This gives you the chance to root out our infiltrator for he will no doubt come looking for you once you start talking about an attack by the Lizardmen. Your warnings will ensure that the Capital is ready for war when it arrives before its gates. If you can take out the changeling you will also be able to prevent him using the Rift to coordinate any attack from within. Furthermore, your story will give the rest of us the opportunity to move in secret through the north lands as we seek to locate Thamous. We have to take possession of the Gems before the Lady gets her foul hands on them. Will you accept this task on our behalf Tonousa?"

Another silence fell, broken only the waves as they crashed against the side of the boat. After some minutes of deep contemplation Tonousa began her answer.

"I think you're idea teeters on the edge of madness but often the best plans do. I will go back to Parandor and do as you say. I will unmask the spy and find the hidden ruby. I don't know how I will do it but for the sake of the survival of the Realm I will try my best."

"One more thing," added Thias as a thought crept into his mind.

"Just one!" sneered Tonousa.

"Remember the words of the prophecy. '*When the Oracles crypt shall be opened'*. Master Ulthirn believed this to be reference to the Oracle of Frasteria, she who was buried somewhere near the ancient Barrow of Harico. It has always been believed the Oracle would offer directions to the location of the entrance to the Underworld. Find out all you can about this Oracle before we meet again. Our lives may depend upon what you can unearth."

"I'll see what I can do but how shall we to communicate with each other across the lands that separate us. It's not like I can send a carrier bird for that could be intercepted with ease."

"She makes a valid point," added Irabo. "How do we let her know of our success or failure?"

"Is there anyone you can trust within the Capital? Someone that you are sure has not been turned by the enemy?"

Tonousa thought for a few seconds and then offered up a name.

"Danisun Dain of the City Watch. I can trust him better than any other. You could send a bird to him with your message but where would you find one?"

Thias looked troubled.

"In Falahorn," replied Irabo without hesitation. "The people there are sure to have one."

"Then that's settled," said Thias with some discomfort. "Tonousa will solve the secrets of Parandor, find the spy and the lost jewel, while Irabo and I will escort Llyat into the Dragonas in search of Thamous."

"What about Heliana, Highroar, and the rest of the crew of the Banshees Wail? Are we to abandon them here in Valameer?" replied Tonousa.

"That thought did pass through my mind," added Irabo. "They need to know that we are alive."

"No they do not!" snapped back Thias. "Don't you see? We can only trust the four of us now. I am certain that none of us have been replaced by the enemy? If we have then our plan is doomed from the outset. Tonousa, you are the only one who can reveal herself to the others but you must stick to the story that you were the sole survivor of our small group. The rest of us must remain hidden from the Lady's penetrating gaze."

Thias was unsure if his new friend would be able to commit to the degree of secrecy required and how Llyat would react when he found out that he would not be reunited with his lover. Now they had a plan in which they all had a critical role to play. Despite the lack of detail it was at least a step forward.

"I know of an alcove in the northern cliffs were we can make dry land," said Thias. "There is a hidden stairway, carved through the rock and which comes out to the south of the Ivory Pass. It had first been used by smugglers long before the Guild took charge of the coastal waters around Valameer. With a bit of luck we may find some supplies abandoned there by passing Guild members."

"That sounds a viable option," agreed Tonousa.

"There is one issue that concerns me," continued Thias. "If you are to return to Valameer claiming to have survived the attack on the Guild, then it would seem rather suspicious if you approached the town by the cliff road considering that the bridge is in ruins."

"You don't have to spell it out," groaned Tonousa. "I know what you are asking of me."

"Then it is settled, we must part our ways, but we will row you as far as we dare to Valameer's harbour without us being spotted," continued the bard.

Sometime later Thias looked on as Tonousa and Irabo said their farewells. They embraced with genuine affection until the female warrior pulled away.

"Good luck." she said.

"You too," replied Thias with the briefest of smiles. "The gods be with you always."

"And with you should any exist," she answered.

With that Tonousa dived over the side of the boat and back into the cold waters of the ocean. There she began her arduous swim towards the town, now bathed in the warmth of the morning rays of Solaris. Once she had disappeared from sight within the swell of the ocean, Thias returned the oars to the sea and began to row in the opposite direction. All the time he manoeuvred the boat to face north. Up alongside the cliff face and with the current in his favour he propelled the vessel forward at good speed. As the oars cut through the water Thias took one last look at the burning remains on the distant rocky outcrop and then closed his eyes in prayer. He realised that he still clutched the amethyst pendant against the wood of the oar in his right hand. It had been there the whole time yet only now it had chosen to make its presence known to him.

It took several hours to reach the cove which Thias had spoken about. During the journey Thias and Irabo had shared the labour of rowing while Llyat remained asleep on the floor. On several occasions Thias had been tempted to kick Llyat and see if he was still alive but whenever he had decided to do so the boy snored loudly and thus escaped a boot in his ribs. The cove was simple small and sheltered shingle beach set in a small recess within the cliff face and shielded from view of the ocean by a large pinnacle of rock that jutted out from the waves. Even the Guild and the distant Bridge of Athuna were hidden by this massive stone pillar. Having brought the boat ashore and beached it upon the shingle, Thias checked around but saw no sign of activity. It seemed that no one had used the cove for some considerable time. There was just one clue that someone been there before, a skeleton dressed in rags and lodged into the rock face. An ancient and rusting dagger protruded out of its rib cage where its heart had once been. It was a warning not to dally. Once the boat was safely secured Thias decided to wake Llyat from his slumber.

"Where are we?" asked the youth as he stretched and scanned his surroundings.

"A couple of miles north of Valameer," replied Thias. "It's an old smugglers cove. We are safe for the time being but gather your thoughts and be quick about it. We do not want to be here when the tide comes in and we have a devil of a climb before us."

Thias pointed towards the rock face above the skeleton and to a series of manmade foot holes that led up and out of the cove. Thias watched as Llyat turned pale for the youth could not believe the chosen means of escape.

"You have got to be fucking kidding!" gasped Llyat.

"Unfortunately I'm not," replied Thias. "There is no other way."

"Can't we take the boat further up the coast and find an easier way?"

"Not this time Llyat," continued Thias. "This is our way forward."

"Where are we heading?"

"North into the Dragonas," replied Irabo. "We are going to find Thamous."

"Let's start then," said Llyat much to the others' surprise.

Thias was perplexed for not once did Llyat ask about Tonousa, Heliana, or even the sailor Theoplous. Then as he led the way to the rock face and took the lead on the climb, the answer came and forced him to smile. The one rational explanation was that Llyat had not been asleep in the boat. He had heard everything and yet still kept silent. His snores had been fakes. The bard then knew that Llyat the farm boy was far cleverer than he made out to be.

25

When Tonousa at last made it into the harbour the inhabitants of Valameer were massed by the water's edge. There they stood and watched the last throws of the inferno that had destroyed the Bards Guild. Those who did not stand and stare in shock were hard at work as they launched their small crafts into the water in order to set out and search for survivors. Despite her predicament and the cold that permeated her body, Tonousa noticed in an instant the difference in behaviour between the residents of Valameer and the professional sailors who manned the trading ships in the harbour, including those from the Banshees Wail. The dirt-rough and scruffy seamen stood idle in stark contrast to the inhabitants of the town, who despite the hour of the day busied themselves in clean white linen robes with golden ropes around their middles which matched the colour of the leather sandals on their feet. As Tonousa at last reached the harbour wall she heard the cry of a young boy.

"Mother! Father! Look... There in the water!"

With considerable effort Tonousa climbed a ladder onto the wooden decking of the old town dock. Several citizens then raced over to aid her and helped her to steady her legs as copious quantities of salt water flowed from out of her clothes. Each seemed to have a question for which they demanded an immediate answer. All were desperate for news of what had happened across the water.

"What has gone on? Are you okay? Are you alone? Are there any more survivors?" were some of the many questions that Tonousa picked out from the chaos in her ears as she tried to regain her land legs. Then she looked back and gazed upon the Guild, or what little was left of it, and saw away in distance the flames that still licked at its base. Despite the plan that had been fixed in her mind she first needed to warn the people of Valameer that it would not be long before their town was attacked.

"I need to see Lady Flurdiana at once," bellowed Tonousa above the clamour. "Your lives are in great danger."

The father of the young boy who had first spotted Tonousa in the water stepped forward from out of the crowd and pointed in the direction of the twin towered building that stood above the others in the centre of the town.

"Come then with me, be as quick as you can," he shouted. "I will take you to her."

"Thank you, I am forever in your debt sir," replied Tonousa while the man then turned to his wife and the agitated citizens of Valameer.

"The rest of you should look to the sea and watch for other survivors. Ailora, take Finian back home and lock yourself inside. Barricade the door and don't open it to anyone except me. Do as I say now and without question." Then turning again to Tonousa he said, "Follow me... this way... now."

"Of course sir, I am ready to leave whenever you are!"

The man moved away from the dock and Tonousa followed as fast as she could. Her legs still trembled from her long swim and she struggled to keep up with his fast pace. On through the network of narrow streets he led, passageways lined with the same white coated buildings that she had marvelled at on her arrival in the town just a few hours earlier. The light from Solaris made its walls glisten and sparkle with a most magical splendour. The man led on and never once looked back. Tonousa knew that her primary objective was to return to Parandor as soon as possible but she could not leave before ensuring she had done all she could to prepare the Lady Flurdiana and her people for the imminent onslaught of the Lizardmen.

Some ten minutes passed before the man brought Tonousa before the twin towered palace of the Lady. On their approach to its vast wooden doors they were confronted by two armed men. Both were dressed in white tunics with green cloth cloaks around their shoulders, buckled under the neck with shimmering bronze broaches. Attached to their belts each carried a scabbard containing a short sword and in their right hand a wooden shield and a trident.

"Who comes before us?" demanded the men in unison as they crossed their tridents and bared access to the wooden doors.

"Darchus Arillius," said Tonousa's guide as he stepped forward. "A survivor of the Guild wishes to speak with the Lady Flurdiana at once. She brings news of grave danger."

"The Guild you say?" said one of the guards.

"As you will have noted Sirs, the Guild burns this morning," said Tonousa. "I must warn the Lady of what happened there and what will soon come to Valameer's doors."

"She speaks the truth," added Darchus. "Her words must not be lost in the smoke and fire that now drifts towards the heavens."

The two guards eyed Tonousa with suspicion. After a brief minute while they whispered together they stepped aside and retracted their tridents.

"Be careful how you speak in her presence and remember that there are many more Trident Guards inside," added one as he swung open the wooden door.

"I thank you kind sirs," replied Tonousa. "Have no fear, I will be most respectful."

Tonousa and the man from the harbour entered into a large rectangular hall. They walked past many marble pillars around which Ivy grew as far as the vaulted roof. Tonousa's legs, having got their second wind, raced forward through the vast empty space towards a raised area at the back of the hall. There upon a bronze chair sat the slender yet stern figure of the Lady Flurdiana. Flanking the Ruler of the town were a dozen more guards dressed in identical manner to those that had manned the main door. On reaching the bottom of the steps that led to the throne she followed Darchus's lead and knelt on one knee in a sign of deference.

"My Lady," said Tonousa.

"You may rise," the highborn answered. "From the look of your garb, I would guess that you are a herald of the City Watch of Parandor. What brings you this far north and in the company of our cordwainer, the honourable Darchus Arillius?"

"Forgive me my Lady but I must draw your attention to the night's tragic events at the Bards Guild," began Tonousa "I am sure you have been told that it has been destroyed. I need to inform you of all that happened there, an attack from within, led by those who dwell in the Eastern Marsh."

"The Guild burns?" questioned Lady Flurdiana. "Does she speak the truth Darchus?"

"Indeed she does my Lady. It was first noticed some hours ago. At first we all thought it was Solaris's light breaking through the night sky, but it was a different type of fire. My Lady, the Guild is destroyed. It is now but a collection of hot ruins."

"And yet I am just told of this now Darchus," she grumbled.

"Forgive me Lady," he replied. "We thought it a priority to find survivors as there seemed to be no immediate threat to Valameer. Even now we have men heading out to sea to search for others like this brave woman. There may be many who have escaped the conflagration and who are now fighting to survive in the ocean. We in the town thought it best not to disturb you too early in the day."

"I thank you for your honesty and consideration Darchus," continued the Lady. "I have not yet broken fast this morning and you were correct in your assumption. Everything must wait until my stomach has been filled!"

"We would have waited longer Lady Flurdiana but this woman that arrived like a fish out of the great water was insistent that she came here at once to warn you."

"Then I shall listen to her council but her words best be important for my stomach waits for no one, least of all one of low rank from Parandor. Please tell me your name, woman of the City Watch. How shall I address you?"

"Tonousa Amberstone, Lady."

"Any relation to the Lord Mathias Amberstone, Phauless Gylewu's book minder?"

"His daughter," replied Tonousa with a hit of pride.

"I have known your father a long time young Tonousa Amberstone," continued Lady Flurdiana. "But given your state of urgency and Darchus's words, I guess you haven't come here to discuss your father or his library."

"I beg your pardon Lady for my frankness but you're so right. I have not come for small talk and pleasantries," replied Tonousa and after which she jumped into her story.

She started with how she had been ordered to investigate the murders in the Capital and how that had led her to the Bards Guild. Then she told in great detail of the subsequent attack by the Lizardmen and how she had only just managed to escape alive. Throughout the unfolding story the Lady, her guards, and Darchus listened to her every word. Tonousa never once mentioned Irabo, the boy Llyat, nor Thias the Bard whose existence she had vowed to keep secret. She also kept back the news from the Grey Keep and the death of her betrothed. That painful message she hoped would fall on someone else to deliver. Right now she needed the Lady to be able to think with clarity and take decisive action. Once Tonousa had finished her story she looked up and awaited a response. The Lady sat unmoved and it was several minutes before she spoke.

"That is such a fascinating story, but tell me Tonousa of the loins of Amberstone, why do you trouble me with the matters of the Bards Guild?"

Tonousa was stunned, as it appeared was Darchus. This was not the reply she had expected.

"Forgive me Lady Flurdiana but don't you see, any attack on the Guild must mean that Valameer will be next," stuttered Tonousa. "If any of the creatures from the Eastern Marsh managed to make it across the bridge before it collapsed they could already have infiltrated your town. You need to mobilise and protect yourselves."

"And get caught up in the in a ridiculous and old rivalry between Parandor and its enemies?" grumbled Lady Flurdiana with a growing disinterest. "If what you have told me is indeed true and the Lizardmen of the Eastern Marsh have sided with those who dwell in Avolire, then there is no reason at all for them to trouble Valameer. We have always distanced ourselves from the feuds between the Capital and that city long forsaken by the gods. Phauless Gylewu tried many times to bring me to his side in the hope of legitimising his family's right to rule the Realm. He has even arranged a marriage between his brother and my body. He no doubt intends using Valameer as a defensive outpost and my womb to perpetuate his family's dynasty. Those in Avolire will not know of this intended marriage and so will not yet see my people as a threat. I do not doubt the truth of your story given the support of our own cordwainer, but I fear no attack from those that dwell in the Eastern Marsh."

"But please, for my sake Lady, ensure that your citizens are protected," pleaded Tonousa. "Don't let them be taken unawares like those of the Guild."

"For your sake! You think too highly of yourself woman," grizzled Lady Flurdiana without moving from her bronze chair. "Be very careful how you speak to me. Now, what would you have me do Tonousa Amberstone? The townsfolk of Valameer are either fishermen or traders who live off the sea. They are not fighters and warriors like those of the Capital. We also have a few farmers, merchants and scholars but they all lack the training of those of the City Watch. Other than my trident guard, who I reserve for my personal defence, we have few weapons and I cannot put a sword in every man and woman's hand."

"Yet we would be proud to fight for you my Lady," interrupted Darchus.

"And I would be glad to have you by my side," she replied as for the first time a hint of a smile formed on her face.

"When our Sovereign Lord calls in his banners against Avolire, will you just then sit back and watch?" demanded Tonousa, frustrated at the Lady's failure to understand all that was happening. "If not for yourself, but for the sake of your citizens, please ready your men however few they may be. I have come here in good faith to warn you and I cannot believe you will sit there and do nothing."

"How dare you speak to me with such venom in your voice Tonousa Amberstone? What would your father say if he was hear how you speak to a highborn?"

"Once again, forgive me my Lady," continued Tonousa, "But my father is not important to this conversation. I just don't understand how you can leave your people undefended. The threat that I talk of is most real..."

Before Tonousa had chance to continue Lady Flurdiana raised her hand from her lap and signalled an end to the conversation. Her voice bellowed out across the marble hall and it echoed back from its sides.

"Enough. I grow weary of this conversation and as I have already told you my fast has not yet been broken. Feel free to show yourself out Tonousa, daughter of Mathias Amberstone, but do not speak again or indeed come back. I am tired of this conversation and your continued presence bores the bowels out of me."

The words reverberated in Tonousa's ears as the Lady turned, moved across the raised platform, and exited through an archway. Her guards followed and left Tonousa alone in the cavernous hall except for the presence of the man called Darchus. She could not comprehend why the Lady had such a callous disregard for her people's safety. There had to be more to it than refusing to get involved in a conflict between Avolire and the Capital.

"Of all the pig ignorant, thick skulled bitches that I have ever seen…" spat out Tonousa, unable to hold in her anger. "I have seen more brains on a butcher's cleaver."

"Please do not let her hear your insults," pleaded Darchus as he put his finger to his lips. "She may be stern and stubborn but she has the interests of Valameer carved deep within the chambers of her heart."

"I can't understand how you can defend her like that," snarled Tonousa. "She is crazy to leave the town defenceless in this way."

"I understand you have not had the answer that you desired but I may be able to help a little. I have some powers of persuasion and status in this town and may be able to convince other townsmen to take up arms, but as the Lady told you, we are simple fishermen and tradesmen. We lack the training and skills to fight in earnest."

"That's as maybe Darchus, but I saw your family, your wife, your son. You cannot tell me that they are not worth fighting for."

Tonousa watched as Darchus looked around and then nodded towards the door.

"Let us not talk about this here," he continued. "Walls of stone also have ears and I would not like you to have to explain yourself to the Trident Guard."

"I can handle myself," replied Tonousa as she sought to calm her frustrations.

"That may be so, but what good will it do you to end up in one of the Lady's death pits?"

"So be it," replied Tonousa as she recalled her prime mission to return to the Capital.

"Might I suggest we go where you will not draw attention to yourself? Somewhere you can find sustenance, hot food, and ale?"

"And where do you suggest we go?"

"The Winking Ogre," answered Darchus. "It's an old tavern near the water front. We can talk with much greater freedom there."

"That sounds ideal for I may have friends there that could be looking for me," said Tonousa as she remembered Captain Highroar's parting words from the previous night.

"Then it is settled then!" said Darchus as he turned and set off at a brisk pace. "Follow me now and let's waste no more time in this unhelpful place."

Darchus again led the way. The further the pair travelled towards the waterfront the more activity they noticed. The citizens were most busy around the docks, assisting numerous exhausted survivors out from the water. As she passed the scene of despair and looked upon those who were barely alive, all that Tonousa could think of was the shape changing abilities of the Lizardmen. It was plain to her that the security of the town had in all probability been compromised already. Wherever she looked she imagined shape shifters and there no longer seemed any point in alerting the townsfolk given that their stubborn asinine leader had refused to come to their aid.

On reaching a small square the pair stopped before a white stone building outside of which hung the sign of a deformed beast. Tonousa knew they had arrived at their intended destination. She strode through the open door without hesitation and Darchus followed behind. She had expected to have entered into a den of debauchery similar to the taverns and whorehouses of Parandor but what she saw was different to anything she had expected. The centre of the white marble walled room had been cleared of all furniture; placed to one side to allow the tavern to be used to treat the wounded and the dying who had managed to escape from the once imposing Bards Guild. Those who had been fortunate and brave enough to escape the fires lay in a sorry state upon the tavern floor while local citizens did what they could to tend to their blistering burns. Amongst the white linen women of Valameer, several fishermen and sailors busied themselves, attempting to relieve the suffering of the distressed.

"I am dumb struck?" muttered Tonousa as she stood in the doorway. "I wasn't expecting this."

"The Lady may prevent us from taking up arms but she cannot stop us caring for those in need," replied Darchus from behind. "We ignore the rich and powerful when great work is to be done."

Tonousa looked about her and her eyes searched the stone confines of the tavern. She saw no signs of food or drink.

"Do you believe that I would bring you here to fill your stomach?" added Darchus.

"I don't know what to think," replied Tonousa amid her confusion and as she watched several people breathe their last in front of her. The shock of the writhing brotherhood of bards began to cloud her judgment.

"We are forced to look after ourselves in Valameer," continued Darchus. "The Lady Flurdiana may, in the looseness of the terms be called our leader, and she does pass some laws and take our taxes, but she leaves us to get on with our own lives, even to the point of defending the town."

"You are good people, a most admirable community," replied Tonousa.

"Oh, do you think so!" smirked Darchus. "Are you saying that if someone was rescued from the sea near Parandor the people would not assist them?"

Tonousa closed her eyes for a brief moment and thought on Darchus's words. She tried to imagine the scum folk of Parandor turning out to help in this way but in her heart she knew things would be different. Save for Irabo jumping into the

Tiaryer to pull young Llyat out from its waters she could not think of a similar example. She realised in that moment how much the people of Parandor looked only to themselves. They could learn so much from those who dwelt in Valameer, people who could step up and reveal the true innate goodness that most men had long banished from their hearts.

"There is one that I know from the Capital who would have helped in the way that your people do now," added Tonousa. "I am sad to report that he is no more for he was consumed by the flames like so many in the Guild. We must find some way to help in here."

"Of course we should," said Darchus. "There must be much we can do."

A scream of intense agony rose from the nearest corner of the room. Tonousa's attention was drawn to an effeminate man dressed in the once fine robes of the Guild. Despite the burnt and bleeding skin that showed through his tattered robes, Tonousa recognised the frame of Master Ulthirn, the man whom the Grand Musician had sent to help Llyat after the incident in the library. She made her way across the tavern floor and left Darchus behind by the doorway. The Guild Master continued to scream in pain as Tonousa reached his side and knelt beside a young woman, a healer, who administered to the suffering man.

"There must be something that you can give him for his pain," suggested Tonousa as she watched his charred face contort in agony.

"Our pain stopping supplies are running out," replied the woman as with great care she mopped the brow of her patient. "How could anyone imagine or plan for an event on such a scale? It is less than an hour since the first survivors were brought here but already the store of poppite is exhausted. We had just had enough for five people, not the vast shoal that we have pulled from ocean."

Tonousa knew of poppite from her time training with the Watch. It was an alchemist's mixture of alcohol and sap from the green seed pods of the poppy plant. From the severity of the poor man's wounds Tonousa knew that even poppite would not bring relief.

"What do you suggest?" she asked. "Is there anything that we can do for him?"

"We could cut away the burned flesh before it festers but I am afraid any more trauma and this poor man will not survive."

"But we cannot just leave him to suffer in this way," pleaded Tonousa.

"We may have to, for we have nothing left to help control his pain," the woman continued. "Although against my beliefs, the kindest thing would be to end his life right now. Do you have the courage and skill to help him that way?"

"You want me to kill him? Are you asking me to take his fate into my own hands?" asked Tonousa, shocked at being asked to do something so brutal.

"You said you wanted to help us," said Darchus while leaning over Tonousa's shoulder.

"I cannot murder innocents," gasped Tonousa through her shock.

"It wouldn't be murder," replied Darchus. "You would be easing them out of their suffering. You would help them meet their gods without further terrors."

"But taking their life in such a cold way is too dreadful to contemplate," rambled Tonousa. "Murder is murder. This man hasn't harmed me in any way; we just need to make him comfortable."

"And where does it stop?" asked Darchus. "We cannot help everyone. We are limited to doing our best for a few that may survive. For the rest a quick death may be all we can offer."

Tonousa looked around the tavern and took in the enormity of the suffering within its walls. She began to see the impossibility of bringing relief to so many and realised that Darchus and the woman were correct in their conclusions. She reached down to where her sword once hung by her side; lost during her fall from the Bridge of Athuna. Her warrior's heart felt vulnerable and naked in its absence.

"I have parted from my weapon. Do any of you have anything else that I could use?" enquired Tonousa as again she looked upon the suffering Guild Master.

"Here," said the healer as she handed Tonousa a small metal knife. "A deep cut across his throat should do it."

Tonousa took the knife and held it in her hand. She studied it for several seconds before she bent down and made eye contact with Master Ulthirn. Unsure if the man could see her through his burned and clouded eyes she hoped he could not sense her intent. She felt sick to her core but somehow the act she was about to commit felt right.

"Enderdetag!" muttered Master Ulthirn repeatedly between his screams.

"The man is talking nonsense!" said the healer.

"No he is not, let him speak," replied Tonousa as the word returned to haunt her."

"Enderdetag. The Prophecy must be enacted," whispered Ulthirn. "Save the Marked."

"The Marked? The Prophecy?" whispered Darchus. "What is the man talking about?"

"It's a long story," Tonousa replied before addressing Ulthirn again. "Is there anything else you need to tell me about the prophecy?"

Master Ulthirn's screams reached a crescendo and with a swift glance back towards Darchus, Tonousa knew it was time to end the man's life. With one swift sweep she severed the man's throat with the knife. Deep into the flesh it went and forced the cherry red liquid of life to squirt from out of the open wound. The dying man cried out one final time through the frothy gurgling of his severed windpipe.

"Earth...anne...oook."

As the man uttered his last, Tonousa felt a great wave of nausea fill her belly. Vomit crept up from her stomach and she slammed her hand across her mouth to prevent the expulsion of its contents. She dropped the knife to the floor and raced out into the street. Once in the open she fell to her knees and allowed her spew to flow out onto the dirt covered cobbles. All colour then drained from her face and as she knelt and looked down at the ground the feelings of nausea stayed with her. She focused her thoughts on all that she had seen over the past two hours and the knowledge that the citizens of Valameer were doing their utmost to end the suffering of others. The selfless nature of the townsfolk, unlike that of their leader, was most admirable and induced much pride. Tonousa imagined for a moment living in Valameer and vowed one day to return and seek to live out her dotage within in the walls of the town of pure white. But then she shuddered and sensed something strange; perhaps the Fates would soon call and take their revenge for the murder she had just committed.

A hand fell upon her back. Without thinking she wiped her mouth, cleared away the residual vomit, and stood to her feet. She turned expecting to see the man Darchus but it was another that loomed over her. He was the last person that she had expected to cast her eyes on.

"I thought it was you from the moment you dragged your sorry looking arse ashore," said the gruff voice of the rotund man before her. "I sought to follow you but lost you in the maze of streets."

"Fuck off Highroar," replied Tonousa as she tried to steady herself on her legs. Then after a brief pause and several deep breaths she continued. "Although it pains me so to admit it, I am very pleased to look upon your pox ridden face. Shit! What a morning I have had!"

"What the fuck happened over there?" demanded the Captain. "One minute it was quiet and then all hell broke loose. I was quaffing away in the Winking Ogre only to be ejected onto the street to make way for the survivors from the great fire that had started across the water. Then Theoplous turns up on a horse and in a severe flux of the agitations. He carried an unconscious wench-friend of yours, what's her name... Oh yes... Heliana, but the bastard didn't stop long to offer much explanation. Perhaps you can tell me what is going on. How the fuck did you end up in the sea?"

"First things first Ligart," answered Tonousa, wondering if the Captain could be a changeling. "Where is Theo now? Where did he take Heliana?"

"He took the girl back to the ship," replied the Captain. "She'll be in my bed I guess."

"If you've touched her you filthy shit, I'll..."

"Don't so be quick to accuse me bitch! I may like to whore and fuck with the best of them but I never fill a woman's quim without her consent."

"Oh I do apologise sir!" sneered Tonousa. "And Theo? Where is he now?"

"He too is still on the Banshees Wail as far as I know, standing guard over your precious friend and waiting for her to wake up. In his passing he said he felt a great guilt in having punched her too hard."

"Please take me back on board your ship Ligart. I have important questions that I need to ask your First Mate and indeed yourself. Even if it does not please you, your crew and vessel are now an official element of my investigation."

"Is it true that the attack on the Guild was led by the Lizardmen of the Eastern Marsh?"

"Yes, Ligart, it was," confirmed Tonousa. "Now please take me back to the ship at once. I need to speak to Theo."

"How could I refuse what comes from out of your sweet lips," replied the Captain with a mighty laugh and breath that could drop a skyfawn at a hundred paces.

Before they could move away the tavern door opened and Darchus exited the building in haste. He was in search of Tonousa and in a state of almost panic.

"Are you okay?" the cordwainer asked as he reached Tonousa's side.

"I've been better," she answered weakly.

"What did they mean?" continued Darchus. "The Guild Master's last words. I have just worked out what he had been trying to say...Urthanock! Why would he utter the Dark Lord's name as he died?"

"Look Darchus, please be patient," continued Tonousa. "I will return soon or send word about what is going on. I will let you know how Valameer can defend itself but right now I must go and talk with a friend."

Without waiting for an acknowledgement Tonousa set off to follow the Captain who was already well on his way to his ship. Darchus stood stunned and bewildered at the entrance to the tavern, gripped with fear for the future and unable to move a muscle.

The Captain led Tonousa back along the dock of Valameer. They passed many citizens dragging more survivors from out of the water. Although she had been plucked from the salty waters by Irabo and Thias she knew she had to stick to a story that did not involve them. Questions started to form on route to the Banshees Wail. The one that remained foremost in her thoughts was whether the attack on the Guild had been planned to coincide with her visit. If so then the spy in Parandor must have tipped off the reptiles. If that was the case it was imperative that she discovered who the bastard was and where he was hiding. It had to be someone close to those who had planned the journey to the Bards Guild and yet there were only a handful of people aware of the true nature and purpose of the visit to Valameer. She fought hard to recall events for she would need to question every one of those who had even the slightest knowledge of her movements. Several minutes later Highroar led Tonousa up the gangplank. As she stepped onto the ship she glanced across towards the glowing mass of rock and stone that was once the Bards Guild. A deep sadness brought on by the scale of death and destruction overwhelmed her. Tears flowed in torrents down her cheeks.

At the back of the Banshees Wail, Highroar opened the door to his cabin and stepped inside. The ornate carved room contained little furniture save for a bed in its centre and a desk up against one wall. There were shelves fixed to the plank wall above the desk and on which rested the Captain's few possessions. At the rear of the cabin, a large window looked out towards the harbour of Valameer but Tonousa was not interested in the view. She made her way to the bed where Heliana lay motionless beneath hessian sheets. Sat on the far edge of bed, holding the young woman's hand, was the sailor Theoplous. On seeing Tonousa enter behind his Captain the First Mate stood up from the bed and offered his hand to Tonousa in a gesture of greeting. Tonousa shook it with vigour after which both hugged in a spontaneous expression of relief.

"I am so pleased to see that you made it to the town," he began.

"You as well!" replied Tonousa.

"And the others? Your Grand Physician? Irabo?"

"I've not seen any of them since I reached safety," lied Tonousa. "I thought if anything they would be here on the boat with you."

"And the Marked?" added Theoplous. "The boy Llyat? What about him? Did you manage to get to safety?"

"Someone is going to have to explain what is going on," snapped Captain Highroar. "I know Lotus Isle folk talk in riddles but you Theo take the fucking ship's biscuit."

Tonousa looked at the unconscious girl on the bed before responding.

"I must assume that Llyat is also dead Theo," lied Tonousa again. "Lost within the Guild for I have not seen him amongst any of the survivors that I have come across this morning`."

"That saddens me a great deal," replied Theoplous.

"Theo what the fuck is going on. Tell me now...That is an order you scurvy swine!" bellowed Highroar.

"I am sorry to say Captain that I have somewhat mislead you. My purpose in taking up your offer as First Mate on this voyage was not just for the work and the money. You see I had a greater purpose in mind. I needed to find a boy. A specific youth known as the 'Marked', a boy that was to fulfil a Prophecy. Furthermore I believed that I had found him. It was the young lad called Llyat Emgar who had made the journey out with us, the servant of the old Physician who had funded this venture."

"Marked? Prophecy? What nonsense are you talking of moron?" fumed the Captain.

"I'm sorry Ligart," said Tonousa. "There is no time for an explanation as there is a much more urgent issue at hand. Who else did you tell about our voyage to Valameer? The attack on the Guild seems to have been planned to coincide with our arrival. Someone knew we would be there and is seeking to disrupt my investigation. There is a spy in our midst. By the orbs of Belanore who did you tell?"

"I told no one and that is the truth." replied Highroar.

"That's a load of horse shit," spat out Theoplous. "You told me yourself what you had heard the Grand Physician and his party discussing during the first days of our voyage. Tonousa, as I told you at the Guild, why do you think I became so interested in the boy? The Captain cannot hold his piss nor his tongue. At the first smell of alcohol the sot was spilling your secrets to his crew. Such a drunkard and whoremonger cannot keep his tongue still for long."

"Enough, you bastard! Another word from you and you'll be swimming back to the fucking Lotus Isles," spluttered the old sea dog as his face turned redder than a radish.

Tonousa waited for Highroar to explode but yet he did not. The Captain thought for a few seconds before he let forth.

"Okay, okay," he continued. "So I admit it. Perhaps I cannot hold my tongue. Strong drink has always been my weakness and I am the ship's parrot when my tongue is loosened. They say I always repeat all I have heard after a good piss-up in The Murdered Wolf. So I have to admit that my crew probably knew of your intentions to visit Valameer but I cannot believe any of them capable of bringing down the Guild."

"I see!" replied Tonousa. "If Theoplous hadn't been with us I have no doubt that neither myself nor Heliana would have escaped."

In the silence that followed Tonousa looked to the girl, still unconscious and breathing with a leadened sonorous tone.

"Was there anyone else, other than your crew, who could have known that we were setting out for Valameer?" she demanded. "We believe that one of the Lizardmen of the Eastern Marsh has infiltrated the Citadel and replaced a member of the Sovereign Council or some other in high office. Please think hard and do not lie for the security and safety of all in Parandor could depend on what you can recall. Are you sure you didn't tell anyone else?"

Highroar paused and tried to remember anything that could be of importance.

"Well!" said Tonousa as her frustration mounted.

"Tonousa, forgive me but there were four others that knew of this journey. The night before we set sail I got involved in a game of cards and dice. The wine had flowed and we began to prattle on about our futures, the murders, Death Tubaria, and of course the Grand Physician's journey to seek the counsel of the bards. There were five of us in that game and by the end of the session all four of the scum knew of your journey."

"Fuck, you cannot be serious!" grumbled Tonousa and it took all her resolve to not punch the Captain in the face. "Tell me the truth and tell me now, who else played the game with you that night?"

"As I recall there was the barkeep, Isambard Hotch, the one legged dead collector, Cassius Underscroft, and that strange foreign fellow, Falaz Al Hizdor. Oh, and that blacksmith you taught a lesson to in the tavern; the one whose friend lost a hand to your blade."

"Nedes, Nedes Karoly?"

"Aye, he's the one," continued Highroar. "They were all privy to the information. They knew where I was taking you but as I remember there was just one person who seemed at all interested; old Isambard."

"Now that does surprise me," said Tonousa as she tried to work out why the barkeep would be so interested in her affairs. "Did he tell you anything more or ask further questions?"

"No, he did not. He kept on talking about ogres being seen around the ruins of Barad Elestor, wherever the fuck that is. Bugger me, you don't think he is a Lizardman? I always said he talked with two tongues."

"To be honest I'm not sure but you have at least given me something to follow up," replied Tonousa as many complex thoughts whizzed through her head.

"So what do you propose to do next?" asked Theoplous.

"I must make for Parandor with haste. I do not have any time to linger here any longer. I must find out who is responsible for the murders. By now the riders that were sent out by the City Watch will have returned to Parandor and news will have reached our Sovereign Lord about the death of his brother at the Grey Keep. There may have even been more murders while we have been away and all under the name of Death Tubaria. I will need that horse you borrowed Irabo."

"Glorius, as you named her, is at this moment tied up in the stables at the rear of the Winking Ogre," replied Theoplous. "But what about us? What do you want us to do? What of the girl Heliana."

"I need you to rally the people of Valameer in case they are attacked," answered Tonousa. "We will require their help, of that I am certain. You may find some resistance from Lady Flurdiana but one called Darchus Arillius appears to be the voice of the town. I am sure you will be able to persuade him to help us in our cause."

"And Heliana?" added Captain Highroar.

"Let her rest and recover," continued Tonousa. "When she is strong enough, bring her back to Parandor, and Captain, if you so much as try to touch her, I will ensure you spend your last moments in the company of Sir Richemanus of the Nightfall. I will have you feel the blunt edge of his axe. Do you understand me sir?"

"I understand very well," replied a much deflated Highroar.

"Don't worry Tonousa," added Theoplous. "I will look after Heliana for you."

"Thank you sir. When you return to Parandor and we meet again. Then you must finish your story and tell me how the people of the Lotus Isle fit into this puzzle. But I must leave now knowing there are five that I need to question as soon as possible."

"Four!" corrected Highroar. "There were four others at the card game."

"No Captain," added Tonousa. "There was one other that knew of our plan to visit Valameer."

"Who" asked the surprised Captain?

"The Lord Commander of the City Watch, Brynn Townsforth."

26

Methladon had heard of the twin Lions of Avolire. There was not a day that had passed since the commencement of his incarceration that he hadn't heard the name of the dreaded felines uttered by either prisoners, slaves, or the Lizardmen that ran the mines. Less than twenty four hours had passed since he had met with the Lady of the Silverwynn in her enchanted room but it seemed much longer. He had been woken in his cell, been beaten at once, and then dragged through the tunnels of the mines. Always he was guarded and kept without food and water by the evil bastard Ssnakash. Methladon was in the company of three fellow prisoners, all who were about to share the same fate in the pit that contained the legendary beasts.

The lethal leonines were not of flesh and blood but comprised two large and hollow bronze statues in the shape of rampant lions. Each sat above a furnace that would be lit before the appointed time of their use. Methladon had known from the moment that the Lady of the Silverwynn told Captain Rhaizen to burn his friends that this would be the method of execution for Dayis and Tycus. It would also be the same fate shared with the third prisoner who had also been chosen by the Lizardmen to die that day. Methladon's imagination rolled through in overtime and he pictured the fiery end with great clarity of insight. Inside each of the hollow lions an unbound prisoner would be restrained, unable to move the smallest of muscles, yet conscious in the knowledge that there was no escape. The stories of the beasts were told daily by the Lizardmen masters in order to terrorise and subjugate their prisoners. Once inside the lion's metal bellies and with the furnace lit the condemned were cooked alive. The sounds and screams made in their dying moments were channelled through bronze pipes and echoed out of the beast's mouths as if they roared. The noise was said to increase in intensity as the steam rose from the flesh that cooked within their innards. Methladon sensed somehow that this method of execution had not been chosen for him. If he had interpreted the true intentions of the Lady of the Silverwynn then the Lions of Avolire would be reserved for his friends. He would be made to stand, watch their suffering, and soak in their pitiful screams. She no doubt had another purpose for his presence at their execution and that was to break him to her will; at least that is what he expected.

"You couldn't keep your fucking mouth shut could you?" swore Tycus through his swollen lips and broken nose. "You had to try and take them on. Now look where it has got us."

"Shut up Tycus!" snapped back Methladon as he was pushed forward ahead of Ssnakash. "I've had enough of your pathetic whimpering. You're almost as bad as Lancet. Everything that I have done so far has been to give me time to formulate a plan of escape. I've been beaten often, tortured each day, and my cock assaulted by a toothless hag. I've had my mind manipulated by some fucking sacred jewel and been shown images of a future that I do not wish to remember. All this I have endured to get us out of this shit hole and all you can do is whine and complain."

"You have not seen the Lions yet Meth!"

"No I haven't but I know the stories well enough," the youth answered as once again the mark on the back of his head began to burn. "I know what is waiting for you and I'm sorry that I failed …"

Methladon did not have time to finish before feeling the crack of a whip across his back.

"Quit talking scum!" hissed the reptile.

Methladon desperately wanted to cry out in pain but to do so would incur another blow. He gritted his teeth and choked out his scream. Then he raised his eyes and looked at this fellow prisoners, each of whom showed different emotions etched upon their faces. Despite Tycus's broken bones he saw an anger in his eyes that was mixed with great apprehension over the fate that he was soon to endure. In Dayis's he just saw fear, amplified tenfold, and mixed with a stink from his tattered trousers. Only the third, a fellow called Thillias, showed any strength in his eyes. Despite being yet another scrawny wretch with few muscles, long emaciated from his time in the mines, he looked determined to face his fate with a firm resolve.

The group marched on through the mines towards the lion pit while Methladon's thoughts focused on the offer that the Lady of the Silverwynn had initiated. He began to question if her request for him to serve in her army had been made on the basis of the images he had seen in his vision. Perhaps she was convinced that at some point in the future the Fates would conspire to have him sit on the throne by her side, but then he came to the conclusion she would not. Uncertain as to whether she would permit his fellow prisoners to live if he agreed to fight with her against the forces of Parandor, he knew it to be an issue he needed to resolve with some urgency. If he tried to bargain for their lives, to save them from their fiery end, it could result in more pain for himself. If he let them die to serve his own ends his mind would be tortured by that memory for the rest of his days.

Some minutes later the prisoners reached the place of fiery execution. The circular pit was not a natural phenomenon but one cleared by the hands of men. The hole was many cubits deep and was lined with thick oak planks. It was some twenty or so cubits in diameter and ladders led down from its sides by which access was gained to the bronze lions. On first seeing it Methladon was reminded of the dog pits on the outskirts of Parandor that his father used to take him to as a boy and where men bet on which animal would be first rip out its opponent's throat. Standing on the edge of the pit Methladon stared, first at the two rampant lions, and then at four white but dirt smeared horses that commanded its centre. Between the snorting animals stood a pale and muscular man, his face obscured by a black leather mask that covered all of his head. The presence of the horses came as a surprise and Methladon pondered on their purpose. Then he began to think who the executioner could be beneath the sinister head covering.

At one side of the pit a viewing platform had been erected. It was held up by large wooden posts and it provided an excellent vantage point from which to observe the events in the arena below. On that platform stood three figures that Methladon knew well. Between Captain Rhaizen and the dwarf Grovrouk, both in full armour, stood the Lady of the Silverwynn. Once again she looked both young and beautiful. Methladon made eye contact with the Lady and attempted to question it was too late to bargain, to join his fate with hers, and save the lives of his companions.

An audience began to gather around the edge of the pit. Mostly they were knights and Lizardmen masters but a few selected slaves from deep within the mine had also been dragged up to watch, either as punishment or reward. All looked on in silence daring not to speak lest the Lady was angered. Methladon then realised what they waited for, the signal from the Lady to start the show. Her voice soon echoed across the cavernous mine and rolled around the centre of the pit.

"Throw the scum in!" she bellowed, her voice amplified as if by some form of diabolical magic.

Methladon felt a boot strike against his back and he was propelled forward over the edge of the pit. There he slid down the sloping wooden panels towards the base and as he fell he caught a glimpse of Dayis and Tycus as they followed him over the edge. He landed on the floor with a heavy thump but before he could clamber back to his feet he felt the weight of his fellow captives land on top of him. They pinned him to the ground and trapped him like a rat in an upturned bucket. As he lay struggling to breathe under the combined weight of the three slaves he heard the voice of the Lady once again echo around the walls of the execution pit.

"Do not attempt to try and climb out," she ordered. "If you try to escape from the confines of this place of death my cold bloodied servants will shoot without mercy."

All around the edge of the pit Lizardmen stood with crossbows readied and primed.

"You don't expect us to die without resisting do you?" shouted Tycus.

"She doesn't expect you to do anything at all," growled the executioner who stood beside the heap of prisoners and whose voice Methladon then recognised. "It is death that awaits you here but you can choose how you will face your end. Step into the lions of your own free will and you will save yourselves a savage beating."

"You are insane Nictis," shouted Methladon from the bottom of the pile. "No one in control of their mind would climb into one of those things."

"Good, this is going to be most pleasurable," replied Nictis. "We have a different plan for you Methladon. It is something that I have been looking forward to ever since that first meeting of ours in your shit filled village. I hope you remember that time when my men butchered all your family and the few low life you called your friends."

Methladon made as if to reply but Nictis continued, lost in his joy of inflicting fear.

"I have an offer to put to your friends and so I need their full attention."

"We are listening," shouted Tycus as the prisoners separated from their knot.

"Good, I trust that the fear of the Lions will help you all make the right decision. Here is the choice. You either all climb into the Lions of your own volition, or you take the ropes attached to these four horses and tie them to the limbs of the bastard Methladon Heyn. Once you have secured the ropes in place you will be allowed to climb out of the pit and will be granted your freedom."

Methladon looked to the four horses and then back towards his fellow prisoners. He made eye contact with Tycus first and noted his friend's dilemma. The voice of the stranger Thillias sounded.

"I'd rather burn in the fires of the Lions of Avolire that carry out your dirty work brother."

'Brother!' thought Methladon. 'Surely not.'

"Is that so," replied Nictis. "That is indeed a shame. You others, do you share this view?"

Methladon looked to Dayis and Tycus but neither of them seemed inclined to speak.

"You see Captain," said Methladon as he stood his ground. "Honour and friendship prevails over fear. We shall all die in the…"

Before Methladon could utter his last word he felt his feet pulled from beneath him and he landed with the full force of his weight upon his back. He sought to work out what was happening when a fist punched him in the face. His head swooned and his vision hazed. Then through the cloud of his bloodied vision, Methladon was shocked to find it had been Dayis who had attacked him.

"This is our chance Tycus," shouted Dayis. "Get the ropes and bind him."

"Then keep him subdued while I do so!" stuttered Tycus.

Dayis punched several more times and then began to kick Methladon as a man would a rabid cur. As each blow was struck, Methladon realised that Nictis had given his fellow slaves no other option. If any of them was to live they had to give up on him. He sensed the futility of resistance and even though his birthmark was on fire his will was at last broken. There was nothing further he could but to accept the last few cards that fate dealt him.

Within moments he felt the ropes tighten around his wrists and ankles. He didn't struggle, just surrendered to whatever would come while deep from the chambers of his heart he focussed on forgiveness. Tycus and Dayis were simply ensuring their own survival and in this struggle of life he had underestimated the mental weakness of both the man from the Bards Guild and dark one from the Lotus Isle.

"Make sure that his bonds are secured as tight as possible!" ordered Nictis.

"Of course we fucking will," screeched Tycus in the throes of mania.

Methladon could not stop thinking of the effect that the horses would have on his limbs and as he ceased to resist he felt a strange sensation seep through his body. The hairs on his skin stood bold and erect as a burning wave spread out from the mark on his neck. The sensation was unique and of a kind he had never experienced before. Even in times of great stress when the three circles burned the sting had never felt as intense as in that moment.

"Both of you, each take two horses," bellowed Nictis. "When I give the order I want you to lead them away and lengthen this bugger. Do not stop pulling once his limbs dislocate for his skin will stretch even further. His arms and legs will then be ripped off and be dragged bleeding through the dirt. Only then can you stop the horses and gaze back at his writhing stumps."

Hearing these orders caused memories of the past to flood through Methladon's mind. In all its clarity, undiminished by the passing years, he saw images of his father seeking to save him from dismemberment. He was the child of the nightmares that had haunted him through the years. The distant memory that he had suppressed for so long was released to further fuel his anger.

"Methladon Heyn, before you are pulled apart," continued Nictis as he pointed at Thillias, "You will at least get to hear the Lions of Avolire. They will roar like never before for today my brother must suffer in their fiery bowels."

Silence fell and all looked at Thillias. The wretched man knelt with his head bowed as if in shame before he then stood tall. In that moment Methladon expected Thillias would also turn against him but he didn't.

"If it is the will of the Lady that I sacrifice myself for the good of Avolire, then so be it," shouted the emaciated wretch. "I forgive her despite her not knowing what she does."

"It is my will. Cease the shit fall from your mouth and get on with it," the Lady shouted back.

Methladon struggled to grasp all that was going on. There was something more than the culling of slaves happening in the pit and he failed to work out why a sacrifice was needed."

"Now my brother," ordered Nictis. "Choose your lion."

From down in the dirt Methladon's blood stained eyes watched the emaciated Thillias walk with great purpose across the floor of the pit towards the two bronze lions and the furnaces that lay beneath them. After a moment of silence and deliberation the waif looked back towards his brother.

"I choose the left."

"Good, very good," replied Nictis as he smiled. "The choice has now been made."

"Do not sacrifice yourself Thillias," shouted Methladon. "Save yourself and help the others in the taking of my life."

"You don't get it do you Methladon," replied Thillias. "We're all dead."

"Don't throw your life away. Take mine instead," Methladon screamed.

"My brother has made his decision so shut your fucking mouth," snarled Nictis.

Thillias walked over to the left lion and opened the panel door that allowed entry into its interior. The man without hope looked back one last time, then turned and climbed into the lion's belly. He pulled on the hatch and closed it behind him.

"Now let's make this lion roar!" screamed Nictis as he moved forward, slipped a bolt, and sealed his brother inside.

The evil Captain took a burning torch from one of the metal brackets that illuminated the pit and tossed it into the opening of the furnace beneath the metal beast. An eerie silence fell and no one, either in the pit or watching from above, uttered a word. The furnace burst into life and Methladon in desperation looked around for some way that he could save the unfortunate man. One step forward and he would no doubt be shot full of crossbow bolts and forfeit the promised freedom of his friends. Without warning Thillias began hammering on the metal interior. It was followed seconds later by the sound of high pitched screams. Then as the intensity of his shouts grew ever louder, the lion roared. It was an inhuman sound, somehow amplified and changed in tone as the dying man's air forced its way through the pipework and out of the beast's mouth. To Methladon, whoever had devised this terrible torture of roasting men alive had been sick of mind.

Tycus and Dayis looked on in horror but soon moved their attention back to Methladon. There was no way now to stop the pair from aiding his execution for the thought of suffering the same fate as Thillias was beyond their comprehension.

"The time is right, my friends," growled Nictis. "Rip this turd apart."

"Forgive me Methladon!" screamed Tycus.

Methladon closed his eyes and he heard the snorts of the horses as they tensed their limbs and made ready to move forward. He felt the ropes around his limbs pull tight and he was lifted from the ground. The pain in the joints of his arms and legs were of an intensity that he could never have imagined but he was determined not give Nictis the satisfaction of hearing him cry out. Somehow he was still alert enough to look around but could not see a way out of his deadly predicament. This was where he would end his days and his demise was imminent. An intense ripple of energy coursed through his body and he felt as if a great fire burned deep within his core. Suspended between the four horses intense bursts of energy shot through his limbs and enveloped the ropes that bound him. The thick restraints burst into flame but not of the kind that raged in the furnace beneath the Lion. They were green, magical, and most bizarre. They contained a heat that even Solaris could not match and the birthmark on his neck glowed like a beacon.

Amid a fluorescent emerald green flash of energy Methladon found himself lying on the dirt floor and free of his bonds. Before he could understand what had happened to him he jumped to his feet and scanned the arena. Dayis and Tycus rushed forwards him to subdue him again but as they drew near Methladon swung out with his fists and dropped them both to the floor where they then lay still. He then heard the priming of the Lizardmens' crossbows and the twangs as they unleashed their bolts. Yet as the arrows approached he felt pulses of energy shoot from his body and the projectiles vaporised before they could reach him. He was both amazed and grateful for whatever was happening although he had no understanding of the force that had taken over his body. Whatever it was it had originated from the mark on the back of his head.

"Captain! Finish him!" squealed the Lady of the Silverwynn.

"My pleasure," roared the executioner.

Nictis took hold of a glowing poker from the side of the furnace. This would be his new weapon. Methladon looked around for something with which to defend himself. He gripped an iron bar that lay on the floor, abandoned without care by those who had prepared the Lions for use, and with it he readied himself for Nictis's attack. Within seconds the two make do weapons collided. Sparks flew as each combatant wielded their iron as hard and as fast as they could. Both had but one intention, to smash the life out of the other.

"I want my voice to be the last thing you hear before you die!" screamed out Nictis.

"You need to change your words, Captain. You are becoming one tedious old cunt," shouted back Methladon between attacks. "You keep promising my death but it's one you will not get to keep."

Over the continued roars of the lion, Methladon swung his metal ever harder. His father's training began to pay off and he sensed that old Nictis was beginning to tire. He was also aware of the Lady of the Silverwynn and the others watching from above. Despite the distractions he could still focus on seeking to kill the swine who had brought so much death and destruction into his life.

"What are you waiting for Nictis?" Commander Rhaizen shouted. "Finish the lad now."

"I'm fucking trying to!" moaned the brute.

Nictis lost his footing as he moved forward to attack. He tripped over the unconscious body of Tycus and landed face down in the dirt. In less time than it took to draw breath Methladon was on top of him. The youth smashed away with his metal bar and pummelled the Captain's head into the ground. The leather mask was soon reduced to a pulp. Slithers of skin, blood, fragments of bone, and lumps of glutinous brain soup, splattered out through the eye holes of the cow hide with each of Methladon's strikes.

"This is for Mal!" he shouted as he landed blow upon blow. "This is for Maria... This for my family... For my brothers... For Llyat... For Lancet... And this fucking one is for me!"

Soon Methladon was covered in blood and dripping lumps of white. Taking a step back he looked down with pride at his work. Nictis's corpse had long ceased to twitch. Then for good measure he hit it several more times as his hate for the beast dissipated within the depths of the pit. Something powerful had taken charge of Methladon and it had channelled his anger. It was scary and yet it fascinated him. In fact it made him feel amazing.

In the silence that then surrounded him, Methladon stood tall and looked towards the viewing platform where the Lady, Rhaizen, and Grovrouk stood and watched with mouths open. The Lizardmen around the periphery of the pit also looked down with trepidation while the few slaves present began to mutter amongst themselves. Methladon attempted to recover, to get his breath back, and plan his next course of action. He saw the Lady of the Silverwynn begin to descend one of the ladders and in her shadow the Commander followed. She approached Methladon with no obvious signs of fear and the youth prepared himself for a further confrontation. The silence was palpable and even the Lions were quiet.

"There is no need to fear me Methladon Heyn," said the Lady of the Silverwynn.

"What the fuck do you want with me?"

"As I told you yesterday, when we met again I would offer you a last chance to join me in my quest. I can see that you still have much fight left in you, but also that something remarkable has manifested within your body. It is a power most strange that has been wakened and I can help you discover its true potential. But in return I demand, no I request, your service both to me and my cause."

Methladon considered his options. If he refused then the Lady would no doubt seek to destroy him and as yet he was unsure as to the ability of his new found powers to provide him adequate protection. He felt a sudden desire to understand the force that had consumed him in his hour of need and whether or not he could learn to control it over time. Whatever it was he was sure it had something to do with his birthmark and yet was also linked to images from his past. As the seconds passed he began to wonder if the Lady had used the force of the sceptre. Perhaps the mystical jewel that had given him a glimpse of a fractured future had been the cause of his new found power. Then he thought about the dagger that the dwarf had brought to her, the one that looked so familiar and perhaps was the source of his mysterious abilities. The Lady had hinted at a connection with the sceptre in the far distant past and perhaps it was something to do with their coming together that had made him invincible.

"What of my friends?" he demanded, pointing to the unconscious Tycus and Dayis. "If I submit to you, will you spare them?"

"How can you show compassion towards those who turned against you?" answered the Lady.

"Because I can. Nictis gave them no other choice. It was me or them. They had to try and save themselves."

"What would you have me do with them then?"

"I would have you keep the promise that Nictis gave them," replied Methladon. "He offered them their freedom if they turned against me."

The Lady smiled. "Commander Rhaizen," she ordered.

"My Lady,"

"See that his friends are set free for it appears young Methladon has seen sense at last. Then prepare my chamber to receive our most welcome guest, the latest member of our alliance."

"My Lady!" repeated the Commander as he saluted.

Rhaizen turned and looked up to those gathered the top of the pit. He then shouted out his instructions. The Lady turned to Methladon who still stood over the fallen body of Nictis with the metal bar still in his bloodied hands.

"Please drop your weapon. You have no need for it in my presence."

It was as if Methladon no longer had any control of his actions. His hands released their grip on the metal bar. With a dull thud it fell onto the dirt covered ground and disturbed a pool of clot. Numerous droplets of crimson splattered across his feet but Methladon did not notice. His mind and body felt free from tension and he dropped to his knees and bowed his head.

"I am forever grateful my Lady," he said. "I most humbly thank you for sparing their lives."

"Your gratitude is noted Methladon Heyn," she replied. "But now rise for you are no longer a simple blacksmith's son but a servant to the freedom of the Realm. Arise Sir, as a Knight of Avolire."

In that moment Methladon Heyn knew that that his life had changed for ever. He had a new purpose in life, not just in the service of the Lady's cause, but to discover the true nature of the power than had been awakened deep within his mark.

27

From his vantage point on a high rock promontory Llyat looked down on the boulder strewn valley before him. It was a mind numbing vista that that filled his presence with awe. The wasteland was vast and devoid of all life save for a few hardy shrubs and the occasional weed grown from seeds blown in on a distant wind. It was a foreboding vision and one which heightened Llyat's concerns over the direction they were to travel. Several leagues away across the valley lay the foothills of what Llyat knew to be the Grey Mountains. The peaks stretched across the land and then down and on forever until disappearing into the Eastern Marsh. It was as if stone wall had been built by the gods across the centre of the Realm in order to prevent the coming together of the wild scavengers from the north and those who inhabited the more fertile lands of the south. Two of the mountains, Skillar and Charibol, were the highest of the peaks and they soared way above the clouds and lay their heads on Solaris's lap. Between these peaks was the one way through the razor sharp range at its western edge. It was known to all as the Ivory Pass.

The journey had been a long and arduous one. It had started with the steep climb up and over the cliffs north of Valameer and then across the plateau that led to the mountains. After the first hour on the trek Llyat had seen no sign of life be it human or reptilian, save for his two companions. The isolation helped his thinking for it gave him both time and space to reflect on the events at the Bards Guild and his subsequent escape. He so wanted release from the unfolding drama but his thoughts continued to pose difficult questions. He tried to figure out his exact role and why his father had been deemed a traitor. Time and again he had tried to make connections between the murders in Parandor, the rising of Avolire, and why the knights in black were looking for him. The knowledge that the First Mate of the Banshees Wail had linked the Enderdetag Prophecy to him added further worry to his many guileless ponderings. Most troubling of all was whether Heliana was safe. So many questions had swept in and out of his head that he felt incapable of rational thought and yet he knew one fact for certain; if he was to be of any help in finding the remaining Gems of Thamous he would have to conquer his uselessness.

During that days slog from distant Valameer, Llyat had listened to the many conversations that had passed between Irabo and Thias, most of which related to seeking the right path that would lead to the town of Falahorn that he understood lay somewhere on the edge of the Dragonas. But there had been several others that he had sought to follow despite getting lost in the detail. During the few rest breaks that Thias permitted, Llyat tried to ensure that all that had happened was fixed into his memory. If he ever got back to Parandor he would have a most remarkable tale to tell, one to rival the shite that spewed from the Fool's mouth. The weather had so far been kind but as all three men stood and stared into the vast expanse of wasteland the smallest drops of water started to fall.

"So, Aquaris decides to torment us again," moaned Thias.

"Indeed so," replied Irabo. "If we race on to the pass we will find cover there amongst its rocky overhangs."

"That would be good, given the look of those clouds building over the mountains," added Thias. "What do you say Llyat?"

"Whatever," replied the youth for the truth was he did not know what else to say.

Llyat felt uncomfortable. He was stuck in the far reaches of the Realm in a place he never once thought he would see. Even Denius Castor's dungpat tales could not have prepared him this experience. His feet pained from the blisters on his heels and his legs ached. Clothes, soaked many hours earlier, still clung to his skin like wet leaves in the woods. Worst of all was the hunger that gnawed away at his stomach. Irabo continued to take the lead and the youthful serf that had been marked out by the Prophecy followed him down the rocky trail that snaked into the lifeless valley below. Llyat looked up towards the mountains as rain poured down from clouds that obscured their snow covered peaks. He so much wanted to be like Irabo and he envied the warrior's great strength of character. His saviour from the Tiaryer reminded Llyat of his best friend Methladon who he saw fall in Maplehill and whose companionship he now so much missed. There were certain qualities that both possessed, bravery, selflessness, and swordsmanship. If fact, they were the complete antithesis of all that he knew himself to be.

As he followed Irabo down the barely discernible path Llyat glanced back to check on Thias's presence. It seemed a long time since that night in Maplehill when he had asked the bard to sing of the Fall of Urthanock. Indeed it was and much water had drained from his bladder since their first chance meeting. Had anyone asked Llyat that night before he fell asleep in the Red Mare to predict where he would be in one month's time, being on an adventure with a bard from the Capital would have been the last thought to have come to mind. Yet as he walked forward the key question that troubled him had still not been answered. He could not understand why everyone referred to him as 'the Marked'. No one had given him a straight answer and yet all had vowed to protect him with their lives. It had to have something to do with his father being denounced as a traitor.

"So why am I the marked one?" asked Llyat, unable to contain this thought to himself. "I never once asked for any of this? What does all of this mean? Why pick on me?"

Irabo stopped at once and turned. Thias pulled up at the rear as the rain fell harder.

"Those are very valid questions Llyat," answer Irabo. "They have troubled me ever since we left Valameer. Thias may be able to shed some light on all of this for I cannot. I think understand this so called Enderdetag Prophecy now and that for some reason Fatumai has ensured that we three are all caught up in its unfolding, but I cannot begin to imagine why she should have chosen you."

"I'm sure this can wait until we find some shelter," moaned Thias as the rain bounced off his head. "We can talk with more comfort then and I promise I will tell you all that I discovered about the Prophecy."

"Then let's move on as fast as we can," replied Irabo. "Remember the bard's promise Llyat and that should spur us on to find cover for our heads."

The three whose fortunes had been entwined in fate's strange game, continued on their journey down and across the valley that stood before the mountains. The rain continued to fall and within his sodden clothes Llyat soon felt a chill begin to take hold. He contemplated telling his companions of his shivers but then thought better of it for he expected that they no doubt felt the same and he did not want to be the first to complain. Once they began to cross the valley floor Thias walked by Llyat's side instead of behind him. When Llyat looked across he noted three dead pheasants tied by their feet and strung around the bard's neck. These birds had been caught earlier during the first hour of their journey. Thias and Irabo had taken four with the use of much stealth from out of a small copse of trees close to the cliff side. They had consumed the first of them for breakfast and Llyat craved to eat another right there and then. Amid his drooling his gaze fell upon the bronze pendant with its embedded amethyst that hung from the bard's neck.

"That's a rather nice jewel," he said, his mouth talking independently of his brain.

"Thank you lad," replied Thias as he raised an eyebrow. "It is just a worthless memory now."

"What do you mean?"

"We were all given them! When we as students started our path of learning at the Guild, we were all presented with one of these. It was something with which to give us identity and bind us in a sense of belonging. I'm sad to say it is all I have left to remind me of what was once my happiest of homes. The memories of the Guild will no doubt stay until the day my allotted lifetime runs out."

Llyat did not respond. He realised that loss of the Guild had wounded the bard's heart and sensed it would be imprudent to question him further. He began to reflect instead and make comparisons between the events at the Guild and the attack on his home in Maplehill. Both he and Thias had lost many loved ones and their homes had been destroyed by fire. The Lady of the Silverwynn, or at least those who followed her orders, had been responsible for both events and Llyat wondered if he would ever gain revenge over the swine who had changed his life. His lip curled as an image the beast in the skull helmet appeared behind his eyes. He swore that if the opportunity came to kill that knight he would take it and his life now held but one purpose, revenge. That is what Cleath Mark or any of the Heyn brothers would have sought.

The rain continued to fall as they progressed at speed across the flat open valley. Another hour drifted before they reached the entrance to the Ivory Pass. Rising up from the valley floor it started as a narrow gully in which a mountain stream trickled down from the base of Charibol and disappeared deep into the rocks and earth below. Over this cut in the land had been built a small wooden footbridge, one wide enough to allow the passage of two men side by side. Irabo marched on towards the bridge where Llyat was surprised to see a group of mountain goats grazing off the sparse vegetation that fought to survive beside the flowing water.

"Do you think we should kill the youngest of the three?" queried Irabo. "That would give us enough food to make it to Falahorn."

"Why not," added Thias. "These young creatures have little meat on them but given what there is for them to eat here I am not surprised."

"I think we should leave them alone," ordered Llyat. "They are a family and they do not deserve to suffer the loss of their child."

Llyat didn't know where this emotion had come from. It was perhaps that the three reminded him of his own family as he began to imagine the pain the others would feel if one were killed.

Neither Irabo nor Thias felt any inclination to challenge Llyat's comment and so continued onto the bridge. When Llyat was half way across he glanced down into the gully and there saw a hideous and yet amazing sight. He stopped for he felt the need to investigate further.

"What the fuck's that?"

Soon all three stared down upon the grey rotting carcass of some weird deformed four legged beast with a long elongated nose.

"That is something I've not seen in a long time," said Irabo.

"What is it?" asked Llyat. "Is it a troll?"

"No my young friend," replied Irabo. "You've been listening to too many stories with make-believe creatures. This is one of the beasts that give the Ivory Pass its name. That down there Llyat is the body of a wormnose, one of the strange grey creatures that inhabit the Dragonas. They are able to live in peace amongst the dragons, wyverns, and hornnoses. If you look to the tusks of the creature then you will see that they are made of pure ivory. The worm noses, for some reason known only to themselves, choose the pass between Skillar and Charibol as their final resting place and make their way down it to die."

"Do you mean that we are walking into a grave pit?" asked Llyat.

"Exactly," replied Irabo. "Even my people, the men and woman of Falahorn, refer to the Ivory Pass as Greynose Grave. It will not be the only such carcass you will see before we reach our goal. Now let's try and find some shelter for Aquaris continues with his spiteful torment. This weather is wretched and I for one am soaked and weary."

Irabo then turned and made his way off the far end of the bridge and up into the pass. Thias was the next to follow and for a brief moment Llyat continued to look down at the creature below. He so hoped that he would get to see one alive before his quest ended. That would add to his story if he ever got to tell it in the taverns of the Realm. After a few moments of quiet reflection Llyat turned and ran to catch up with his friends. Irabo had been true to his word. As they progressed further and deeper into the pass they came across more rotting carcasses of both wormnose and hornnose, all in different states of decomposition. Some were just bleached bony skeletons, scatted on the earth and rocks amid the rising ground, but others had died in more recent days and were not yet stripped of their flesh. In their advanced states of decay they spilled out their innards in a putrefying soup of blood and organ mush. The dreadful smell of the putrefying creatures hit the back of Llyat's throat and sought to make him vomit. All three turned pale from the foul odours and yet they would need to get used to the stink for the journey up through the pass would take longer than a day. Their character and resolve was about to be tested to the limit.

An hour later the three companions came across one particular carcass that had been stripped of its innards by some scavenging creature. Whatever had carried out that gruesome task had left the grey leathery skin intact and stretched across the wormnose's mighty rib bones to form a natural tent. It provided a perfect shelter from the rain and once inside the three men felt more at ease. Even the putrid stench no longer seemed to sting their noses. Llyat helped Thias to build a small fire inside their makeshift shelter. He had tried to ignite the fire using two flints that he had found but to his immense frustration they failed to create a spark. Thias smiled in a kind way and whispered a word of magic. In an instant the small amount of kindling they had found in the barren wastes of the Ivory Pass burst into flame. The bard then placed some old branches off some long dead tree upon the fledgling fire. Irabo meanwhile busied himself as he plucked away at one of the pheasants. Llyat warmed his hands upon the fire and held the hope that his clothes would soon dry out. He longed for his gambeson that the Grand Physician had given him but it was a wasted wish for his prized jacket had gone up in the flames of the burning Guild along with all his other possessions; all that is except for one. He had managed to salvage the old man's blade, the sword called Destiny's Song which still hung from his waist.

Once his hands began to thaw before the fire Llyat returned again to the question that most troubled him.

"Why have I been chosen to be the Marked?"

"As I promised you some hours ago, I will tell you all that I know," replied Thias. "But I warn you that it is somewhat fractured information that I pulled from many sources during my brief time in research at the Guild."

"Please tell me anything you can," continued Llyat. "Help me make some sense of what is going on."

"Well first off, let me take you back to the time we were together in the library at the Guild. Do you recall that I saved you from the cursed hand that would have petrified you?"

"Fuck, yes!" replied Llyat. "How could I forget? Then I knocked that masslewort stuff on me and started to glow."

"That's right," said Thias. "So tell me Llyat, do you know what masslewort is used for? Do you know of its purpose?"

Llyat tried to think back to the events of the library but after all that had happened his thoughts seemed a scrambled blur. Then as if a page in his mind had been turned, a memory of aiding the Grand Physician reformed. A vision came back of the dead stable boy and the strange markings that that triggered the journey to Valameer in order to seek the help of the Bards.

"It's used to detect magic, isn't it?" he spluttered. "Sprinkle the powder and if magic has been present then a glow is given off. Forgive me, but I've forgotten the name given to the light produced."

"That Llyat is the Kundalish Aura," continued Thias. "And before you ask, yes, that is what you displayed in the Guild after the powder fell upon you."

"But I can't see what that has to do with me being marked?"

"He has a point," added Irabo, who had been following the conversation.

"Fair enough," continued Thias. "As I said, my knowledge is bitty. During my stay at the Guild and while attempting to shed light on the dark resurgence of Death Tubaria, I kept being pointed to the Prophecy of Enderdetag. With Master Ulthirn and the Grand Musician's help I managed to deduce the following. 'The Marked' is the one person capable of entering the tomb of the Oracle of Frasteria.

Legend states that person is a boy raised in the presence of pure magic that was harnessed from out the Underworld."

"Bulls bollocks!" snapped Llyat. "My parents were Rukave and Lyrusa Emgar. They were not great wizards or wielders of magic. They were simple sods and we lived In Maplehill all our shit filled lives. We were just common serfs who knew nothing at all about magic. The first time I ever came into contact with anything of the sort was at the Bards Guild. I have no special powers and I can only just manage to swing a sword. I am just a dolt raised in one of the cesspits of the Realm."

"But yet you displayed Kundalish Aura. How are we to explain that?" replied Thias.

"There must be some mistake!" said Llyat while he quivered, unsure how to take on board the facts being presented.

He began to consider if the bard was teasing him and he doubted he was speaking the truth. Yet whatever was happening there was no denying the fact that he had glowed. Then without warning Llyat felt queasy but he was not sure if the rotting flesh of their shelter or the shocking prospects of being somehow important was the cause of his sudden discomfort. He jumped to his feet and ran outside where he then fell upon his knees in the rain and spewed up over the rocks.

After his third painful wretch and the expulsion of his sparse stomach contents Llyat felt a tap on his shoulder. He turned around and saw Irabo standing over him. The warrior smiled, took Llyat's wrists, and applied pressure to them. Several seconds later Llyat's feelings of sickness had gone.

"You are going to have to teach me how to do that," said Llyat as a broad grin spread across his face.

"Of course, but first, come back inside and keep warm."

Irabo helped Llyat to his feet and the pair returned to sit by the fire.

"I am sorry Llyat," said Thias at last. "I didn't mean to scare you with the story but you did say that you wanted to understand what is going on."

"This shite is so difficult to get my head around," replied Llyat.

"I think it might be best if we talk about something else," suggested Irabo. "I think our young friend here is not ready for any further shocks. My belief, for what it is worth, is that Fatumai has chosen Llyat, either alone or with others, to carry out her bidding. It is also my belief that she has mapped out his whole life. We Thias are just pawns in her game."

"But I can't be born out of magic? My parents were so nothing."

"And yet the Lizardman that killed the Grand Physician said that you were a traitors son?" continued Thias, "Where and when could your father have committed treason? I hate to be blunt but he may not have been the one who had seeded you. Now how I wonder could he be connected to Avolire?"

"I don't know," answered Llyat with a whimper. "In all truth I have no idea. The first time I ever heard the name Avolire was the day that my village was destroyed."

"It appears that whatever fate has in store for you young Llyat that the cursed place in the north has been shielded from you, and you from it."

"The hand of Fatumai looms large in all of this," added Irabo. "If Llyat is indeed the Marked, I think it would be best to explore the details at a later time. Give the boy a chance to digest what you have just told him. If I were him, I would need time alone to think things over, if as you suggest the parents he has always known were perhaps not his true ones."

"I take your point," replied Thias. "We'll discuss this again when Llyat feels ready, if that is of course if he wants to."

"Sure," replied Llyat not knowing what to think or say anymore.

The youth so longed to be back in the Capital and wrapped in Heliana's arms. Darker thoughts appeared and he began to wish that he had never made the journey to Valameer. A blackness then covered him and told him he should have died in the Tiaryer. Too many conflicting emotions rattled though his confused mind. Llyat was however changing for at least he had not fainted to escape his confusion. This was an option he could no longer countenance. He had to take charge of his life.

Before Llyat could voice further concerns Thias and Irabo struck up another conversation.

"I understand Irabo that you and your kind put a lot of faith in this fate shit," began Thias.

"That is true," replied Irabo, concerned as to where the bard was leading him.

"In my time as a traveller crooner, I've heard and sung many a tale about the origin of the deities and the interactions between them. As a follower of Fatumai, what is your take on the relationship between the different gods?"

"What is there to tell? I am sure such stuff will not interest Llyat."

"Oh please, do tell," said Llyat. "It may help take my mind off all that is happening."

"As you so wish," replied Irabo, "What do you want to know?"

"Tell us the creation story that you believe in, your take on how the gods came into being," continued Thias. "The structure of their family and how each is related and so forth."

There followed a brief pause as Llyat watched Irabo think on how best to construct his story. He looked on as the young warrior pondered and stared into the flames of the small fire. Llyat too was drawn to the flicker of the flames, the shadows and images that were cast upon the grey leathery hide of the wormnose carcass. Soon he found himself listening with great interest to Irabo's story of the birth of the gods. Characters came alive in his imagination and his mind projected them onto the flames and the dancing shadows that surrounded him.

"At first there was nothing," began Irabo. "That was until the great explosion in the heavens and the sudden appearance of the creators, the Brothers of the Beginning. Egredor was the elder and he represented the Land of Life and all that would be created on it. His brother Kha was given charge of the Underworld and the power over death itself. They formed the balance in the heavens that we know of today. Egredor bestowed life upon the world and Kha took it away. Each brother knew their strengths and promised never to interfere in the others work. Egredor was the father of the world and created not just man but all the other creatures and plants that dwell in this Realm. Kha was responsible for ensuring the smooth passage through death and control over departed spirits in the afterlife. All was peaceful until the arrival of the third creator, born out of the beauty of life itself and the one that came to influence man's behaviour. She was called Chalis and she was the goddess of love."

Llyat was captivated by the unfolding story for myths and ancient legends had always fascinated him although he never understood why.

"In time the three creators learned to co-exist and they worked together in harmony to create the Realm as we know it," continued Irabo. "Each gave their own spiritual energy to the cycle of life but the peace between the three was destined not to last. Egredor fell in love with Chalis and together they produced seven children. You know them as Solaris, Mona, Aquaris, Fatumai, Bycphy, Thinestar and Hamthor. To each of these children Egredor donated power which allowed them to govern their own elements within the world that he had created. Kha grew jealous of his brother's love and was driven into seclusion, racked with paranoid thoughts. He no longer wished to play by the rules that he and his brother had devised and in a jealous rage he set out to destroy all that Egredor and Chalis held dear."

Llyat sensed that Thias sought to pick up any clue that could assist in their current quest.

"After a lengthy battle between Egredor and Kha, the god of destruction got the upper hand over his brother and his lover. In the depths of his depravity Kha swallowed his brother's children whole. Tormented by despair and in the belief that her children were dead, Chalis threw herself from the heavens and crashed to earth with a force that shaped the land now called the Dragonas. It has ever since remained a place void of warmth and love and still relishes its birthed bleakness. For many years Egredor sought out his brother who had fled into hiding but at last he found him. In their final battle Egredor cast his brother down into the Underworld but not before slicing open his belly and pulling each of his children alive from within its stinking confines. While within Kha's belly Egredor's daughter Fatumai had used her divine power to ensure the survival of her siblings and for that act we still worship her today as the goddess of Fate. We of my land are convinced that Fatumai will always be there to protect us. Each day she manipulates our actions in accordance with her grand design, no matter what comes our way."

"It's very interesting that you mention Chalis as being the one who created the Dragonas," said Thais.

"Why is that?" asked Llyat who failed to see the point that Thias was making.

"I found another legend about the place we are heading too," continued the bard. "The story said that after the fall of Chalis to this world, and when she lay dying, she shed five tears. It was the water from those tears that gave life to the first dragons. A tear for each one of the different races of dragon that are now found within the Dragonas."

"Are you saying there more than one type of dragon?" squealed Llyat with surprise.

"Of course he is," said Irabo with a smile.

"I am sorry," replied Thias. "I forgot for a moment that you come from Falahorn. You will therefore know this better than anyone. Please explain the different types of dragons for Llyat."

"Oh it's quite simple," continued Irabo. "There are four distinct beasts, each identified by their colour. One for each of the elements that governs life. I am sure you know what they are Llyat."

"Yes I do, I am not so dull!" replied the youth, unsure if Irabo had meant to sound so condescending. "Earth, Wind, Fire and Water."

"Correct. There is a dragon for each of the elements. However, I must make a small correction for the prime element at the beginning was not water but ice. As I said, the difference between the dragons is their colour, red for fire, brown for earth, white for wind and blue for ice. Apart from the wing span of the wind dragons being greater than that of the other three, the only other major difference between the four is that the ice dragons do not breathe out the flames of the furnaces of the Underworld but instead emit the frosty manifestations of the hidden ice world. Their breath is reputed to be cold enough to freeze stone."

"But there were five tears of Chalis," said Llyat as he looked across fire. "What of the other?"

"The fifth tear seeped into the ground and created the wyverns. They are dragon like creatures but with only two legs instead of four. Just like the dragons, wormnoses, and hornnoses of the Dragonas, they are now on the verge of extinction. Hence those that dwell in their homeland, the residents of the town of Falahorn in particular, have devoted their lives to the preservation of the creatures. They believe it to be vital to the future wellbeing of us all to help these incredible beasts survive, whatever the cost and even if it means sacrificing their own lives."

Llyat looked back down into the fire and once again his imagination took hold. He saw each flame flicker and leap as if a different dragon, each locked in fiery combat against the next as they pushed for dominance of their race. As the images intensified he began to wonder which would be strongest of the four. Then his thoughts moved on to Thamous, the great wyvern that they had set out to find, and he began to ponder as to how difficult that task would prove to be. The lands of the Dragonas were said to be enormous and there was a possibility that there could be more than one wyvern out there. Perhaps the inhabitants of Falahorn would point him in the right direction.

A blood curdling howl reverberated through the valley and then inside the carcass as the travellers huddled in shelter from the rain. Llyat was jolted out of his trance. Whatever had made the noise was less than a league away.

"Please tell me that was just the wind," whispered Llyat as his right hand fell upon the hilt of Destiny's Song.

"Kulkulkath!" gasped Irabo as he jumped to his feet, drew his weapon, and then approached the opening of the canopy. "It sounds like there is just one of them. I was so preoccupied in getting out of the rain that I forgot that the beasts can often be found wandering through the Ivory Pass."

"Thanks for finally remembering!" sneered Thias. "Can you see anything?"

"Not a thing! The rain is too heavy. Let's just pray for two things. First that there is only one of the buggers, and second that it passes us without picking up our presence. It will not be easy to take on a kulkulkath in this weather amongst all these wet rocks and slippery ground. With their many legs they will have a distinct advantage."

Llyat tightened his grip on the hilt of his sword as he stood up from besides the fire and joined Irabo at the exit from the belly of the wormnose. He looked out into the rain and knew exactly what he was looking for and why Irabo was so spooked. Among the stories that Denius Castor had told around the fire of the Red Mare he had learned of the giant hairy creatures that inhabited many of the remote lands of the Realm. The beasts were the size of a cow and had a passing resemblance to a giant scorpion. Although they were said to be hairy they were not covered in fur such as would be found on the bear or fox. The hair of the kulkulkath was much coarser and similar in appearance to that found on the legs of flies and spiders, but on a much greater scale. The knowledge of how to best to overcome a kulkulkath was something that Llyat had always meant to ask Denius Castor but his father did not like Llyat delving into such practices given that the creatures had no relevance to where they lived and worked. He had only been allowed to learn the details of the beasts that posed a direct threat to Maplehill, the skyfawn and the nighthowlers. Neither of those came this far north or so he had been told. Had they done so then they would have provided hearty meals for the ever hungry kulkulkath.

"Do you see anything?" asked Thias as he took hold of a smouldering stick from the fire.

"Nothing, nothing at all," replied Irabo.

Llyat stared out of the shelter and saw only the rain that continued to pour down between Skillar and Charibol. Then he heard the sound of rocks moving against each other as if dislodged from the steep slope of the land. He held his breath and listened. Above the sploshing thuds of falling water drops and the whistle of the wind that echoed through the pass he heard a strange noise, no doubt made by many legs as they scuttled and scampered over the hard ground. He glanced towards Irabo for he knew that the warrior of the City Watch had also heard them.

"There is one out there," whispered Irabo, "and it is close. Did you pick up its distinctive six feet patter?"

"What do you suggest we do?" whispered Thias. "We can't take on a full grown kulkulkath."

"That is why I am so concerned," replied the warrior.

As Thias and Irabo continued to debate the possibility of an attack Llyat listened as the beast scuttled and circled around their hiding place. Then, as all fell quiet, he stuck his head out into the rain for he was certain that the sounds were moving away.

"I think it's buggered off," the youth whispered.

Llyat then sneezed. It wasn't of the refined type but a most explosive one that echoed down the pass and throughout the valley floor. Llyat wiped the dipping mucous from the end of his nose as he realised the enormity of his error. The sounds of the beast's legs fell away. The creature had stopped and it no doubt listened for further sounds from the prey that it hunted.

"Quick, get back inside Llyat, and lay flat on the ground," ordered Irabo as he grabbed the youth by the neck and threw him into the rear of the wormnose carcass. "Thias kill the fire and get down in the dirt. Our lives depend upon it."

Llyat looked on as Thias then covered the fire with his cloak as he too dropped to the ground.

"Do not even twitch the smallest of your muscles," continued Irabo in a whisper. "It, or they, have been hunting us by sound. If that creature sticks its head in here you must remain still and quiet. A kulkulkath's vision only picks up movement not fine detail. The smell from this carcass is strong enough to mask our own scent."

Llyat remained as still as he could without stopping breathing. He listened again to the creature's footfall as it moved around their shelter. Then after a moment of silence the beast's head appeared at the entrance. There it paused with its pincers readied to snap and its poisonous tail cocked and primed to strike. Seconds passed like hours and Llyat wondered how long they would have to wait before the creature got bored and moved off to hunt some other prey. He looked to the shadowy black shape of its head and despite the dark he saw enough to confirm its nature. Just as Denius Castor had described it was covered with thick course hairs through which two black spheres that passed as eyes bulged forward. The monster pushed its gruesome head forward into the belly of the wormnose. Llyat felt the urge to scream and run but the only way out was into the jaws of the beast. He clenched his back cheeks so as not to expel his fear and just when he could no longer control his terror the beast turned and began its retreat down into the valley.

The three friends waited for the sounds of feet on rocks to disappear before Irabo made the first move towards the opening to their shelter. Once again he stared out into the rain that had at last begun to ease.

"Bugger me!" swore Irabo. "That was close, but it seems to have gone now. Llyat if you to sneeze like that again I swear I will thrust you in the creature's jaws myself."

"That's a bit harsh," added Thias as he stood up and then helped Llyat to his feet. "I am sure the lad didn't do it on purpose."

"Listen well Llyat," growled Irabo. "Prophecy, or no prophecy, you almost got us all killed just then. You must be more careful."

"I'm sorry, I didn't mean to do it. I think I've got a chill coming on."

"Just be more diligent in the future," grumbled the warrior of the Watch

"I will try, honest. I couldn't help it, believe me. It's this fucking weather."

"Well it looks to be easing off now," added Irabo as he once again looked out into the pass.

"So now what" asked Thias? "How far is it to Falahorn?"

"Another two or three day's trek," replied Irabo "Let's hope the gods are with us and we don't come across any other such beasts."

"Two to three days!" muttered Thias. "That's a long time to go without being hunted. There must be more of them out there."

"We could take the higher path," added Irabo as he pointed up towards the rocky ledges of Skillar. "The kulkulkath do not like to climb where it is cold and I would feel much safer being out of their reach, even if it means extending our journey by a day or two."

"Are you sure that they won't climb after us?" asked Thias

"I am positive they will not," replied Irabo. "I have heard a lot about them. Our Man-at-Arms, Danisun Dain, once devised a training exercise in the Howling Hills and to get there you had to cross an area well known for its kulkulkath colonies. Two cadets were sent for nine days, to survive on their instincts and hunting skills, deep within the shadows of the Howling Hills. This was deemed to be essential training by our Lord Commander...."

"Yes, yes, yes, I get the point," snorted Thias as he stopped Irabo's flow before turning to Llyat. "Do you think you will be able to make the climb lad?"

"Of course," replied Llyat despite being unsure. "I will give it my best."

"Then it sounds like we have a plan," said the bard. "Irabo, I think we'd better take some of this wormnose rind with us despite its horrendous smell."

"If you'd eat that, you'd worry a barn rat!" moaned Llyat at the thought of rotten meat.

"I don't think we will find much else to eat on the steep face of Skillar, so we must be prepared," ordered Thias. "Come on, we need to move away from here and strike out for Falahorn."

28.

The head of the skyfawn flew through the air, severed from its body by a curved blade that had swung down from on top of a chestnut steed. Having travelled a significant distance the creature's head hit the ground and bounced once before coming to rest in a small ditch by the side of the dirt path that passed as the coast road between Parandor and the town of Valameer. Tonousa praised the gift that Theoplous had given her for the sailor's blade had replaced her own after it had been lost during her fall from the Bridge of Athuna. Wielding the weapon with great skill she protected herself from the claws and beaks of the ravenous skyfawn pack that targeted both her and the horse she had named Glorius.

It was on the afternoon of the fourth day of her journey to the Capital that the flock of screaming skyfawn had intended to make their kill. Until that point the journey from Valameer had been uneventful with no sign of any Lizardmen or knights in black armour. Tonousa had known that the journey back to the Capital would dangerous and that it would take longer than her time on the Banshees Wail. She had also calculated that if she stopped only when necessary and rode on through the night, then she could make Parandor within four to five days. So it was that she limited her breaks to two hours while all the time praying that her luck would hold and that the horse not go lame.

From atop of the brave steed, Tonousa at last got the upper hand over the remaining skyfawn. Three ended up diced as her blade slashed their bellies and spilled their bloody innards across the road. The last creature she had managed to just wound but it fled knowing it too would die if it persisted in its attack. Tonousa spat down onto the ground as the creature departed and hoped that soon it would be eaten by some other beast; one that would find it an easy target. She felt no sorrow for its eventual fate, just a feeling of satisfaction that she had got the better of it.

Taking hold of the reins and having sheathed her blade, Tonousa set off as fast as the exhausted Glorius could take her. Down along the dirt road she raced, through the rocky outcrops and over the grass lands that lay before her. For the rest of that day and through the night that followed Tonousa continued her journey without further incident. The rest periods grew longer for Glorius toiled long and hard. But the breaks gave Tonousa time to recuperate, take in sustenance, and focus on the tasks she faced on reaching Parandor. It was now down to her alone to uncover the murderer who sought to resurrect the cult of Death Tubaria and her head was full of uncertainties. If Thias had been correct and there was indeed a Silverwynn spy in the Capital, then she would have to be very careful with who, if anyone, she trusted this information. The traitor could be any of the Sovereign Council who were close to Phauless Gylewu and who by now may have established a network of agents and informants, perhaps even including one or more of those who had been involved in Highroar's card game. Then there was her own Lord Commander to consider. He had known of the journey to Valameer and the Physician's attempt to seek the council of the Bards. It pained Tonousa to contemplate his possible involvement such heinous crimes. She also had been tasked to track down the heart shaped ruby, said to be fixed to a golden necklace, and one of the five Gems of Thamous needed to prevent the forces of Avolire from opening the portal to the Underworld. If the bard was again correct, the ruby necklace was hidden somewhere in the Capital. Yet, given the size of the city and having no one to help her search, it would be like finding a mite in a midden. Then there was the issue of the Oracle of Frasteria, hidden somewhere near the Barrow of Harico, and within its mysterious defences. She struggled to think where she should begin if she was to have any chance of success.

Later that day while sat before the small fire that she had made to keep warm, the challenges of the investigation weighed heavy on her mind. The heat from of the fire was not the only thing that warmed her for she felt sure there was another who could help. Danisun Dain was without doubt the one person she could trust. She would seek him out, tell him her story, and seek his assistance. In addition to being the head of recruitment, Man-at-Arms, and keeper of the armoury, Danisun Dain, was one of her closest companions in the Watch. Other than Irabo and the Lord Commander he had been the one who had stood by her throughout Xix Blackfayer's assault on her character. Danisun was well respected by the men that served under him. Their friendship was the strongest of all in the Watch and because of it Tonousa felt able to confide in him. She could not even begin to conceive of Danisun turning against the Realm. Then as her thoughts drifted she began to hope that Irabo had not yet reached Falahorn. It would be unfortunate if a bird came to Danisun before she had the opportunity to take him into her confidence.

On the fifth day of her journey south Solaris climbed into the heavens and peeped through the scattered clouds that drifted across the deep blue sky. As the light spread across the land, Tonousa spotted the slums which stood before the North Gate and the walls of Parandor. Glorius was forced to canter and the steed accepted the prompt for it too sensed it was nearing the end of its exhausting journey. Woman and beast made their way through the shanty town but the nearer she got to the gate the more troubled Tonousa became. The slums were far too quiet for her liking and there were few of life's' unfortunates out on the streets. Those that she passed looked at her with great suspicion and mistrust and she sensed that something significant had happened during her brief absence from the Capital. Her intuition spoke sinister events brewing deep within the dens of misery and she readied herself against a possible attack.

Once she had reached the large gate that was set into the circular wall of the gatehouse she slowed down to a walk and at last brought Glorius to a halt before its solid presence. Within moments she was greeted by another of the Watch, a warrior she recognised as Karkis Snouth.

"Tonousa Amberstone," said Karkis with surprise as he approached the horse. "Now there is an unexpected sight for my weary eyes. Where the fuck have you been?"

"And greetings to you too Karkis," replied Tonousa as she dismounted. "When did those who guard the North Gate decide to forgo the ritual greeting demanded by the Sovereign?"

"I beg your forgiveness Tonousa," replied Karkis as he took hold of the horse's reins. "I sense you are unaware of recent events. Your disappearance has been a cause of great concern in the Capital and even your father has denied knowledge of where you could be."

The guard's ignorance of her travels reassured Tonousa for it appeared her visit to Valameer was not yet common knowledge.

"Karkis, I've had a very long journey and an exhausting number of days on the roads of the Realm. Please stop talking in riddles and tell me what's going on. Then explain why you are not at your usual post at the South Gate?"

"Once again I beg your pardon Tonousa but I had orders from the Lord Commander to take the place of Yarrior Hilton."

"Why, what has happened to Yarrior?"

"Townsforth, for some reason during your absence, sent fifteen riders out to scout the lands south of the Grey Mountains. Yarrior was included as he is an accomplished rider. I was sent here to take his place. Ambrose Bluehill has been rushed through the final stages of his training and now mans the South Gate with Lolye Throissler. Yarrior returned exhausted yesterday and is resting."

"I see," replied Tonousa. "Was Danisun Dain also sent out? If so has he returned?"

"Yes Tonousa, he was. I believe that he made it as far as the Grey Keep and the edge of the Eastern Marsh."

"But has he returned Karkis?" repeated Tonousa as the words caused her to fear for his safety.

"Yes he has and that is why you sense the great unease outside this wall."

"Right, I see," stuttered Tonousa amid her uncertainty. "What is going on; tell me at once?"

"You don't know do you," gasped Karkis? "The news Danisun brought confirms that those shits who dwell in the Eastern Marsh have declared war on the Realm. The Grey Keep has fallen and Xix Blackfayer has called a War Council. They say Phauless Gylewu has so far refused to take part for he is in deep mourning over the loss of his brother. The death has affected him to a great extent and I fear that we are in danger of losing control in the slums. There is a rumour going around that the Capital will soon be locked down as it was in the old days of the plagues."

"The Council... Karkis? When is it due to begin?" asked Tonousa as she realised the seriousness of the situation.

The blow that Avolire had dealt to the brother of the Sovereign Lord had been discovered and from Karkis's revelations Tonousa realised events were moving at a much more rapid pace than she had anticipated. Now she had even less time to discover the identity of the spy, something she had to do before the enemy's siege plans were finalised. Danisun needed to be found without delay and taken into her confidence.

"Where is he?" asked Tonousa. "Where is Danisun Dain now?"

"He's in the Citadel. He went there this morning on the orders of Commander Townsforth."

"Thank you Karkis," answered Tonousa as she attempted a smile. "Look after my horse and see that it is fed and well-watered. Get a message to Edwardis Treveyn if you have to, but for now I must leave and find our Man-at-Arms."

Karkis signalled back towards the gate house and a few seconds later the gate began to open. Tonousa marched forward at pace leaving Glorius behind with her young comrade. She made her way through the narrow streets that led up to the Royal Citadel and on her way she stepped around many beggars as if they didn't exist. So preoccupied was she in her thoughts that she was lucky not to have been hit by unsavoury emissions from above. A quarter hour later Tonousa arrived at the Barbican entrance of the Citadel. Two guards in armour with the crest of Gylewu on their shoulders guarded its entrance.

"I have an urgent message for Lord Commander Townsforth and Danisun Dain of the City Watch," shouted Tonousa with authority as she approached.

"And who may we be speaking too?" asked the first.

"Tonousa Amberstone of the Watch."

There was a brief pause as the two guards eyed her with great suspicion. Tonousa felt frustrated and her anger began to grow.

"Look I haven't got all fucking day!" she snapped out. "As I have told you already, I am Tonousa Amberstone of the City Watch and I have vital information for Commander Brynn Townsforth and his Man-at Arms, Danisun Dain. I understand from those at the North Gate that both of those I seek are at this moment inside the Citadel."

"The information you have been given is correct," replied the first guard. "However, the War Council has begun and both are present at that meeting. I will escort you to them but do not overstep your position or overstay your welcome should you be granted an audience. I do not want your blood on my hands Tonousa Amberstone."

"Listen very carefully as I will say this but once," ordered Tonousa as she gripped the handle of her blade. "I have information concerning a great threat to this city. Take me to the Council now or else be prepared to witness my wrath. Do not have me send you limbless to Fatumai's healers."

The two guards looked at each other again before the first then turned and led Tonousa through the Barbican gate and into the street beyond. She marched at double pace amongst the shadows of the buildings while the urgency of her task drove her forward. Soon she began to think on why the knights of the Citadel had been so hostile but it was something she would address later. War was coming and this was not the time to load further burdens upon the Watch.

The guard led the way into the courtyard and then to the gates of the Keep itself without speaking. As the pair traversed the ground floor of the building they passed numerous servants, courtiers, and the Fool called Lolly. Up the grand staircase they went and once again Tonousa's eyes widened on seeing the magnificent stained glass window that depicted the fall of Urthanock. Beyond the stairs they scuttled through the first floor halls of the Keep until they at last approached the solid oak door that led into the Sovereign's war room. Voices of the

Council seeped through cracks that surrounded the door and begged attention from those waiting in the hall. The loudest mouth was that of Xix Blackfayer and it was obvious that he was in the midst of asserting his authority over all others present.

"It tells us nothing!" Blackfayer shouted. "How may we be sure that it is these so called Knights of Avolire who are responsible for the massacres that the villagers spoke of?"

Before the solid door Tonousa's mind raced while she thought of all that she had learned over the past few weeks. She realised that Blackfayer had received word that the Knights of Avolire were on the move and she then understood why the slums, the City Watch, and the Royal Guards were so spooked.

"I came across a knight clad in strange metal armour. It was extremely light and allowed for swift and agile movement in combat," said another, young but also wise for his years, and who Tonousa recognised as Danisun Dain. "From the wound to his throat it was obvious that these warriors do have a weakness. There is a small gap between the chest plate and the helmet, no doubt to facilitate movement. It could be that the dead knight had borrowed another's suit, someone larger than himself, however I believe there to be a design fault and that knowledge may help us in the future. Either way he never stood a chance once his opponent's blade had entered his throat."

"And what was the armour made from" asked another voice that Tonousa knew to be Sir Rayner Byddin, Head of the Royal Guard.

"I don't know," replied Danisun Dain. "It was of a metal I have never seen before. I must assume it is the legendary orichalcum. Finding the warrior's corpse on the road confirmed my suspicions as to what was afoot."

"Now then," began the guard beside Tonousa. "Do you want me to take you into the Council chamber or would you prefer to enter alone. It may be inappropriate for you to barge through the door but to be honest I would prefer not to announce you."

"I don't know what lies Blackfayer has been feeding you of late sir…"

"Nothing! Nothing at all," replied the guard. "I'm sure you will hear the truth soon enough and I sincerely hope you get to see this day out."

With that said the guard turned and marched off through the hall and back towards his post. The knight's strange behaviour implied something significant had occurred that involved her in some way or other. Whatever it was it made others treat her with open hostility. All was not well in Parandor but she could not work out what it was.

Tonousa turned towards the door that barred her way and struck it three times with her fist. Behind the wood all fell silent. A few seconds later a murmur grew and the first voice to speak clearly was that of Blackfayer.

"Who the fuck can that be," shouted the Sovereign Advisor. "Cragtalon, tell whoever it is to fuck off and bother somebody else."

"Yes Sir! At once," came the reply.

Tonousa did not have to wait long for the doors to open and as soon as the gap between them was wide enough she brushed past Cragtalon and strode into the centre of the chamber. The first she sought to make eye contact with was Lord Phauless Gylewu but she could not see him anywhere. Then her eyes me those

Blackfayer who stood up from his seat and glared with an intensity that would have withered most men.

"What is the Amberstone bitch doing here?" he snapped.

"I beg a brief moment of your time for I bring important news to your Council Lord Blackfayer, urgent information of interest to my Lord Commander Townsforth and Dansiun Dain."

"Sir Cragtalon, Sir Redglade, I want this woman removed and flay the cunt that allowed her in here," bellowed Blackfayer.

Tonousa's hand fell upon the hilt of the curved blade that hung at her side and she signalled her intentions to the two Knights that approached.

"I don't think so. I have not ridden for five days to be welcomed like this. I demand that you hear me out."

"Tonousa, this isn't a good time," shouted Commander Townsforth.

"Now is exactly the time. You will all hear me out if you value the survival of the Realm. I bring you word of the death of Abrahamus Marus, the Grand Physician who was a guest at the Bards Guild of Valameer and much more."

"Abrahamus is dead!" gasped a woman.

Tonousa turned her head and watched Lady Thinata Fullbane begin to fan her face in her usual affected manner. The room fell silent and in that briefest of moments Tonousa looked around and noted all those present. Sat around the black onyx war table were all the members of the Sovereign Council and one other of the highborn. Also present was Danisun Dain standing out with his magnificent ginger beard and Commander Townsforth. To the left of the marble chair reserved for the Sovereign Ruler stood Blackfayer, while to its right sat the Lord Chamberlin, Gilebin Ystafell. Sandwiched between the Lord Commander and Lady Thinata Fullbane sat the Court Judge, Lady Llys Emeny, who looked skeletal in contrast to the fat whale whose excess of lard encroached upon the judge's twiglet thighs. Lady Fullbane was not an official member of the Council but her presence had been tolerated as she had already been in the room when the others turned up and it would have taken an age to have removed her. The head of the Royal Guard, Sir Rayner Byddin, sat to the left of Commander Townsforth which seemed odd given their past disagreements. Opposite the two great warriors sat the faith leader, the Royal Priest Heward Teulu, whose presence brought a moderating influence on those fuelled by the product of their loins.

"So speak then!" ordered Blackfayer after a brief pause. "Explain to us why our Grand Physician is dead. How did it happen and what else you know."

Tonousa caught the eye of her Lord Commander who nodded his approval. She then proceed to describe to the Council how she had been ordered by Phauless Gylewu to investigate the murders related to Death Tubaria. She described how the investigation had led her to the Grand Physician and his servants. Clues then pointed them to the Bards Guild of Valameer and the possibility of the resurgence of the Knights of Avolire. Then to the shock of all she described how the Guild had been attacked by the Lizardmen of the Eastern Marsh and that during the ensuing battle the rest of her party had perished. Tonousa also lied about various other facts and left the clear impression that none other than she had survived. She prayed that her fabrications had passed undetected.

"This confirms my worst fears Lord Blackfayer," said Danisun Dain. "Added to the massacre I witnessed at the Grey Keep these facts prove that the Lizardmen are massing to attack us. They intend to move on Parandor. This is confirmation they have joined forces with the Knights of Avolire..."

"Which we have still yet to prove," hissed Blackfayer.

"I too saw the marks on the body that Tonousa has described," interrupted Townsforth. "As did you Xix if my memory is correct. The wounds implicate the Knights of Avolire in the murders we have uncovered."

"To me, all the stories seem to add up," added Lady Emeny.

"I agree with both Emeny and Townsforth," added Lord Ystafell. "This points to the need to lock down the Capital, declare war on the Eastern Marsh and those murderous swine from Avolire."

"Why do you all take the word of the Amberstone bitch with such ease," snarled Xix.

Tonousa knew that Blackfayer felt ill of her but he'd never shown such venom before.

"Considering who her father is, why should we be believe anything that she says" he added?

Tonousa's ears pricked. Something was very wrong.

"What has this got to do with my father?" she demanded.

"Later Tonousa," shouted Commander Townsforth. "Now is not the time."

"Lord Blackfayer, tell me what has happened to my father," demanded Tonousa "If you don't speak of your own volition then my blade will loosen your tongue."

"You see members of the Court, the same hatred flows in her blood as in that of her father," hissed the snake as he addressed the chamber. "The daughter of the traitor Mathias Amberstone shows the same disrespect for the Council that her father did."

"Traitor!" gasped Tonousa, unable to comprehend what was being said. "My father?"

"We were planning to tell you in private upon your return," added her Commander. "We didn't expect you to come straight here. I wanted to break the news to you in a more gentle way, over time, and in a less threatening manner."

"Gentle!" gasped Tonousa. "What is his treason? What is he accused of?"

"The murder of six people in the Sovereign's Household and the attempted resurrection of the cult of the Death Tubaria," smirked Xix, his face full of evil intent.

Tonousa wanted nothing more than to launch herself across room and strike the smile from his face but she knew such an action would condemn her to a slow and painful death. She had much to achieve and would not be able to do it from the confines of a prison cell.

"My father is no traitor," she roared as she tried to restrain herself. "Didn't you listen to anything I told you? The reason for Marus's trip to Valameer, the marks that point to Avolire, surely you understand? Had you listened with an open mind then you would recognise that it is the Lady of the Silverwynn who is responsible for all that is happening."

"That old crone must be long dead," chipped in Lady Fullbane.

"Or at least withered so past her age that she could not even raise a fart," agreed Lady Emeny.

"I am telling you that my father is no traitor," shouted Tonousa. "I demand to see him. I must be able to talk to him. It is my right as his daughter."

"I'm sure that you could at least allow that Xix," added Danisun Dain.

In the pause that followed Tonousa realised that Blackfayer was mulling over her request. She knew the spite that the man felt for her family but even Xix would find it difficult to deny her the right to visit her father. Thoughts of the Lore of the Dead once again bubbled up. She remembered how her father had told her that the book had been stolen and the ritual of Kha had been ripped from its pages. At last she came to realise that the plot to bring down the Realm was not confined to the Dark Lord's resurrection. It was much more ambitious for it involved the Gems of Thamous. The secret plan was all about power and who would rule the lands that stretched from the Dirmark to the coast beyond the Badlands. In that moment she understood that whoever had taken the Lore of the Dead was using her father to divert attention away from the spy who lurked amongst the highborn. While all fingers pointed to her father the need to identify the hidden one became even more urgent. Tonousa's relationship with her father had always teetered on the edge yet she knew deep in her heart that he was innocent and she was determined to prove it.

Well Xix," added Danisun Dain. "Will you at least allow Tonousa to see him?"

"Yes, I will relent," smirked Blackfayer. "But she must not be left alone with him, even for one minute. She must be accompanied by another from the City Watch and I appoint you Danisun Dain to that task. You will be responsible for the bitch now."

"Thank you my Lord," answered Tonousa as she released some of the tension in her fists.

The woman warrior then turned and made her way to the door. Danisun Dain joined her a few seconds later and together they began their journey through the corridors of the Citadel and on towards the tunnels of the Underkeep. On they strode through the flickering torchlight of dank passageways and through the screams of unfortunates being tortured. Amid this foul palace of death Tonousa began to question her great friend on all that had happened since her departure for Valameer. She demanded to know what it was that her father had done to be condemned as a traitor.

"I had just arrived back from the Grey Keep when I found the Citadel in disarray," he responded. "The previous night there had been an attempt on the life of Phauless Gylewu. A swine, cloaked, hooded, and with an assassin's dagger in his hand was discovered in our Sovereign Lord's bed chamber. The bugger managed to escape the guards by a daring leap from the window. However, that was not before he had managed to slash out and cut Phauless deep across the arm as the Sovereign tried to protect himself. Blackfayer's guards conducted a detailed search through every nook and cranny but they found no trace of the assailant. Since then the Citadel has been locked down with all entry to it restricted."

"What has that got to do with my father," asked Tonousa? "Are you saying that they believe him to have been the assassin? My father creeping about and using a knife; I don't think so!"

"Not at all," added Danisun as they moved forward. "As the Royal Guard are few in number Blackfayer recruited the assistance of the Citadel's servants to search their master's rooms in secret. You will not be surprised by that method for that is how the slimy little shit operates. It was when one of your father's servants looked through his belongings that they found it. Then all fuck broke loose."

"Danisun, tell me please; I need to know. What did they find in my father's chambers?"

"They found it Tonousa. The book that was responsible for Tullage's murders all those years ago; the Lore of the Dead."

"You have got to be fucking kidding me!" exclaimed Tonousa.

"That is what I said the moment that I heard that they had arrested him. Why in the name of all the gods would he be caught up with the schemes of Tullage?"

"Did they catch the assassin?"

"No, they did not," continued Danisun. "They didn't even find the dagger that wounded our Sovereign Lord."

"But it can't be my father," replied Tonousa as she fought to control her emotions. "It just can't be, I won't believe it."

"Yet all the evidence points to him being guilty."

Tonousa at last began to understand the hostility that she had faced since her return. Everyone, Karkis Snouth, the two guards at the Barbican, and the slithering Blackfayer, had all treated her the same. Somehow she had to prove her father's innocence and the only way she could do that was to complete her mission in Parandor and discover the true identity of the one who had infiltrated the Capital. Finding Thamous's ruby disappeared from her thoughts.

"Danisun we go back a long time, do we not?" she said.

"Tonousa, you have my full attention. Ever since you turned up at the war room you've been acting out of character. The story that you told to the Council has so many holes in it. But you know that you can trust me. Tell me the truth, all that you know, and then maybe I will be able to help you."

"I have reason to believe that at least one of the Council, and perhaps others, is in fact a changeling from the Eastern Marsh. The Capital has been compromised and we are all in the utmost of danger. You weren't the first person to discover what had happened at the Grey Keep."

"What do you mean?"

"I ran into Lord Phauless Gylewu's clandestine investigator, the Bard of the Royal Court. You know who I mean; the young fop in the greens and the reds."

"You mean Lolly, the fool?"

"No I don't mean the fucking jester," she snapped before dropping her voice to a whisper. "I refer to Thias Calavan. I ran into him up in Valameer. He had been there a week before I arrived and he had just come from the Grey Keep. He told me about the attack of the Lizardmen, the disappearance of the dwarf Grovrouk the Despoiler, and the murder of Lord Raorick."

"And you didn't think to send some communication south?"

"I assumed that our Commander would have sent the riders north as soon my party had left for Valameer. I also knew it would be just a matter of days before you discovered the massacre yourselves. What I did not want to do was to have any communication intercepted by the spy that lurks within our midst."

"Tonousa, this is most interesting," continued Danisun. "I am not going to press you further here in the Underkeep where anyone or anything could be listening from the shadows. We will discuss this later and debate the issues once you have seen your father."

Danisun led the way through the corridors and Tonousa followed like a dog as her anxiety grew. She tried to fight her way through her scrambled thoughts and put together what little pieces of the jigsaw she believed she had identified. She reckoned that even Danisun, a man whom she had known for many years, would be hard to convince of the truth. Soon the Man-at-Arms opened one many solid iron doors and began to descend a small flight of steps into the deepest level of the Underkeep. At the bottom Tonousa found herself inside a small anteroom lined with dark and mouldy bricks. From its end a short passage led to a small alcove which had no windows. The fourth wall was constructed from a mesh of iron bars. Nostrils detected the prisoner before she saw him. Her father, chained and manacled to the wall, had been forced to sit in a growing pile of his own excrement. Half asleep and leaning against the wall of the anteroom was the unmistakable figure of the prison keeper, a brute called Tharik Mastisan. The muscular dullard snored like a muffled pig and the sound reverberated across his leathers and rattled the huge ring of rusting iron keys that hung from his belt.

On reaching the bars Tonousa looked down at the old man before her and was shocked to see the extent to which he had been beaten. Blood seeped from his many wounds and covered the purple contusions underneath his exposed skin. The congealed blood around his mouth pointed to the loss of many teeth. For the briefest of moments she thought it may be a joke and that the man was neither her father nor so badly hurt after all, but then the prisoner managed to open one swollen eye and whimpered.

"Tonousa, Is that you?"

"Yes father," she replied. "Is it true what they are saying? Did you have the Lore of the Dead all this time?"

"No Tonousa, I swear I did not. Like I told you the last time we met, the Lore of the Dead was stolen long ago from the library vault. I thought it was Xix Blackfayer at first playing some cruel trick on me, considering what I had already told you?"

"Let me interrupt," spat out Danisun. "What has your father already told you?"

Tonousa turned and looked in all directions. She focused on Danisun's eyes and then on to Tharik who was still content in his slumber.

"Blackfayer ordered the pages containing the ritual of Kha to be burned," she began. "He was fearful of a further uprising from any remaining followers of

Lord Tullage. My father kept this information to himself, even during the recent series of murders, because someone had stolen the book from his library. They both feared the second coming of Death Tubaria."

"So are you telling me Xix knew about the theft?" asked Danisun.

"Who is that person with you Tonousa?" asked her father. "It doesn't sound like Townsforth."

"It is Danisun Dain, my Lord," replied the Man-at-Arms. "Mathias, is it true that Xix Blackfayer knew that the Lore of the Dead had been stolen?"

"Yes my friend," whimpered the shell that was once Lord Amberstone. "Someone else must have known the secret that we thought was ours alone. Someone is manipulating the Sovereign Advisor and undermining his support. I can say with all honesty that the last time I saw that cursed book was just before it was stolen."

"Is it really eight years since Lord Tullage tried to resurrect Kha?" asked Danisun

"Correct," moaned the old man.

"Father," continued Tonousa. "Before or after the theft of the Lore of the Dead did anyone come asking questions about it or what it may contain?"

"I don't see the point in asking…"

"I beg to differ Danisun, this has everything to do with what is going on," replied Tonousa. "If the ritual of Kha had been erased by my father and Blackfayer and the lore then later stolen, perhaps the person behind the theft did not know of the burning of the pages. Given what I have deduced, I am sure that this ritual of Kha it is no more than a deliberate subterfuge. It is some form of ruse to distract the Council from a far more sinister plot."

"Sorry, hold on a minute!" spluttered Danisun. "Explain what exactly you are getting at."

"Whoever is responsible for the murders in the Capital, whoever our spy and assassin is, he is trying to force our hand. He wants us to locate something for him but without telling us what it is. He is leaving both clues and misinformation to ensure we do not grasp his true intentions. He is hoping both to startle us and force us into making mistakes."

"Tonousa, slow down," responded the confused warrior. "You are talking in riddles. We came here for you to make peace with your father yet you seem intent on asking him vague questions that don't make any sense."

"It's something I have thought about a lot since my incarceration," muttered Lord Amberstone. "Someone wants me out of the way because of what I know. It must have something to do with the contents of that bugger of a book and whatever else is contained within its pages."

"What is it that you could have known that was so dangerous?" asked Tonousa.

"I know very little about its content."

"Please father," continued Tonousa. "If I am to clear your name then it is imperative that you tell me all that you know. In the years that you had the book in your keeping, who else apart from Xix and yourself showed any interest in it? Had anyone else tried to examine the book's contents?"

"Please daughter, I need a drink," gasped Lord Amberstone. "Can you find some for me?"

"Of course father, I can try," replied Tonousa as tears welled in her eyes.

The heart cut stoic had not agreed with her father on much that they had shared in life and yet it distressed her to see him so feeble and so frail. She became so consumed with finding water that she forgot the reason for Danisun's presence.

"Danisun, please find him some water and maybe some bread too. Wine if you can."

"I'm not supposed to leave your side but I will see what I can do".

Without further comment Danisun returned to the stairs and exited the room.

"He's always been a good man," groaned her father once Danisun was out of hearing range. "He reminds me of the selfless citizens of Valameer who always see the good in others no matter how they behave."

"Father, I have just ridden from Valameer. The Bards Guild was destroyed by the Lizardmen of the Eastern Marsh and even when the town appeared to be their next target the cow headed Flurdiana was not willing to authorise its defence."

"As has always been the way of that bitch," replied her father. "She leaves all planning and work to her people and is lucky to rule over such valiant men as those from Valameer."

A loud snort from Tharik's snout caused Tonousa to turn. The lump who kept the keys remained in a deep slumber. Realising her words were for her father's ears only she began to whisper through the bars that restrained him.

"Did anyone come to see you father about the Lore of the Dead before it was stolen? Has anyone else shown any interest in its contents?"

"Only two."

"Was one of them the Lord Commander of the City Watch?"

"No," replied her father after a moment's thought. "If Townsforth had showed any interest in the Lore then it was never recorded in our ledgers. My librarians pride themselves in their record keeping and they would never fail to note who examined a tome of such importance."

"Father, I don't have much time before Danisun returns. What were the names to the two who did show interest?"

"Lady Llys Emeny was one of them."

"And the other?"

"I believe it was Sir Rayner Byddin," he croaked through parched lips. "Yes, it was without doubt Sir Byddin. He came to us saying that he wanted to research the ruins of Barad Elestor for someone had told him a story that a weapon forged with powerful magic had been hidden there. This was over six years ago Tonousa and my memory of that day is rather patchy but I can remember parts of the conversation with great clarity for he swore me to secrecy. The bastard threatened me saying that if I loosened my tongue or ever spoke about his visit then he would ensure that I would spend my last hours with Sir Richemanus of the Nightfall. It seems Byddin's words have come to pass. I have lost everything Tonousa; my execution date has already been set by Blackfayer."

"What" gasped Tonousa? "When?"

"Tomorrow morning when Solaris is half way on his ascent."

"Xix doesn't waste any time does he?" snarled Tonousa as she turned to move towards the stairs. "Can't he see that you are being set up? He's trying to cover his own mistakes by having your head placed on a spike."

"Where are you going?" asked her father.

"To talk to Xix," replied Tonousa. "I must make the snake see sense."

"Why bother Tonousa, all is lost. He will execute me anyway, guilty or not. I am a dead man breathing his last hours with a dear daughter. They will realise as soon as there is another murder that I am not the one they are looking for but by then it will be too late for me."

"Don't be such a fucking martyr," snapped back Tonousa. "I will confront Xix and put the scrawny shit straight. I will even talk to Phauless Gylewu himself if I have to. The Sovereign Lord chose the City Watch to run this investigation, not that snivelling creep Blackfayer. I am sure that Phauless Gylewu will allow you to contest your innocence given your loyal service over so many years."

Tonousa thought for a moment and realised she had no lead as to who had infiltrated the Court. Deep down she knew she couldn't approach Xix or the Sovereign Lord over her father's innocence without some solid proof of another's wrong doing. Yet she would need to move with haste if she was to have any hope of finding something useful by the mid-morning of the morrow.

"Do you have a good alibi for all of the murders perpetrated in the name of Death Tubaria?"

"I'm afraid I do not daughter. Ever since your mother died, I have kept myself to myself and spent my evenings in solitude. That's why I offered to run the Royal Library for our Sovereign Lord. You see, I liked the silence and the isolation that it brought."

"Sadly that is not helpful," replied Tonousa.

"Leave it be girl. I'm a dead already and I will join your mother in the morning."

"But I can't let them..."

"You are going to have to Tonousa and that is my final demand of you," he added. "Please be a good child and honour this last request. Leave me now so that I may prepare for my end. Let this moment be our last goodbye."

"But father..." shouted Tonousa as tears poured over the edges of her lids.

Tharik stirred but Tonousa failed to notice.

"Goodbye dear Tonousa," said the old man as he closed his swollen eyes and hung his head low. Weary bones slumped back against the wall and skidded through the excrement on the floor.

"Father!" screamed Tonousa as she rattled the iron bars of the cell door "Damn you Father!"

"You heard what that traitor said," bellowed a rough voice. "Fuck off."

Tonousa turned and stared into the face of Tharik Mastisan. The brute glared back with squinting pig like eyes. She wiped the tears from her cheeks and then made her way back up the stairs and out into the dark corridors of the Underkeep. As she did so she took one last glance towards her father. As soon as the iron door closed she dropped down onto her rump and rested her back against the wall. Amid a cascade of emotion Tonousa broke down and wept. It was the first time in years that she had lost control of her spirit but it allowed the sufferings of the past weeks to drain from her tormented mind. She cried as she thought about the impossible tasks ahead, uncovering the killer, finding the ruby, and discovering all she could about the Oracle. On top of everything else her father had been condemned to die, no doubt framed by Blackfayer in order to cover his own sorry arse.

For what seemed like forever, Tonousa sat by the door of the cell and wept. No one heard her pain and her sounds of woe were drowned by the cries of others suffering greater tortures within the confines of the Underkeep. Danisun Dain eventually returned with water and bread and she sobbed as he passed. Then after just a couple of minutes he returned to join her in the dim light of the corridor where he held out his hand to help her to her feet.

Once upright Tonousa wiped her reddened eyes. Trying to compose herself she smiled at Danisun who at once put his arms around her. He pulled her in close, hugged tight, and allowed her stress to dissipate amid her tremulous breaths.

"Did you know that he is to be executed tomorrow?" asked Tonousa, placing her head on the leather armour over Danisun's chest.

"I have just heard, Gibbs the cook told me. Said it was a time of dark omens when one of the Sovereign Lord's own household conspires against him."

"It not right," moaned Tonousa. "He may be difficult at times but my father would never harm another creature. Can't you see he's being framed for crimes he hasn't committed?"

"In cases like this Tonousa, I would most times disagree and let Richemanus of the Nightfall take the traitor's head, no matter who they were. My cause is for the Realm and our Sovereign Lord but after seeing you talk to your father, it is quite clear that something is not right. The attack on the Grey Keep, the missing dwarf, this stolen Lore, and now the attack on the Bards Guild of Valameer. You need to tell me all you know Tonousa if you want me to help you and I need nothing but the truth. Let go of your secrets; what really happened in Valameer?"

29

"Llyat, are you sure you're okay?"

To Thias it was quite obvious that Llyat was ill. The youth did not look at all well; his skin was pale and clammy and two streams of mucus dripped from the end of his nose like hot trails of wax down a candle. The continuous sniffing combined with sporadic sneezing and coughing fits pointed to the strange, but not so common, sweating sickness. The recent close encounter with the kulkulkath amid the lower levels of the Ivory Pass had also taken its toll.

"I'm just tired, that's all," Llyat replied as he continued to struggle up the steep mountain trail.

"Are you sure lad?" asked Thias again. "You don't look that great."

"I'm fine," Llyat snapped back as he turned his head to scowl at the bard. "I'm just run down. Given all that I've have been through, I'm just exhausted, that's all. I've not had any decent food for three days, just that fucking half cooked pheasant, and I am pissed off from walking along this high mountain with no real idea where we are going…"

"Oh, I see… That response proves that you're not well Llyat."

"What do you mean," demanded the youth?

"Because this is the fourth time that we have had this same conversation in the past hour."

It was true. It had indeed been the fourth time that the same question had been put to Llyat as the three men had traversed the high mountain trail that led along the steep sloping side of Skillar and the answer had always been the same. Still the group continued to trek northwards out of the Ivory Pass. For most of the way Irabo took the lead for he knew the area well having originated from Falahorn, the ancient town located between the far end of the pass and the Dragonas beyond. The path's base was composed of rough gravel and the climb through it had so far been without incident. There were no further signs of kulkulkath save for the occasional scuttles in the distance which warned of their ever watching presence. The footfall of the creatures was such as to indicate juveniles rather than adults which would no doubt have attacked already; but what concerned Thias and Irabo most of all was the state of Llyat's health.

"So what do you suggest I do then?" continued Llyat. "I'm sure I will be fine."

"Take it from someone who is experienced in living rough and navigating the wilderness," continued Thias. "You look like bird shite in the snow."

"He's right Llyat, but I didn't think it the right time to comment," added Irabo who had stopped walking in order to address his companions.

"Llyat, I don't know what is wrong with you but you do look very pale and you are not acting like your usual self. You have been sniping at everything we have said over the past hour or so and you are beginning to slow us down."

"I'm not …" replied Llyat but before he could speak further Thias lost his composure.

"That settles it," ordered the bard. "We are going to rest right here and now. Llyat must gather his strength. He's no good to us dead or even half dead."

"I'm telling you, I am fine," replied the sickly youth.

"And I'm telling you that you are not," snapped back Thias. "If you could just see yourself you would agree with me. You look like something that has crawled out of the Underworld, died, and then been left to putrefy under the heat of Solaris. We are going to stop here and rest for the night. Somehow we must get you to a place of safety as soon as possible. Without you we will not be able seek Thamous and his Gems. I can tell just by looking at you that you will not make to Falahorn if we do not break from our toil."

"But I am telling you I feel fine. Why will you not listen? "

"And I am telling you that you are not," snapped back Thias. "Please do not make me use my last reserves of magic to keep you subdued. We still have the kulkulkath to contend with and we will need all the strength we can muster if we come across more of the bastard beasts. I cannot afford to waste my powers so I hope you understand that what I am saying is for your own good."

"But..."

"Don't argue!" snapped Thias bursting out of his temper. "Just do as your fucking told."

Llyat did not respond further and neither did Irabo. Thias's body language and tone of voice left his companions in no doubt that it was the end of the matter. Solaris had begun to descend behind the mountains as the three companions completed their second day on the high pass around Skillar. Then on seeing an appropriate level area of the path, Irabo ordered that they would stop for the day and to create a fire with the small amount of wood that the three had carried up with them from the lower reaches of the pass.

Once the fire had been built and ignited from flint and dried moss taken from the gravel path, Irabo began to roast the last remnant of well hung pheasant. There in front of the fire the smell of the blistering bird filled six nostrils. Thias noted with concern that the heat had no effect on Llyat who continued to shiver. It was clear that there was something serious going on inside the boy.

"Well that's the last one," announced Irabo once the bird had been sliced and shared. "It might be some time before we eat again."

"How long until we reach Falahorn" asked Thias, mindful of the seriousness of journeying on without sustenance?

"Just one more day now," continued Irabo. "If it hadn't been for the Kulkulkath, we might have been there by now. I estimate at least half a day before the path descends towards the Dragonas. Falahorn lies right on the edge of it."

"Ah yes, "replied Thias, as he took a mouthful of bird and spat out a quill that had been missed during the plucking. "The town that protects the dragons."

"We are not the only ones," said Irabo in response. "There are others who have always watched over the beasts. It is not just the men from Falahorn."

"Yet Falahorn is the one place the stories always talk about," continued Thias between munching morsels of his share. "So tell me Irabo, why did you leave Falahorn? What brought you all the way to Parandor and to your place in the City Watch?"

"That's a very long story," replied Irabo smiling.

"Tonight we have all the time in the world," sniggered Llyat.

Thias noted that the illness had taken control of the youth's thoughts and words. Ignoring Llyat's comment, Thias winked at Irabo across the fire and they both screwed their foreheads in recognition of their companions growing delirium.

"We need a tale to help us all settle tonight, another for my repertoire of Ballads. A good one might even inspire me to write a new song for Phauless Gylewu himself," said the bard with a wry smile.

"As I have already stated, it is a long story and there isn't a great deal of substance to it. I was born in Falahorn and lived there most of my childhood. The town, being the first beyond the Ivory Pass, was the hub that linked the border towns and villages of the north of the Realm, with those of the south. Well, I call it a town although to see it you will feel it more like a small village. It is however far more than what it seems. At first glance you will find it comprised of two rows of wooden buildings built into and between the dusty rock boulders that boarder the Dragonas. My parents were simple farmers who tried to scratch a living off the barren wastelands that surrounded their settlement. They would often travel south to Valameer through the Ivory Pass in order to sell their wares to anyone prepared to pay even the lowest prices. Mum and Dad had five hungry mouths to feed, including myself and my twin sisters."

"So when and what brought you south?" asked Thias while he looked across the flickering fire.

"My sisters died in their second birth year due to malnourishment. To be honest they starved. Food was scarce that year and my mother's tits had dried up. When I was twelve years old there was a plague in the northern parts of the Realm that people said had leached its way out of the Eastern Marsh. The pestilence took my parents from this world and I tried to fend for myself for several months with the help of some friends. Then the hunger in my stomach and a desire to travel the Realm and visit Parandor drove me to leave Falahorn. You see I then believed in the tales of the golden streets of Parandor."

"You as well?" giggled Llyat following which he launched into a fit of protracted coughing.

"Yes!" replied Irabo with a worried grin. "I did not know at the time that those stories were designed to entertain children and dimwits. It's one I believe originated in the Bards Guild."

"More than possible!" added Thias.

"I first made my way to Valameer. During my time in that coastal town and in the view of the mighty Bards Guild, I became friends with a young cordwainer's apprentice who went by the name of Darchus. He helped me to find work in the town's stables. It was from Darchus that I got the cart, the one that took the Grand Physician to the Guild. I stayed in Valameer for several years but then I grew despondent over the antics of the Lady Flurdiana. She couldn't rule over a dung heap even if she tried. The highborn half-wit didn't give a toss about anything but food, nor did she have a gnat's worth of diplomacy. The woman didn't care about her subjects either and left them to run the town themselves; but of course they still had to pay her exorbitant taxes. The people became secretive and organised a clandestine committee in order to dupe her and care for those in most need. I think even Darchus would have left Valameer had he not fallen in love with a girl called Ailora."

"And so was your real reason to leave driven only by politics?" asked Thias. "You wanted to go somewhere where people were respected and well governed by the ruling classes? Am I correct?"

"That was the plan, although I could not have put it such eloquent terms," replied Irabo before spitting out a bone that had caught between his molars. "I made my way down the coast towards the Capital. There I worked on many farms and offered my labour in exchange for something to eat and a place to sleep the night. I even hunted skyfawn for an extra bowel of gruel."

"It's a shame that you never came to Maplehill," chirped up Llyat as he broke through his delirium. "You could have helped us out with our skyfawn problem and had a few Blessed Beasts with me and my mates. I could have told you some right dirty jokes to help you pass your life away. Have you ever heard the story of the maid with three quims?"

"The secret to defeating skyfawn is to eliminate their nest," continued Irabo. "Yet how to do that is a story for another day. After many months of travel, I found myself at the gates of Parandor and on entering the city I came across a poster that told of ongoing recruitment into the City Watch. After some deliberation I decided to join up and that was that. You see, that's my simple story. Not much to tell in the way of exciting adventure and I doubt it would entertain old Phauless Gylewu."

"That would be for him to decide," laughed Thias. "And we could give it a new twist!"

All then laughed, including Llyat who didn't get the joke. After several minutes silence under the watchful gaze of Mona, Llyat spoke again as his thoughts broke from the fog that confused them.

"You said that Falahorn is a simple village but I know from the stories of old that it protects the Dragonas and all the creatures that live within it. What did you mean when you said it's more than a village?"

"I'll leave that one to you Irabo," replied Thias.

"As you no doubt know Llyat, from the songs and tales you have heard from the bards, in particular the one about Mighty Xenvagen and the Knight that slew him, that Sir Belquin vowed to exterminate the all the dragons and at least drive them out of the Dragonas."

"I always thought knights were supposed to be noble and just!" shouted Llyat as he thought back to the conversations with Cleath Mark and Methladon Heyn before their fall. "I remember the tale that said Xenvagen captured and threatened the life of the young daughter of the Mayor of Griginor. After that Sir Belquin dressed up in his green armour, sought out Xenvagen, and killed the creature."

"You know your history well," said Irabo smiling. "Then you will also know that is was Sir Belquin that who having decapitated the mighty beast, tethered it to a horse and dragged it through the streets of Griginor. That display of disrespect for the once magnificent creature lead to the creation of a secret warrior sect. Its followers were so appalled by what they had witnessed that they made a vow to protect all other dragons from harm. They even began a quest to discover a way to communicate with the mighty winged serpents of the north. These warriors left Griginor and established the farming community of Falahorn. There under its buildings and farms, hidden from sight and the knowledge of passing travellers, they constructed vast numbers of tunnels, caves, and secret entrances. They took generations to build and their purpose was to house the nests, the breeding dens of the dragons, and of course to give them sanctuary should they be attacked by those who supported Sir Belquin's cause."

The story of the resistance group in Falahorn had not been a surprise to Thias. He had heard of such rumours and had himself passed them on to others during his travels across the Realm. The bard then looked towards Llyat and saw that the youth continued to shiver. He prayed the lad had not contracted the lethal sweating sickness and tried to convince himself that it was just a simple chill caught from walking through the cold rain as they had traversed the barren valley. Yes, that would be it, plus the fact that Llyat was run down and his brain addled given all that he had been through this past month. Then Thias looked across the fire towards Irabo who sat picking remnants of meat from between his teeth with a splinter of bone that he had found near the base of the fire.

"I'm guessing from what you have told us that you were referring to those known to the rest of us as Berserkers, the legendary hidden horde of Falahorn?" said Thias.

"Yes indeed, the very same."

"I'm sorry to interrupt but I am more than confused just now," jumped in Llyat's mouth. "What is so special about these warriors that protect the dragons and why do they need to hide in tunnels like wriggle worms? What kind of a dumb shit name is Berserker?"

Irabo laughed out loud as did Thias for they both knew that Llyat had asked the same question that most others had done when they first heard mention of the fighters from Falahorn.

"As years passed under the Dragonas and while searching for a way to communicate with the dragons, the Berserkers developed the ability to live as one with the beasts. They outgrew the use of chainmail and iron plated armour and as generations came and went, with the help of a little dragon seed, their skin grew much tougher. So hard did it become that neither fire, ice, or iron have any great effect upon it. They go bare chested and wear thin trousers around their lower bodies. They do however have one additional striking feature of attire. The pelt of the wolf-like nighthowler is used to adorn their heads. This animal disguise sometimes gives them the advantage of surprise and it helps them approach their enemies in silence without the tell-tale sounds of moving armour. I am sure Thias that you have also heard the legend that the Berserkers are capable of changing into nighthowlers. That is but a story yet there is some truth behind it. They are known to drink a potion that clouds their thoughts, one that helps detect friend from foe and heightens their physical strength. When they drink this strange brew their eyes turn deep red, just like the nighthowlers themselves, and that is story behind the legend."

"Awesome," said Llyat after yet another sneeze. "I want to meet one of those fuckers!"

"I'm sure I can arrange that," replied Irabo. "Falahorn is our destination and from the Berserkers we must try and discover the location of Thamous. We must therefore seek one out and pray that once again Fatumai favours you."

"You really do believe in all of fate shit, don't you?" sneered Thias while he stoked the fire in an attempt to keep the flame alive. "How can you be so sure that our lives are predestined and that we have no choice in the actions that we make?"

"Ah, how I wish Tonousa was here for this discussion," replied the warrior. "As much as she tolerates my beliefs, I would like to hear her counter my arguments again for she always makes me smile. I guess she must be back in Parandor by now. By the will of Fatumai, I hope that she has unearthed the traitor and found the ruby. But in answer to your question Thias, then yes, I do believe in the control exerted over us by Fatumai, or to be more accurate, the Moirai."

Moirai was not a word that Thias knew despite his travels far and wide across the south of the Realm. Even in the Sovereign Court such a word had never been uttered in his presence and he was clueless as to who or what it meant. As the bard contemplated its significance he glanced across to Llyat who had lain down upon the shale floor in an attempt to find some comfort. It was obvious at once that Llyat needed much rest for his energy reserves were fast draining from his body.

"Moirai?" said Thias a few seconds later. "Please say more Irabo."

"Forgive me then," continued the warrior with a little reluctance and regretting having used the term at all. "I was so caught up in talking about Falahorn and the Berserkers that I used a word of my people's dialect. The translation of Moirai is simple. It means 'Fates'. They are the weird three who carry out Fatumai's bidding."

"Then I guess all in Falahorn believe in Fatumai?"

"Indeed," agreed Irabo. "And I think that she is at work right now."

"What do you mean?"

A sudden snore from Llyat's resonant palate caused them both to snigger.

"I see what you mean," said Thias. "Llyat's fever has been up and down all day but at last it seems he has gone to sleep and we shall have some peace."

"He so does need to rest," added Irabo. "This is no simple chill but something much more serious. I fear for his life,"

"Me too," replied Thias as he lowered his voice to speak with a greater directness. "Are you certain it will take just one more day before we reach Falahorn? I do not think the lad's heart will sustain him longer than that."

"As do I," replied Irabo. "The Moirai, or Fates if you have it, are playing a strange game today."

"If we get to Falahorn..." began Thias.

"When we get to Falahorn," spat back Irabo.

"I'm sorry! When we get there, do you think that your people will be able to help him?"

"I'm sure they will try," replied Irabo. "They beat the plague and a common fever should be easier to remedy."

Thias sighed. "I'm pleased you think the same. I thought perhaps he might have the sweating sickness. If so we could all be dead by the time it would take to reach Falahorn."

Thias looked down at Llyat and felt comfort in the fact that the youth was at least now asleep. He also felt reassured that their guide to Falahorn was a skilled warrior and knew the land well, including the high pass over the mountain. Watching the flames of the fire dance before him and feeling their weak warmth against his face, Thias's thoughts began to drift but Irabo's voice broke in once again.

"So what do you believe in? What are your thoughts on fate and destiny?"

"It's difficult to understand and make sensible conclusions. I would like to believe the gods care for what we do but I have spent my youth learning tall tales. How can we sift out the truth from the dream stories of the ancients? Perhaps one day before I die I may come to understand the real truth. Like I said down in the Ivory Pass, I do believe that Llyat is the Marked that the Prophecy of Enderdetag speaks of. I am also sure that the threat from Avolire is real and serious. I've not mentioned this to you before but I am greatly worried. If the prophecy is to be believed and that the Marked must vanquish the Lord of Fear, which we must assume is Urthanock, then somehow the Underworld must already be unlocked. It must be seeping its evil back into the Realm. My biggest fear is that the Lord of Fear has already returned in some form and is manipulating events from the shadows, pulling the strings of the Lady of the Silverwynn and her Knights of Avolire. I sense we are only just beginning to scratch the surface of what's going on and that so far we have been rather naive. Things are not as clear as they seem. There is much more that we need to understand before we can hope to succeed in our quest, seal the doors of the Underworld and vanquish Urthanock forever. We must cling to the hope that Llyat will live to fulfil the prophecy."

Irabo thought for a brief moment before replying.

"Who knows what lies ahead for us, but even if you are a non-believer, I carry enough faith in Fatumai to know that the fate of we three, the fate of Parandor, and even that of Avolire has been pre-determined. It has already been played out in some arcane game of the Moirai. Believe me, we all have our roles to fulfil and we must not try and fight against what will be. Good will surely prevail in the end."

"I very much hope that you right," said Thias as the urge to sleep took hold over his body.

"You look very tired my friend. I tell you what; I'll stand guard tonight and keep the fire going until we use the little wood that we have left. We may be safe now from the kulkulkath but there are other beasts that roam the heights of Skillar that we need to watch out for."

"Like nighthowlers," replied Thias yawning?

"Exactly!" said Irabo smiling. "I do not mind taking most of the watch tonight for it will allow you to regather your strength."

"What about you?"

"I can rest once we reach Falahorn."

"Is that wise. I don't think I would be able to carry both you and Llyat."

"I'll be fine, believe me."

"So be it," replied Thias, "If you insist I will not decline the offer."

Thias then tried his best to make himself comfortable upon the gravel floor. The ground was hard, cold, and uneven. As he moved from side to side he imagined he was back in the Guild, lying upon on a thick feather mattress with woven cloth covers to keep him warm. Such visions had often aided his sleep as he had travelled the Realm and when for much of the time he had been forced to sleep out in the open. However in the south the grass lands provided a far more comfortable place to rest. The last thing he remembered before drifting into a deep slumber was Irabo stoking the fire and the crackle of the burning wood.

The bard woke with a start and sat bolt upright. He had no conception of how long he had been asleep. It could have been minutes or even perhaps hours. Something significant had taken place and it had wrenched him from his slumber. He was however too confused to work out what it was. In an instant he stood up tall, tried to gather his senses, and then scanned his surroundings. It was early morning as evident by the glow cast by of Solaris in the sky but the light's full glory remained obscured by a grey mist that rolled in over the high mountain pass. The fire was well out and he noted that Llyat remained motionless, still far away from the world of consciousness. Irabo stood before them both, sword drawn and readied for battle.

"Irabo?" whispered Thias. "What is it? Did you also hear something? And where did all this fucking fog come from."

"All in good time," whispered Irabo. "I don't know what's out there but it's bad and it is close. It has been circling ever since Solaris rose this morning and I'm not sure what kind of beast stalks us. For sure it is not human."

"Do you think it could be a dragon?" asked Thias as his voice trembled.

"No, it's too small for that."

"Skyfawn then?" added the bard.

"That is a possibility."

"I wish we could see more," said Thias. "I've never seen fog like this. It's too thick and strange to be natural."

"That's what I thought at first," replied Irabo. "But we are high up and the air is cold. There is much moisture up here for Solaris to heat up but it may also be that the clouds are themselves falling down upon us."

"Are you sure that this has nothing to do with dragons?" shivered Thias.

"I doubt it very much. They don't venture this far south. Remember the one that we saw in the distance from the Bridge of Athuna? That one continues to puzzle me. Something strange must be happening out in the wilds of the Dragonas…"

Before Irabo could say more, a whoosh swept past their heads. Some beast was flying fast and a waft of displaced air passed across Thias's face which caused the hairs on his head to stand on end.

"I think we better leave talk of the fog until later," whispered Thias. "We need to wake Llyat up and get moving."

"I agree; let's go," replied Irabo without hesitation.

Thias scuttled across to Llyat and nudged him in the back with his foot.

"Llyat, wake up," he ordered, "We have to have to get moving."

The youth did not respond. Thias then fell to his knees and shook the youth with vigour.

"Llyat, for fucks sake wake up!" he snapped. "We're in deep shit."

Still Llyat did not move and it was then that Thias realised the seriousness of his companion's sickness. Llyat was both pale and clammy. He was just about breathing although his chest barely seemed to rise and fall. It was obvious that he had something far more serious than a chill.

"Irabo," shouted Thias despite the presence of the creature that circled in the mist. "I need some help over here."

The warrior responded at once and made his way across to Thias.

"What is it? What is wrong?"

"Llyat," replied Thias. "This is very bad, I can't wake him."

Irabo knelt and shook the limp torso with all his strength.

"Llyat," shouted Irabo. "We need to move."

Llyat groaned but still he did not wake.

"It's no good we're going to have to carry him."

"Shit," swore Irabo. "That will slow us down too much. Whatever is hunting us will sense our struggle and we will never make it to Falahorn."

"We can't just leave him here to die. Come on, help me."

Thias managed to pull Llyat up from the ground and slung one of the youth's arms around his neck. After some moments of deliberation Irabo took Llyat's other arm and threw it over his shoulder while in his other hand he readied his blade.

"Don't worry Llyat, we'll look after you," said Irabo. "The beast will have to take us before it can have you."

"Warrr...teerrr." moaned Llyat through his pale and cracked lips.

"We'll find you some as soon as we can lad," added Thias. "Which way Irabo?"

"Over there," answered the warrior as he pointed with his sword. "Let's go."

Thias staggered forward as fast as the weight on his shoulders would permit and together the three made their way along the mountain trail. All the while through the mist the ghost like flutters continued. Without warning a high pitched shriek ahead forced Irabo and Thias to a stop.

"That has to be skyfawn," said Thias.

"I agree, but let's not wait for the proof," answered Irabo.

Again they set off along the path while the fog got thicker and Llyat grew heavier.

"Can you see where you are going?" asked Thias after a further few minutes.

"Only just," replied Irabo. "My vision is just about as good as..."

"As what?"

Just as the words left Thias's mouth he heard the sounds of gravel moving under his feet and he braced himself for what he thought was an impending rock fall. Llyat felt suddenly twice as heavy and he realised he was holding him alone. He looked to the floor on the side where Irabo had walked and to his horror saw that the path there had disappeared.

"Irabo?" bellowed Thias. "Irabo, where are you?"

No reply came but before the bard could shout again he was struck in the back by a blow of sufficient force to send both himself and Llyat crashing down into the dirt. Thias twisted around in order to face his assailant. That was when the creature landed on his chest and as he stared forward he looked straight into the face of the skyfawn, its beak and razor sharp teeth ready to snap and bite.

Thias tried to raise his blade in order to fight for his life when a further disturbance of the air enveloped him. Through the mist he saw the head of the Skyfawn fly to one side having been separated from its neck. The beaked cranium rolled off the path and disappeared over the steep edge. Then much to his surprise he caught the shadowy outline of the large man who had saved his life. Thias tried to stand but he was pushed back down by force of the man's great fist.

"You had better have a very good reason to be up here on Skillar," growled a deep bear like voice. "If not, prepare to meet your gods!"

30

All who dwelt within the Citadel knew that Xix Blackfayer's chambers were located on the first floor of the Keep, sandwiched between those of Grand Physician Abrahamus Marus and Lady Calendrial Lorst. As she made her way up from the Underkeep, Tonousa filled in the gaps in her story and allowed Danisun to hear the parts that she had kept from the Council. After a long search of her soul she told him of those who had also survived the attack on the Guild, Irabo, Thias, Llyat, and Heliana, players her story had hidden away from those who would seek to interfere with her investigations. Despite their trusted relationship, Tonousa knew she would still have great difficulty in persuading Danisun Dain of the truth of her story. While she led them both through the corridors she prayed that her words resonated truth for her father's life depended on her being able to recruit Danisun to her cause.

"I think you have just about convinced me," he replied after he had listened to and then contemplated all that Tonousa had told him. "So let me see if I have got this right. Irabo Basequin, the bard called Thias Calavan, and the Grand Physician's servant are at this moment heading north into the Dragonas. That is most interesting even if a bit of a stretch of the imagination. It is hard to believe that they would try to locate a mythical dragon who will tell them where the some fabled jewels are hidden. It sounds like a story you would hear in a tavern. Marus's serving girl you say is hiding with a sailor named Theoplous, the First Mate of the Banshees Wail, and that they may be on their way here by sea. I know how sea dogs occupy themselves when locked way alone with a wench and the girl may not be as was when and if she returns to the Capital. You say that you are tasked to find a ruby that is hidden somewhere here in the Citadel but yet you admit you haven't a clue where it could be, or even how to begin your search! Then, when you have done that, you are tasked to discover the identity of the traitor, the spy that has infiltrated these walls; the same swine you believe has been feeding secrets to Avolire and some old crone called the Lady of the Silverwynn. At the same time as pulling off these miracles you must prove your father's innocence before the morrow. By the gods but you have your work cut out Tonousa!"

"There you have it in one," she replied as they continued their trek through the Keep.

"Is there anything else I need to be aware of? Are there other facts that you have forgotten to tell me or deliberately omitted from your story?"

"No, I have told you everything..." answered Tonousa. "Now that I think more on it, there is one other detail that I need to tell you. When the three reach Falahorn they will send a carrier bird to you. It is important that no one knows that the three are still alive, not even Townsforth. I must be able trust you with this so please do not let me down."

"But surely you cannot suspect our Commander!" exclaimed Danisun with much surprise.

"I am sorry to say this but he remains a key suspect... Don't look so shocked for Townsforth knew of our journey to Valameer and very few others did. Someone let the Lizardmen know that we were on the trail of the traitor. Our sudden deaths away in distant Valameer would have made people forget about spies in Parandor, don't you agree?"

"Tonousa, you are blind to something fundamental and your mind is clouded because of your love for your father and..."

Danisun didn't have time to finish his sentence before Tonousa turned, grabbed the neck of his uniform and threw him up against the wall. There she held him in her firm grip as she felt the anger boil inside her chest. Forcing herself to breath she relaxed for she also knew that she needed to save her anger for Blackfayer. As she glanced around she saw numerous servants who had stopped to see what had caused the sudden disturbance. With care she released her grip on her friend.

"I do apologise Danisun. I didn't mean to cause you harm but I have been through so much of recent that I am finding it hard to hold myself together."

"Shit Tonousa, I have never seen you like this before. I didn't mean to insult you so please forgive me, but there is no time left to prove your father's innocence. I think you are hate driven by the thought of another having set your father up. You are clearly not thinking straight. Tell me where you are taking me."

"If I do that Danisun, then you'll try to stop me. You shall see soon enough."

Tonousa knew that Danisun was right in his assessment. She was being driven by vengeance. He whole being wanted to inflict great pain on those responsible for the recent murders and the incarceration of her father. Her anger steamed like a pot on the boil and she sought to contain it until her confrontation with the Sovereign Advisor who with luck was still in his private rooms. That was a fair assumption to make given that it was common knowledge that once the Council concluded its work, Blackfayer always returned to his chambers to down several potent drinks. A few minutes later the two members of the City Watch stood before the wooden doors to Blackfayer's apartment.

"You cannot be serious," muttered Danisun as he realised where Tonousa had brought him.

"Believe what your eyes tell you; just watch and learn," snapped back Tonousa.

Her face flushed with hate as she pushed the great oak portal open and stepped into the space beyond. Blackfayer's private antechamber was a most impressive room. Round in shape it reminded Tonousa of a smaller version of the library tower in the Bards Guild. A wooden desk sat in its centre, covered in books and papers, all scattered in a mess as were the documents on the shelves that clung to the walls. She found it inconceivable that anyone could work in such a disordered way, in particular someone of such immense authority. Besides the table rested a carved wooden chair and beyond it yet another solid door that led off to the bedroom and toilet closet. To one side of the room hung the golden cord, a standard requirement of all chambers belonging to the elite and whose function was to summon servants as and when their owners required. It also acted as a method for calling the Sovereign Guard in the event of danger.

Tonousa closed the door behind her and moved into centre of the room. Danisun followed. Part hidden by shadows the two others present were startled by the forced intrusion and were for a moment struck dumb. Nearest to Tonousa stood Arfon Caddick, the private fetch-all of the Sovereign Advisor. He dropped the manuscripts that he had been holding as the door reverberated from the insult to its surface. The house slave bent down and scrambled on the floor in an attempt to rectify this new addition to the general clutter. Behind Caddick stood Xix Blackfayer with a face so purple it looked like a ripe boil. The Sovereign Adviser moved to his desk and placed the manuscript he had been reading upon its surface. The hue of his face changed through various shades of crimson, his fists blanched, and his teeth bared in a snarl. There was however nothing he could do to prevent Tonousa from speaking the words she had carried with her. The warrior's eyes fired like blood oranges as she glared back at the snake of a man.

"How dare you force your way in here," screamed Blackfayer. "You have no right."

"I have every right," shouted back Tonousa.

"Sir, shall I call the guards?" squealed the bewildered Arfon.

"At once," yelled Blackfayer.

"Yes Sir!" bellowed the servant as he made for the door but Danisun held out an arm of restraint and stopped further progress.

"Not so fast young friend," he ordered with great authority.

"Fuck you all!" screamed the Sovereign Adviser. "I'll call them myself..."

Blackfayer cut short his sentence as Tonousa's sword thrust beneath his chin and prevented any movement of his throat. The most hated of the highborn had the sense to fall silent. Tonousa then glanced at Danisun and uttered her next command.

"Lock the door from the inside. Do not let anyone in."

Danisun manoeuvred away from the bemused and frightened Arfon, slid the iron bolt across the door, and sealed all four inside the chamber.

"Look bitch!" said Blackfayer as soon as Tonousa's blade had released its pressure on his throat. "I don't know what you intend to achieve by this outrage but if you hope to save your father then forget it. You too will pay for this with your life."

"Shut your foul worm mouth and sit down," snapped Tonousa as she jabbed her blade forward and nicked the skin over Blackfayer's throat.

With force of will and the tip of her steel she pushed him back into his chair. As his rump touched the firm wood Tonousa glared at the man she hated above all others. Xix Blackfayer took a deep breath and wiped away a trickle of blood as it seeped from his neck wound. Never before had Tonousa felt such a level of contempt as she did for the man at the end of her sword. His assault on her privates when they had first met was nothing compared to the anger that now cried for release.

"Before I order the warrants for both your arrests please have the courtesy to explain the reason for this attack. It will need to be documented on your death certificates. You know what it is like these days, so much paperwork to complete," sneered Blackfayer.

"Spit shit from your mouth all you like," snapped back Tonousa. "I know you have worked out why we are here."

"The City Watch has no jurisdiction in the Citadel. I must remind you of that."

"I think that you'll find that we do," growled Tonousa. "Our Sovereign Lord authorised the Watch to look into the murders linked to the cult of Death Tubaria. I hope you can remember that. This interrogation is a direct result of that order."

"You can't just..."

"I'm afraid she can," added Danisun before Xix could continue. "Yes, this is an official investigation for you have fallen under suspicion. We believe you have conspired and condemned an innocent man in order to cover up something more evil. We are here to find out what that is. Tonousa has the backing of the Watch and we will bring its full force down upon you if you do not comply with our attempts to get to the truth. Cross her and you take us all on."

In the silence that followed, Tonousa and Xix Blackfayer stared each other out. It was the Sovereign Advisor who spoke first.

"I will humour you both then," he sneered. "What little good it will do you."

"Why was the Lore of the Dead not reported missing when it was stolen?" asked Tonousa.

"I beg your pardon?" demanded Xix.

"I'll repeat the question," continued Tonousa, her eyes alight and piercing. "Why was the Lore of the Dead never..."

"Yes, yes, yes, I heard you the first time. Why should you ask such a question of me? Isn't that a question you should put to your father? He was the librarian after all?"

"I have already asked him and do you know what he told me?"

"I shudder to think."

"This is serious Xix," added Danisun. "Especially given what we have already discovered about that book."

"And what do you dimshits know about it?" sneered Blackfayer.

"We know that you ordered the pages that contained the Ritual of Kha to be burned."

Silence fell again and as Tonousa waited for an answer she sensed that the mere mention of the book had unnerved Blackfayer. Then while she scanned his face, doubt crept slowly into the space between her ears. Was the Sovereign Advisor as guilty as she thought or just yet another counter in the much larger game of a devious mastermind? Blackfayer spoke again.

"Arfon, if you repeat anything that you hear me say from his moment on, to anyone you understand, you will spend the rest of your shitty life cleaning my piss pot with your tongue. Do you understand me?"

"Yes sir, I get the message loud and clear."

"You better fucking had!" grumbled Blackfayer as he turned his attention back to Tonousa.

"Yes it is true that I had the pages that contained the Ritual of Kha destroyed. You would have done the same had you found yourself in my situation? We believed at that time there were members of Tullage's cult still at large within the Capital. Even though that bastard of a book was kept locked in our Sovereign Lord's library, by your father you understand, I could not take the risk of the Ritual falling into the cult's hands."

"Thank you for that Xix," replied Tonousa. "You have confirmed that my father speaks the truth. I do have another question that you must answer. My father also stated that some years ago the Lore of the Dead was stolen from his care and the book then disappeared. He reported this theft to you and yet you never informed or registered the crime with the Royal Guard or indeed the City Watch. Please explain why!"

"I...I don't...but..." stuttered Blackfayer as his face turned lily-white.

"Come on, what do you have to say man?" continued Tonousa. "Tell me the truth or I swear in the presence of your gods, I will cut that forked tongue out of your mouth."

"The book was not reported stolen because I believed that the threat had been neutralised. Given that we had the important pages burned, no one would be able to continue with Tullage's plans. The incantation was no more. It was lost forever, and don't forget that Tullage was manacled in the depths of the Grey Keep's dungeons. The book was useless so why should I have bothered to have reported its theft?"

"And yet there are rumours that Tullage passed the ritual by word of mouth to someone else. They say further that it was his cell mate, the dwarf that later killed him."

"Keep to the point Tonousa," ordered Danisun. "Stick to the facts not the hearsay."

"Yes... quite," she replied. "So then tell me this Xix; why did you had my father arrested for an irrelevant crime that took place some years ago?"

"Because you stupid bitch, the book was found in his rooms, on his bed for all to see."

"Don't you feel that was a little too convenient" asked Danisun? "We smell rat like interference, a setup, or however else you wish to name it! What other reasons could you have for eliminating Tonousa's father?"

Tonousa glanced at her colleague and understood his reasoning.

"What do you mean?" asked Xix. "I am at a complete loss as to where you are going with this."

"Let me make it clear then," continued the Man-at-Arms. "Whoever left the book on Lord Amberstone's bed meant it to be found. It was a perfect distraction following the attempted assassination of Lord Gylewu. Can you not see man, it was an ideal opportunity to frame Tonousa's father for that crime. The two events are without doubt connected."

"Perhaps. However there is a more obvious solution," added the Sovereign Adviser.

"Well spit it out then, say what you have to say," replied Tonousa.

"Your father is the one who took the Lore of the Dead from the library ..."

Tonousa's anger flared again as the words slithered out from Blackfayer's lips. She felt an intense urge to thrust forward with her blade but she was not yet finished with her interrogation.

"You know that is lie," she barked out.

"Is it?" continued Xix. "As you have already pointed out, it wouldn't be the first time he has told untruths to save his skin."

"A lie to which you were an accomplice," added Tonousa. "Believe me when I say this Xix. If my father is executed in the morning I will stop at nothing to ensure that all know the truth behind your betrayal. Our Sovereign Lord for one will be most interested to hear what I have to say."

Three distinct rings of a bell broke Tonousa's concentration. She scanned the room and as she looked for its point of origin her eyes moved from Blackfayer to Danisun and beyond. He gaze at last fell upon the servant Arfon who stood at the side of the room with the golden cord still in his hand. Tonousa realised at once the imminent danger that she now faced.

"You see bitch, you may have bolted the front door but you forgot about the back entrance," snarled Xix. "Your father will die tomorrow at my command and there is nothing that you can fucking do about it. My servants are very loyal to me."

"How long do we have?" asked Tonousa as she readied her blade.

"Seconds you bitch," replied Blackfayer as he straightened his robes and then pointed to the wound on his neck. "You will rot in the dungeons for a very long time for this. I give you my word on that."

Tonousa lunged forward towards the Sovereign Advisor.

"You dishonourable bastard!" she screamed.

Before Tonousa could strike the impact of a heavy blow to the back of her head dropped her to the floor. Her blade fell too and both bounced off the hard stone. Forcing herself back onto her knees she felt the back of her head and was relieved to find the skin unbroken. She brought her hand back forwards and sought to confirm the absence of blood but her vision had begun to blur. Tonousa's eyes then closed and she slipped into unconsciousness. As she slumped forwards she heard Blackfayer's voice for the final time.

"Thank you Danisun. Your assistance was most timely and has been duly noted."

All was death dark as Tonousa walked through the vast open space that surrounded her. There appeared nothing but an all-encompassing blackness and yet something supported her weight as she moved forward in her trance. Drifting amid the lightless void, shapes began to materialise. She began to focus on the shaded walls of buildings and the people who formed there out of the gloom. Prying phantom eyes watched her movement through the shadowlands. Heavy black storm clouds formed above her head and while she walked she began to feel drops of rain upon her bare face.

For what seemed like forever Tonousa continued on through the streets of her altered consciousness while increasingly aware that she was being followed. Someone or something was hiding deep within the folds of her thoughts and yet every time that she turned to look for her own shadow it would disappear along with that of the one who stalked her.

"You are being watched," said a voice inside her head, one although familiar she could not recall. "Avolire is watching."

Twisting and turning she sought out its owner but saw nothing but black wisps of mist. Suddenly the creature came before her, one black as the night sky save for the cherry red eyes that tried to stare her out. Tonousa screamed and the creature opened its mouth to reveal row upon row of sharp needle like teeth that dripped bucket quantities of fetid saliva. It too started to scream with a high pitched screech that scrapped like sharp talons across Tonousa's eardrums. In an instant it was no longer a creature from the darkest reaches of the Underworld but the blackened face of Tonousa's mother, breaking through the soil from the pit in which she had been buried many years in the past. Rotted, blackened, and stinking flesh, hung in pieces from the yellow stained bones. Then jaws began to move.

"Avolire is watching you Tonousa," said the sad and gruesome corpse. "Be mindful of your decisions. Your guard must never drop or their will be grave consequences. "

The warrior woman closed her eyes and prayed for the image to be gone. She counted the seconds, no more than ten, and then opened her eyes only to find herself on the deck of the Banshees Wail. The cabin doors banged open and shut with each rise and fall of the vessel in the storm battered sea. Her stomach knotted and she retched from her boots. Nothing came from her mouth. Her eyes looked to the ocean which had turned red and clotted. From out of the pink wave foam several sea monsters swarmed and snapped their hideous jaws in attempts to crush the puny boat that tossed upon the crimson swell. A giant wave then swept the vessel up and threw it high into the tempest. The ship flew through the air and Tonousa, all alone upon its deck, stumbled forward and flew through an open door into the night sky. Down she plummeted through the void, always in complete silence and for what seemed like another eternity. It was as if she were falling through the very gates of the Underworld itself and into its deepest pit. Then all ended.

A while later a small glow appeared that allowed a degree of feeble light to manifest itself around her soul. It constricted her, pushed her, and she begin falling again. Down she tumbled, lost in swirling madness and with no sense of where she was headed. She saw the faces of the Sovereign Council about her and as one they stared and laughed. Each tormented her with the knowledge of her father's innocence even though they knew he was about to die. Somehow she recognised that Blackfayer was not among them and she struggled to understand why that would be.

"Traitor's bitch," each from the Council cried as Tonousa fell through their shapes. "Guilty of treason. Guilty of heinous crimes against the Realm."

Another face then appeared; that of Lady Thinata Fullbane, and it filled her vision.

"Avolire is watching," advised the rotund Mona lookalike. "You must know who to trust."

"But where do I start?" pleaded Tonousa. "How can I do this alone?"

"You are far from alone," replied Fullbane's mouth. "A path will form before you. Make sure that you take it."

Tonousa landed with a thump and found herself lying upon wet sand amid a vast estuary from which the sea had just departed. Upon the shore she saw a burning city with two great armies at war before its walls. In the sky dragons swarmed through the air and engulfed the city in fire that belched from their gizzards. She looked towards the burning citadel and witnessed the approach of three cloaked figures that soon began to obstruct her. Silhouetted against the bright glare of the inferno she could not make out their features but nonetheless felt their eyes as they pierced her soul and judged her actions. She started to argue with them despite being unaware of the cause of any disagreement. Then she found her true voice and shouted out.

"He is innocent! He is innocent."

"But his death allows our game to continue," cackled the first of the three.

"Avolire will rise and Parandor must fall," growled the second while the third held a card to her lips and did not speak.

"Follow your instincts Tonousa Amberstone; let the Moirai guide you," added the first which even though female reminded her of Irabo.

It couldn't be him. No, it couldn't be. It had to be a trick of her mind.

Tonousa woke with a start, sat upright, and surveyed her surroundings. It took her no time at all realise that she was back in her own bed amongst the fifteen that made up her dormitory in the barracks of the Watch. She began to look around and attempted to re-orientate herself while a dull throb from the back of her head triggered the memory of being hit from behind. Feeling sorry for herself she soon deduced that there could have been but one person to have struck her. It had to have been Danisun Dain. For a while she struggled to understand why he above all others would have downed her in such a manner but her logic soon provided the likely answer. He wasn't the spy that she sought. The Man-at-Arms had acted in her best interests because she had lost control and attempted to harm Blackfayer. Had Danisun not intervened then rather than being confined to the barracks she would by now be rotting in the dungeons and next in line for execution. Even though she had great faith in Danisun Dain, she wished that he had given her some warning and not hit her quite so hard.

Tonousa swung her legs off the bed and felt the hardness of the floor beneath her feet. Then as she attempted to stand she became aware that she was not alone. Someone else stood over her and she immediately recognised the silhouette of Commander Townsforth.

"I can't believe that you were so stupid Tonousa," he said once he was sure she was fully conscious. "Thank the gods that Danisun intervened or you would now be facing the same punishment that your father will within the hour."

Tonousa attempted to stand but fell backwards onto the bed. She felt dizzy and the pain in the back of her head grew ever more intense. Then, as she attempted to stand for a third time the impact of the Commander's words registered inside her troubled mind.

"Did you say within the hour?" asked Tonousa as she rubbed away at the source of her pain. "How long have I been out?"

"You slept up to the end of the day and then right through the night. Given all that you appear to have been through, with the loss of your comrades, and your father's betrayal, we decided it was best to leave you at rest."

Tonousa looked towards the one window in the room where the light from Solaris confirmed that morning had arrived. Danisun Dain must have hit her really hard to have been out of the waking world for so long. She felt relieved that he had not killed her but realised he was more skilled than that. Her hands wandered over her body and she confirmed she had been left clothed in the leather armour of the City Watch. Her weapon however, the sword that Theoplous had given her in Valameer, was nowhere to be seen. Once she had regained her balance she turned her back on her Commander and without warning headed off towards the dormitory door.

"And where do you think you are going?" demanded Townsforth.

"To see my father," she replied. "To get him to plead his innocence and to buy himself time."

"Haven't you heard anything of what I have just said?" continued the Commander. "He will be executed within the hour and by now will already be on the route for his appointment with Sir Richemanus. There is nothing you can...."

"I have to try something..."

"I'm under strict orders from Blackfayer to keep you under observation. You must not approach the Sovereign Advisor under any circumstances."

"Fuck Xix Blackfayer! This is my father we are talking about. I will not stand by and let him die when I know he is innocent."

"You must see sense Tonousa," replied the Commander as he grew ever more frustrated.

Tonousa did not hear his voice as she marched out of the dormitory and on through the central hall of the barracks. Those present in the long chamber looked on with trepidation as she bustled through the room to the door that led into the courtyard. She didn't care who watched her leave for she had but one thought on her mind; to see her father one last time.

Solaris was half way up his daily climb when Tonousa stepped out in to the cool morning air and made her way across the dirt covered training ground in the shadow of the Barbican. As she hastened her step she found herself consumed by thoughts of the black axe that Richemanus wielded and how its blade was kept blunt to ensure a prolonged and brutal beheading. Rarely was a sharpened sword used at executions and never on traitors. There were only two circumstances when the use of a sword could take precedent. The first was when the executioner had a vast number to behead in any one day. The second was because the sword was Sir Richemanus's favourite weapon. He was proud of his skill level and liked to show off on the rare occasions he was allowed to do so. But Tonousa's father would face the blunt axe to reflect the severity of his crime. The Nightfall's axe edge was kept blunt such that a single strike to the back of the neck would not sever the head from the torso. It required numerous attempts to remove it and the first blow just broke the bones. Subsequent strikes were required to smash through the connecting flesh and sinews, bit by bit, crushing skin, bone, and tendon alike into a bloody pulp. These repeated blows caused the head bounce on the block as if confessing to the crimes it was found guilty of committing.

Tonousa shuddered and she tried to make sense of all that had occurred since her return to the capital. Whoever was responsible for the recent murders had obviously framed her father, either to draw the investigators attention away from himself or instil panic and uncertainty amongst the general populace of Parandor. Someone else must have known that her father and Blackfayer had covered up the theft of the Lore of the Dead and the swine was using that knowledge to his advantage. She was tormented by the idea that perhaps her father had been close to discovering the identity of the mastermind behind the devious plot and she was determined to get to her father before the answer died with him. Tonousa knew she had to get to the Stukeley Knoll before it was too late.

The Knoll was a small natural hill situated in the east of the city. Amid crammed in buildings that made up the distinctive style of the Capital in that district, the dirt track from the edge of the city streets snaked its way up through the mud streaked grassy slopes of the hill to the structure that was known by all as the Richemanus Folly. This infamous contraption consisted of a row of gallows placed upon a wooden platform and where the dead were left hanging for all to view while bathed in the light from Solaris. Once hung, bodies were preserved in a covering of salt and cumin seed broth that deterred the carrion that would otherwise feast on the swinging flesh. Keeping the bodies intact for a greater length of time sent a clear message to the populace and reminded them of the fate that would befall them should they too be foolish enough to embark on similar crimes. Amid the ropes stood the grey blood streaked stone decapitation block. Surrounding the gallows was a further raised platform where the members of the Sovereign Council and selected members of the Court could stand and pass their judgement over the condemned. Then could even piss on those about to die if they felt so inclined. The wretches who made their final journey to the Folly came from the dungeons and hell holes of the Sovereign's Underkeep, or from the many stone lockups spread across the Realm. The most infamous of these had been the Grey Keep. Even though incarcerated many miles from the Capital, those who had committed the most serious of crimes always found themselves back in Parandor and forced to perform upon the stage of the Richemanus Folly

As Tonousa approached the Knoll she noted that a significant crowd had already gathered. The scum-mass jeered and jostled in anticipation of yet another glorious show. She recognised numerous members of the highborn as they mounted the viewing platform and doubled checked to confirm who was present. The important were all there save for one noticeable absentee. Lady Thinata Fullbane had not showed up, no doubt because the wooden stand was too weak to support her bulk. Tonousa pushed her way through the crowd and on up the hill towards the Folly. All the while she searched for a sign of her father's presence. Then she spotted Danisun Dain standing motionless in the crowd and staring at the gallows. For a moment she wondered why he would turn up at her father's execution but then she spotted many more members of the Watch scattered about the crowd as they too waited and watched over the gathered multitude. She began to think that they all must looking for her but then realised it was simply her paranoia whispering in her ear. The Watch was there to ensure order amongst the sweaters, the cursers, and the sots. At least she had arrived in time to witness her father's wrongful execution.

Before Tonousa could gather her thoughts the crowd fell silent. She looked up to the viewing platform and saw the distinctive shape of the Sovereign step forward, face the mass of onlookers, and then signal for silence. Tonousa listened to the words that flowed from his mouth but her eyes were fixed on the large stone block with its gully shaped to receive a neck. There was still no sign of her father and as the crowd twitched in constrained excitement the Sovereign continued with his speech. Tonousa heard the words that sealed her father's fate. She also knew in her heart they had been written by Blackfayer and she vowed to take her revenge; the snake would die at the end of her blade.

"It is with great sorrow that I address you my subjects once again in this place of death. After the disgraceful attempt on my life and the murder of numerous innocent members of my household, we gather to celebrate the end of the terrors that have stalked our great city. I bring before you the traitor from within House of Gylewu. This man whom we had all trusted in the protection of the knowledge of the Realm, and as a respected member of my Court for many long years, dared to invoke dark magic. He cast its evil shadow upon this kingdom with the sole intention of bringing death and destruction to us all. He has sort to profit from his evil and bring misery to our feet. My friends and subjects, I give you the traitorous book minder, Mathias Amberstone, Lord of the Swine."

With the last of his words riding the wind, the Sovereign pointed behind and from out of shadows the large imposing figure of Sir Richemanus strode forward. The executioner was dressed in his darkest of garbs and the vision of the beast man struck terror onto the faces of the watching children. The leather mask that covered much of his face did not extend over the hairless head of the monstrous man. The bald pate added to the fearsome sight that would disturb the sleep of the youngest watchers for years to come. Tonousa was mesmerised as the executioner stepped forward with his infamous black axe clutched so firmly in his right hand that his knuckles blanched. His left hand held a wooden implement, carved in the shape of a violin and yet without strings. Attached by his neck to this object of restraint was the man whose loins had given Tonousa her life. As both the executioner and victim stood before the block, the crowd roared with excitement and spewed out their insults. 'Traitor' and 'fucking bastard' were the most popular of those hurled forward by the crowd. From where she stood Tonousa noted two facts of significance. Her father had not been subjected to further beatings and those members of the Watch who had been posted amongst crowd made no attempt to suppress the growing agitation of the masses. It would not take much to set off a riot.

Two eyes flicked towards the nearest member of the Watch. She did not know the fat youth's name but she recognised his belly shape as it rolled out from underneath armour two sizes too small. But it was not his figure that so held Tonousa's attention but rather the sheathed blade that hung from his waist. Amongst the cheers and insults Tonousa thought to grab the weapon and rush to her father's rescue. It was just a crazy idea for there was no way that Tonousa, despite all her skills, could overcome all those present.

From on high the crowd was again ordered to be quiet. Xix Blackfayer had taken centre stage having elbowed his Sovereign Lord to one side.

"Silence," he shouted. "We must allow old Amberstone his final words before we send him to meet Lord Kha in the Underworld. I advise you not to heed them for his mouth has been proven to spew nought but shite."

Tonousa's anger rose again. She wanted nothing more than to sever the Xix's head from his shoulders with one swift swing of a blade but that act would have to wait a while longer. She struggled to understand how she could obtain her father's secrets from under the watchful eyes of the Council, the crowd, and the City Watch. Before she could formulate a coherent plan she heard the voice of her father speak out. Its strength was muted, yet proud, and those who heard it all agreed he had confessed to the crimes of which he had been accused.

"Good subjects of Parandor, I come to this place to die by my own will in accordance with the justice of the Realm and the law of Phauless Gylewu. I have been judged and must now depart this world. I will not speak against that judgement and I do not come here to accuse others of what they say that I have done. I can offer you no evidence that would confirm my innocence and so will not waste either your time or my own in speaking on it."

The words hit Tonousa hard. She sensed he was hinting of something significant to someone present. Perhaps it was to her he was directing a clue, one perhaps yet undiscovered within his chambers. Maybe her mind was folding in under the strain of the past few weeks. Words came back to her from her traumatised dream and they seemed to be somehow important. Lady Fullbane's whispers forced their way into her consciousness: 'A path will form.' She looked over the heads of the crowd and to her father who had at the last minute decided to cast out more words.

"I pray that the gods will work to watch over our Sovereign Lord and allow him to reign long over you all. There has never been a gentler nor a more merciful ruler. He was to me a peaceful and honest Lord, just like his father and grandfather before him. Let me say this; should any person seek to remember me and enquire as to the cause that I die for, then I require them to follow their eyes and seek the truth within the walls of the Citadel."

Once again Tonousa felt her father was giving her clues and yet it all seemed such a great mystery. Whatever the vital piece of information had been transmitted she knew that she would only hear it once. In her desperation she tried to think of ways to stall the execution but then a feeling of helplessness swamped her soul.

"And thus I take my leave of this world and all of you dear people. I will seek out those who collect the dead as I cross into the Underworld and request that you all pray for me in that endeavour. The time will soon come when you all must seek a safe crossing. Lord Phauless Gylewu have mercy upon me."

The crowd erupted into cries of "traitor", "fucking bastard" and every other curse word ever uttered under the cycles of Solaris. The heaving multitude then began to throw rotten fruit towards the Folly, some of which hit her father in his face as Sir Richemanus removed the executioner's violin. Tonousa's eyes remained fixed upon her father as he then knelt behind the block and stared down towards the wooden deck. Although she could not see his eyes, she wondered if he too was crying and if so over what. Perhaps he would even be thinking of her. The pain she felt was too much to bare and yet there would be no further fuss. Neither was there a drum roll. After what seemed like an age in a world of madness she heard the voice of Phauless Gylewu ring out.

"Sir Richemanus, send the traitor Amberstone out of this world."

Tonousa couldn't make out what the executioner replied due to the background roar from the crowd. She guessed it had been no more than a simple grunt.

"Close your eyes Tonousa; there is no need to look upon at this," said a voice from behind.

Tonousa sensed Danisun Dain by her side but she did not avert her gaze. The great black bladed axe plummeted down towards her father's neck. Her screams were drowned by the cheers of the crowd as it made contact with the flesh of the highborn Lord. All were however silenced as something most unexpected then happened. The blunt axe passed clean through her father's neck and the separated head bounced forward into the crowd and out of Tonousa's line of sight. Her father was no more but something was not right. This was not the way it was supposed to have happened.

"It looks like Richemanus has been sharpening his axe," shouted out Blackfayer from the viewing platform. "Executioner, we all expected the kind of show that we have grown to love and indeed pay you for. What were you thinking man?"

Richemanus did not have time to reply before the first screams sounded amongst the crowd. Soon the entire mass of the assembled panicked and pushed back from what lay in front of them, the spot where Amberstone's head had come to rest. Tonousa looked to the members of the Sovereign Council and saw that they too were shocked. Lady Emeny had fainted and was being supported by Blackfayer and Heward Teulu. Lord Ystafell had turned ghost white and had vomited onto the Folly. Sir Dustfury began to shout orders at Sir Lightmain and Sir Cragtalon. Knights rushed forward to escort their Sovereign Lord away from the ensuing melee. Whatever was happening was linked to the execution and had its origin at the place her father's once proud head had come to rest.

Tonousa threw a glance at Danisun and then to the fat youth of the City Watch.

"Fuck this!" she shouted and she rushed towards the man.

"Tonousa," screamed Danisun, "What are you doing…. Oh Shit!"

Tonousa snatched the hilt of the fat man's sword and drew it. Then turning at pace she drove straight into and through the fleeing crowd, unaware that Danisun and lard boy were in hot pursuit. She pushed and shoved her way through the mass of screaming men, woman, children, and crones. On she raced to the source of their fear and panic. A path opened up before her and soon she came before her father's head. There she too recoiled in horror and dropped the blade that she had stolen. Rooted to the spot she stood and stared at her father's head.

"What the fuck are you playing at?" shouted Danisun. "You're in deep shit now Tonousa having stolen an officer's blade… What are you gawping at?"

Tonousa pointed to the head that lay on the ground. The old man's cranium glowed with an intense ethereal light that was mirrored by the glowing torso still on top of the Richemanus Folly. It had been this intense light show that had sent the crowd and the Sovereign Council into disarray. Tonousa edged forward and as she looked down at her father's remains she noticed something else that had struck terror into those who had seen it appear. There etched into her father's forehead and oozing crimson were the marks of the foul magic that was still at work in the Capital. It was unmistakable and yet how it had formed was a complete mystery. The three circle curse brand was clearly displayed for all to see.

"You know that I now have to arrest you," said Danisun. "It is the law of the Watch."

Tonousa did not reply. She no longer had to prove her father's innocence for the proof was there for all to witness. Avolire and the cult of Death Tubaria had struck again. While Danisun shackled her hands behind her back Tonousa realised that all was lost. There was nothing she could do now to counter the power of Avolire. If there was any hope left then it lay in the hands of a bard, a simple farm boy, and her friend Irabo, lost somewhere out in the wilds of the northern lands. They alone could save the Realm. Tonousa knew that she had tried her best but it had not been anywhere near good enough.

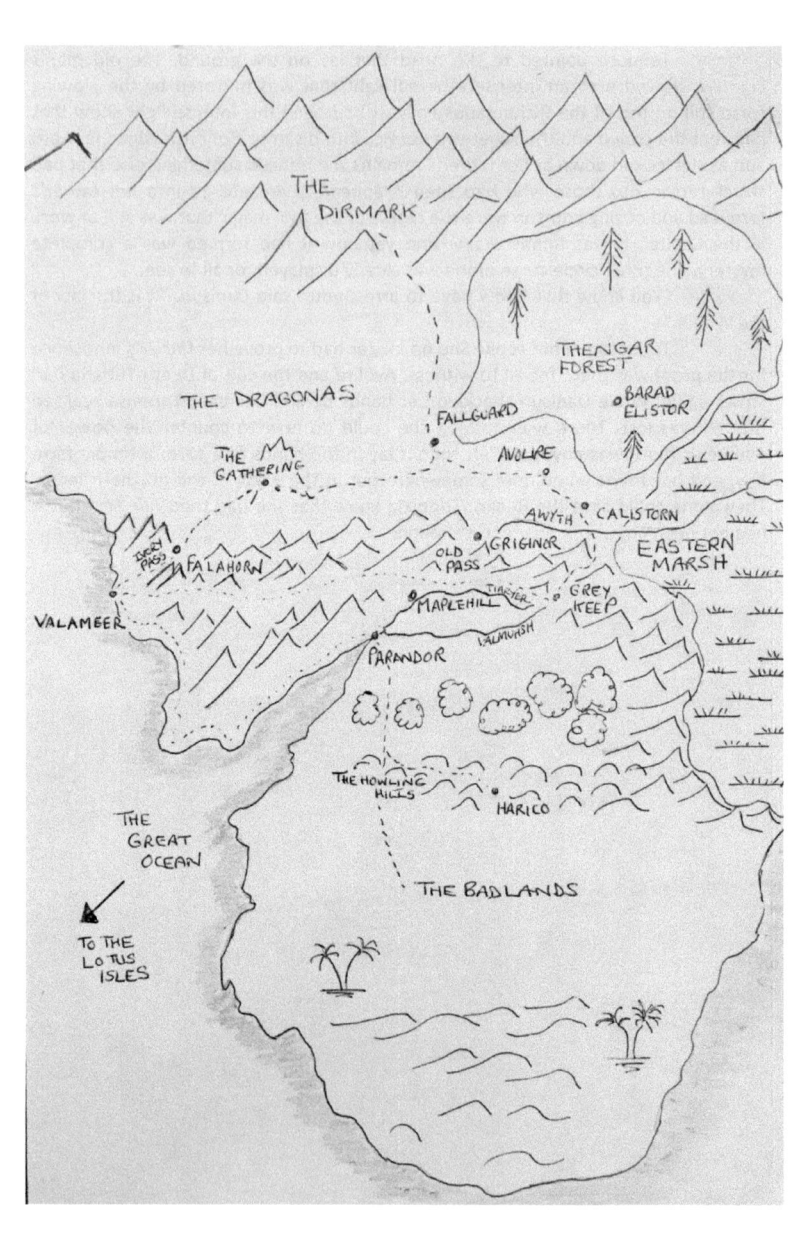